FLAMES OF BETRAYAL

The Horus Heresy®
SIEGE OF TERRA

Book 1 – THE SOLAR WAR
John French

Book 2 – THE LOST AND THE DAMNED
Guy Haley

Book 3 – THE FIRST WALL
Gav Thorpe

Book 4 – SATURNINE
Dan Abnett

Book 5 – MORTIS
John French

Book 6 – WARHAWK
Chris Wraight

Book 7 – ECHOES OF ETERNITY
Aaron Dembski-Bowden

Book 8 – THE END AND THE DEATH:
VOLUME I
VOLUME II
VOLUME III
Dan Abnett

SONS OF THE SELENAR (Novella)
Graham McNeill

ERA OF RUIN (Anthology)
Dan Abnett, Aaron Dembski-Bowden, John French, Guy Haley, Nick Kyme, Gav Thorpe and Chris Wraight

FURY OF MAGNUS (Novella)
Graham McNeill

GARRO: KNIGHT OF GREY (Novella)
James Swallow

The Horus Heresy®

Book 1 – HORUS RISING
Dan Abnett

Book 2 – FALSE GODS
Graham McNeill

Book 3 – GALAXY IN FLAMES
Ben Counter

Book 4 – THE FLIGHT OF THE EISENSTEIN
James Swallow

Book 5 – FULGRIM
Graham McNeill

Book 6 – DESCENT OF ANGELS
Mitchel Scanlon

Book 7 – LEGION
Dan Abnett

Book 8 – BATTLE FOR THE ABYSS
Ben Counter

Book 9 – MECHANICUM
Graham McNeill

Book 10 – TALES OF HERESY
edited by Nick Kyme and Lindsey Priestley

Book 11 – FALLEN ANGELS
Mike Lee

Book 12 – A THOUSAND SONS
Graham McNeill

Book 13 – NEMESIS
James Swallow

Book 14 – THE FIRST HERETIC
Aaron Dembski-Bowden

Book 15 – PROSPERO BURNS
Dan Abnett

Book 16 – AGE OF DARKNESS
edited by Christian Dunn

Book 17 – THE OUTCAST DEAD
Graham McNeill

Book 18 – DELIVERANCE LOST
Gav Thorpe

Book 19 – KNOW NO FEAR
Dan Abnett

Book 20 – THE PRIMARCHS
edited by Christian Dunn

Book 21 – FEAR TO TREAD
James Swallow

Book 22 – SHADOWS OF TREACHERY
edited by Christian Dunn and Nick Kyme

Book 23 – ANGEL EXTERMINATUS
Graham McNeill

Book 24 – BETRAYER
Aaron Dembski-Bowden

Book 25 – MARK OF CALTH
edited by Laurie Goulding

Book 26 – VULKAN LIVES
Nick Kyme

Book 27 – THE UNREMEMBERED EMPIRE
Dan Abnett

Book 28 – SCARS
Chris Wraight

Book 29 – VENGEFUL SPIRIT
Graham McNeill

Book 30 – THE DAMNATION OF PYTHOS
David Annandale

Book 31 – LEGACIES OF BETRAYAL
edited by Laurie Goulding

Book 32 – DEATHFIRE
Nick Kyme

Book 33 – WAR WITHOUT END
edited by Laurie Goulding

Book 34 – PHAROS
Guy Haley

Book 35 – EYE OF TERRA
edited by Laurie Goulding

Book 36 – THE PATH OF HEAVEN
Chris Wraight

Book 37 – THE SILENT WAR
edited by Laurie Goulding

Book 38 – ANGELS OF CALIBAN
Gav Thorpe

Book 39 – PRAETORIAN OF DORN
John French

Book 40 – CORAX
Gav Thorpe

Book 41 – THE MASTER OF MANKIND
Aaron Dembski-Bowden

Book 42 – GARRO
James Swallow

Book 43 – SHATTERED LEGIONS
edited by Laurie Goulding

Book 44 – THE CRIMSON KING
Graham McNeill

Book 45 – TALLARN
John French

Book 46 – RUINSTORM
David Annandale

Book 47 – OLD EARTH
Nick Kyme

Book 48 – THE BURDEN OF LOYALTY
edited by Laurie Goulding

Book 49 – WOLFSBANE
Guy Haley

Book 50 – BORN OF FLAME
Nick Kyme

Book 51 – SLAVES TO DARKNESS
John French

Book 52 – HERALDS OF THE SIEGE
edited by Laurie Goulding and Nick Kyme

Book 53 – TITANDEATH
Guy Haley

Book 54 – THE BURIED DAGGER
James Swallow

Other Novels and Novellas

PROMETHEAN SUN
Nick Kyme

AURELIAN
Aaron Dembski-Bowden

BROTHERHOOD OF THE STORM
Chris Wraight

THE CRIMSON FIST
John French

CORAX: SOULFORGE
Gav Thorpe

PRINCE OF CROWS
Aaron Dembski-Bowden

DEATH AND DEFIANCE
Various authors

TALLARN: EXECUTIONER
John French

SCORCHED EARTH
Nick Kyme

THE PURGE
Anthony Reynolds

THE HONOURED
Rob Sanders

THE UNBURDENED
David Annandale

BLADES OF THE TRAITOR
Various authors

TALLARN: IRONCLAD
John French

RAVENLORD
Gav Thorpe

THE SEVENTH SERPENT
Graham McNeill

WOLF KING
Chris Wraight

CYBERNETICA
Rob Sanders

SONS OF THE FORGE
Nick Kyme

Also available

THE SCRIPTS: VOLUME I
edited by Christian Dunn

THE SCRIPTS: VOLUME II
edited by Laurie Goulding

VISIONS OF HERESY
Alan Merrett and Guy Haley

MACRAGGE'S HONOUR
Dan Abnett and Neil Roberts

Audio Dramas

THE DARK KING
Graham McNeill

THE LIGHTNING TOWER
Dan Abnett

RAVEN'S FLIGHT
Gav Thorpe

GARRO: OATH OF MOMENT
James Swallow

GARRO: LEGION OF ONE
James Swallow

BUTCHER'S NAILS
Aaron Dembski-Bowden

GREY ANGEL
John French

GARRO: BURDEN OF DUTY
James Swallow

GARRO: SWORD OF TRUTH
James Swallow

THE SIGILLITE
Chris Wraight

HONOUR TO THE DEAD
Gav Thorpe

CENSURE
Nick Kyme

WOLF HUNT
Graham McNeill

HUNTER'S MOON
Guy Haley

THIEF OF REVELATIONS
Graham McNeill

TEMPLAR
John French

ECHOES OF RUIN
Various authors

MASTER OF THE FIRST
Gav Thorpe

THE LONG NIGHT
Aaron Dembski-Bowden

THE EAGLE'S TALON
John French

IRON CORPSES
David Annandale

RAPTOR
Gav Thorpe

GREY TALON
Chris Wraight

THE EITHER
Graham McNeill

THE HEART OF THE PHAROS/
CHILDREN OF SICARUS
L J Goulding and
Anthony Reynolds

RED-MARKED
Nick Kyme

THE THIRTEENTH WOLF
Gav Thorpe

VIRTUES OF THE SONS/
SINS OF THE FATHER
Andy Smillie

The BINARY SUCCESSION
David Annandale

ECHOES OF IMPERIUM
Various Authors

ECHOES OF REVELATION
Various authors

DARK COMPLIANCE
John French

BLACKSHIELDS: THE FALSE WAR
Josh Reynolds

BLACKSHIELDS: THE RED FIEF
Josh Reynolds

HUBRIS OF MONARCHIA
Andy Smillie

NIGHTFANE
Nick Kyme

BLACKSHIELDS: THE BROKEN CHAIN
Josh Reynolds

Download the full range of Horus Heresy audio dramas from
blacklibrary.com

THE HORUS HERESY®
SIEGE OF TERRA

FLAMES OF BETRAYAL

Dan Abnett, Aaron-Dembski-Bowden, James Swallow and many more

BLACK LIBRARY

A BLACK LIBRARY PUBLICATION

Garro: Knight of Grey first published in 2023.
Era of Ruin first published in 2024.
This edition published in 2026 by
Black Library, Games Workshop Ltd.,
Willow Road, Nottingham, NG7 2WS, UK.

Represented by: Games Workshop Limited – Irish branch,
Unit 3, Lower Liffey Street, Dublin 1,
D01 K199, Ireland.

10 9 8 7 6 5 4 3 2 1

Produced by Games Workshop in Nottingham.
Cover illustration by Neil Roberts.

A CIP record for this book is available from the British Library.

ISBN 13: 978-1-83609-021-2

Printed and bound in the UK.

THE HORUS HERESY®

SIEGE OF TERRA

It is a time of legend.

The galaxy is in flames. The Emperor's glorious vision for humanity is in ruins. His favoured son, Horus, has turned from his father's light and embraced Chaos.

His armies, the mighty and redoubtable Space Marines, are locked in a brutal civil war. Once, these ultimate warriors fought side by side as brothers, protecting the galaxy and bringing mankind back into the Emperor's light. Now they are divided.

Some remain loyal to the Emperor, whilst others have sided with the Warmaster. Pre-eminent amongst them, the leaders of their thousands-strong Legions, are the primarchs. Magnificent, superhuman beings, they are the crowning achievement of the Emperor's genetic science. Thrust into battle against one another, victory is uncertain for either side.

Worlds are burning. At Isstvan V, Horus dealt a vicious blow and three loyal Legions were all but destroyed. War was begun, a conflict that will engulf all mankind in fire. Treachery and betrayal have usurped honour and nobility. Assassins lurk in every shadow. Armies are gathering. All must choose a side or die.

Horus musters his armada, Terra itself the object of his wrath. Seated upon the Golden Throne, the Emperor waits for his wayward son to return. But his true enemy is Chaos, a primordial force that seeks to enslave mankind to its capricious whims.

The screams of the innocent, the pleas of the righteous resound to the cruel laughter of Dark Gods. Suffering and damnation await all should the Emperor fail and the war be lost.

The end is here. The skies darken, colossal armies gather. For the fate of the Throneworld, for the fate of mankind itself...
The Siege of Terra has begun.

CONTENTS

GARRO: KNIGHT OF GREY

JAMES SWALLOW

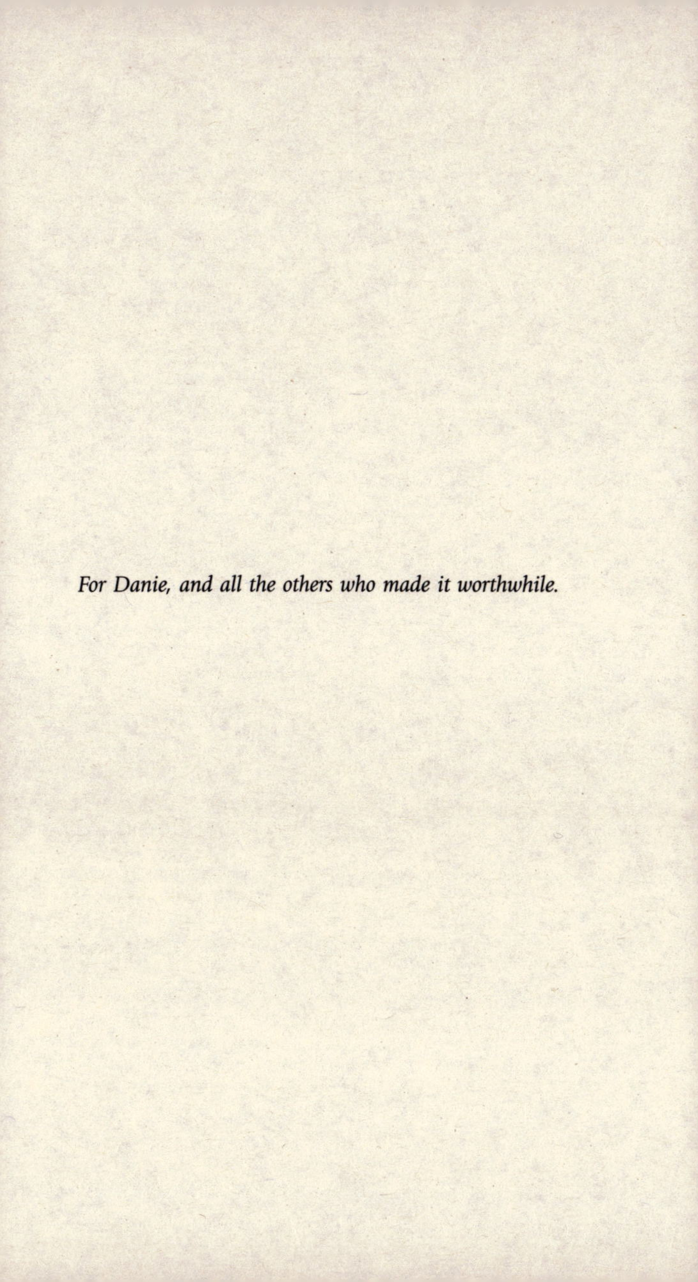

For Danie, and all the others who made it worthwhile.

DRAMATIS PERSONAE

The Knights Errant

Nathaniel Garro	Former Agentia Primus, former battle-captain of the Death Guard
Helig Gallor	Former legionary of the Death Guard

The XIV Legion, 'Death Guard'

Mortarion	Primarch
Typhus, the Traveller	First Captain

The Imperial Army

Maed Kostagar	Captain, Dilectio Tier, Marmax garrison
Rold Greff	Trooper, Dilectio Tier, Marmax garrison

Others

Euphrati Keeler	The Living Saint, former remembrancer

'Those who embrace their own fate fear nothing.'

– *Last Books of Sight,* Hirundus Iago [date unknown]

'There must come a moment when the soul knows: this far, and no further. But we are cursed never to hear that warning until it is too late.'

– attributed to the remembrancer Ignace Karkasy [M31]

ONE

Dining on Ashes
The Last of the Few
You Know Her

With one heavy footfall after another, the warrior giant advanced up the narrow spiral stairwell.

His ceramite boots were too wide for stairs that had been built for the tread of common men, the shoulders of his power armour far too broad for the tight, human-scale confines of the towering minaret. The edges of his wargear's pauldrons would catch on the walls from time to time, gouging lines out of the fire-blackened granite to mark his passing.

He was forced to negotiate places where the sides of the passageway had been blown in by shell impacts, picking his way over heaps of sooty debris, and often, the grisly remains of slain defenders.

The damage and the carnage grew ever worse the closer he got to the top. The tower had been home to a lascannon nest that rained beams of crimson hell down on the enemy throughout the night's fighting, drawing concentrated fire in return. At length, he emerged into the smoggy cold of the day as the spiral stairs deposited him on the highest level that still remained intact. The beheaded ruin of the minaret hummed with a hard breeze that carried particles of gritty, dirty sleet with it.

The dead – men and women in the grey carapace armour of the resident garrison – lay where they had fallen, half-buried in drifts of ash and broken brickwork. Some still clutched their guns to them, the muzzles of the rifles glistening with the oily rainbow sheen of heat-damaged metal. He saw burst flesh seared from within marking many of the soldiers, and toxin-bloated faces on others that stared sightlessly at the sky. Death had touched them with terror and agony in their final moments.

Compelled by a sudden impulse, the warrior checked his air sensors, then removed his grey-hued battle helmet and mag-locked it to his hip. He looked up past the missing roof of the tower, to snatch a glimpse of what the fallen had seen.

Above, the forbidding sky had a strange, sickly hue, lined with striations of black cloud reaching from north to south, and on the wind were sounds that might have been voices, if one listened for them. Hundreds of metres up, above the perimeter of the great aegis field, metal birds caught the weak sunlight as they wheeled and turned around one another, trading streaks of sun-hot plasma from their guns. The keening whine of their engines and the faint chug of their weapons reached him over another, steady sound coming from far away – a low drumming like the beating of a gigantic heart.

Past the atmo-fighters locked in their endless dogfight, the strange storms of brassy lightning, and up into the higher ranges of the reddish Himalazian sky, shapes loomed in the heavens. Great baroque forms floating in near-orbit, some on fire, others crackling with arcane energies. Starships as big as city-states drifted there, their numbers and their masses so great that their proximity tormented the planet's gravitational and magnetic fields, warping weather patterns from pole to pole.

The skies of Terra were no longer the domain of the Imperium of Man, the warrior reflected. The skies belonged to Horus Lupercal, *may his name be blighted,* to the treacherous Warmaster and the Traitor Legions at his banner. Only the stone and the mud were held by those who remained loyal to the Emperor, and even those elements were in danger of slipping away.

After a breath, the warrior took another step, moving onto an unsteady outcropping of broken masonry and laser-scarred ouslite. He let his gaze drop to the riven battleground beneath the minaret, and the fields of destruction rolling away to the broken horizon.

The spindly tower was the only one to have survived the recent onslaught, emerging from the cracked and shattered domains of the gigantic Colossi Bastion, reaching to the burnt sky like a skeletal, accusing finger atop a beheaded mountain. A vast, seemingly endless landscape of rubble stretched towards the gutted shell of the bastion's sibling fortress, Corbenic Gard, and in the direction of the City of Sight. Ahead of the warrior, the Anterior Gate and the outer dominions of the great Imperial Palace still stood intact, but in the eerie red corpse-light, the huge, maze-like conurbations resembled forms scrimshawed out of old bone.

His face turned towards the heartbeat sound, towards the Lion's Gate and what lay past it. Eyes narrowing, he raised a battered monocular scope to look across the great distance, searching the canyons of debris and the towering wall of thick, abyssal smoke obscuring much of the battle zone's reaches.

He picked out forms in bright crimson moving in packs through the destruction: some on foot, others riding slab-shaped tanks or speeders blurred by anti-gravity fields as they navigated the shattered avenues choked by the spill of ruined buildings. All were drawing back, likely towards more adequately reinforced strongpoints, abandoning the kill boxes and poisoned quadrants that remained from their last engagement.

These were the rearguard elements of Brother-Captain Raldoron's forces, sons of the IX Legion, the noble Blood Angels of Sanguinius. In the past desperate hours, Raldoron's army, and that of the White Scars Legion under the command of the Khan himself, had made war on Horus' invaders. It had been a brutal and harrowing skirmish in a conflict that daily set new standards in horror and destruction – and ultimately, it had counted for little. The line the Blood Angels and the White Scars had fought so hard to maintain could not hold indefinitely.

The word had finally been given. The eastern bastions could no longer be adequately secured by the loyalist forces, and they were declared indefensible, surrendered in the face of the enemy advance.

The enemy.

How those words burned in the warrior's heart.

Once, in what seemed like another life, a whole other existence, he had marched alongside those whom the Blood Angels and White Scars had fought to a standstill. In the time before the great betrayal at Isstvan, in countless righteous battles and noble crusades, the warrior had been proud to be a part of the XIV Legion, the Death Guard. Now he had only shame, sorrow and rage for those who had once been his oathsworn brethren. Their broken vows to Terra and the Emperor were wounds upon his heart that would never heal, and that he could never forgive.

He looked past the withdrawing Blood Angels elements – the sole loyalist forces remaining on the field, the White Scars having already decamped and moved off in search of better odds – and away to the wall of curdled smoke marking the edge of the traitors' advance.

It wasn't *just* smoke. One who studied it carefully would see that the hazy mass moved against the direction of the wind, with apparent conscious intent. Even from kilometres away, he saw the glitter of reflected light off the millions of tiny wings that made up the plague swarms.

And among the haze strode huge forms as tall as hab-blocks, unhurried and inexorable, moving as one in deliberate lock-step. Each massive footfall sounded across the distance to the warrior's ears, the steady drumbeat rhythm of corrupted steel and corroded iron against the earth.

The giant bipedal war machines of the Legio Mortis were on the march, each passing moment bringing them ever nearer to the walls of the Inner Palace. Within hours, they would be within optimal range and a new rain of fire would begin. Oath-breakers of the Mechanicum, bound to Horus' perfidy, the Warlords, Reavers and Iconoclasts of the Death's Heads would leave only radioactive dust in their wake. Somewhere at the feet of those killer god-machines marched phalanx upon phalanx of tainted Death Guard legionaries, and the warped things they had allied with.

His brothers were coming for him, he could feel it in his blood and bone. They were coming for them all.

In every corner of the Palace's gigantic span, a thousand small battles were being fought, with countless battalions of soldiers, aviators, gunners, war devices and legionaries deep in their own brutal engagements. Whole districts had been laid waste, filled with the bodies of unburied dead left to decay and fester by comrades who had no time to tend to the innumerable fallen. The pall of the worst war this planet had ever known hung over everything, the dense reek of aerosolised vitae, spent promethium and cordite changing the atmosphere into a constant funereal haze. It was no exaggeration to voice the thought – these desperate times had the colour of the end of days, of an apocalypse that would, in its fullness, soon erase the rule of mankind from the planet of its origin.

No living soul on Terra could ignore the whispers in every shadow, and the terrors – some conjured by tricks of the mind, others real in fang and talon – lurking in the darkness. There could be no rest, no respite, no quarter asked for or given. Hell had disgorged itself upon the planet, rising from the depths of nightmares and falling from the blackness between the stars. Whole worlds were ending here in every passing second, some of them the lives of ordinary men, others the futures of those who would be left behind.

And yet… in *this* place, in *this* moment, there was only desolation. In this lacuna amid the bloodshed, the sullen peace of the grave held sway.

A new sound caught the warrior's attention, a trickle of stone fragments and the juddering buzz of damaged motors as something moved beneath one of the rubble piles. Warily, he crossed the open space to the source of the noise, and with one gauntleted hand, he shoved away a fallen piece of ceiling. The action revealed the remains of two bodies, Army troopers most likely assigned to the lascannon crew. They had fallen together, united in death, but what killed them was still here.

A foetid, bloated shape trembled in the daylight, nestled between the bodies of the dead men. No larger than a fuel barrel, it lay atop the corpses. On one surface, a cluster of insect eyes regarded the warrior blankly, and two filth-caked propeller modules protruded from its flanks, blades turning in weak, jerky motions. A cluster of chitinous mandibles scraped and wavered in the air.

A blight drone: halfway between a machine and an engineered life form, fleshy wattles and mollusc-shell animated by foul processes the warrior loathed to imagine. Trapped under the fallen roof, the drone was trying to repair its own damage by opening the dead men to use their bones, sinews and skin as replacement parts.

His jaw set in a hard line, the warrior's disgust expressed itself in swift violence. He stamped the drone into a pulpy mess, and as it died with a squeal, it let off a puff of reeking vapour. He recoiled, grimacing as faint traces of the poison touched his bare face. The warrior's transhuman physiology endured the toxin with ease, but where the vapour's heavy droplets fell on the dead men, their bodies turned to black slurry.

The warrior drew himself up, and spat to clear his lungs. His dark, wary eyes sat in a face criss-crossed with trophy scars from past wars, beneath a heavy brow that carried the brass service studs of a ranked battle-captain. His skull was shorn and he wore no beard, his pale face reminiscent of some ancient Hellenikai statuary from the age before Old Night. His aspect was rigid and searching, a man one might think was bound by great duty, yet lost to his cause. A warrior destined to live and to die alone.

But not today, it seemed. Someone was coming up the narrow stairwell, following in his footsteps, someone equally unsuited to the human-scale confines of the passageway.

His hand dropped to the great power sword sheathed at his belt, fingers tightening around the hilt. He sensed no immediate danger at hand, but it would take only a heartbeat to draw the blade. He had learned through bitter experience that to lower his guard was to invite ill-fortune.

Presently, a figure emerged from the broken mouth of the stairwell, another giant man-shape in powered armour rising into the daylight. Both wore the same stripe of wargear: Mark VI Corvus-pattern plate, heavy in form like that of the Blood Angels below on the battlefield, but drained of colour. The ceramite of their greaves and gauntlets was a shade of grey like slate, like an ocean storm.

'Well met, kinsman,' said the new arrival, his words bereft of warmth.

Nathaniel Garro, former battle-captain of the Death Guard, former Agentia Primus of Malcador the Sigillite, inclined his head in a nod. 'Helig Gallor,' he said, recognising the other warrior by the pattern of his movements more than his voice. 'You are not yet dead.'

'Despite all attempts of the fates,' came the dour reply. Gallor removed his helm to mirror Garro's aspect, revealing a familiar, ever-grave expression.

Gallor too had once been a son of Mortarion, one of the Death Guard Legion, and his path mirrored Garro's in the warrior's rejection of perfidy against Terra. Both were remnants from the ideal of a Legion that no longer existed, the last of a handful of loyalists whose gene-sire primarch had turned his back on the Emperor and embraced treachery. Both had, for a time, found new direction as Knights Errant under the command of the great psyker Malcador, as agents of the Emperor's right hand.

But despite their shared circumstances and common origins, there was little comradeship between the two warriors. Garro considered Gallor to be imprudent, even undisciplined. For his part, Gallor thought of Garro as stiff, haughty and arrogant.

Gallor nodded towards Garro's shoulder pauldron. 'You no longer carry the mark of the Sigillite upon your armour.'

'It has not proven to be an issue.' Garro gave a curt nod. 'Malcador generously released me from my service to the Throne... As if a mere etching on ceramite was all that tethered me to that duty.'

'Only in death does duty end.' Gallor repeated the old, rote maxim without conscious recollection, the words coming from the deep reservoir of hypnogogic training that had been imprinted on both legionaries as initiates.

'Aye. So what duty has compelled you to seek me out in these bleak days, brother? I have not laid eyes on you since the mission at the Saturnine Wall.'

'Bleak?' Gallor echoed the word, deflecting the question. 'They are, at that. But tell me, do you not carry a flame of hope in your breast, safe beneath your armour?' He pointed to the ornate golden eagle across the cuirass that shrouded Garro's torso. 'I wonder. Do you not hold an ephemeral light in your spirit? Isn't that your way now?'

Garro's lips thinned at the veiled challenge, uncertain where it was leading. 'I believe what I believe. That the Emperor protects.'

'He cannot protect everyone,' said Gallor. 'He is mighty, but He is no god.' Then the other warrior cocked his head. 'Or is He?'

Garro said nothing, refusing to be baited. Long before the Siege of Terra had begun, even before the Warmaster's betrayal, there were those who considered the Emperor of Mankind as more deity than mortal. They had many names – the followers of the *Lectitio Divinitatus:* Truekind, Imperiads, Lightbringers – and many expressions of their devotion, such as it was. Garro did not consider himself among any one of these groups, but he did *believe.* He did have *faith.*

It was only when called upon to fully quantify that conviction that words failed him. 'I have faced death many times, against impossible odds, and still I live,' he murmured. 'There must be a reason, by the Throne. Once, I was told that I was *of purpose.* I choose to hold to that still.' He looked away. 'Call it what you will, brother. I care not if you think I am deluded.'

To his surprise, Gallor gave a rare – if bitter – laugh. 'I would not dare to! And in days as dark as these, who am I to challenge what gives a warrior succour? No, I only sought to know if your attitude has shifted on such matters. I see it has not.'

'Oh, it has,' Garro corrected, a grim solemnity sweeping over his expression. 'My faith has been tested, again and again, but never as gravely as now.' He gestured towards the ruins heaped at the horizon. 'Terra burns about us, in such profusion that a single sword, a single boltgun cannot hope to turn back the fire. I have lent my aid to the Palace's defenders wherever I can, wandering between the battlements and donjons, and yet the taint of futility is forever at my back.'

Gallor nodded. 'I feel it too.'

When Horus' fleet had come, when his ships had darkened the

sky, some stirring of martial exhilaration had been reborn in Garro's twin hearts. He stood with his ersatz kinsman Garviel Loken and made ready for a battle of such glory that it would be sung of for ten thousand years; but the reality of the grinding, monstrous siege-war had burned through that. The great imperious scope of the Palace city-state, once the venerated jewel of Terra, had become a hellish crater filled with shed blood and the detritus of brutal war.

An inescapable foreboding filled his soul. As if sensing the great cogs of some unseen mechanism turning about him, Garro felt the fates were aligning in ways he could only guess at. And now, with his lost Legion on the approaches, and with his former primarch marching somewhere among their number, the true power of something he rarely knew gripped him.

Fear.

'He is out there,' said Garro, voicing the thought.

'Mortarion.' Gallor knew of whom he spoke, grimacing around the name. 'Our traitor lord, come to plague us anew.'

'Aye.' Words pushed to be spoken, but Garro held them back, suddenly uncertain.

What could he say to Gallor that would not cast a greater pall over their conversation? That he dreaded what would come to pass at the moment Mortarion stood before them. That he could not escape the sense that he was living on borrowed time, and worse, that Nathaniel Garro's end would come before he had the chance to fulfil his purpose in this life.

And most treacherous and terrible, the words he dared not utter, that he could barely even countenance – the awful possibility that Horus Lupercal might actually take Terra for himself, despite everything they had done to defy his heresy.

A chill cut through Garro's blood and his hand tightened on the hilt of his sword. *I will die a thousand times before I let that come to pass.*

He released a held breath and studied Gallor anew. 'You did

not answer my first question. You have not said why you are here. You have reason to distract me from my musings. Did someone send you?'

'In a way,' allowed Gallor. 'There is something you need to see.'

Garro's kinsman would not be drawn further, citing both his own reticence and the possibility of long-ranging traitor observers watching their position. Instead, Gallor silently led him back down to ground level and across the broken landscape at a loping, swift pace.

They moved through shallow canyons of debris and over burnt-out combat vehicles, skirting deep craters where seething bowls of heat still sizzled from macro-shell impacts. Presently, the battlefield levelled out into the remains of some great plaza. Once beautiful mosaics and elegant stone friezes had been fused into masses of black glass, and the nubs of tall statues were all that remained of a sculpture orchard in the centre.

They came to a small forward observation post, little more than a clump of plastek bivouacs, in the process of being torn down by a crew of Blood Angels Legion serfs. Four warriors of the IX Legion watched them arrive from afar, giving the two Legionless cursory nods of greeting but nothing else.

Garro noted the elegant uniformity of the faces of the Blood Angels. Despite their war-scars, they remained handsome in aspect, echoing their winged, angelic progenitor. But their nobility seemed muted, as if the war had knocked it out of them. He knew from shared battles in the past that beneath the Blood Angels' dignity there lay a murderer's fury when provoked, and Garro imagined that shackled rage lying closer to the surface now, ready to be released.

'In here.' Gallor halted by a camouflaged yurt, pulling back the door flap so that Garro could enter. Ducking his head, the warrior passed inside, into shadow.

Gallor followed him, moving to a pile of storage crates, delving into one to retrieve something. 'I asked our cousins to guard this for me while I sought you out,' he explained. 'I wanted to gauge your disposition before I showed it to you.'

Garro folded his arms. 'I am in no mood for games and obfuscation, know that,' he said. 'What do you have there?'

'See.' The other warrior showed him the glittering shape of a hololithic diamond. Reams of data or imagery could be stored inside its complex crystalline structure, preserved and virtually indestructible. He inserted the gemstone into the reader matrix of a tactical projector in the corner of the space.

With a soft hum, the projector came to life, breathing out a smoky sphere of holographic light. The diamond's lattice translated its contents into three-dimensional pictures that wavered and danced between the two warriors.

Garro saw aerial views of other bastions along the fighting line – he recognised Corbenic when it was still intact, the massive fortresses of Gorgon Bar and Marmax. Gallor's gauntleted fingers moved with delicacy, manipulating the projector's controls to dash forward through the data stored on the diamond.

'Like you,' he went on, 'I too have wandered the edges of this siege, from the Europa Wall all the way to the Helios Gate, providing what assistance I can to those who need another gun or another strong arm. There has been no shortage of those at disadvantage.'

Garro nodded. 'When there are no orders given, we make our own.'

'Indeed.' Gallor hesitated, and Garro sensed he was framing his next words with care. 'In my travels, intelligence has come to me, some of it useless, some of it accurate. A few days ago, I encountered a flyer crew whose craft had been shot out from under them, the survivors retreating on foot towards loyalist lines. They gave me this...' He tapped the diamond. 'And they told me a story.'

Gallor went on, insisting that he had spoken to no one else of what the aircrew had said. He had brought it straight to Garro, keeping it secret from the Blood Angels he marched with, from everyone. At first, Garro did not understand why his kinsman was acting with caution, but as the other Knight Errant unfolded the tale, the reason became clear.

South of the Colossi Bastion stood its sister-citadel, Marmax – another gargantuan holdfast built to the Emperor's own design and fortified beyond that by His steadfast son, Rogal Dorn of the Imperial Fists. Like the now abandoned Colossi, the domains of Marmax were also in heavy contact with traitor forces – something that would only worsen with the renewed advance of the Death Guard and the Legio Mortis.

Soldiers perished in droves each day upon the battlefield, but Gallor's story spoke of a peculiar anomaly among the tally of the fallen. In a sector of the Marmax Bastion's north-western face, where the fighting was among the most violent, the defenders of a zone called the Dilectio Tier were *holding* their ground while all around them were crumbling.

'They defy the odds,' said Gallor, with a scowl. 'Day after day, so I was told.' As he spoke, he dialled in the projector's images, finding the location among the clutter, zooming in to enlarge the tier until it filled the interior of the yurt. 'They should be dead and ashes twenty times over, Garro. And yet, *they hold*. These common soldiers, these ordinary humans have beaten back attacks that should have annihilated them.'

'You suspect something... *corruptive*... at work there?' Garro hesitated to find the right phrasing. He had almost said the word *daemonic*, before he stopped himself.

'At first,' Gallor noted. 'But the reality appears to be quite the reverse. I sought to learn more, and in doing so I discovered that someone is moving among these soldiers. A voice, Garro. Not quite a leader, but a...' He frowned. 'A confidante, you could say. This person is rallying these soldiers to fight far beyond what their normal abilities should allow.'

'A psyker, then.'

'Unclear.' Gallor shrugged. 'You are better qualified than I am to answer that.'

Garro's expression mirrored his kinsman's. He was growing impatient. 'Speak plainly! What do you mean?'

'You know her,' said the other warrior, as he dialled in on a group of figures captured in the image of the embattled fortress, enhancing and sharpening it until distinct faces were visible.

Garro saw a frozen frame of dozens of Imperial Army troopers, caught with their arms and lasrifles raised to the air in a shout of victory. They looked battle-worn and weary, but their eyes were alight with that same defiant martial zeal Garro had felt on the day Horus came.

In the middle of the group was a woman in a threadbare civilian oversuit, and all the troopers around her had a hand upon her shoulders or her back. Not in the manner of supplicants touching some holy object, but like friends, united in a simple moment of human connection.

He knew her.

'Keeler.' The name fell from Garro's lips in a hushed breath.

'The Saint,' said Gallor.

Garro shook his head. 'She never chose that name. Others laid it upon her, forced her to carry its weight. The truth is far more complex.'

He had thought her safe and protected, deep in one of the Emperor's most secure refuges, but to see the woman like this, her laughing face bare to the sky and open to attack at any instant... The raw shock of it made Garro's hands draw into fists.

Euphrati Keeler: once a remembrancer sent into the Imperial fleets to document the work of the Great Crusade through her picter and her artist's eye, she had passed beyond that life when events conspired to draw the woman into the Warmaster's machinations.

It changed her in ways that no one could ever have expected, and soon the threads of her fate became entwined with those of Nathaniel Garro. As Gallor had said, some knew her as the so-called Saint, the voice of the nascent Imperial Truth, of the divinity of the God-Emperor of Mankind. Some said she was touched by the Emperor's power, even that she might be a conduit to His greatness.

Garro knew her as something else. A guide. A light in the darkness that showed the way ahead. The woman who had counselled the warrior time and again since the tragedy at Isstvan.

Without her, he mused, *I would have been lost.*

But she was supposed to be in hiding, protected from danger until the fires of the Siege of Terra were put out.

'What is she doing there?' Garro bit out the words.

'I would say, she is doing the same as you and I,' said Gallor. 'Lending aid where she can.'

'She is in harm's way,' he retorted. 'This...' Garro gestured at the hololith. 'This is too great a risk. I must take her from Marmax, get her away before this reckless behaviour claims her life!' He stared into the image, trying to see into Keeler's thoughts.

What could compel her to put herself in so great a danger, to hide in plain sight in the middle of a warzone?

'I brought this to you because I know of your beliefs.' Gallor eyed him. 'Which I do not share. But that said, I do have faith of a kind – in *you.* Our differences aside, battle-captain, I understand that the Keeler woman has importance to whatever Imperium will come after Horus Lupercal lies dead. I will accompany you.'

'Gratitude,' offered Garro. 'But you need not.'

'I know,' Gallor replied, 'and yet I will. You may consider it misplaced nostalgia on my part, if you wish, for the days when we were Death Guard. When that meant something.'

'Very well.'

Gallor removed the hololithic diamond and the projector image vanished. He weighed it in his hand, then added something more. 'I will say this,' he went on. 'Prepare yourself for disappointment. She does not seem like the kind of woman who bows easily to the will of another. Man, legionary… or god.'

TWO

Marmax
Only Truth
Whispers

Fire, smoke and fury crackled across the wide saw-tooth stonework of the Dilectio Tier, spilling over the ferrocrete slabs, roaring around rank after rank of the beleaguered defenders.

The spent powercell of her laspistol burned Maed Kostagar's stubby brown fingers as she cracked the weapon's barrel and plucked it out. Swearing animatedly under her breath, the captain tossed the hot cylinder along the battlement, into a waiting bin that was already near brimming with dead batteries from her company's rifles. One of the runner-servitors would come and drag the bin back to a charger maw, if of course the runner wasn't already cold meat and iron, lying somewhere she couldn't see in a pool of its own oils.

Kostagar tried not to think about running out of loads, or stubber rounds, or med-packs, or fighters, and she rammed a new cell into the gun's breech, snapping it closed with a flick of her wrist. The old weapon hummed to life again, reliable as daybreak, rewarding her trust and care better than any of her ex-husbands ever had. But the batteries her troops hoarded were starting to go stale, becoming harder to recharge, and holding their wattage for shorter and shorter periods. Kostagar tried not to think about that as well.

She popped up out of cover and killed the closest of the coven-scum scrambling up the incline of the walls towards her. This outcast – as the troops had come to name their kind – was wrapped in soiled green sashes and made his way up the steep slope using crude hand-held claws welded from bits of corroded iron. His face was painted with something foul, a daub in the form of three rough circles framing wild eyes and a gaping mouth.

Kostagar's beam-shot shrieked through his chest, and exploded open the outcast's back in a welter of superheated blood. The attacker tumbled away down the slope, crashing into dozens of his comrades climbing up beneath him. He took some with him as his ragged corpse vanished into the battle-fog, but there were so many still coming. Each hour, it seemed as if a new army had come to besiege them.

Some had the claws or memory-metal ladders, others tools like miners' picks or impact hammers; some used cables dangling from cleats fired into the stone by pneumatic launcher. They came climbing up the outer tiers of the Marmax Bastion, chanting and screaming for blood, killing everything in their path. Tier after tier had already fallen to their predations, forcing Kostagar's forces to seal the stairwells and elevator tubes to the lower levels, and barricade themselves in place.

The men and women around her were a patchwork of survivors from ten different companies, that in her wisdom – or perhaps, her foolishness – she had managed to pull together. Their uniforms and battle gear were a mismatched collection of whatever they could salvage, whatever they had carried from the routing of their own units. She had them spread thin across the main approaches, doing the work of a force ten times their size, with half the firepower.

Dress guards and regular line infantry. Field police and rear-echelon servicemen. These and more, they carried lasrifles and stubbers, ballistic rod-throwers and quarrel launchers, and the only thing they had in common was the will to fight. The will to *keep* fighting, and damn the bleak truth of the end massing at their gate.

Kostagar had an assassin's eye, aiming and firing with care, and everywhere she landed a las-bolt, an invader died.

No one knew exactly where the outcasts had come from, with their madness and their bodies caked in filth and triad-shape tattoos. Some of the junior officers said that the traitors had brought them to Terra from worlds they had taken, that they were inductees chem-conditioned to serve as shock brigades. Others whispered fearfully that they were what became of those taken captive by the turncoats, persona-wipes thrown back at the very bastions they might once have manned.

Kostagar doubted the latter was true. The traitors did not take prisoners. And what she feared most was not the erasure of her mind, but the warning the outcast attacks presented.

Today, the Dilectio Tier was besieged by the enemy's human auxiliaries. That meant soon the *real* invaders would come, the Legions of dishonoured Astartes at the banner of the Warmaster.

The outcasts were just the start of this particular battle in the ongoing siege of the Imperial Palace, blunt instruments with little military artifice sent in to soften up the lines around Marmax. They would spend their cheap lives choking the guns of the fortress, eating into the morale of the defenders, whittling them down. Preparing the way for the hammer blow that would inevitably follow.

'What are they doing?' came a reedy cry, from a young man in carapace armour with a drum-fed stubber, firing bursts into the invaders' line. His eyes were wide. 'Are they breeding these whoresons down there like rats? There's too many of them!'

'So we keep shooting,' said the captain, drawing a startled

flinch from the youth. *Greff. His name is Rold Greff*, she remembered. He hadn't seen her there, crouching nearby in the same revetment. 'Until they get the message, eh?'

Greff nodded woodenly, but she knew the cast to his gaze. The lad was lost behind it, terrified that each thump of his heart in his ears would be the last.

Like him and all the others firing down at the advance of the climbers, Kostagar was running on stale recaff, lho-sticks and precious little sleep. She knew that the shadow of fatigue lurked at her back, and if she let it come close, it would embrace her. Drag her down. Dull her thoughts.

And if that happens... The enemy would take the advantage and engulf them.

The outcasts kept on coming, attacking out of the smoke at random intervals that were impossible to predict. Eventually they would wear out the resistance of everyone on the Dilectio Tier, just as they had the defenders on the levels beneath.

We are the last here. If we fall... the Marmax Bastion will be lost.

In the flyer silo on the far face of the fortress there was an aircraft that could, at a push, have evacuated everybody still fighting on this tier. But the order from the Master of the Siege, the primarch Rogal Dorn himself, was to hold. And so they would, until they could do so no longer.

Then a peculiar silence fell across the battlements, as if by random chance the drone of all the guns paused at once, and the screaming of the enemy was briefly stilled.

'Stand fast,' said a voice. *'I know it is hard. I know every breath is a struggle. Every step feels like a marathon. But you can do it. You* can *hold this line.'*

The voice was not a shout. It did not come as some martial roar or chest-beating exhortation. It was not a hymnal or a sermon. But not a whisper either, instead something strong, constant and honest. Everyone listened. Everyone heard it.

'I know what you have seen,' it said. *'The horrors you have witnessed and the sacrifices you have made. I know how empty your bellies are, how you wish you could make it all just* stop *for a moment, so we might rest. I know the darkness that you feel, the hollow in your hearts. The despair and the fear. But I also know how* strong *you are. I believe in all of you. You* can *do this. You will survive this.'*

Across open vox-channels or broadcast by speaker-horns, even carried on the stiff breeze itself, the voice was there for all of them.

For Kostagar, the voice recalled warm memories of her older sister Galae, long dead now but never far from her thoughts. She had always known the right thing to say whenever little Maed had jolted awake from a nightmare or been caught by some sorrow. Others heard it differently, but to the same effect. A gentle speech that cut through fear and heartened those who listened.

'Stand fast,' said the voice, *'and look to those at your side. You fight for them. They fight for you. Together, we are defiant, no matter what we face.'*

Despite herself, the captain's round face split in a grin. A swell of renewed confidence blossomed in her chest, and she dared to believe that perhaps they *could* prevail today, that they *could* hold the Dilectio Tier for a little longer.

At her side, Greff seemed to have grown in stature – or was it that he was just standing taller than he had a moment before? The young man was no longer cowering. He was still afraid, but now he refused to let his fear rule him.

'Stand fast!' Kostagar echoed the words, and the shout went down the line of the battlements, repeated back to her over and over.

'Stand fast!' 'Stand fast!' 'Stand fast!'

Out of the chorus came gunfire, as the defenders fought

back. Las-bolts split the smoke, sundering air molecules with shrill, steam-kettle screams. Stubber weapons, heavy-gauge man-portables and mag-fed shoulder-arms alike, rained shot into the scrambling mass of the outcasts.

The enemy forces withered under the defensive barrage and they fell back. Siege ladders and cables snapped away, attackers retreated. It soon became a hectic collapse, as the lines of the outcasts were broken. They fled desperately into the fire-smoke that billowed constantly from the levels below.

The war cries of the invaders faded to nothing. The attack had been repelled once more, and for a moment Kostagar and her troopers could breathe again.

She sank to her haunches and checked the charge on her las-pistol, blowing vapour from the coolant fins down the long, ornate barrel. She had made it through another battle and lived to tell the tale.

Greff and the others sent up a ragged, insolent cheer that carried down the long walkways, as if they were terrace hooligans at some scrumball match, heckling the losing side. The captain let it go. She was too far past enforcing pointless notions of propriety on her troopers.

I'll let them yell, she thought. *The time might come when that's the only weapon they have left.*

'Maed,' said the voice, from close at hand. 'You're injured.'

'I am?' As the words left her mouth, Kostagar felt thick, warm fluid trickling down from her brow. She reached up and found a shallow cut that was bleeding badly, from where a splinter of stone had struck her in the melee. She hadn't noticed the pain. 'Oh. It looks worse than it is,' she said, and glanced up to see who had spoken.

'Still, it could get infected. Let me help.' Unremarkable in a common worker's oversuit and a scrounged heavy-weather jacket a size too large for her, at first sight Euphrati Keeler looked no different to any other human surviving the Warmaster's onslaught. She opened the field pack she carried over one shoulder, dug inside for adhesive bandages, and set to work cleaning and dressing the captain's wound.

Keeler's kindly, moderated voice was more soothing than the anti-chems she applied to the cut, and Kostagar smiled slightly. 'Thank you. Thank you *again*, Euphrati. I don't know how you do it… but your words are better than any doggerel or empty platitude.'

'I just help people to remember their own courage,' she said, dismissing the compliment. 'Nothing more.'

From anyone else, that might have sounded like false modesty, but Keeler meant every word. Kostagar had met few people in her life she would have described as truly 'selfless', but this woman was one of them. She had appeared back when the fighting was still concentrated on the lower tiers, and offered her help with the wounded. Desperate for any aid, the captain was only too happy to accept her. Soon word spread about the woman with the kind eyes who carried a battered old picter, now and then snapping image captures of the battles, always giving time to those who needed it.

Like Kostagar's long-passed sister, Keeler seemed to know the right thing to say to someone, and the right moment to say it. She didn't flatter or cajole; she just brought the truth when it was needed.

The captain met the other woman's gaze. 'You know, without you… we wouldn't have survived this long.' She took a breath, framing a question that was almost a whisper. 'Did someone *send* you, Euphrati?'

'I saw a need.' Keeler looked away, finishing the application of the bandage. 'In all this horror, a person like me can only do one of two things. I could help, or I could flee. And I am tired of running.'

Kostagar rose to her feet, ready to press the question further, but a shout from further down the battlements drew her attention. Greff sprinted back to the captain's side, panting hard in the thin Himalazian air. 'Gunfire, ma'am,' he reported. 'Quad two, from down in the fog! Sounds like big-gauge bolters!'

Her jaw set. Were the outcasts coming back already, unwilling to grant the defenders even a minute of respite? She saw the same question in Greff's eyes and shook her head. 'I want to look for myself.'

Greff led her back along the battlements, picking a path through breaches in the high walls and sections where servitors worked to shore up the damage. Kostagar noted Keeler trailing behind her, and she saw the weary nods and weak smiles from her troops as the woman passed among them.

The captain heard the fighting before they got there. The flat bang of boltgun discharges sounded up the sides of the fortress like peals of thunder, and she dared to step up to the edge of the crenellations and risk a look down the wide stone slope. It was hard to see through the churning smoke, but Kostagar spotted brief splashes of heavy muzzle flare, jets of ejection flame lighting the haze from below.

There were other sounds. Loud screams of agony that were suddenly cut short, and the thudding boom of krak grenades. She saw something go spinning, wheeling away, as if thrown from one of the lower levels, out into the air to tumble to the ground far below.

'That was a person,' said Greff, chancing his own head to take a look. 'An outcast?'

'Are they fighting amongst themselves?' Kostagar wondered aloud. If so, it was new behaviour for the enemy.

The guns down below went quiet and the troopers on the quad stiffened, raising their lasrifles, anticipating what would come next.

Kostagar had her pistol drawn before she was even conscious of doing it, and she raised it up in a silent command. *Hold your fire.*

'Do you see?' Greff's voice dropped to a terrified hiss. He jabbed a finger towards the roiling mass of the smoke. 'Ma'am, look there!'

At first it was only the suggestion of movement, the vague outline of shapes drifting through the black haze. Things that could have been men, or something far worse. Kostagar heard the crunch of ceramite on breaking stone, and through her boots came the tremor of a giant's footfalls.

'I see,' she said.

Hulking forms sheathed in pitted, battle-worn power armour were making the ascent up the side of the bastion from the burnt-out level beneath. Kostagar's heart leapt into her mouth.

Legionaries.

No more outcasts, no more madmen and conscripts. These were the warlords of the Emperor's own design, a single one of them the fighting equal of every soldier under her command. They carried guns and swords scaled for hands bigger than a man's head. They were clad in wargear that could turn the hit of tank shells.

It was said their kind could not be killed, and for many years of her life Maed Kostagar had thought that to be propagandist hyperbole spun by the Council of Terra. But then she had been promoted from her home stationing among the plains of Indus to one of the coveted posts in the Imperial Palace. And there, she had seen a warrior of the Legiones Astartes in the flesh for the very first time, and come to question her cynicism.

Wherever the Legions walked, they brought destruction. Now two avatars of that fate climbed the stone at her feet, slow, steady and inexorable. The shades of their armour were indistinct, but the captain had seen the hordes of the Death Guard before, and she knew these could be no other.

She took aim with her pistol, and the troopers followed along with her. This would be their only chance to put up any meaningful resistance. Perhaps a lucky hit might save their lives. Kostagar knew that if even one legionary made it up to their tier with violent intent, no one would survive.

But as the captain's finger tightened on the trigger, a delicate, long-fingered hand came to rest on her wrist and she heard the voice again.

'Maed, please don't,' said Keeler. She was standing right next to her, out of cover on the lip of the battlements. 'Let me speak to them.'

Are you insane? The words were forming on Kostagar's lips as Keeler stepped past her, deliberately making herself fully visible. 'Euphrati, no!' She grabbed at the civilian's sleeve and tried to yank her back.

Keeler shook off her grip and called out, 'Welcome, Nathaniel! It is good to see you again!'

The warrior leading the pair halted in his climb and looked up, the faceted eyes of his battle helmet finding the two women. Kostagar was aware she was pointing her weapon directly at the legionary's head, and slowly she lowered it. The warrior gave a nod in return.

'By your leave, captain,' he said, his words carrying up across the battlements. 'May we cross your lines?'

'If she vouches for you,' managed Kostagar, recovering her power of speech, 'then I suppose so.'

'Like we have a choice?' Greff muttered the words under his breath.

The captain gave him an admonishing glance as she stepped back. 'Secure that talk and look sharp.' Greff had the sense to look chastened, and he retreated before the two grey-armoured giants rose above the ramparts and climbed over.

It took all of Kostagar's self-control to stand her ground

before the towering warriors, and her knuckles whitened around the grip of her gun. She couldn't bring herself to holster it, not while every fibre of her being was screaming *danger!*

Keeler stood between the legionaries, dwarfed by their size, but utterly unintimidated. As one, the warriors reached up to remove their helmets, revealing faces mapped with scarification.

Kostagar stared at them. The one who had spoken, the one Keeler had called 'Nathaniel', had different wargear from his comrade, and his aspect had a strange kindness to it that she did not expect. The other, who seemed younger, was watchful, nursing an air of distrust.

'Here you are,' said the older legionary, looking down at Keeler. 'It vexes me and pleases me in equal measure to find you.' He glanced in Kostagar's direction. 'Captain. I hope you will forgive our unannounced arrival. I am Nathaniel Garro, I am...' He halted, as if correcting himself before he said more. 'I am a servant of Terra and the Emperor of Mankind.' Garro gestured at his comrade. 'He is Helig Gallor. My brother in arms.'

'You are Death Guard.' *Or were they?* Now she saw them clearly, the colours of their armour were subtly different from that Legion. Still, everyone held their breath when she said the words.

Gallor grunted. 'Once. But not since the betrayal.'

The captain decided to leave that statement where it lay. 'My name is Maed Kostagar. I am company commander of the Dilectio Tier, Marmax garrison.' She gave a nod. 'What brings you to our particular piece of this hell?'

'They're here for me,' Keeler answered for Garro.

'Aye,' said the elder legionary, and his steady gaze went back to the other woman. 'We must talk, Euphrati.'

As he stood upon the watch-balcony, the ruins passed beneath the primarch's jaundiced eye, a repeating landscape of beheaded towers, shattered walls and the broken remains of pretty sculptures. All wreckage and destruction now, city-sized heaps of rubble that bore no resemblance to what they had once been when whole.

The war-barge *Greenheart*, carrying Mortarion's command post, floated low over the debris like a galleon crossing a stone sea, engines humming with power above the marching lines of the Death Guard and their auxiliaries. With mechanical regularity, the weak, spoiled light of Sol appeared and disappeared through the crimson sky as the bodies of the Titans walking with them passed in front of it, causing moments of brief eclipse. Striding high at the edges of their lines, the great machines rocked and swayed to the pace of their thunderous footsteps.

The Death Lord's thin and skeletal fingers reached for one of several censer spheres hanging from his ragged robes. Plucking it like a fruit from the bough of a tree, he rolled it in his pallid palm until the chems inside began to seethe. Threads of virulent smoke emerged from the holes in the sphere's surface and Mortarion held it to the vents of his breather mask, inhaling deeply.

The earthy reek of a particular poison filled his throat, and he felt the philtre warring with his flesh, trying to destroy it. But the ruin did not spread, it only curdled and became consumed by blood that was itself more toxic than the most lethal venom. His uneasy, altered flesh was new to him, and even now the primarch was still learning the gifts it granted. The potential that had been unlocked by his acceptance of the Grandfather's Mark changed and grew every day, and he no longer feared it. He had chosen to embrace it.

Mortarion drew in every last atom of the gaseous mixture, savouring the burn. The poison had been captured from the high crags of Barbarus, where no common humans could venture without suffering an agonising death.

Barbarus: the primarch's adopted home world, its blighted

skies since ripped asunder by the petulance of the Lion and his Dark Angels. It would forever be a dead rock, and what true traces of it still remained were few. One less now, with the sphere's contents dispersed. He crushed the globe and tossed it over the balcony's corroded balustrade, into the wreckage of the Imperial Palace's outer domains.

Let it die. The notion whispered in his mind, perhaps from the depths of his own thoughts, or perhaps from other, more ephemeral dominions. *Let Barbarus die, and Terra with it. Let all the worlds die and be reborn anew.*

It was a fitting thought. Tall, gaunt and hooded, with a great scythe across his back, Mortarion resembled the avatar of death's messenger from the myths of thousands of human cultures. He looked down at his hands and examined scars on his pale flesh, repetitions of marks in a triad formation.

Life. Decay. Rebirth. The three true states of existence.

He felt nothing at the prospect of destroying something as beautiful as his father's house. For what was beauty, after all, if not a bright and shining lie? He had never truly understood the depths of the concept, never drowned himself in the ideal like his brother Fulgrim. Beauty – forced and forged by the hand of men – was something ignoble in his eyes. It was fakery.

What Mortarion sought was only *truth.*

A wet sigh announced the opening of the iris door leading into his chamber, and the primarch turned from the balcony, even as two of his Deathshroud moved to intercept the unexpected visitor. Mortarion's silent praetorians were shaped in his image, each armed with a manreaper blade, which they brought to the ready.

A coven-conscript – his face a mask of odorous blood, his emerald jerkin torn into rags – crashed into the room as if kicked, collapsing to the floor. The Deathshroud advanced on the mewling human as a second figure entered.

Typhus. Once, the primarch would have considered the other warrior his oldest, closest friend, his trusted brother... But those days were long past. Now, Mortarion's relationship with his First Captain, the so-called Traveller, could only be described as *complex.*

A mist of miniscule flies buzzing about the horned growths at his back, Typhus gave a bow that was just on the right side of respectful. ***'My lord,'*** he rumbled. ***'News from the forward reaches.'*** He indicated the cowering helot. ***'The probing attacks on the fortress at Marmax have stalled. They have been beaten back.'***

Mortarion's sinews stiffened. Retreat, and notions allied to it, were not something that his Death Guard readily indulged. ***'My orders were to advance, only advance. Until attrition or victory.'***

'Yes.' Typhus nodded again. ***'And yet...'*** He gestured at the coven-conscript, who had prostrated himself on the deck, begging for his life. ***'This one fled the line. He* survived.'** The Traveller turned the last word into a savage insult.

'Who defends this bastion?' Mortarion waved away his praetorians, advancing towards the First Captain. ***'The Warmaster's prognosticae spoke only of human soldiers garrisoned there.'***

Typhus kicked the conscript. ***'Answer your master's question.'***

'Fighters!' The trembling man stared at the deck, too afraid to meet the gaze of the hulking figures around him. 'Can't beat them, never defeat them, too strong, too wilful, they don't break, won't break...'

'Impossible,' said Mortarion. ***'Not against the numbers I dispatched.'***

'And yet...' repeated Typhus, with a curl of his lip.

'Explain!' The primarch growled the demand, but the conscript could only babble, his nerve breaking.

'Ah, no,' Typhus grunted. ***'His terror has snapped his mind. We'll get little sense from him now of what happened up there.'***

'Intelligence can be gleaned in other ways,' said Mortarion. He reached down and grabbed the man by his throat, hauling him off the floor. The primarch placed the fingers of his other hand around the conscript's shaven pate. Before his victim could protest, he squeezed hard enough to crack the man's skull. Carefully, forcefully, he broke the bones without crushing the delicate grey matter within.

The convict was still alive when Mortarion opened his head with a sickle-bladed execution knife, revealing the pulpy corpus of his brain. With surgical dexterity, the primarch reached in and found the man's hippocampus, deep amid the whorled mass. As the body collapsed, the Death Lord consumed the piece of brain matter in a single swallow.

Within moments, the omophagea node in Mortarion's chest dissolved it, the arcane bio-processes in the artificial organ separating out the chemical chains of memory until he could smell them in his nostrils like the content of the spent censer.

He closed his eyes and concentrated, listening to recollections that were not his own.

Let it die, came a whisper, *let it die.* To his surprise, the words were not from his thoughts but from those of the dead man. Whatever power spoke to Mortarion in those quiet moments, it also talked to the conscript. Perhaps to all touched by the Grandfather's Mark, he mused.

He concentrated on what he needed, separating it from the chaff of trivia that formed much of the dead man's life.

Then, entering the blurred memory-dream of the attack on Marmax, he was inside the tiny confines of the little human's limited body, sensing echoes of elation and mad fury, ghosts of abject terror and bloodlust. Roaring guns, screaming attackers, crashing stone. It was a wild deluge, like viewing a hololith through a torrential downpour, but Mortarion had done this before, and he knew what to look for.

The potency of the consumed memory was already starting to fade, and so the primarch pressed deeper. *Let it die,* said the whispers.

Light blazed at the edge of the recollection – not a physical illumination, but a figurative, subjective one. Through the eyes of the dead man, Mortarion saw the moment that had sent him running, panicking.

A line of common troopers firing in his direction, each one of them with a face lit by dogged defiance; and among them, unarmed, almost unnoticed, a woman kneeling. Speaking.

What was she saying? The fading memory did not hold that recollection, but it had captured something vital – something that the dead man could sense by instinct but not articulate with words, like an animal unconsciously catching the scent of fear.

Mortarion knew, however. In the forbidden books he had read, in the prohibited works he had absorbed, in the partnership he had made with the Grandfather, his understanding had grown to encompass such knowledge.

Witchery.

There was an aura-light around the woman that could not be seen, as if she were a prism through which a far more potent psyche had granted some of its power. That invisible light touched the humans around her, gave them strength and made them bold.

She intrigued him. That potential crackling through her blood was a priceless thing, rare and rich. He could only wonder at what nourishment it might bring if gifted to the Grandfather.

Let it die, said the whispers.

The memory faded to nothing, and Mortarion's last impression of the man he had killed was the sensation of hot blood running in streams over his hands.

He blinked back to awareness, to find Typhus watching him expectantly. ***'Did that illuminate you, my lord? Your taste for learning was sated?'***

'I saw enough,' he replied, turning away. ***'We will continue with the pace of our advance as planned.'***

The Traveller remained where he was, ignoring the dismissal

implicit in his primarch's tone. *'Must we? The Legion marches at the speed of its slowest element, and for what account? We could be at Marmax in hours. Instead, we slowly pick our way through ruins while our enemies regroup on the horizon.'*

Typhus was eager for battle, and he had made no secret of how he chafed at the primarch's measured advance. He and his company would have cut away and prosecuted their own invasion, if Mortarion had not forbade it.

'We will wet our blades in good time.' Mortarion touched the edge of his war-scythe. *'Patience, Calas.* **Patience.***'*

The use of his old forename drew a grimace from the Traveller. *'Would we move at so leisurely a pace if I told you that our scry-scouts have sighted the Sigillite's agents in neighbouring sectors? Knights Errant, my lord. The warriors in grey.'*

'You should have led with that,' Mortarion retorted irritably. *'How did this information come?'*

'From a blight drone,' replied Typhus. *'Before it perished, it captured an impression of an old friend. The traitor of the* **Eisenstein.***'*

Garro. The whisper gave him the name, and a tremor of cold amusement unfolded in the primarch's chest. *If he is here, then he has come for the woman of the light. There can be no other reason.*

Mortarion gave a racking, dust-dry snort. For days now, he had felt the threefold hand of the Grandfather guiding him, directing him towards the faint aura flickering atop the bastion, to the light of something so pure amid so much horror that it shone like a beacon. Now came this news, the presence of the traitor, confirming what he knew to be true. It had to be fate, he decided, the Grandfather moving over events to bring them to pass.

An opportunity was here, a chance to take all these prizes at once. To obliterate Marmax and capture the woman in the memory, so her blood could be water to Nurgle's gardens; and to rid the galaxy of the oath-breaker Garro, by the little-death of his submission, or the greater of his murder.

INTERVAL I

The starship Endurance: before Isstvan

'What answer do you expect of him, my lord?' Typhon posed the question with deceptively little weight.

Mortarion considered his reply as they marched along the corridors of his flagship, his Deathshroud praetorians at his side. All about them, the warriors of the Death Guard were at their stations or setting to their preparations for the attack on the planets of the Isstvan System.

How many of them sensed the import of what was going to come, of the great upheaval that would begin on those inconsequential little worlds? How many were invested in Horus Lupercal's great plans for rebellion, and the changed galaxy that it would create?

When the moment came, when Mortarion gave the fateful order to open fire on the other Legions, how many of his sons would pull the trigger? Not out of their own intent or understanding, but because they were *commanded* to do so?

Will they do it because they are tools? *Or because they* understand *this?*

Mortarion released a breath. 'What do I expect, kinsman?' He glanced back at the First Captain, who feigned a casual smile. 'I expect to find the truth.'

Typhon's expression stiffened, and he halted. 'But why him? There are others who are unswerving, loyal legionaries to which the question of obedience does need not be asked. Grulgor. Kalgaro. Crosius. And more.'

'That is exactly *why* I need to know Nathaniel Garro's mind,' he replied, pausing beside an oval viewport. 'Because the battle-captain is fiercely independent of action and impetus. Because he rejected membership in the Davinite lodges...'

'Because he is Terran-born, and not a child of Barbarus?' Typhon cocked his head and absently fingered his dark beard.

'That too.' Mortarion gave a nod. 'He is respected, not just by his men and by other company captains, but by warriors in our sibling Legions. Garro's stance on what will come to pass on Isstvan is a bellwether. If he agrees to it...'

'Aye, if a warrior as loyal as "Straight-Arrow Garro" would bow to the insurrection, then who could argue its necessity?'

'Just so.' Mortarion turned to move on, but Typhon had more to say.

'You know he will never take a stand against the Emperor. Garro will never turn his back on the Throne.'

'Perhaps. But I will not dismiss a warrior of note without due consideration.'

'You are too fond of him.' Typhon sniffed. 'If I were commanding the Legion, the matter would have already been dispatched.'

Mortarion eyed his old friend from the depths of his hooded

robes and his tone sharpened to a razor edge. 'But you are not, Calas. And the choice is not yours to make. If you wish to retain your post as captain of my First Company, you should remember that.' They began to walk again.

'I meant no disrespect,' Typhon said quietly. 'But I believe we will have to kill him. Garro will not turn.'

At length, the primarch gave a nod, reluctantly accepting the possibility. 'If it needs to be done... have the brute Grulgor see to it. But only on my word.'

They found Garro with his men, and on the primarch's arrival, the battle-captain and his command squad went to their knees before their liege-lord and the First Captain.

Mortarion bid the legionary to his feet. 'Stand, Nathaniel, please. It becomes tiresome to look down upon my men.'

The faintest hint of doubt and uncertainty lurked in the warrior's eyes as he stood, but to his credit the battle-captain did not flinch from his gene-sire's searching, measuring gaze.

Mortarion smiled thinly. 'You ought to watch your step, Typhon. This one, he'll have your job one day.'

Still chastened from his primarch's earlier censure, Typhon said nothing, remaining as silent as the voiceless Deathshroud.

Garro took a breath. 'Lord, what service may the Seventh Company do for you?'

'Their captain may step forward,' said Mortarion. 'He has earned a reward.'

The moment of confusion on the battle-captain's face was brief. 'Sire, I deserve no special–'

Typhon spoke over him before he could finish the thought. 'That is not a refusal forming upon your lips, is it, captain? Such false modesty is unwelcome.'

'I am merely a servant of the Emperor.' Garro bristled. 'That is honour enough.'

Mortarion felt Typhon's gaze on him, and his words unspoken. *You see? Garro will never turn his back on the Throne.*

He pushed that thought aside and beckoned to a Legion servitor lurking close by. As it ambled forward, a tray of containers held before it, he addressed Garro again. 'Then instead, Nathaniel, might you honour me by sharing my drink?'

The men called them *the cups;* it was not anything as archaic as a ritual, not so rigid an act as that. Just a gesture shared between warriors of the Death Guard, a small way to toast their indefatigable nature and reaffirm the concord of the XIV Legion.

The reputation of Mortarion's sons was one of obdurate strength and unbreakable endurance – their repute carried before them, the vow that no obstacle, no toxin, no venom could stop them in their tracks. This truth had been born in the poison fogs of Mortarion's adoptive home world and spread to every corner of the Death Guard's campaigns, on worlds so hostile and toxic that no other Legion would dare to face them.

With the cups, they proved that truth over again. In the echo of a gesture that he himself had begun on Barbarus, in the aftermath of any engagement where Mortarion participated, he would select warriors and share a drink.

But not ale, wine or amasec. The draught would be of poison.

The servitor finished the work of mixing the chemicals and poured measures of the lethal brew into three plain metal cups. Mortarion took the first, the second he gave to Typhon and the third he placed in Garro's open hand. The battle-captain studied the mixture dubiously, catching the molecular scents of the cocktail of toxins.

'Against death,' said the primarch, saluting with the cup. He drank the contents in a single, long pull. The fire of the poisons bit into Mortarion's body and he savoured the blood-rush as they warred with his enhanced physiology. It made him feel *alive.*

Typhon followed suit, never one to be seen to show reticence, but even he could not drink as swiftly as Mortarion had. Then Garro warily repeated the salute and drank as deeply as he dared. For a moment, the battle-captain's colour rose and the primarch wondered if he had gone too far; but Garro held his own, fighting the response of his flesh, *enduring* as only a Death Guard could.

Mortarion could not resist a cold smile, pleased by the display of fortitude. 'A rare and fine vintage, would you not agree?' Garro could only nod, the savage burn of the toxins temporarily robbing him of the ability to speak. At length, the primarch put a hand on the legionary's back. 'Come, Nathaniel,' he said, dismissing the others with a nod. 'Let's walk it off.'

They paused at a balcony above one of the *Endurance*'s vast loading bays, where several of the Death Guard's companies were staging for the drop on Isstvan. Mortarion studied them grimly. These sons of his were doomed to a sacrifice that they had no idea was coming, and although their deaths were a regrettable cost of the rebellion to come, he did not weigh the cost cheaply.

What Mortarion was about to do would alter the course of his Legion's future forever. Old oaths sworn and given would be shattered beyond repair. *Some will call us traitors,* he thought, *and they may be right.*

He glanced at Garro, considering what the battle-captain would say if he were to reveal the whole of the truth to him. How would he react to word of Horus' sundering?

'You are a respected man,' Mortarion noted. 'There's not a captain in the whole of the Legion who would not acknowledge your combat prowess... Even Commander Grulgor, although he may hate to admit it.' Garro reluctantly accepted the words of praise as his liege-lord went on. 'The men trust you. They look to you for strength of character, for leadership, and you give it.'

Garro's discomfort grew distinct. 'I do only what the Emperor commands of me, sire,' he said, after a moment.

Of course he does. Once more, Mortarion felt the ghost of Typhon's warning in his thoughts.

'It is important to me to have unity of purpose within my Legion,' insisted the primarch, 'just as it is important for my brother Horus to have unity across the entirety of the Legiones Astartes.' Carefully, he probed for the response he wanted, searching for some possibility that Garro might choose Legion over Throne when the ultimate moment arrived. 'The Death Guard must be of one mind,' he went on. 'We must have singular purpose or we will falter.'

Affirm your loyalty to me. Mortarion stared into Garro's eyes, willing him to make the vow anew. But the words he sought to hear remained unspoken.

Perhaps Typhon was right, perhaps the primarch did grant the battle-captain more latitude than he deserved. But Garro represented something that Mortarion wanted to hold fast within the Death Guard, no matter whose banner they marched under.

Honour. A simple quality at its heart, but one many were hard-pressed to retain.

He posed a question to the warrior, about the Davinite lodges, and in the reply Mortarion finally saw that what he hoped for was not there.

'We are set on our path by the Master of Mankind,' said Garro. 'Tasked to regather the lost fragments of humanity to the fold of the Imperium, to illuminate the lost, castigate the fallen and the invader. We can only do so if we have truth on our side. If we do it in the open, under the harsh light of the universe, then I have no doubt that we will eventually expunge the fallacies of gods and deities... But we cannot bring the secular truth to bear if any of it is hidden, even the smallest part. Only the Emperor can show the way forward.'

Garro will not turn. Typhon's voice was as clear to Mortarion as it would have been if the First Captain had been standing at his side. *We will have to kill him.*

So be it. The primarch made his choice and covered it with a nod. 'Thank you for your candour, battle-captain. I expected nothing less.'

Garro nodded, believing that he was in receipt of an honour in this moment, unaware that his words would be his death warrant.

I will keep him close, Mortarion decided, *and with that, learn the faces of any others among my sons who share his sentiments. And when the moment comes…*

…Nathaniel Garro will die for his Emperor.

THREE

Duty & Love
Attack Warning
Helbrute

Although it was technically classed as a single level of the Marmax Bastion, it would have been wrong to name the Dilectio Tier a 'floor' of a particular building, as if it were the upper storey on some ordinary hab-construct. The footprint of the tier, if set out on the grid of the Palace-city beneath it, would have encompassed several metropolitan blocks. It had its own independent power core, a landing pad cupola, operations centre and dozens of barrack quads – although many of these were empty, their population thinned by the constant attacks.

As such, Garro saw that Euphrati Keeler had plenty of space to call her own in the chambers Captain Kostagar had granted to her. Keeler's rooms were off the main corridor nexus of the tier, and she explained that being there made it easier for the soldiers of the Auxilia to come and find her when they wished to talk.

Garro looked around, taking in the space, the low ceiling and the heavy stone walls. Electro-candles burned here and there, casting a warm light, and in one corner he spotted a familiar bundle of bound pages printed in crimson ink, lying in an open crate. His own copy of the *Lectitio Divinitatus*, bequeathed to him by his long-dead housecarl Kaleb, was rolled tightly in one of the pouch-packs affixed to his wargear. He had not considered it for some time.

Across from a hammock, there were several empty chairs around a makeshift table made from another storage box, and a battered old auto-samovar that could have made black tea for fifty people. The rooms might have been a place for Keeler to lay her head, but they were more than that.

'This feels familiar,' Garro noted, gesturing around. 'Another place, but the same scenario. Are we destined to repeat events, you and I? Perhaps this is the Emperor's influence on the path of our lives, drawing us into the same circles?'

She shook her head. 'This isn't like it was at the chapel on Hesperides.'

Then, in a secret church on the orbital plate above Terra, Keeler had been actively spreading the word of the God-Emperor's divinity. She had done so with such vigour that it made her the target of a cursed Assassin sent by the Warmaster himself. Garro had killed that man before he could fulfil his mission, but to this day he still felt as if he hadn't protected Keeler well enough.

'I don't preach here,' she went on. 'I don't even read the...' The woman nodded towards the papers in the crate, without finishing the thought. 'It is enough for me to just... Just *be*.'

Garro frowned at that and sighed, suddenly as weary as if he carried the weight of the world. 'What are you doing, Euphrati?'

Keeler smiled faintly. 'Whatever I can, Nathaniel.'

Garro grew a scowl. 'Don't be glib, it doesn't suit you.'

She laughed. 'If you believe that, then you may not know me as well as you think.' She wandered to where her old, dented picter lay in the hammock, and toyed with the device. 'Once, I was renowned for it.'

He ignored her attempt at deflection. 'When last we met, I

begged you to leave Terra, but you insisted on remaining. If you had accepted my counsel then, you would be light years away now.'

'And *safe*? Is that what you were going to say?' Keeler shook her head. 'Do you think anywhere in the galaxy will be safe until this is over? And even then, if the Warmaster is defeated?'

'Horus *will* die,' Garro insisted. 'And the iterator, Sindermann... He could remain in your stead.'

'Kyril has his own work to do,' she countered. 'His path was never mine to choose for him.'

At length, Garro went to the crate and picked up the battered copy of the *Lectitio Divinitatus*. 'The word of this... It needs a light, a voice to guide it. We both know what happens when there isn't one to keep the seekers on the true path. And you are the light, Euphrati. If you go in harm's way, you put that in jeopardy!'

'You're wrong,' she shot back. 'I am keeping the word alive, in the only way I can!'

'By needlessly risking your life?' Garro's voice rose, and he caught himself before it became a shout.

Keeler's tone was wounded. 'Is that why you are here, old friend? To say *I told you so?* That does not suit *you*.'

Garro stared down at the book, frustration and duty and a dozen other sentiments warring within him. He turned the pages, briefly losing himself in the action, and the silence between them lengthened.

When he spoke again, he took a different tack. 'Do you remember the gallery you showed me, that day on the Hesperides plate?'

Keeler nodded, clasping the picter. Alone with Garro, she had presented the legionary with still images captured by the device, but each one was of a possible future where she would perish. There had been countless variations, but only one where Keeler lived – the one where Garro watched over her.

She nodded in the direction of the corridor. 'You can see the Byzant Minaret from the battlements up here.' The slender tower was the setting for one of the death-images, Garro recalled, in which Keeler's end came at the point of a sword. 'Well,' she corrected, 'the ruins of it, at least.'

'I know,' said Garro. 'I was there when it was destroyed. I confess I was relieved to see it crumble. That meant one less ill fate that might come to pass.'

'I meant what I said,' she said. 'The Sigillite drew an oath from me, and from Kyril, and the rest of us. We cannot preach... So I found another way to help. It is for the best.'

Garro studied her, seeing the micro-expressions and subtle tells that only a transhuman could have detected. 'Do not hold back from me,' he said gently, cutting to the truth of it. 'I know you mean what you say, but I can see the doubt in you.' Keeler opened her mouth to speak but he held up a hand, finishing his thought. 'I know it, because I have also known that uncertainty. You helped me find my way past it.'

'I refused to hide in some dungeon chamber in the Blackstone,' she told him. 'Yes, I have my misgivings, but I knew I could do more out in the world. I felt it in my bones. I could no more sit aside while this siege rages than you have.'

'Yet you are still uncertain as to what lies at the end of your road.'

She glanced up at him. 'When did you get to be so perceptive, battle-captain?'

'It's how I was made,' he admitted.

Keeler sighed. 'Is it odd to say that among this madness, the fighting and bloodshed, I found a kind of peace?' She shook her head. 'Don't answer that. But I tell you, the acts of walking the corridors, talking to the troopers holding the line... I found myself exploring my own questions about the nature of the God-Emperor as well as theirs. And in doing so, they were inspired by me. I didn't mean for it to happen. But if less of them die when they hear my voice, if I give them something like faith to hold on to… How can that be a bad thing?'

'You would not ask that question if you were certain of the answer.'

'No. I suppose not.' She broke his gaze and looked away. 'There is an irony to this, don't you think? Our roles are reversed, Nathaniel. Once you were the one seeking guidance, but now it is I who searches for it.'

'If that is so, then let me illuminate you.' He put down the booklet and crossed to her side. She seemed so small and fragile in the candle-glow, but Garro knew that was a misconception. Euphrati Keeler had a reserve of inner strength greater than many warriors of his experience. 'Think of the good you can do, the inspiration you can give, if only you live beyond this day, beyond the reach of this damnable heresy.' He reached out and took her hand, enveloping the woman's slender fingers in his great ceramite gauntlet. 'The danger you have placed yourself in, in this citadel… It is too grave. In any other soul I might think the act was a death wish! You are too important to risk yourself for such a small and inconsequential battle as this one, for just the lives of Kostagar and her meagre force of troopers. The good captain would say the same, if only you asked her.'

'No…' Keeler shook her head, and pulled her hand from his grasp. 'How can you say that to me?' A new fire burned in her eyes. 'None of these battles are inconsequential. You shouldn't be so fixated on some idealised path to destiny that you lose sight of what you are fighting for! This entire bloody insurrection was born out of that kind of short-sightedness!' She put her hand, fingers spread, on the breastplate of Garro's armoured cuirass. 'However the trappings of it may appear, this conflict burning about us? It's not for the God-Emperor, not for His primarch sons or even for your brother Legions. It's for the common folk of the Imperium, the ones who have the most to lose! People like Maed and her troopers. Tell me you still see that, Nathaniel. *Please.*'

He held his silence, weighing his words before he replied. 'I... see it.' But for a moment, he had not. It was easy to lose perspective in a war so vast it had set the galaxy aflame. 'There is truth in your words,' he went on, 'but never forget that I am unlike you. I am a warrior of the Legiones Astartes, and I was bred to instil fear and awe. My kind cannot engender what you do. Faith. *Love.*' Garro shook his head. 'A speaker, a saint... She can inspire. But ultimately, a legionary is only a creature of martial duty... And my duty is to preserve your life at any cost.'

'Even if it is against my wishes?'

'Even if.' He gave a wan smile. 'You once told me I would save you, Euphrati. Please, let me do that.'

'You will,' she said firmly. 'It is not quite time yet. But soon. Very soon.'

Garro took a breath to form another question, but before he could utter a word, a clanging alarm bell sounded down the corridors.

'The attack warning,' said Keeler. 'The heretics have returned.'

'Throne and blood.' Gallor watched the colour drain from Captain Kostagar's face as she stared through her monocular, into the army of figures beneath the oncoming mass of warsmoke. 'There's so many of them... I can't even begin the count.'

Gallor nodded gravely. 'They've picked up the pace. The main elements of the Death Guard advance will enter attack range within an hour. I'll warrant their vanguard will be here in minutes.'

She frowned. 'I don't see the Titans. I had expected their bombardment...'

'That is not the Death Guard way,' he noted. 'The war machines will hold off in case heavy fire is required. The attacks to come will be ones of attrition, fought close and hard. They will want to see your faces when you die.' He ventured to the edge of the battlements and looked down. Shapes moved in the haze, but he couldn't register anything more than vague forms. 'Now would be the time for you to commit any reinforcements, captain.'

Kostagar gave him a shocked look and a bark of incredulous laughter. 'Are you new to this battle, legionary? We *were* the reinforcements. No one else will be coming.' She waved in the direction of the other distant bastions lined up past Marmax, disappearing into the far reaches. 'Each of these fortresses is an island unto itself. We are all that is left of this one's populace.' She lifted the monocular again, scanning the enemy lines.

'Then, with respect, perhaps it is time to withdraw.' Gallor checked his boltgun, his nerves tingling with a pre-sense of imminent violence.

As a former warrior of the XIV Legion, he knew their tactical doctrines by heart. The initial probing attacks were over, and the next strike would be a reconnaissance-in-force. After that would come what the sons of Barbarus called *the march* – the steady, inexorable movement of their lethal infantry advance, rolling over all resistance, grinding it brutally beneath their boots.

'My orders were to hold,' Kostagar replied, clutching what defiance she still had. 'And I will, until I… Until…' She faltered as she saw something through the monocular. Her expression shifted again, towards abject fear and cold revulsion. 'What in the name of blades is that?' Horror marbled every word she uttered.

Kostagar pointed at a war-barge moving through the Palace-city's rubble-choked boulevards, far off in the middle of the main Death Guard force. Atop the corroded, copper-green prow of the vessel, figures were visible amid a cloud of drifting, swirling black motes. One was tall, lost in the shadows of a dark cloak; the other was hulking and bloated. An aura of ghastly menace surrounded them.

Gallor didn't need to see their ruined faces. He knew their names.

'He is here,' said the legionary, but his words were for his kinsman, as Garro approached from behind. 'Mortarion has come. And Typhon's with him.'

'It is said he calls himself *Typhus* now,' said Garro, moving to stand alongside. 'He always was... twisted inside. Now his outer aspect mirrors his true nature.'

Kostagar let the monocular drop. 'That... that's a primarch. One of the changed ones.'

'Aye,' said Gallor.

She nodded, staring at the stones at her feet. Sweat dripped off her face, and Gallor frowned. He had seen this in common folk before – the shock-effect of facing a post-human being, of grasping that abrupt realisation of what the Emperor's sons really were, and of what they were capable.

But this was worse, for what Kostagar saw down there was a corrupted version of that, an engineered demigod transformed into something monstrous. Something *daemonic.*

'After due consideration,' said the captain, 'I've decided to re-evaluate the orders I was given–'

Heat like the heart of a star obliterated the woman before she could finish the thought. Propelled by preternaturally fast reflexes, Gallor and Garro were already in motion as the sun-fire pulse of the enemy plasma cannon screamed in, diving away from the strike point.

But Maed Kostagar never saw her death coming. The plasmatic blast ate a hemisphere of stone out of the battlements, turning ferrocrete blocks into acidic vapour, heating others around it to the point of brittle fracture. Fires started everywhere there was something combustible, and troopers screamed as their uniforms caught alight and their carapace armour melted like wax.

The smallest mercy was that Kostagar would not have felt any pain, likely would not even have known she was dying – the violent force of the plasma blast reduced her to atoms faster than her nerves would have registered it. But now a good soldier was dead and her people were in disarray.

Gallor lurched back to the seething heat of the broken battlements and saw the massive, bloated shape of the captain's killer, rising before a horde of screaming outcasts.

It resembled a venerable Dreadnought of the Legion, but only in the broadest of ways. Swollen and overlarge, the bipedal mutant was a fusion of corroded armour plating and oozing, ashen skin. Thick wattles of diseased, reeking flesh protruded from around the edges of the rust-caked metal, as if the heavy plates were barely able to keep the organic matter inside from bursting out into the air.

One entire arm of the bestial thing was the bulbous plasma cannon that had erased Kostagar from the world, jets of superheated steam shrieking from coolant vents down the serrated length of the glowing barrel. Where the other arm should have been, there was a writhing nest of slime-coated tentacles, each as thick as the torso of a human. Some of these were anchored in the sloping side of the bastion's outer wall, allowing the creature to make the slow climb upward, and others whipped at the air, showing hook-toothed maws at their tips.

The hulk had no head, only a torn orifice in the centre of its chest where ropes of rotting epidermis had been peeled back and nailed in place. In the hole there was a face made of dozens of maddened, rheumy eyes that rolled to show yellowed whites, above a flapping skeleton jaw that opened and closed like the working of a mantrap.

'*Helbrute.*' Garro named the thing with a sneer of disgust. 'The Death Lord has sent one of his accursed to destroy us.'

'It won't die cleanly,' said Gallor, as the creature crashed upward over the fortress' steep incline, knocking aside the outcasts at its feet in its eagerness.

'But it *will* die,' Garro noted. He raised his gun – an exemplary model of a master-crafted Paragon bolter – and fired into the Helbrute's hide. The whistling cadence of Kraken rounds sliced through the air and Gallor drew his pistol, snapping off a cluster of shots in the direction of the monster's torso.

Orange sparks flared off the Helbrute's armour, but it showed no signs of slowing its climb. Both the legionaries knew that they could not allow the thing to reach the Dilectio Tier. In the confines of the corridors, it would kill everything that drew breath.

Gallor found the nearest of the Army troopers who still showed some degree of clarity and gestured down the line. 'Kostagar is dead, you are in command now. Muster the men, concentrate your fire on the outcasts.'

'B-but that... that *thing!*' The young man's eyes were wide with abject terror.

'Is our concern,' Gallor said bluntly. 'Do as I say. We'll avenge your captain, aye?'

'Aye.' The trooper stiffened as he accepted his new burden, and Gallor turned away.

Garro handed him a magnetic disc attached to a length of heavy-duty polymer cable. The cable ran to a reel set into the stonework of the battlements, and the other legionary had already locked another to a tether point on his backpack. 'Ready to take a stroll, Helig?'

Gallor accepted the disc and locked on himself. Similar mechanisms were often deployed in null-grav environments, safety lines that would keep fighters from drifting off into the void. Here, the cables allowed defenders to descend along the steeply angled sides of the Marmax Bastion without fear of falling to their deaths.

'Guns only,' added Garro. 'We cannot chance the use of blades... A single ill-judged sword swing could cut our cables, and I have no desire to plummet to the ground below.'

Another plasmatic blast screamed through the air, lashing the battlements with flame, and Gallor banged his mailed fist on Garro's shoulder pauldron. 'Go now!'

The Helbrute weapon's powerful release was brutal, but it ran hot and the recharge cycle was long. In the pause between shots, the two Knights Errant threw themselves over the edge of the fortifications, sparks rising as they dug in the heels of their ceramite boots and the fingertips of their gauntlets to slow their descent.

Gallor felt the tug of the cable at his back, heard the buzz of the line reeling out. Raising his bolt pistol again, he paced rounds up the Helbrute's torso, aiming for the eye-cluster.

Around him, streaks of laser fire fell in a deadly rain as the troopers on the line opened up on the chattering outcasts. The Helbrute rocked back and emitted a reedy scream, exhaling a noxious breath that curdled the air about it.

Dangling precariously over the dizzying drop, the legionaries kept up their own salvo of bolt shells, but the monster brought up its tentacles to cover its torso with the thick bulk of greasy flesh. Impacts tore out chunks of sizzling meat, leaving gaping wounds oozing chalky pus, but the hits did little to slow the thing's advance.

Garro pulled on his cable, reeling back and swinging wide as the Helbrute lit off another shrieking plasma bolt. This one slashed horizontally across the bastion's stonework, carving a blackened furrow through the ouslite cladding. Across the slope, the slide on Gallor's pistol snapped open as he expended the last round in the magazine. He bared his teeth in annoyance as he slammed a fresh load into place. The Helbrute soaked up every hit they landed on it, and the thing never lost a step.

Guns would not be enough to stop it. A more radical approach was required.

Gallor jammed his pistol back in its holster and pulled his combat knife instead, turning it in his fist. Garro caught sight of light flashing off the weapon's monomolecular edge, and called out, 'What are you doing? I said no blades–'

'I know what you said,' Gallor snapped back. 'Cover me.' He flicked the knife backwards and cut his own tether. Gravity snatched at him and the warrior dropped like a stone, sending up sheets of sparks as his armour scraped down the side of the fortress exterior.

'Fool!' He heard Garro shout the word at his back, but still the battle-captain did as he was asked, bracketing his comrade with heavy fire.

At the last second, Gallor kicked off and launched himself directly at the Helbrute. He collided with the creature, leading with the blade, stabbing wildly at its exposed flesh.

The monster screeched and rocked back, but its clawed feet held firm, metre-long iron talons digging deep into the stone. Gallor took off the tips of thrashing tentacles whipping at his back, sending gushes of foetid blood sluicing into the lower tiers. He grabbed fistfuls of sallow, doughy meat and ripped them away. The Helbrute writhed, trying to shake him off, and when it couldn't, the beast clubbed him with the massive barrel of the plasma cannon.

Gallor saw a ball of light building in the weapon's pre-fire chamber, and the air around it shuddered in a heat haze – but then more shots from Garro's Paragon clipped the steaming coolant pipes and mechanisms feeding the cannon.

The Helbrute let off a premature shot from the plasma weapon, a catastrophic misfire that ripped open the emitter muzzle and sent particles of bone and fulgurite glass into the air. Gallor pressed himself into the fortress wall to duck the inferno, but even at a fraction of full power, the blast boiled off shreds of his wargear's outer shell. The fire exposed the muscle fibres and power train of the armour beneath, and cooked the warrior's flesh within.

Wounded and enraged, the Helbrute sent its writhing appendages snaking around him, trying to hold him down. The trapdoor mouth opened in a ululating scream, and it brought the broken end of the plasma cannon down on his chest.

Glowing blinding white, the shattered maw of the useless gun was still hot enough to melt ceramite, and with a crackling hiss, the Helbrute drove it through the layers of Gallor's chestplate and into the meat of him.

The legionary let out a cry of agony as sub-modules of his wargear went offline and the infernal heat enveloped him, boiling the blood in his veins. Unlike poor Kostagar, Gallor would be made to feel every moment of his burning end.

Dimly, he was aware of Garro crying out to him, but the screaming from the Helbrute's broken-toothed maw drowned out the words.

If I am to perish, then this abomination comes with me. Gallor grabbed blindly for a cluster of knurled cylinders dangling from his belt, fingers closing around them.

He ripped the krak grenades free, the arming pins spinning away, and with a yell, the legionary rammed the devices into the orifice of the Helbrute's face.

The creature reacted, releasing its grip on Gallor as it tried desperately to pull the grenades from where they had lodged. To his dismay, Gallor's armour responded jerkily to his movements, malfunctioning around him as he began to slide towards the sheer drop.

A heavy shape blurred past him on the end of a whickering cable, and Gallor was suddenly moving across the fortress walls instead of down. Garro had him in his iron grip, pulling the other legionary away.

Behind them, the krak grenades went off in a ripple of thunder and the Helbrute came apart, the discharge smothering its cohort of outcasts in ashes and fire. A toxic wash of acidic blood steamed in the light falling from the great aegis far above, and in the lull that followed, Gallor heard the cheers of Kostagar's troopers and the creaking of strained cable. With only a few degrees of motion in the fused joints of his armour, he could only tense himself against the storm of pain in his flesh, as his bio-implants fought the damage within him.

'Fool,' Garro repeated, shifting his position to take Gallor's weight. Moving hand over hand, he began the slow process of climbing back up the slope towards the Dilectio Tier. 'It almost killed you.'

'Almost,' admitted Gallor, wheezing out the words as his body forced him into a healing trance. 'Perhaps the next one our gene-sire sends… will be more of a challenge.'

FOUR

The Fate We Choose
No Turning Back
The Challenge

Another of the empty barracks in the core of the Dilectio Tier had been turned into a makeshift recovery space, and Greff – the trooper Gallor had summarily promoted into command of the defenders – had provided a medicae servitor for use by the Knights Errant.

For a while, Garro stood sentinel beside the angled support pallet where his brother-warrior lay silently. The helot tottered closer, using a manipulator to inject philtres and antigens into Gallor's neck, but in truth its help was hardly needed. Despite the horrible plasma burns the legionary had suffered, he was fully capable of healing himself, given time.

But that was a commodity no one had in surplus within the Marmax Bastion. On the tick of every minute, a salvo of laser bolts streaked into the flanks of the fortress, sending crashing shocks through the dense stone. Dust and debris trickled from the ceiling above as the Death Guard used their ranged weapons against the stronghold, forcing the defenders to remain in cover or be atomised.

Mortarion could have ordered the macro-guns and nuclear launchers under his command to open up in an instant, had he truly wanted to wipe Marmax off the map; but that was not the tactic here. The invaders barraged the tiers to keep the troopers pinned in place while the real attack was being prepared.

There was little else to be done but wait, and so Garro was in the process of cleaning and reloading his Paragon bolter when Gallor suddenly jerked awake, twitching sharply enough to knock the doddering servitor off its iron feet.

The younger warrior's damaged features were briefly caught in a moment of shock as he looked down at the half-melted wreckage of his own battle armour.

'My wargear…' Gallor managed, his voice as dry as kindling.

'It was almost your coffin,' Garro explained, bringing him a canteen of water. 'I am sorry to say it is damaged beyond our capacity to fully repair, at least with any tools to hand in this place.' Gallor took the canteen and drank it dry as Garro went on. 'The plasma damaged the joints, destroyed the circuitry.'

The lasers hit again, and Gallor cocked his head, quietly assimilating the situation. 'Very well,' he said. He discarded the container and leaned up, rising unsteadily off the pallet where Garro had placed him. Leaked blood and processor fluids soaked the mattress where the warrior's genhanced body had gone into overdrive in order to keep him alive. He closed his eyes and Garro knew he was taking a mental inventory of the damage that had been done to him.

Neither needed to say it out loud. Gallor's risky ploy to kill the Helbrute had succeeded, but he had almost died in the attempt.

His eyes opened again. 'Thank you.' Gallor spoke quietly, grudgingly, and his tone made it clear he would not be open to criticism of his actions. 'How long have I been hibernative? What has transpired in that time?'

'Not long,' said Garro. 'Only hours. I think your mind refused to surrender fully to the healing trance. And as for the enemy...' He gestured at the dusty air and they both listened to the steady chorus of energy impacts.

Gallor nodded to himself, and he ran a hand over his head, tensing as he touched patches where the outer epidermis had been burned all the way down to the nerve sheath, mentally shunting away the pain. 'The next assault will be the one that breaks through.'

'Likely,' admitted Garro.

Gallor rose stiffly, and made a growling noise as he surveyed the damage wrought upon his ruined armour. 'For a moment... when I awoke... I thought my spirit had been severed from my body.' He shook his head. 'Fanciful. The mind playing tricks upon me.'

'You don't consider such things possible?'

Gallor eyed him. 'I'm not like you. I put no stock in the numinous.'

'And yet you came to me with the news of Keeler. You came here. You almost died protecting her and... the *numinous* things she represents.'

'Yes. It seems I am what you accused me of out there, captain. I am a fool.' Before Garro could respond to that, the injured warrior took a juddering, limping step towards him. 'You know they will all die, yes? When the march reaches us, every last one of the defenders will be massacred, even with Keeler's inspiration to motivate them. Her words can't protect them. The Emperor cannot protect them. Their only choices are retreat or perish.' He paused. 'And as for you and I... There is no question Mortarion will see us dead before he moves on from this place.'

From the gloom of his memories, a voice pushed out of Garro's eidetic recall and echoed in his ears, as strong as if the man who had said the words were standing beside him.

He let me see. The Vindicare Assassin Eristede Kell, corrupted and dispatched by the Warmaster to kill Euphrati Keeler on the Hesperides plate, had spoken to him in the moments before Garro ended his life. *And I've seen you dead, Death Guard. Your heart broken and bleeding black.*

Kell's utterance had the conviction of someone bereft of any doubt. Was it possible that Horus had somehow shown the Assassin a skein of the future where Garro's life was forfeit? He looked at Gallor's damaged flesh, at the black blood congealing on his body where the legionary's bio-implants warred with his near-fatal injuries.

The question weighed him down. *Is it finally time?*

'She can't die here,' Garro said quietly, then he repeated the statement with force. 'She can't die here! I will not allow it!'

'But if Keeler refuses to leave–'

'Are you whole enough to fight, Helig?' Garro's words were as fierce as the roar of the lasguns, and he stared into the other warrior's eyes as he spoke.

'Always,' said Gallor, bristling at the challenge.

'I assumed as much.' Garro picked up the other warrior's bolter and pressed it into his hands. 'These are my commands: secure the landing cupola on the far side of the tier. There's a heavy cargo carrier in there that should still be airworthy. Strip it to the bulkheads and pack every last one of Kostagar's troopers inside, and Keeler with them. Take them to the Inner Palace, low and fast, beyond the range of the Titan guns. Take them somewhere safe.'

'Look around,' Gallor said sourly. '*Safe* is a relative term, kinsman.'

'Do as I say!'

Gallor grimaced. 'Suppose I agree to that. You know what will happen when Mortarion's spotters see the troopers abandoning their posts. They'll come in force, and swiftly with it.

We both know the Death Guard can take the pace if they are motivated. That carrier won't make it off the pad.'

'Aye,' admitted Garro. 'So I will provide something else to occupy their attention.'

The younger warrior's scalded face twisted in a grimace as he caught Garro's meaning. 'You're not coming with us.'

'We go where we are needed.'

'You want me to... to run? While you stay back and sell your life like a cheap token?' Gallor was affronted by the suggestion. 'Where is the honour in that?'

'It is not a matter of honour. It is one of *need*.' Garro shook his head. 'I have no doubt you can fight, despite your injuries, but on this day I need a man I can trust, not a warrior.' He put a hand on Gallor's shoulder. 'You might not believe in what I do, but you believe in duty. And yours is to save Keeler and the other survivors.'

Gallor angrily shrugged him off. 'What do you think you will achieve? The great Battle-Captain Nathaniel Garro, the hand of the Sigillite, the hero of the *Eisenstein*, will single-handedly halt the Death Guard advance? Mortarion's guns will rip you to shreds in the blink of an eye! This is arrogance.. Nothing but fatalistic hubris!'

'I do have my pride, it must be said,' Garro countered. 'And I have no wish to die for nought. But today there is need. And we both know it.'

'My words fall on deaf ears.' Gallor stepped away. 'You will do whatever you wish, no matter what argument I present. That has always been your way.'

'I know my duty–'

'An excuse!' Gallor shot back. 'You took the *Eisenstein* and ran for Terra, and said it was because of duty! Those of us on the ship, the Seventy, we had no say in it! And so we found ourselves orphaned sons, cut out from the Legion we called home.

Because of a choice *you* made, Garro.' Now he was bringing it into the open, the other legionary's long-buried resentment could not be held back. 'We were imprisoned on Luna because of you. Distrusted by our cousins in the other loyalist Legions, and named betrayers by our own. We lost all that we were because of your decision! And now you seek to make another grand gesture, the consequences of which you won't live long enough to see!'

Garro stood in silence. The other loyal Death Guard who had come with him on his desperate race to carry warning of Horus' betrayal, they had followed him because he was their commander. But in the time since that act, he had never dwelled on the question: had they *agreed* with his choice?

He had been arrogant, he realised, assuming they felt as he did.

'If we had not fled the Dropsite Massacre at Isstvan,' Garro began, 'we would be dead... or turned. Is that what you wish for, Helig?'

Gallor took a shuddering breath. 'We might have been able to stop Mortarion before he committed to the Warmaster's perfidy, and the pacts he has made since. We could have...'

'Changed his mind?' Garro shook his head. 'No. I wish that were so, but that point was too far gone. Typhon and that bastard Word Bearer Erebus made certain of that with their machinations. Only now, in retrospect, is it clear. We lost our Legion a long time before Isstvan. The rot was already there, but we did not see it.' His remorse weighed heavily in his words. 'Never forget, we are not the ones who sundered our oath. *We* are the only unbroken.'

'And because of that, there is no place for us.' Gallor's ire faded, turning bitter as another rain of dust fell from the stonework above them.

'You are mistaken.' Garro stiffened. 'My place is here, now.

And yours? For the moment, it is with Keeler and the others. It will take a Knight Errant to get them through the aerial defence cordons to the Palace's inner dominions.'

'You trade your life for theirs? You, a legionary. A warlord of the Emperor. For a handful of common soldiers and a woman reciting pretty words.' Gallor scowled. 'You know, I thought if I came here with you, I might understand you better. But I still don't.'

'The moment we value those people as less than us,' Garro told him, 'we take the first step down the path beaten by Horus. Keeler reminded me of that, and now I do the same for you.' He let the silence hang for a moment, then spoke again. 'I regret the circumstances that forced me to drag you and the others into this. I regret the deaths of those I called my battle-brothers... Tollen Sendek. Meric Voyen. Solun Decius. And the rest. But we *all* would have perished over Isstvan had we not fled the massacre. At least here on Terra, you and I can choose the manner of our own fates.'

'There is little comfort in that,' Gallor noted.

'Agreed.'

At length, Gallor checked over his bolt pistol, gear packs and the few remaining krak grenades, making ready. 'It vexes me that I must abandon you. It feels like a betrayal.'

'That you live is all that matters,' Garro told him. He reached into a pouch and found the booklet of folded pages within. 'Here. I want you to take this.'

Gallor looked at the papers and raised an eyebrow. 'I have no interest in that.'

'This was bequeathed to me by a man named Kaleb Arin,' Garro went on, weighing the dog-eared copy of the *Lectitio Divinitatus* in his hand. 'He was my housecarl. An ordinary soul, but without doubt one of the most loyal and honourable men I have ever known. The words on these pages... They gave him guidance. They gave him purpose. It's yours now.'

'I have no interest,' Gallor repeated, but Garro shook his head.

'I am not asking you to believe,' he said firmly. 'Just read. And perhaps then, you will have the understanding that escapes you.'

For a moment, Garro thought the other warrior would turn his back, and the silence between them was filled by the keening of another laser barrage.

Then finally Gallor reached out and snatched the booklet from him. 'I will consider it,' he rumbled.

'You've made your decision?' The new voice came from the doorway across the room, and both of them turned. A figure stood watching them; Garro was certain that Euphrati Keeler had not been there a moment before, certain his enhanced senses would have heard her approaching. Yet they had not.

'How long have you been listening?' said Gallor.

'Long enough to know what is intended.' She looked up at Garro. 'We don't have to leave, Nathaniel.'

'You know that is not so,' he countered.

'The Emperor protects,' said the woman. 'He has done it before, He will do it again.'

'You are right.' Garro drew himself up. 'The Emperor does protect. Through *me*.' He gestured at Gallor. 'Through *us*. It is why we are here.'

She blinked, and doubt darkened her face. 'You believe He sent you, is that it?'

When Garro spoke again, his voice dropped to a softer register. 'Euphrati… You are not naïve. You cannot believe you would survive a Death Guard assault.'

'She does not want to.' Gallor fixed Keeler with a hard, searching gaze. 'Do you see it, Garro? Staying here, in the path of the fighting, facing certain annihilation. It would take away the burden of the choice she must make. Free her from it.' He addressed her directly. 'But that is the way of a weak spirit, and you are not weak. The battle-captain would never venerate someone undeserving.'

A lone tear followed the curve of Keeler's cheek before falling to the flagstones at her feet. 'I… I cannot carry this burden any more. I am spiralling, falling, out of control. Can you know what it is like to be the one others look to for guidance, but to have none for yourself? Yes, I think you do.' She brought a balled fist to her chest. 'I am hollow inside. Every day, I give all that is in me… But the well runs dry. I am afraid I will become the echo instead of the voice.'

Garro went to her, and once again, he took her hand in his. 'Neither of us had a choice in the paths that destiny placed us on. But we cannot falter. We must go on, for the alternative is ruin and destruction. *You* taught me that, Euphrati.' He felt a swell of certainty in his chest, a renewal of his resolve – cold, strong and clear, like the waters of a mountain stream. 'I learned the lesson you imparted to me when I first came searching for you. Do you remember what you told me?'

'You are of purpose.' She nodded. 'The Emperor has a duty that only you can shoulder.'

'And at last I see what that purpose is.' Garro returned the nod. 'Perhaps I can inspire as you do, in my own way, not with words but with this.' He placed his hand on the hilt of his sword. 'I see my path now, without obfuscation. From the core of my being, you have my thanks.'

Keeler looked away. 'I wish I had your certainty, Nathaniel.'

'You do,' he told her. 'You need only to rediscover it. Helig will make certain you have the time you need to do so.'

Garro turned back to the other legionary and offered his hand. Gallor took it and they clasped each other's vambraces, the ceramite of their gauntlets clanking as they met in the martial gesture.

'I will not wish you good fortune,' said the younger warrior. 'Those words would be… disrespectful. I will only say this – if you are to walk the martyr's path, then fight well, battle-captain.'

'We are legionaries,' Garro replied. 'That is what we were made to do.'

He began to stride away, but Keeler reached out and grasped his hand once again. 'I don't want this,' she said, swallowing a sob. 'I don't want you to go.'

'Neither do I,' he admitted, a strange flutter of unfamiliar emotions unfolding in his chest. 'But I must.'

Something made him turn in place, and Garro found Gallor staring back at him, a new expression of grim concern etched over his scarred features. 'Do you hear that?' Gallor raised a hand, as if trying to cup a sound out of the dusty air.

Garro strained to listen, and for a moment he did not comprehend what the other warrior meant. But then his blood chilled as the reality became apparent.

There was nothing to hear. The guns of the Death Guard were quiet.

From the deck of his command barge, Mortarion could hear the crackle of the fracturing stonework across the surface of the Marmax Bastion. The concentrated salvos of beam fire had heated the great granite slabs to incredible temperatures, causing the stone to slag and become molten in certain spots, and it drooled down the sloping flanks, undermining the structure of the upper tiers. Now he had halted the bombardment, the constant chill of the katabatic winds returned to caress the oppressed fortress, and the masonry split along faults and fissures as it cooled.

Marmax would die slowly and by inches, eventually collapsing in on itself like a gigantic tooth rotted from within. *One more marker against my father's hubris,* considered the primarch, *one more of His creations falling before the undeniable truth. All things decay.*

Let it die, said the whispers, and Mortarion nodded to himself. *All things must die in order to be reborn.* The Grandfather had shown him that singular truth when his Legion had been becalmed in the madness of the warp, and the Death Lord had learned the lesson well.

Beneath the prow of the hovering barge, the advance orders of Mortarion's pestilent legionaries waited in stillness, the only sound above the mutter of anti-grav motors the rasping, bubbling chorus of their breathing. He cast a glance across the ranks of hulking forms in rusted, discoloured armour, many stained with glistening ichor, others newly blessed with transformed flesh that oozed from the crevices of their wargear. Even the ever-present clouds of black flies that weaved and danced about the Death Guard mass seemed muted, crawling upon the exposed skin or soiled metals of Mortarion's sons rather than buzzing in swarms.

The Legion was waiting for him. Mortarion raised his pallid, skeletal hand, preparing to give the signal for the terminal phase of the attack – the advance that would leave nothing alive inside the shell of Marmax – and hesitated.

Something was moving on the flanks of the battered citadel. A figure in storm-grey armour and a war-cloak, leaping from one shattered battlement to another, descending towards the broken ground like a falling comet.

Animated as if by their own will, cluster-cannons on the barge's flanks twitched and moved to track the figure, and legionaries with long-bolters among Typhus' Grave Wardens took it upon themselves to take aim.

'Hold your fire,' growled the primarch, his voice carrying. His raised hand became a fist, and unseen, a curious and twisted smile emerged in the shadows of his hood.

'Why?' Mortarion turned to find his First Captain watching him from close by. Deep in his musings, he had allowed himself to dismiss Typhus' presence. ***'A single warrior? I'll have him in ashes before his boots touch the earth. Why tarry, my lord? Must I ask this question again?'***

'Because I wish it,' he muttered. And in truth, Mortarion already knew who it was that had dared to show his face to them.

The winds brought a shout of defiance to the war-barge, carried over the heads of the thousands-strong Death Guard forces, and the shout was the primarch's name – not a hail or a greeting but an accusation, a *challenge.*

'Mortarion!' The warrior in grey called out across the silenced battlefield. *'For Terra's sake and by the will of the Emperor of Mankind, I name you traitor!'*

Traitor. The last word echoed about the ruins surrounding them, repeating off the broken walls and into the haze of war-smoke. Mortarion's smile became brittle, fracturing into a sneer. A swift, stony fury came upon him at the denunciation, indignant rage steeling his limbs.

'I have betrayed **nothing,'** he hissed, answering the whispers in his mind before they could begin anew. The primarch strode to the edge of the observation gallery and gripped the corroded rail there, tightly enough to compact the metal. He was aware of his warriors in the ranks below looking up at him, eager for his next order, conflicted by his inaction.

The shout came again. *'You are corrupt! You have destroyed what you were sworn to protect! If one shred of what you once were still remains, then show it now! Face me, gene-sire… If you have the courage!'*

'Garro.' Typhus uttered the name like a curse. ***'It appears time has not diminished his arrogance, only nurtured it.'*** The great growth upon the Traveller's back shuddered. The plague swarms nesting within the Destroyer Hive that shared the legionary's transformed body sensed the warrior's need to make murder, and they wanted to fulfil his desire. ***'Grant me the right of dispatch, my lord. Say the word.*** **Say it.'**

For a moment, Mortarion considered the possibility. He need

only nod and Typhus would have his Grave Wardens gun down the Knight Errant. And they would not kill Garro with that opening salvo, *no*. They would likely cripple him, breach his armour and render him unable to fight. Only then would his death begin, a long and tormented process that might last to the Fall of Terra and Throne, and beyond.

It was a tempting prospect. But as with everything Typhus offered his liege-lord, it came with a cost.

If Mortarion granted the kill to the First Captain, then the sacramental power of Garro's death would belong to Typhus the Traveller, not to the Reaper of Men.

Mortarion had learned that in his new, changed existence, the boon of Grandfather Nurgle required sacrifice. His body and those of his warriors had been remade, literally transformed into the undying ideal that was the dark soul of his Legion – but the bargain had to be paid for, again and again, and the only coin of value was *death.*

The death of a hero, of a *believer*... That had great worth. Not just as a murder-gift to Nurgle and his gardens of decay, but to the corrupted spirits of Mortarion's warriors. The changed way was still fresh upon them, and while many embraced the new flesh, others wavered. With this kill upon his scythe's blade, such a righteous kill indeed, the primarch would reaffirm his mastery of the Legion.

'No,' he told Typhus. ***'You are denied. Garro's life belongs to me. Once, he pledged it to my name. It is mine to end as I see fit.'***

In spite of himself, Typhus snorted in derision. ***'My Wardens will obliterate that conceited fool! The oath-breaker is not worth sullying your weapon–'***

'You would have me turn away from a challenge to my name?' Mortarion's rasping voice became flinty.

'I question this.' Typhus moderated his tone, but he did not back down. ***'One legionary calls you to conflict? You give Garro***

more honour than he deserves!' Then he paused, taking a husking, gurgling breath. ***'Or is it that I do not see your full intent, my lord?'*** He nodded to himself. ***'Yes. That's it, isn't it? Garro has always been a splinter in your eye. He is the Death Guard you could not turn to your will, when the moment came. He is your lapse… Your failure.'***

Belying its name, Mortarion's great war-scythe, *Silence*, cut through the foetid air with a sharp hiss as the primarch drew it from across his back. Tainted sunlight flashed off the corroded arc of the blade and before Typhus could pull his own weapon, the cutting edge was pressing at his neck.

'Take care how you speak to me, my brother,' intoned the Death Lord. ***'In times past, I have indulged you. I let myself be blind to your ambitions. But those days are over. Remember your place, First Captain.'***

'I meant no disrespect,' said Typhus, unwilling to move even the smallest degree while the blade threatened. ***'I have always been truthful with you. Even if you dislike what I say.'*** At length, he found the will to back away a step, to distance himself from the weapon's killing arc. ***'I speak truth now. It is vanity to answer Garro's challenge. It is beneath you.'***

'Perhaps so,' allowed Mortarion, ***'but the decision is mine to make.'*** He returned *Silence* to its place and spoke again. ***'These are my commands. Have the Legion stand down… And give me fighting room.'***

With each step he took, Garro tensed for the shot that would kill him.

He wondered if he would hear it in the moment before he died, the subsonic thrum of the bow wave before an incoming bolt shell or the scream of torn air about a beam blast. Or did death come unspoken to those it claimed?

For now, the question went unanswered. Not a single warrior

in the foul army before him raised a weapon in anger, but he could feel their seething hate for him.

As Garro dropped the last distance to the churned ground at the foot of Marmax, a humming cloud burst from the waiting legionaries. Countless numbers of oily black insects rose from where they had been resting, beating at the icy air with millions of gelid wings.

The swarm writhed over the ground, forming into something like a great black curtain – and with stolid, theatrical grandeur, that curtain parted and so did the ranks of the corrupted. The Reaper of Men was coming to answer Nathaniel Garro's defiance.

Garro took a deep breath and planted his boots firmly amid the mess of mud, burnt stone and rock fragments. Slowly, he removed and stowed his helmet; tactically, the gesture might have been unsound, but it felt wrong – even *dishonourable* – to do this hiding his face behind armour plate.

His bolter was mag-locked across his armour and his sword was at the ready for the draw. He let one hand drop to the hilt of the ancient blade, fingers tracing the studs that would activate its power field. These small, instinctive, pre-battle rituals gave him focus; they let him briefly forget the nature of the foe marching towards him.

But only for a moment.

What strode forth out of the Death Guard ranks barely resembled the primarch Garro had known, now a creature seen through a despoiled lens. Tall and emaciated, a hooded cloak draped over metallic battle armour; but the cloak was putrefying, rancid cloth where before it had been heavy, dark material, and the armour – once the magnificent, master-crafted work of combat artisans, shining bare steel and bright brass – was now creaking, rotten and rust-rimed.

And worst of all was the figure who wore them. Garro had once bent the knee to a sallow, hard-faced master with a gaze that knew fury, knew sorrow, and knew honour. The monster he saw before him now, wreathed in poison dust, consumptive and decayed, was death incarnate.

Horrified, ashamed and saddened beyond measure, Garro met the gaze of his liege-lord and gene-sire for the first time since the great betrayal at Isstvan. And he asked the only question that he could.

'What have you become?'

'I am what we have always strived to be,' Mortarion intoned, eyes flashing in the dark beneath his hood. ***'Undying. Unstoppable. Unmatched.'***

A pall of fear rose in Garro's hearts and his hand tightened on the hilt of his sword. 'What did it cost you, my lord?'

The question seemed to surprise the primarch, and he hesitated before replying. ***'The price… The price was everything.'*** Through his breather mask, Mortarion took a deep inhalation of the toxins whirling around him, as if sustaining himself with them. ***'Garro,'*** he wheezed. ***'You were one of my best. I have not forgotten. You can be again. You can rejoin your battle-brothers. There is still time.'***

Of all the words he thought Mortarion might utter, the last Garro expected were these. After everything that had taken place since Horus Lupercal's heresy had commenced, Garro had embraced the path of the outsider, the outcast.

'He will win,' said the primarch, as if plucking the thought of the Warmaster from Garro's mind. ***'It is inevitable. The sons will soon kill their father, as is fitting. And a new world will beckon.'*** Mortarion reached inside his cloak, and when his skeletal hand returned, there were two corroded metal cups in his grip. Black fluid, dark as night and oil-thick, shimmered in them.

He offered one of the cups to Garro, and compelled by an impulse he could not resist, the warrior accepted it.

Garro stared into the depths of the cup and sensed something powerful uncoiling around him, as if the air itself were transforming. A boundless grief, a longing he had buried deep within, reawakened.

The breaking of his Legion's oath had left him bereft in ways he could not articulate. He thought of Gallor's anger and bitterness, of the younger warrior's unanswered sorrow at what they had lost.

There was an undeniable part of Garro that wished time could be turned back, that what was sundered could be remade. *And perhaps, in one way, it could be.*

'Might you honour me by sharing a drink?' said Mortarion.

INTERVAL II

The planet Barbarus: after reunion

The shuttles touched down in an area beyond a city the locals called Safehold, in a sector of cleared grasslands that helots were busily turning into the planet's first starport. A sleeting deluge of black rain was falling, hissing where it landed, giving everything a bone-deep chill.

Nathaniel Garro was the last to descend the ramp of his transport, letting the others file out before him, a handful of warriors among a mass of human auxiliaries brought down from the fleet in high orbit. He saw other figures disembarking from the rest of the craft in the shuttle flight – more towering legionaries like him, clad in newly forged, newly liveried armour.

When the majority of them had left the surface of this planet over a solar year ago, they had walked with the tread of men. Now they returned as transhumans, reforged by the great science of the Emperor of Mankind and His scienticians. Garro heard them laughing and calling out to people in the crowds who waited for them, the prodigal sons returning to the death world that had borne them.

Not all of those taken from Barbarus to be uplifted had survived the process. Many perished passing through the gauntlet of the change, their bodies rejecting the implants with terminal effect. In the usual scheme of things, neophyte legionaries underwent the implantation regimen and enhancile conditioning over a cycle of several years, and at a far younger age – this had been Garro's lot, plucked as a stringy youth from the Albian outlands on Terra when he was only thirteen winters old, for induction into the Legion. The new intake had no such consideration, forced through a crash-course process that turned these men into Legiones Astartes with uncommon rapidity.

Some said that it was only the Emperor's personal intervention in the programme that had kept the Barbaruns from dying to a man, but Garro thought otherwise. After a year in their company, he was firmly convinced that the sons of this blighted world were too stubborn to die easily.

The process of *reunion* was well under way. After finding and reuniting with his lost son Mortarion, the Emperor had presented the primarch with the war fleet and the warriors that were his bequest – the XIV Legion, known since their inception as the Dusk Raiders. Mortarion's first act had been to cast that name aside and rechristen them as the Death Guard, in echo of the fighters he had led in his rebellion against Barbarus' cruel rulers, the Overlords.

Garro was no longer conscious of the new insignia on his armour, the white skull upon a six-pointed star rendered in dark green. Like many things, it was another change to take on and assimilate before the Legion returned to their first calling – the prosecution of the Emperor's Great Crusade.

Taking his first step onto the surface of the planet, Garro looked across a bleak landscape of grey hills, past granite tors and distant mountains, and up at the soured sky. He tasted faint toxins on the damp breeze, the weak traces of the poisonous mists that wreathed the higher ranges of Barbarus' atmosphere, and at his feet, stiff blades of metallic-looking grass crunched under his boots. The planet was hard and unwelcoming, and he did not doubt it hid a thousand ways to kill the unwary. That was the truth of a death world: nothing weak could exist there.

He skirted the landing field, avoiding the crowds. The people gathered around their changed brethren, many of them marvelling at their new forms, some daring to reach out and touch their faces and the surface of their grey-green armour. Garro avoided their gazes, instead following the approaches to Safehold. Nearby, he saw evidence of construction and more transformation – buildings and machinery transplanted from the fleet, brought down in hopes of accelerating Barbarus to the level of the rest of the Imperium. In a way, the planet was being uplifted too, and Garro had learned that new initiate cadres from the Barbarun populace were already being selected. As the Legion had once taken its tithe of young men from Terra, now it would do the same here. And perhaps, at some future point, there would come a time when there were no more Dusk Raiders among the Death Guard.

He shook off the thought, finding himself at the foot of a great black wall near the city gates. Assembled out of rough-hewn stone slabs, it was carved with countless names in the local Low Gothic script. Garro reached out and ran the fingertips of his gauntlet over the letters, inclining his head in solemn respect. This, he understood. A memorial for the dead.

'Why do you bow to them?' Hearing the voice, Garro looked up. A woman in a military uniform stood a short distance away, arms folded over her chest, eyeing him gravely. The way she unconsciously favoured one leg told him that she had been badly injured once in her life, but her manner was that of someone who would not let such a thing prevent her from fighting. 'They're all cinders and the lands are better for it.'

Garro drew back his hand. 'These are *not* the names of your war dead?'

'These are the names of the Overlords and collaborators we slaughtered to free Barbarus,' she corrected. 'Written in stone so that any creature who might try to rule our world knows how much it'll cost them.'

'Ah. A warning, I see. Forgive my error.' He nodded. 'So tell me, how do you venerate those who perished fighting these Overlords?'

The woman frowned. 'We keep them here.' She touched her heart and head. Then she took a step closer. 'You're one of the Newcomer's warrior-breed.'

'Newcomer?' Garro didn't know the reference.

'Your Emperor.'

'He is *your* Emperor as well,' noted the warrior. 'He is Mortarion's father.'

'So I hear.' The woman sized him up, frowning. 'The iterators He sent here say your kind are remade in His image, yes? You are changed, just like He's changed our fathers, cousins and brothers.'

'Yes.'

'Why just the men?' She drew herself level to stare Garro in the eye. 'Seems a waste of good resources.' She nodded at the wall. 'Women shed their blood to carve those names as much as men did.'

'We'll ask that question of the Emperor when next we see Him,' said another voice. Garro turned to find Mortarion's wolfish comrade in arms striding towards them. Typhon gave a nod and held back a grin.

'Is that you, Calas?' The woman gave the other legionary an

incredulous look. 'What happened to the man I knew from Heller's Cut?'

'That skinny young fellow is in here somewhere.' Typhon's expression hardened, as if he didn't care to be reminded of his past. 'Don't you have a post to mind, soldier? Be about it. Lieutenant Garro and I have things to discuss.'

'We do?' Garro watched the woman depart.

'I've been observing you.' Typhon's steely gaze bored into him, and Garro found his intensity disquieting. 'Most of the Terran-born men in the Legion have embraced the reunion with gusto, welcoming their new brethren, training in live-fire exercises with Mortarion and the rest of us… As we have each learned the ways and manners of the other.' Typhon pointed a finger at him. 'But you, Garro. You could not do so at a remove, as others have. I think something in you needed to see the world where your primarch grew to manhood. To feel its air in your lungs, its mud under your boots.' He opened his hands, taking in the landscape around them. 'Am I right?'

'Your insight does you credit,' said Garro. 'Yes. I wanted to know Barbarus for myself. To walk the path the primarch did, albeit for a brief time.'

'And now you are here, what do you think of it?'

Garro looked at the wall of death, considering what it represented, and then away towards the distant, forbidding crags. 'I am beginning to understand.'

'The Legion is undergoing a seismic shift,' said Typhon. 'The Dusk Raiders you knew are gone. The Death Guard rise in their place.'

'It is the will of the Emperor and Mortarion.'

Typhon was silent for a moment. 'The primarch is in the process of reorganising the Legion into something… better suited to his command style. Your Great Company, Garro. The Seventh. It is currently without a captain to lead it.'

'That is correct.' Garro tensed, suddenly uncertain as to where the conversation was leading him.

'Would you like the glory of that posting, lieutenant?'

He considered his next words carefully. 'I would welcome the duty of it. But as for glory… I don't care for that.'

Typhon laughed, as if he had just scored a victory. 'It seems everything I've heard about you is true, Garro! *Good.* In the wars to come, Mortarion will need a man he can rely on to lead the Seventh.'

'The primarch has my blade and my oath,' said Garro. 'It will always be so.' But he couldn't keep a thread of doubt from his voice, and Typhon heard it.

'You have misgivings,' said the other warrior. 'You ask yourself, how can you hope to become part of a Legion bequeathed to a world and a master you have never known?'

A chill ran through Garro's blood. Typhon spoke the words as if he had plucked them from the hidden depths of the warrior's thoughts.

The other legionary went on. 'You feel… you are not one of us?'

At length, Garro shook his head, finding the resolution that had previously escaped him. 'No. Perhaps I did have reservations, but not now. You…' He indicated Typhon and by extension, all of Barbarus. '*You* are one of *us.* Even if you and your kindred were born here, the sons of this planet remain children of Terra, even if millennia separated us. You are grown from those who struck out into space before the Age of Old Night. We all rise from the same birthworld. We are all humans, tracing our lineage back to that place.'

'Indeed?' Typhon placed a hand on Garro's shoulder and his smile returned. 'Well, *captain.* Perhaps one day I will meet you there. I will walk your path, and see it for myself.'

FIVE

Reaper of Men
No Quarter
Fall of a Champion

Garro looked into the cup, and in the tiny sea of darkness it held, he saw oblivion.

In the past, this Death Guard tradition was a celebration of their fortitude, a customary ingesting of poison that the powerful physiology of a legionary could resist, endure and overcome. But like everything else about Mortarion's sons, it had been twisted into something new.

Garro was certain that the cup contained blood, or something like it.

His primarch's vitae, gifted like an offering – and if he were to drink from it, what then? It would be submission.

Sundered from his Legion for so long, Garro would be changed and remade just as they had been, but he would be *part* of them again. For what seemed like an age, he had buried the sorrow of his self-imposed exile beneath a righteous fury towards his former brethren. But now, just for a moment, the warrior allowed himself to acknowledge a singular truth.

'I did not wish this,' he said quietly, his words caught on

the wind. 'To turn against the Legion I pledged my life to. I did not want to draw weapons against my battle-brothers. It is anathema to me.'

'Every path across the moor is thorny,' intoned the Reaper of Men, as he watched the legionary with severe, yellowing eyes. ***'But there is always a way back. Nothing is constant, Nathaniel. The universe that surrounds us is not fixed. It is malleable, forever in states of change and evolution. Decay and rebirth. My eyes were opened to it in the warp.'*** He gestured to the sky and the distorted light from the war raging over their heads. ***'This truth goes beyond Horus and my father. Beyond this conflict, or any other. You can see it too. If you wish. You can become greater, as we have.'***

Garro looked up. 'That... is not our fate, my lord. I am a warrior, gene-forged and uplifted in the Emperor's name. You are His son, cut from His flesh, bred to be a war god made manifest. We were not created to evolve. We were made to fight and to die for the glory of the Imperium of Man.' His hearts felt hollow as the words fell from his lips. 'We are but weapons. Instruments of fate. Knights of Grey and Lords of Destruction.'

Oblivion beckoned. It would be easy to tip back the cup, to swallow the contents and let his burdens be taken away. As Garro held that thought in his mind, he felt empathy for Euphrati Keeler. He understood how obliteration could seem like the better of every option, the seduction of the impulse to let go and fall towards the darkness.

But at the far end of that spectrum was the singular instinct that had guided Garro's hand from the very start, the purpose that could never be denied.

'We can be more than weapons if we wish,' said Mortarion. ***'We can defy fate.'***

'No.' Garro shook his head. 'We are the tools of higher powers, of the greater players. If you cannot see that, sire, then you are blind.' At the legionary's words, the primarch's cold expression shifted towards anger, and Garro brought his reply to its core. 'The difference between us, the truth I have learned since I broke with your command, is that I *accept* it. You still believe you can determine your destiny, but you are wrong.'

Mortarion released a low growl and pointed at the cup in Garro's hand. ***'I would have your answer.'*** The primarch's rasping tones carried back to him. ***'Will you return to us, or will you perish here?'***

Garro raised the cup, and with deliberate slowness, he tilted it until the oily contents drooled out to spatter and hiss against the broken stones. Then, with a flick of his wrist, he tossed the empty hemisphere into the dirt at Mortarion's feet, as a ripple of terse reaction flowed through the silent Legion watching them.

'Mistake.' The primarch drank down his own cup and savoured it. ***'You have no concept of what you have rejected.'***

'I know full well,' Garro replied, his gaze raking over the other Death Guard, over the ranks of monsters that had once been his brethren.

'Step aside, then, and I will gift you with a swift death.' Mortarion's lip curled. ***'Call it a mercy, in honour of the past times you served me.'***

With a crackle of unchained energy, the power conduits embedded in the metal of Garro's great sword came to life as the legionary drew the weapon. The crystalline metal of it sang as it cleared the scabbard to hang in the air before them.

'I regret I must decline,' said Garro.

The blade was called *Libertas* and it shone like a beacon through the battle-smoke. Of unknown age, as ancient as mountains, the weapon carried by Garro was his talisman, but even he did not know the fullness of its origins. Some believed it had been forged before the age of Old Night, in echo of the great Terran blades that had come before it – *Kusanan of the Valorous,* the *Xkal*, the *Vhorpul* and the *Zul'fiqar*. For Nathaniel Garro, the weapon was as much a part of him as his hands, his limbs and his hearts. A thousand enemies had perished upon its monomolecular edge, a thousand foes had been cut down never to rise again.

But it had never been drawn in anger against a son of the Emperor, fallen or otherwise.

Mortarion gave a solemn nod and his giant war-scythe, *Silence*, fell into his waiting hands.

'So be it,' he intoned.

It was not an *attack;* it was an *explosion* of steel.

It was an assault like no other the legionary had ever experienced, a howling torrent of blades that came at Garro as if the air itself had transformed into razors.

Thunderous bangs of metal on metal sounded across the battleground, and each blow the warrior managed to parry hit so hard he feared the shock of them alone would break his bones and tear his muscles.

Garro had not one instant to consider how he might try to counter-attack. His every iota of thought and skill was pulled unto the overwhelming challenge of simply staying alive for the next second, and the next, and the next. He dodged and spun, fighting to keep out of the reach of the war-scythe's massive head, but Mortarion's weapon was everywhere at once.

It defied logic. A blade as large as a human was tall, heavy as starship metal, and yet the primarch made it move as if it were a paper streamer caught in the breeze. Great, thick sparks of actinic green-blue jetted when *Silence* and *Libertas* briefly crossed one another, some starting fires in the dry dust where they landed.

Garro had battled mutants and aliens, beasts and monsters alike, but nothing and no one like Mortarion. His recollection dredged up the memory of a sparring match he had once fought with a member of the Emperor's personal guard, a cold-eyed Custodes named Khorarinn; it was said that the Adeptus Custodes were to the Emperor what the Legiones Astartes were to the primarchs, and to face one was to face a titan. But even drawing on the hard lessons he had learned that day did little to give Garro an edge.

Mortarion cut hissing arcs through the air, knocking back the Knight Errant with each sweep, pressing him towards the corner of a fallen structure – the remains of a covered arcade that had once been part of an ornamental garden. Garro would quickly run out of room to defend himself unless he altered the language of the fight.

Retreating, he swung *Libertas* – not to parry the war-scythe, but to cut cleanly through a pillar holding up what remained of the arcade's roof and the ruins piled upon it. Stone and tile groaned, and tonnes of heaped debris slumped from where it was balanced above, rolling forward in a glittering rock-slide.

Mortarion was forced to step back or be buried, giving Garro precious seconds to extend the distance between them. Amid the growling din of the falling rubble, he heard the muttering snarls of the Death Guard as they cursed him and cried out for his murder.

The reprieve lasted scarcely a moment. As Garro jumped free of the churning clouds of dust from the collapsing building, a flicker of ill light off filth-encrusted brass flashed across his path. In a fluid motion, Mortarion held *Silence* aside in a lazy, whickering spin, and drew his other signature weapon with his other hand.

The drum-shaped gun was known as the *Lantern*, and it was known that the Emperor Himself had gifted it to His son on the occasion of their reunion. Garro had seen its awesome power many times during the Great Crusade, when Mortarion had used it to bring the light of final, fatal illumination to those who defied compliance. Now that power was turned upon him.

Blinding and brilliant, a crackling searchlight beam of pure white energy burst forth from the weapon's muzzle and cut a fiery slash through earth, stone and debris. It atomised everything it touched, leaving a wide, glowing scar in its wake.

Garro charged away, feeling the searing halo-effect of its lethal radiation across the bare skin of his shaven head, and for a moment he feared the white fire would engulf him, but then the *Lantern*'s light died and he went into a turning roll, coming up with his Paragon bolter aimed straight back in the same direction.

Gripping the boltgun in an iron hold, Garro fired round after round at the towering figure in ragged robes, desperately hoping to find a weak spot or some tiny, momentary advantage.

Mass-reactive Kraken shells blurred across the distance between shooter and target, and Mortarion brought up his arms to protect his head. His corroded vambraces clanked together like steel gates slamming shut and the bolt-rounds impacted there, bright globes of detonation and shock-sphere effects pummelling the Reaper of Men where he stood.

Mortarion leaned into the bolt hits and held his ground, weathering everything Garro had thrown at him. The Knight Errant let the Paragon weapon's emptied magazine fall away, ramming a full replenishment back in its place, but the primarch was already moving again, his monstrous beam-gun forgotten for the moment, his war-scythe returning to the fray.

Garro twisted away to avoid the whistling downward arc of *Silence*'s falling blade, but the blow was not meant to strike him. With the deft delicacy of a chirurgeon's scalpel, the curve of Mortarion's scythe hooked the frame of Garro's bolter and wrenched it out of his hands before he could finish reloading it.

The master-crafted gun spun high into the air, and with a

second flick of his whipcord arm, Mortarion's blade caught it and smashed it down against the fallen brickwork.

Garro bit down on the red flash of pain searing through his gun arm, the bones dislocated by the primarch's showy attack. With a savage jerk, he snapped his limb back into its socket, and looked up.

Mortarion was aiming the shimmering muzzle of the *Lantern* directly at him, the air around it lensed by its incredible heat.

'End him!' A shout rose to Garro's ears, and he recognised the voice. *Calas Typhon,* or whatever grotesque creature he had become, was calling for his execution.

Garro straightened, tightening his grip on his sword. If these were to be his last breaths, he would take them in defiance.

But the blazing annihilation of the kill-fire never came.

'Not yet,' said the primarch. ***'You have forsaken the right to die quickly.'*** Mortarion's skeletal fingers curled away from the *Lantern*'s trigger-bar, and the weapon snapped back. Then, with slow deliberation, he unlatched the beam-cannon's holster and threw it, the great pistol and all, into the clasping hands of one of Typhus' Grave Wardens standing close by. That done, he saluted Garro with the head of his scythe, bringing the blade to his eyes. ***'This ends in** the **old way. Blade upon blade. With metal and blood.'***

Garro hesitated, glaring at the primarch's hooded visage, his anger slowly building. *He is toying with me.* The warrior knew that Mortarion could have finished this confrontation in seconds, had he wished to. But just like the Death Guard advance on the Marmax Bastion, the pace of their fight was not being determined by tactical need or capability. It was done for show, in some arcane manner, for sacrament.

Mortarion wants to kill me by inches, Garro told himself. *He wishes to make me pay for my challenge.*

He will make an example of me.

Garro gave a slow nod, and with *Libertas* gripped in his mailed fist, he brought the hilt of the power sword to his chest, over the golden eagle of his armour's cuirass, and beat it twice upon the site of his primary heart.

'So be it,' Garro intoned, repeating the Death Lord's earlier words. *Every second this battle goes on,* he vowed, *is one moment more for Helig and the Saint.*

Mortarion drew in a gale of smoke-filled air, filling his lungs with a rumbling wheeze, and the war-scythe rose, held fast in his pallid fingers. The Reaper of Men exhaled and the reek of a tomb deadened the ground about him.

But this time the Knight Errant did not wait for the primarch's assault to commence. To be Death Guard was to fight as an inexorable force, to resist as an immovable object – but time spent as Malcador the Sigillite's Agentia Primus, outside the strictures of his old Legion, had taught Garro the value of boldness.

Libertas glowed with coruscating blue fire as the energy matrix in the blade ignited. Garro launched himself off a stone ledge, his power armour turning the leap into a gunshot-quick attack, and he sprinted towards his foe.

The legionary's weapon led the dance, shrieking through the air, crackling with power enough to scorch away the clouds of toxic dust gathered around the fighters.

The Grave Wardens and the warp-flesh legionaries surrounding the makeshift arena reacted to the ferocity of Garro's assault, beating their weapons on their armour at a slow, steady pace, and those who stood too near drew back lest they be hit by a glancing blow.

Mortarion slipped out of every stab and lunge by the barest of margins, the glowing point of *Libertas* spearing towards him, tearing at his robes with each near-hit. The pestilent flies droning about his shoulders buzzed angrily and swarmed away, swirling to avoid the edge-effect of the power sword, others burned to a crisp on the wing as the blade passed through them.

The primarch released a dry, corpse-breath exhalation. He had expected to face the same man with whom he had shared the cups aboard the *Endurance* many years ago, but he was quickly learning that Nathaniel Garro *was* a changed man after all.

More with anger than by design, Mortarion swung *Silence* in a tight sweep that would have taken the head from a human's shoulders without slowing. Garro ducked beneath the flashing blade. The legionary reversed his power sword and was already extending away from the clash – but he could not resist the chance to jab a back-thrust into the primarch's guard.

The tip of *Libertas* caught Mortarion's right vambrace and gouged a bright score a half-metre long in the discoloured ceramite. The first mark of the duel went to the legionary, not the lord.

A dark and serpentine rage uncoiled in the primarch's chest at this insult. There had been a time when Mortarion of Barbarus held to a taciturn character, rarely showing emotion, seldom giving voice to even his deepest fury.

Even when his hands had been around the throats of the Overlords who had oppressed his people, Mortarion had controlled the anger that fuelled him. But the Mark of Nurgle had opened new doors in his soul, and the Grandfather's embrace had transformed him in a myriad of ways – not just in body and mind, but in spirit. His eyes had been opened to the numinous truths that he had spent a lifetime hating.

Now he let his anger rise like acidic bile, relishing the novel sensation. *It will not be enough to beat Garro, to shed his blood and kill him,* decided the primarch. *He must be humiliated. Demeaned. And when it is done, I will grant him my consent to perish.*

Mortarion twisted his war-scythe, hand sliding over hand as he inverted the mighty weapon's course, bringing the heavy pommel at the far end into play. As big as an ambull's talon, the brass striker could crush a human skull into paste or punch a hole through ferrocrete. He aimed it at Garro's retreating form and the blow connected with a sickening crack before the warrior could escape.

The legionary spun away, batted back into a pile of fallen brickwork, trailing splinters of broken armour plating behind him. Mortarion heard the air explode from Garro's lungs and the whine of overstressed servomotors as his wargear took the full brunt of the hit. At his back, the Traveller's Grave Wardens rattled their rusted blades and manreapers in chorus, sounding praise for their master's punishing blow.

Garro's world spun around him, an earthquake of agony rolling across his torso from one side to the other.

For dizzying moments – for what seemed like an eternity – he lost his grip on time and rode out a storm of torment. The legionary's armoured form crashed through a jagged mass of broken masonry, and his nerve-shunts reacted, racing to protect him from a bolt of pain-shock that would have burst his secondary heart.

Reacting without conscious thought, Garro staggered out of the crater he had made with his landing and lurched up, boots scraping over compacted layers of stone, metal debris and the half-buried corpses of the luckless. His head swam and briefly a giant shadow passed over him, as the light of the sun fell behind the clouds. At his back, the battered form of the Marmax Bastion resembled a gargantuan tomb marker, and Garro's unseated thoughts played tricks on him. He imagined his name up there in twenty-metre-high letters, etched by laser into the surface of the stones.

Here lies Nathaniel Garro: Terran. Legionary. Martyr.

'Not yet,' he coughed, dispelling the grim portent, ejecting a string of blood-laced spittle from his mouth. '*Not... yet.*'

Tiny, jewel-bright icons flickered around the circumference of his power armour's neck ring, warning him of system malfunctions and integrity breaches. With just one direct hit, Mortarion had been able to crack the ceramite sheath of Garro's breastplate and damage the synthetic muscles beneath. Multiple redundant systems inside the complex weave of the armour's technology reacted to the impact the way a body would react to an infected wound – isolating and containing it, shunting function away to other elements. He could still move, but there was a tremor in his steps, now a fraction off balance.

Garro shook out of the post-impact daze, feeling his blood rush hot as his implanted organs dumped booster endorphins and chem-philtres into his veins. He drew himself to his full height, striding out of the dust. *Libertas* was still in his hand, locked there.

And suddenly, he could feel there was something *more* at play around him.

At first, Garro thought the sense of sunlight-warmth on his face was a side effect of the pain-shunts, but it brought with it a strange kind of clarity – almost a *peace* – that was at once new and familiar to him.

Unable to stop himself, Garro's gaze was drawn up towards the highest tiers of the Marmax Bastion's ruined pinnacle, sensing, *knowing* that kind eyes were looking down on him.

Keeler? Her name was on his lips, so close that he almost whispered it.

Was this how the troopers on the battlements had felt when she spoke to them?

Was this the power of the Saint? Not the fire of martial oratory or the clarion call to die well… but the simple drive to live?

Heavy footfalls resonated through the rubble beneath his boots, and Garro turned back to find Mortarion advancing on him once again. The primarch looked up in the same direction and nodded to himself.

'Her time will come,' he husked. ***'You will not save her.'***

'We will see!' Garro replied with a lethal slash that cut across the axis of Mortarion's approach, and the primarch sidestepped the attack. He parried the blow with the length of his scythe and the legionary spun his sword about before the Death Lord could turn the move back upon him.

Silence's great arc of blackened steel chopped at the debris and ruins, seeking Garro like the fanned head of a giant metal cobra. He fought to deflect the strikes with lateral counter-blows from the broad edge of *Libertas*' blade, impact upon impact sounding in loud ringing clangs, as if a death knell were tolling.

The blunt face of the scythe-head clipped Garro's right pauldron, cracking the grey-white protective sheath around his shoulder, and he spun into the hit, the momentum carrying him back. Typhus and the Grave Wardens hissed their approval once again as the hit was followed by a second and then a third.

Garro staggered over the ruins, fighting to claim a moment to gather himself. The legionary took a wheezing, pain-laced breath of the heavy air, and his scarred face formed into a scowl. The damage Mortarion was inflicting on him was meticulous and deliberate, set to slow him – but the primarch was taking his time about it, pulling each of his blows, deliberately drawing out the fight.

In his own dour way, Mortarion was playing to the gallery. Not just to Typhus and the Grave Wardens, not just to his misbegotten and malformed warrior-sons, but to the Warmaster and the dark, Chaotic forces that Horus had allied himself to.

The turbulent sky above them was illuminated with burning ships and rods of god-fire. Was Horus looking down on this scene even now, watching his brother? Were the Ruinous Powers weighing Mortarion's actions, measuring his worth as their daemonic avatar?

The legionary's seething anger rushed hot, his fury boiling

over at his primarch's arrogance. A tiny splinter of Garro's spirit had hoped that he would be able to find some measure of humanity still alive in Mortarion, but this act of hubris showed him that if such a thing did exist, it lay beyond his reach.

Sworn to the Death Guard's banner years before he had even laid eyes on his gene-sire, Garro had longed to follow a primarch who was everything he wished Mortarion could be, but the cruel lie was exposed.

Mortarion cannot be redeemed. None of them can.

With a snarl, Garro bolted forward again, dashing inside the primarch's reach, acting in the instant while Mortarion's attention was split. Grasping the hilt of *Libertas* with both hands, he swung the power sword up, cutting through the crackling curtain of the Death Lord's foetid robes and scraping the edge of the rusted plates of armour protecting Mortarion's throat. The opening was fleeting, miniscule – but it was there.

Mortarion jerked away, scarcely avoiding a cut that would have slashed open his throat. The tip of the blade sliced through the primarch's tattered hood and carved a deep furrow across the sunken cheek above his breather mask, a trickle of foul green-black ichor oozing from the wound.

Mortarion bellowed – half in shocked surprise, half in pain – and in blind reflex, he struck out with his war-scythe. The heavy shaft of the great weapon cracked Garro across the chest and he was swatted away as if he weighed nothing, back into the wreckage of the collapsed arcade.

The primarch's clawed hand went to the site of the cut on his pallid face, as his Death Guard beat their blades in a deafening refrain.

Dark blood, oil-thick, slipped through his emaciated fingers and ran away in rivulets, as if the fluid had a mind of its own.

He cut me. The realisation burned more than the pain of

the wound, which even now was waning, transforming into a blessed warmth as the sallow flesh knit itself back together across a newborn scar. It seemed an impossibility that this turncoat oath-breaker, this wretched dogmatic, could dare to strike Mortarion – far less to draw his blood. And yet, he had.

Let it die. Let it die. Let it die. Let it die.

The whispers in his head grew to drown out all but the voice amid the exhortation of rusted steel banging on bloated ceramite: the Traveller's voice, echoing to him as if spoken directly into the primarch's ear.

'This game has gone on long enough, my lord,' said Typhus. ***'Garro cannot be redeemed.'***

'Aye,' he muttered, ***'it would seem so.'***

Despite the unfettered power of the blow that had put him down, the Knight Errant was still alive, struggling to drag himself up from where he had fallen. Sparks fluttered from the joints of his leg where Garro's augmetic limb twitched and juddered, the bionics within malfunctioning as he tried to put his weight upon it. As Mortarion approached, Garro grasped towards his sword. It lay fallen just out of his reach, sizzling in a puddle of greasy meltwater.

Before the warrior could reach the weapon, the Death Lord turned his war-scythe to bring the great brass pommel to bear, dropping it to hammer into Garro's chest, smashing him back into the rubble. He lifted it high once more, and with savage precision, struck down again and again, beating against the golden adornment across the fallen warrior's chest – the honour-forged cuirass that bore the head of a virtuous, defiant eagle.

Garro's artisan-wrought wargear was a gift from the Terran Court to the old Dusk Raiders Legion, a boon bestowed by the will of the Emperor Himself. Only one example of its martial artistry existed, and had it not shrouded the battle-captain, it might have hung in some gallery of treasures.

Mortarion destroyed it, blow by blow, smashing the golden metal into fragments, beheading the noble eagle, beating Garro against the stone until his face was a mask of blood. The cuirass cracked down its length and split, exposing under-layers and the armour's damaged works beneath.

'Your honours and your laurels are meaningless,' said Mortarion, stepping back to take a long breath. His words could equally have been directed towards his distant father or the wounded, bleeding warrior at his feet.

The swarms of black flies churning over the battlefield sensed the vitae spilled across the ground and they came in their masses, seething and droning, turning the air into a living, reeking haze.

Garro coughed out a thick gobbet of dark, arterial blood, and the insects went into a frenzy. They could taste the stink of death-to-come in the air, and they were eager to feed upon it. The legionary gasped as he laboured to breathe, but still he lived, and still he struggled to right himself. Resentment burned in his gaze, and virtuous hate fuelled its fire.

Mortarion raised *Silence*, pointing with the heavy pommel, aiming it at Garro's chest and the shattered armour. ***'Perhaps… I will not destroy you.'*** His words echoed through the buzzing swarm, the flies vibrating at the same timbre, mimicking his speech. ***'The spark of life that is Nathaniel Garro will gutter out… But your body? That will be renewed. Evolved and reborn.'***

The swarm's razor-saw choir shifted and changed, the sound becoming something like mocking laughter. Every one of the pestilent insects was a mote of consciousness granted un-life by the Grandfather's will, a collective daemonic form that could fill dying flesh as oil might fill an empty flask. It had no uttered identity beyond the mutter of iridescent wings and the clatter of chitinous mandibles – but those few cursed to see it walk when clothed in human meat had given it a name. They called it the Lord of Flies.

'No...' Garro forced out the denial, his eyes widening as understanding came to him.

'In death, you will serve what you betrayed,' intoned Mortarion. ***'I gave you the chance to return to us of your own free will, battle-captain, and you refused that tribute. But it will come to pass. The Lord is eager to manifest within a new host. Your flesh will be a fitting one.'***

It was better than the Terran-born deserved, mused the primarch, but with the daemon at his side, his dominance of the Legion would be renewed along with it. Garro had witnessed the Lord of Flies possess three of his comrades – Solun Decius, Meric Voyen and the World Eaters exile Macer Varren – and each time he had been party to the daemon's defeat and dissolution. There was ritual power to be mined from the act of allowing Garro's flesh to be taken as its next chosen vessel.

Mortarion's eyes narrowed, and he smothered a tiny ember of dismay at the prospect. He saw now his hope to make the Knight Errant bend the knee had been a wasted one. There was no other choice. Typhus was right; Garro could not be redeemed. This would be the only way to bring him back into the Death Guard fold.

With a moan of effort, Garro lurched forward. He forced himself up onto the broken, spitting metal of his augmetic leg, snatching at his sword, stabbing it into the earth as a makeshift support for his weight.

The primarch pressed the war-scythe's heavy blade against Garro's chest and pushed him back before he could fully rise, holding him in place.

'How did you think this was going to end, Nathaniel?' Mortarion cocked his head, staring down at his once favoured warrior. ***'You believe you are some righteous champion, anointed by my father? It is delusion. Can you see now, the lie of that? Can you see, that every path He laid out – for me, for you and your brothers – they culminate in death?'***

'Only in death…' rasped Garro, 'does duty end.'

'No,' said the primarch, as the swarm gathered to him and he stood tall. ***'Not for you. You will die and rise, die again and rise again, for eternity under my command.'*** A sickening crackle sounded from Mortarion's back as the filth-encrusted plates across his torso buckled and split. ***'This is how you end, Knight Errant. In shadows and decay.'***

Mortarion's armour parted in jagged fault lines and great sails of glistening, semi-transparent matter unfurled from within. Briefly drooping across his back to touch the polluted ground, the malformed sheets stiffened in the light, growing firmer by the second, drying and strengthening. The new-made pinions were shimmering, ghastly things, corpse-beetle black and oleaginous silver. Maggots writhed in their wet crevices, fatty fluids dripping as the extensions lifted out to their full width.

Mortarion's gigantic insect wings curved down to blot out the weakened sunlight falling upon the battlefield, and as Garro was shrouded in dimness, the buzzing of the daemonic flies became a deafening howl.

SIX

Hand of Death
Libertas
The Rest is Silence

'Is it done?' Gallor demanded an answer from Greff, limping towards the trooper as the young human dithered in the smoky corridor. 'Are we ready to depart?'

'We, uh, we are, ser legionary.' His head bobbed. 'As well as we can be, I mean.' Greff gestured in the direction of the landing pad. 'The men asked if we'd make it out and in honesty, I can't speak to that. The carrier's heavily overloaded–'

Gallor cut him off with a shake of the head. 'Content yourself that the decision is no longer in your hands. If we die, it won't be you to blame.'

Greff blinked. 'That's not very reassuring.'

'It wasn't meant to be.' Gallor looked past him, towards the sections of the Dilectio Tier that had already been evacuated. Dusty light filtered in from that direction, cast up by the clash on the battleground beyond. 'Anyone who wants to stay behind, they can do so. And they will die. If they are lucky.' His hard, matter-of-fact statement echoed off the walls.

'And if... they are unlucky?' Greff's knuckles whitened around the grip of the lascarbine in his hands.

Gallor looked back at him. 'You have heard the stories about the horrors the Warmaster has brought to Terra. The creatures out of nightmares. The things they do to the living and the dead.'

'Yes.' Greff swallowed hard. 'B-but I didn't believe them.'

'That was your first mistake. Whatever you have heard... the truth is worse than you can imagine.' He sniffed the air, ignoring the fear on the trooper's face. 'Keeler isn't on board the carrier. Tell me where she is.'

'She, ah, she was near the battlements, gathering her things.'

'Who guards her?'

'I...' Greff's mouth dropped open. 'Oh, Throne. I didn't think to–'

Before the trooper could finish, a woman's anguished cry echoed down the passageway to them, and Gallor bit down on a curse. He broke into a hobbling run, cursing his damaged wargear as he went.

'Go to the carrier!' He shouted the order back over his shoulder. 'Be ready to lift off the moment I return!'

Gallor did not pause to be sure if the trooper was following the command. He disliked working with these humans. Some could be well disciplined and follow directions, but others had an unpleasant tendency to lose focus whenever danger was at hand.

He had no time or interest in playing nursemaid to Greff and his fellow soldiers. His prime mission – Battle-Captain Garro's last command – was to preserve the life of Euphrati Keeler and he would apply himself to that.

'Keeler!' He shouted her name as he reached the outer ring of the battlements. The weapons emplacements, hard points and barriers lay abandoned, home only to the cold winds off the distant icy mountains. 'Show yourself!'

He heard a stifled sob and found her crouching in the ruin of a blasted gun dome. She was pressed into the cover of the broken stone walls, staring down at the debris-strewn wasteland at the foot of the bastion.

'Come away,' he demanded. 'We have to go, now!'

'Do you see him?' Keeler ignored his words. 'Helig, look!'

A sound reached Gallor's hearing – a deep, sonorous crackle like the breaking of stones – and he automatically tensed. He knew the noise: the shattering of ceramite armour.

A sickly dread tightened around his chest as the legionary spied the figures duelling far below. He let out a snarl of anger as he saw Garro take a mortal blow and crash to the ground. Gallor's ire became shock as he realised that the cadaverous, skeletal giant who had landed the hit could only be the primarch. *Mortarion.*

'Gene-father?' he whispered. 'I cannot believe that is… him.'

'It is,' Keeler said quietly. 'It's what they will all become, when Horus wins.'

'If,' Gallor countered, silencing his own misgivings before they could take root. He put his hand around Keeler's arm and applied pressure to pull her away, but she remained in place. He sensed he could not move her unless she wished it. *How was that possible?*

The woman nodded towards Garro, gasping in anguish as he took hit after hit from the Death Lord's great scythe. 'Mortarion will kill him.'

'Yes.' A terrible certainty settled on Gallor. It felt impossible to look away, as if to do so would be the gravest cowardice imaginable.

We will watch Nathaniel Garro die, he told himself. *We must bear witness.*

Down in the arena of ruins and blood, the thing that was Mortarion changed anew, growing great and monstrous wings that rose up to throw darkness over the place where Garro had fallen. A dense swarm of shimmering plague flies swirled around them, droning madly.

Gallor stiffened, dreading what might come next, dreading what he would see when the primarch's dark acts were ended. *The body of a fallen champion? Or something worse?*

'Garro gave his life to distract the traitors,' said the warrior, finally breaking the spell of the desolate moment upon them. 'We must escape, or his sacrifice will count for nothing.'

Keeler stood up and turned her gaze away – but not towards Gallor and the way to the landing pad. She stared in the opposite direction, towards the towers and the great halls of the Imperial Palace itself, far beyond the line of battle.

Gallor grimaced. 'He's gone, Euphrati.'

'No,' she said distantly. 'Not yet.'

The agony was infernal, as deep and murky as the foul, cloying gloom that engulfed him.

The world closed in, shrinking down from a battlefield, to an arena, to a blood-spattered spot on a slab of broken pavement. There lay Nathaniel Garro – Dusk Raider, Death Guard, Knight Errant – and he was dying with each thrumming double-beat of his augmented hearts.

Dark, bioengineered blood, the red of it so deeply shaded it was almost black, pooled about his body and gathered in the lines of his skin. Garro saw it painted over the palms of his armoured gauntlets and the dusty stone where he had collapsed.

He tasted the rich copper-iron tang of it in his mouth and felt the burn of his omophagea organ unlacing the genetic structure of the fluid, sifting it for memory chains. It would drown him in his own recollections unless he could break free, but to move, even to breathe, was like a forest of knives in his chest.

Garro had known pain. He had made it his companion in

war after war. But never like this. This was suffering beyond any he had experienced before.

'I will end this,' said the voice of death itself. *'You will endure, and you will* **rise.'** The Reaper of Men loomed over him, each word he spoke the cold wind from a sepulchre, each word repeated in the violent buzzing of the black swarm. *'But first, you must perish.'*

Garro tried to find the energy to speak, to spit back the defiance in his bones, but he could not.

And then another voice spoke for him. *'No.'* The Saint's whispered words fell through his mind on threads of golden gossamer, delicate but unbreakable. *'Not yet.'*

The sun-warmth he had felt before drenched him anew. Garro's pain receded, the tide of it drawn out and banished. A power from beyond the bounds of his flesh and blood stiffened his sinews and steeled his nerves. He moved. He *rose.*

What seconds ago had seemed like an impossible task was now inevitable. His jaw set, his defiance burning brightly, the wounded Knight Errant embraced this new, fiery strength, and came to his feet once again.

Garro looked down at his bloody gauntlet, and for an instant, he saw the ghost of Keeler's hand in his, as it had been back in the fortress. Her touch was still upon him, and by means that he could only guess at, she was *renewing* him. She was channelling an incredible strength into his flesh, acting as the conduit for something greater than both of them.

He had become like her. In this brief moment, Garro was the avatar for a power beyond the mortal.

The darkness about him receded, and with a heavy tread, the Reaper of Men did something rare for a Death Guard – he *retreated,* drawing back step upon step. His insectile wings rippled and twitched, and the gaunt face in the hollows of his hood creased in anger and confusion.

'You cannot resist me,' hissed the primarch.

'I can,' Garro answered with a furious snarl, dragging *Libertas* up from the dust in a blazing arc of blue light. 'I will. *I must!*' Shouting his rage and defiance, he threw himself into his attack.

Mortarion's hesitation lasted scarcely a blink, but it was enough for the embattled legionary to come at him, sword rising high.

The Death Lord reacted with lightning speed and *Silence* swung through a tight, humming arc, the corroded steel of the war-scythe's great head meeting the powerblade with a thunderbolt crash.

Blue fire erupted at the point where the edges of sword and scythe crossed, casting jumping shadows across the broken ground. Mortarion leaned into the parry, but Garro stood his ground, giving nothing, matching him strength for strength.

Impossible. The Knight Errant was no more than a legionary of the line, strong and powerful in comparison to any ordinary human, but in no way the equal of a primarch. Mortarion should have been able to cut him in two with a single sweep of his weapon; more than that, Garro should already have been dead.

But he stood there, matching Mortarion's effort blade to blade, as if the primarch were battling his own doppelgänger.

A shrill, ear-splitting shriek went through the black swarm of bloated, festering insects and the mass reacted like a living thing. They recoiled from around Garro's form as if repelled by an invisible force, many of them flashing into sizzling ash, the rest of them retreating back and away. Something in the fallen legionary had become toxic to the Lord of Flies, anathema to the daemon's very presence.

Mortarion drew in a deep, wheezing breath, and he tasted it on his curdled lips.

Witchery.

The burning metallic rasp of psionic spoor was all about him, spilling from Garro's weakened aura – but not from the legionary himself.

No. The Knight Errant was no psyker, his soul born without that elusive key to the immaterium. This power was coming from somewhere – *someone* – else.

Mortarion was still coming to grips with the new, preternatural senses the Grandfather's Mark had given him, but he had instinct enough to perceive the source of the energy about Garro.

'Your Saint cannot save you,' he growled, his attention returning to the play of blades. *'You are already dead, Nathaniel.'*

'Then in that, my lord, we are the same.' Garro's eyes were alight with martial fury.

A hollow rasp of laughter burst from the primarch. *'Such a staid, hidebound fool, captain. So rigid in your spirit, so brittle in flesh!'* He shook the scythe, the metal clashing together again. *'You turned your back on greatness, on immortality itself! You swore an oath to me and my Legion, and then shattered it because of your cowardice and fear!'*

'My oath remains unbroken!' Garro shot back the retort. 'You betrayed the Emperor!'

'No, my son. There is only one traitor here.' Behind his mask, Mortarion's lip curled. *'You have always set yourself above others because of your origins. You think yourself superior because you were born on this planet. Because being Terran makes you closer to my father, yes? But that means nothing.'* Venom boiled in his throat as he decried his wayward warrior. *'My birthplace matters not. I was reborn on Barbarus and my foster-father there was no less a monster than the one in this palace. The Death Guard grew in that world's poisoned garden, and only they know what it is to be truly loyal...'* He threw a nod towards Typhus and the phalanxes of Plague Marines. *'Every last traitor from our ranks will be purged. In time, nothing of the old way will remain.'*

'You have... broken my heart.' Garro's eyes darkened. 'I would have done anything for you, Mortarion. If only you had not betrayed us. But you have become the lie, and led my brothers to ruin! You are the thing you always swore to hate and revile! You deceive yourself and the Legion pays the price!'

Their blades broke contact with an oscillating wail and the combatants circled one another, searching for an opening.

'You think you know me?' Mortarion gave a shake of the head. ***'The most desolate horror you have ever experienced is only an ember against the inferno of my suffering. I have seen what lies in the darkest shadows. I have fought the chaos at the edge of death!'***

'I believe you,' said Garro, with a weary exhalation. 'But still you blind yourself to the truth, gene-sire. How can you claim to loathe sorcery even as you make pacts with the things that live in the warp? You betray Terra, the Legion, the Emperor... And you betray *yourself.*'

'Kill it!' The bellowed cry came from Typhus, standing atop a collapsed pillar. He brandished his manreaper, shaking it at the sky. ***'Kill the traitor weakling! Let it die!'***

'Let it die!' Mortarion's pestilent warriors beat their weapons together in a cacophony of rusted steel, echoing the Traveller's demand.

Let it die. Let it die. Let it die. Let it die.

The whispers in his ears joined in the chorus, and Mortarion knew that it was the voice of the warp reaching out to him. The Grandfather's guiding hand pushed him towards the ultimate act.

He glared at his former legionary and saw clearly that this moment had always been here in his path, waiting for him to meet it.

Each step Mortarion had taken – beginning with his rebellion against his Overlord foster-father on Barbarus, his turbulent brotherhood with the man who had become Typhus the Traveller, the reunion with his gene-father, and finally the Death Guard's rebirth by Nurgle's blessing – all these things had been ordained. Each one stripped away the lies that Mortarion had been told about himself, piece by piece, until none remained.

The Knight Errant would perish today, and his murder would mark the fruition of Mortarion's complete truth. Garro was the primarch's final connection to his Legion as it had been before the Great Change, the emblem of the last tiny part of him that still remained human. It had to be obliterated.

Let it die.

'I will,' he vowed, marshalling his power for the fatal strike.

The great jagged blade of Mortarion's war-scythe carved smoke as it fell in an arc of befouled steel. The cursed weapon pulsed with the Grandfather's rancid consecration, and the legionary's desperate attempt to parry it met with failure.

Even bolstered by the fortitude of his Saint, Garro could not stop the fall of *Silence*. The scythe splintered the Knight Errant's venerable blade across its width, breaking the power sword *Libertas* in two.

Mortarion's weapon punched through the last intact layers of the legionary's armour. The point of the scythe-head pushed into bone and flesh. It found his primary heart and punctured it, ripping it in twain.

Wounded mortally, blood surging into his chest cavity, Garro went rigid and his agony became total. The steadfast battle-captain reached out with one trembling hand and clutched at the head of the scythe, his gauntlet sizzling as the ceramite burned on contact with corrupted metal.

The blade wedged in the legionary's chest, Mortarion let the weight of *Silence* force Garro to his knees. Inky threads of toxicity were already eating into the Knight Errant's wargear, and where the scythe met flesh it was poisoning him, dissolving his veins and nerves.

The primarch watched the shadow of death lengthen over Garro's form. This time, he would not rise.

Pinned in place against the blood-washed rubble, Garro's body shook as one by one, each of his implants and vital organs began to shut down. His genhanced flesh and bones – the greatest weapons that the Emperor's science had gifted to him – were not immortal. His end was at hand. Nothing could stop that now.

What would come next? Abyssal darkness? Or would there be some shining, transcendent moment of clarity as the light of life faded?

To Garro's surprise, what freed itself within him was a smile. He released a wet, broken chuckle. He understood his purpose now. Everything was made clear.

'You... know this,' said Garro, labouring out every last word. 'When I die, Mortarion... Your humanity dies with me.'

'As is my wish,' intoned the primarch, tightening his grip on *Silence*'s shaft. ***'I no longer care for such concerns.'***

'Lie,' managed Garro, panting through a blood-filled breath. 'I know... truth. Hidden in your heart. You lie... to yourself. You always have.' He gritted his teeth and gave a bitter laugh. 'In this moment... *you sow the seed of your final defeat.*'

Mortarion hesitated, frozen in place, as Garro's utterance registered with him. Even now, on the precipice of death, the legionary's words were inescapable. They were undeniable.

From somewhere high atop the broken flanks of the Marmax Bastion, a flash of white light blossomed into being and the drumming rumble of thrusters came like a clarion call.

A machine in the shape of a winged bullet blasted itself out of the landing pad and cut a curving turn up and around the fallen tiers of the bastion. Typhus screamed wordlessly and every projectile weapon on the ground opened up at once.

The gathered Death Guard host bracketed the craft, vomiting bilious fire and lethal ejecta into the air. A webwork of criss-crossing rocket-shell contrails and ropes of searing tracer clawed after the heavy carrier as it skidded through the smoke, overstressed engines howling as they pushed it towards the sky. Some of the ground-fire clipped the fuselage and it veered wildly to avoid a terminal strike that might bring it down.

Then, finding its pace, gaining traction against gravity and drag, the carrier shot towards the distant towers and armoured precincts of the Inner Imperial Palace. A double peal of thunder sounded as the craft breached the sound barrier and raced away at supersonic velocity.

Garro's hazy, pain-misted vision caught sight of the silver dart as it receded. He knew that Helig Gallor was at the controls, with Euphrati Keeler and whomever remained of Kostagar's surviving defenders in his charge.

'She is safe,' he gasped, 'and you have failed, Mortarion.'

Whatever plan the Death Lord had, to take the Saint as his prize for Horus Lupercal, to turn Garro to the banner of the Warmaster's heretics, it was now a ruin.

And the price of it was the life of a martyr. *I pay the cost,* Garro told himself. *As I was always meant to.*

This was the purpose towards which Nathaniel Garro's path had been wrought. The moment in which he placed the existence of the Saint before all else. The moment when he saved her.

'No…' Mortarion's grave-rasp rose into a furious snarl. ***'Even in your death you hinder me.'***

'Aye,' he breathed, gathering every last iota of strength still in his body, before the will leaked out into the thirsting dust along with his blood. 'I deny you your victory. You will never have… what you wish. Such is the fate… of oath-breakers.'

And then, with a final bellow of effort, Garro pulled himself up the blade of the scythe, forcing it through his torso, the razored tip bursting out of his back, all so he could bring himself closer.

Close enough for one last strike.

The broken stub of *Libertas* still in his other hand, Garro rammed the shattered sword into Mortarion's throat, burying it to the hilt. Toxic vitae spewed in a virulent spray, gushing down over the neck ring of the primarch's rusted armour.

As Garro sank back into the blood-thickened mud, Mortarion ripped the broken sword from the cut and let out a gurgling, monstrous howl of pain. He pressed a hand to the wound, holding his flesh together. The righteous blow filled his throat with hot bile and sickly ichor, and despite the Mark of the warp on his flesh, the primarch's new injury would not be quick to close.

Darkness closed in softly from the edges of Garro's vision, and the discord around him faded, becoming distant. The twinned sound of his primary and secondary hearts, the pulsing force of life that had been his companion for so long, had been reduced to one single throbbing drumbeat.

The sound began to slow.

Sunlight flashed off the mote of silver in the sky, marking the fading glimmer of Keeler's escape. He felt a wave of sorrow for the Saint. She would have to go on without him and bear the great burden of the Imperial Truth beyond this day. More than anything, Garro wanted to be by her side to carry on the fight against the great Chaos, but he knew he would not live to see another battle. He took meagre comfort in the knowledge that the war against the heretics would not falter, not if it took a century, a millennia, or more.

Death drew near, the shadow of it falling across him. Garro had been to the brink of this chasm before, but always managed to pull back.

Now he was falling, destined to it. The instances between the beats of his heart grew longer, their force fading.

Garro looked up, and as his vision clouded he beheld an

image of death. What men of ancient ages past would have called Thanatos, Azrael, the Grim Reaper, Mortarion had become in reality. The gaunt, hooded primarch was not death in peace, death in nobility or death in honour – he was the horror of it, the decay and destruction of that ultimate end.

But Garro's final conscious act would not be to surrender to that. Defiance filled his spirit as the shadows blurred the world about him, and as time lengthened and slowed, a light – *a golden, beautiful light* – came into being before him. Mortarion and his twisted Legions, the ruins and the vista of the battle beyond, these things faded as the light grew and grew.

Through the heart of the glorious illumination came a great figure in magnificent, gilded armour, as if stepping through it like a doorway. The figure in shimmering, perfect gold looked towards the fallen legionary and met his gaze.

Is this real? Garro's thoughts became a torrent of emotions and impressions.

Is this my failing mind manifesting a last surge of life before the end?

Or is it Him?

There were no words. The golden warrior gave a paternal nod and extended an open hand. The legionary knew that if he took it, if he accepted and truly *believed* without doubt or hesitation, there would come a time when he might rise anew.

Trembling, the son of Albia and Terra, the Dusk Raider, the Death Guard, the Knight Errant, reached out to take the offered hand. As he did so, he saw that the metal of his gauntlets, the flesh and bone beneath were becoming dust and crumbling into the winds. But it did not matter. The rough substance of his being was no longer important. It was his soul that would live in eternity.

He should have been afraid, but in that moment he was elated. For within it, his purpose had at last been fulfilled.

The God-Emperor knew his name; and Nathaniel Garro's duty was at an end.

ERA OF RUIN

ANGELS OF ANOTHER AGE

JOHN FRENCH

'Pity the dead. Pity that they will not see the ages to come, and all the wonders that their acts have wrought.'

– Words etched on the Stones of Remembrance,
Dome of Unity, the Imperial Palace, Terra

Kystos Gaellon is on the remains of Marmax South, Section 52, Hold Point 78, when his father dies. He's been there for thirty-five minutes. That time is an estimate. Everything in the Wasteland is an estimate. He has started to think of the Wasteland as a state rather than a description: a land wasted, burnt, and starved, and cut, and beaten down to the root. A place where dead souls walked.

Gaellon came to Hold Point 78 with two other warriors. Neither of them is of his Legion. There is... There is Su'lok of the White Scars, and Nerron of the Imperial Fists. Gaellon must repeat their names under his breath to remember them. The Wasteland takes names, just like it takes everything else. None of them have any ammunition left. Gaellon is a Blood Angel. He has been killing with his sword alone for... a length of time that he cannot estimate. Su'lok has a chainglaive, but the teeth have broken and the mechanism that turns them has jammed. Nerron has a mace that hangs in his one arm. The other side of the son of Dorn's body is a ruin. Every armour plate from thigh to shoulder is shattered. Burnt flesh is visible in the gaps, and bits of bone through the flesh. He has no arm from the shoulder down – the Wasteland took it. Soon it will come for the rest of him.

Hold Point 78 was one of the many emplacements built during Rogal Dorn's fortification of the Palace. It was part of the line of battlements called Marmax South. It had been a district of habs and institutes for the mortals who studied the Great Crusade. The war masons kept the shells of the buildings and filled them with rockcrete to make a string of artificial cliffs. On top of those they set crenellations and gun emplacements. Now the whole line is rubble, and Hold Point 78 is a tor of smashed rockcrete and girders rising from the cratered ground. The only reason Gaellon knows where they are is because one of the remaining wall sections still has its line-location code stencilled on it.

'You know this place?' asks Su'lok. The White Scar has come to stand beside Gaellon.

'I was here before,' says Gaellon without looking around. 'It's part of the Southern Marmax line.'

Su'lok grunts at that. In the recent past he would have asked how it was possible that they had found themselves on the edge of the Anterior defences that were several hundred kilometres from where they had been fighting. Now all of them know there is no point asking the question. This is the Wasteland. Time, space and distance no longer mean what they once did here.

'I was on this section of the line,' says Gaellon, quietly, half to himself. For a second he thinks of Baeron. If this really is Hold Point 78, then his brother died near here. The thought should not surprise him; Gaellon is rarer now for being amongst the living. The Imperial Palace that was, and the Wasteland it has become are a land of dead angels. To be alive here and now is the aberration.

The land around them is rippled ochre as though a soft blanket of dust has been laid over the devastation. The sky is a rust haze which blends with the land at the point where there should be a horizon. Gaellon lifts a finger and slides it across the distance. In his mind he sees a brush dip into ink and then drag across parchment.

'What are you doing?' asks Su'lok. The White Scar is looking hard at Gaellon. He's watching to see if the Blood Angel is still on the right side of sanity. That's what the Wasteland does – it eats reality and then it eats trust.

'A brother died close to here,' says Gaellon. 'I was thinking how he would have looked at this.'

In his mind the brush dips in another shade of ink.

'Kinder to have died already than to see things come to this,' says Su'lok, and spits. The White Scar has not had a helm since they broke out of Hasgard Fort. Tracks of dried blood mark his scalp and cheeks.

'Something is coming!' It's Nerron, who is looking out from next to a slumped firing lip. The son of Dorn is standing straight, refusing the offer of the tumbled wall as a support. Blood is slowly oozing from his wounded side. Gaellon and Su'lok go to stand beside him.

'I don't see anything,' says Su'lok.

Nerron does not answer. He is scanning the murk, helm moving from side to side. There are cracks in his eye-lenses, and a cobweb of fractures across the helm's crown. Whatever he saw before is gone now. That does not mean it was not there, or that it's not there now. All it means is that the Wasteland won't let them see it yet.

The world has been empty and still for Gaellon for the last three hours. Both the emptiness and time are subjective, he knows. They could have walked past battle and slaughter and not realised it. Similarly, it is not actually quiet. It just seems that way to them. These are the last moments of the greatest battle ever fought by humanity. The Eternity Gate has closed. The Legions and allies of Horus are in ascendancy. Bombs are falling in a deluge. Titans are roaming the maze of ruins that were once cities. Billions remain alive outside the last defences, waiting to die or fighting on in defiance. All that slaughter comes with noise: the screams of the dying, the shriek of weapons inhaling to fire, the thunder of falling towers. That sound is not here. Not in this part of the Wasteland.

Gaellon squints at the distance, and murmurs to himself.

'A heap of broken images, where the sun beats, and the dead tree gives not shelter…'

'What?' snaps Su'lok.

Gaellon shakes his head but does not look around.

'A fragment of ancient poetry,' he said. 'It came to mind. I am not sure why.'

Su'lok grunts.

'The sons of Sanguinius are a strange breed.'

'I recall many poets of great worth amongst the Fifth Legion,' says Gaellon.

'There are, but this war demands laughter and scorn and nothing else.'

'There must always be art and beauty, even when all seems broken.'

'Are all of your kind high-minded poets then?'

'No,' says Gaellon dryly. 'Some of us are painters.'

Su'lok laughs then. The sound cracks through the quiet like the fall of a lightning bolt.

Gaellon is about to speak again when he sees movement in the distance. Su'lok sees it at the same time and points.

'There!' says the White Scar.

Six hundred and forty metres out, a ripple rises in the ochre-dust softness of the landscape. Gaellon activates the power field on his sword. The lightning crackles down the tongue of steel. Nerron and Su'lok do not move. Their weapons have no power. None of them posture or seek cover. They are here to sell their lives.

The ripple in the dust is gathering pace, broadening, curling into a crest of powdered red.

Gaellon feels the need to say something, to add a frayed piece of poetry to the moment. He is a poet as well as a warrior. All the Blood Angels are masters of a craft or art. Words are his, and to give them voice now, in the face of the slow murder of this world, seems as great an act of defiance as drawing a sword.

He opens his mouth…

Then he feels his father die.

Black fills his sight. Pain steals his words.

There is blood falling in the dark somewhere far away. Blood and feathers.

'May I confess something?' Baeron asked. The vox crackled with static. It had been doing that more and more in the last few days. The cheers for the victory at Saturnine were only a few hours old, but there had already been an assault on the lines since then. The fresh dead lay in steaming heaps on the maze of obstacles and wire at the base of the Marmax South fortifications. Two kilometres of crenellated wall separated the two Blood Angels, but the vox let them talk and their helm sight let them pick each other out across the distance. Two figures in scuffed and scratched crimson amid the grey rockcrete and clusters of drab human troopers.

'Confess what?' Gaellon asked. Baeron cocked his head and looked away. It was a gesture that he had made when they were both youths scrabbling for survival in the dust of Baal. It meant the same now as it had then. 'You are thinking of the future again,' Gaellon said. Baeron did not answer and kept his gaze on the horizon.

It was dawn. The clouds and dust had peeled back from the fresh blue of the sky. The towers and buildings of the Anterior stood out against the gold of the new day. Plumes of smoke rose to smudge the sun, as if someone had trailed black ink into orange. It was as though the skies of Terra were gilding the victories of the day before. Even the smell had changed. A fresh wind had diluted the reek of spilled fuel, corpses and burning plastek. For this small slice of time, one could almost dream of peace. It would be a brief moment, Gaellon knew. Another attack would come soon. As line adjutants both Baeron and Gaellon were linked into the main command interface. They knew that the analysts for this section had said that it was likely to suffer persistent main-force attacks in perpetuity. In perpetuity – the battle had given the phrase a new meaning: for the duration of conflict, until the enemy broke through, or were defeated. The war had redefined eternity just as it had everything else.

There were not enough Legion warriors to hold this line. That was a fact. So, Sanguinius had placed hundreds of his veterans amongst the human units. One angel to ten thousand humans, sometimes more. They were there to ensure smooth execution of commands, but more than anything else they were there to fight and be seen. The soldiers in their trenches and gun emplacements would hear the war cries of Baal, and see that angels fought beside them. The moments where the line adjutants would see each other were rare. The dawn of that morning was one such moment.

'I am still waiting for a confession,' said Gaellon.

'I find myself thinking what the echo of these times shall be,' Baeron said. 'All times have an echo. The plagues that almost killed mankind before it had even left this earth led to the flowering of art that we struggle to match. Even the Imperium is a work of art crafted from the trauma of Old Night.'

'And you are wondering what will come from these times?'

'Attack incoming.' *The voice from the command bastion came from the vox. The human officer's voice was calm, but the signal squawked with static.* 'All line sections. Marmax South. Attack incoming. Main force, infantry, armour, full air-support element. Expect contact imminent.'

The only answer that Baeron would give to the last question Gaellon asked him was an echo of the shout he bellowed to the human soldiers around him.

'Rise! Weapons ready! Rise!'

Can a death echo across the sky? Can it fill an instant, and an eternity? An absence that collapses the world around it. An implosion in being.

To others, the death of Sanguinius, primarch of the IX Legion, the Archangel of Baal, is not yet a fact. It will become real to them soon. Rogal Dorn and the Emperor will see the broken Angel, and the blood that flows from the wounds. For others, it will never be a physical truth. It will be words coming from a mouth struggling to speak…

'Sanguinius is dead…'

It will become a fact printed on a signal scroll…

The primarch of the IX has fallen…

It will become a story blurred by time into myth.

'Horus slew the Angel who had been his closest kin…'

To Gaellon, the death of his father is a physical fact.

The link between the primarchs and their warrior sons is a mystery that will soon pass beyond living knowledge. The Blood Angels, like all the Legiones Astartes, were once human. The organs implanted into them changed them, melding their flesh with traits of the primarch from whom they were templated. The organs and process that created a warrior of the Blood Angels caused changes at the genetic level. The effect on the mind, and the soul? Those were mysteries that not even the primarchs knew the truth of. A bond was formed between primarch and Space Marine at the level of the spirit that went beyond flesh. Body and soul. For some, that link might be distant. To the Blood Angels, the depth of their bond with their father is revealed only as it is severed. For Gaellon, it is a revelation of pain.

Black.

White edges of pain tearing through him.

Black.

Copper and iron on his tongue.

Black.

No... No, this can't be. This cannot be.

Black.

Falling, always falling, without wings to catch his descent.

Black.

A brush dipped into red ink...

Black.

A crimson smear across white...

Black.

He is dead...

Black.

I am dead...

White.

Gaellon is standing. In front of him the ripple in the ochre dust breaks like a wave running to the shore. Things burst from under the murk. They are daemons. They are shaped by ideas of rage and hate and fury. Their skin is red and glossed. Smoke fumes from them. They roar as they come.

Su'lok is shouting. Nerron has braced, mace ready. Gaellon sees and hears none of this. He is feeling his heart ripped out by silver claws, and the strand holding the soul to the body snap. He is seeing red and black ink run down the face of a blank canvas in a memory that never happened.

Calm...

Stillness...

The sigh of brush on parchment...

Gaellon stood on a floor of pale stone under a wooden canopy. The floor is marble taken from the last bones of a mountain that once gave its stone to the temples of Terra's long-dead gods. The pillars that support the canopy are not from Terra but Caliban, chosen, felled, and shipped to the Throneworld as a gift of the Lion. It was raining. Water drummed steadily on the stones beyond the canopy's shelter. Curtains of grey shifted across a view of bridges spanning streams which ran between blossom-heavy trees. The rain was semi-artificial, of course, just as the scene it moved over was. This was one of the decorative domes of Hatay-Antakya, Spire of a Thousand Gardens, Terra's Emerald Hive. Gaellon blinked as he looked at the gravel paths and the pink petals dancing on the grey surface of the pools.

'The past…' he said to himself. 'I have fallen from pain into the past.'

This was a memory of the time that he and a hundred of his brothers had been granted leave to see the gardens of Hatay-Antakya while serving as an honour guard to Sanguinius when the primarch came to Terra. It had been a rare moment. Each of the hundred had spent their time in the gardens working on pieces of art to present to the primarch. All Blood Angels were craftsmen and artists. Gaellon had turned his will and hand to several creative disciplines – sculpture in stone and wax, lacquering, and glass making – but in his heart he was the poet he had been when he first ascended to the Legion. Baeron had been a painter. Watercolour and ink had been his mediums, and with them he had seemed to reach the truth under the surface of the world. Gaellon watched the memory of his brother tapping small piles of pigment into bowls beside his palette. A stretched rectangle of parchment sat on a frame in front of the view.

'I am dead,' said Baeron, without looking around.

Gaellon nodded reflexively.

'On the line at Marmax South, three weeks ago…'

Baeron frowned and removed the lid from a flask of ink.

'Did I die well?'

Gaellon thought of the Death Guard lumbering out of the gas-fog, of the bolt-rounds buzzing through the air, as thick as the clouds of flies swarming over the corpses. He thought of the last time he had seen Baeron alive, wading into a tide of bloated figures, rounds exploding on the remains of his armour, axes and cleavers hacking at him as he fired and struck, and kept going forwards as he was torn apart.

'You died with honour,' said Gaellon. Then closed his mouth, for a second. 'I am sorry, my brother,' he said at last.

'Why?'

'I would have liked to have seen you again in life.' Baeron's expression did not change.

'We were all made to die, brother. I was lucky to reach that end when I did.'

'How so?'

Baeron looked at the parchment, considering. Then he took a brush with a fat, tapered head. He dipped it into water then splashed it into the ochre pigment on the palette, swirled the liquid into the dust then dipped the brush back into the water flask. Yellow murk spread through the clear liquid. Baeron mixed more water into the pigment. His movements were relaxed, fluid, as though he were in tune with the spin and flow of the water in the flask.

'I died in the past,' he said, and raised the brush to the parchment. 'I died in an age of sorrow, and betrayal, and bitterness…' The brush swept across the white surface of the parchment. Yellow fog spread across the image. The brush moved again, dabbing, flicking, moving back between palette and parchment. 'I died knowing that the Imperium that we believed in would never be as it was…' The brush dipped and water swirled into a heap of red pigment. The remains of the ochre blended with the red, and now Baeron's movements were a blur. Red ran into yellow, images formed brush stroke by brush stroke, and suddenly Gaellon was not looking at a picture, but the view from the Marmax South line as the sun rose and the enemy came.

The Death Guard came closer, growing in smudges of black – bloated, rolling figures, haloed in flies. 'I died as an angel of a past age,' said Baeron's voice. And Gaellon felt the watercolour blur of dust and poison gas roll over him. He was there again on the line, moving, driven by memory, watching the last time he had seen his brother alive.

Baeron came around the edge of a ridge of rubble. Six figures were on the other side. They were human. All of them wore the gas-hoods issued to troops in the Anterior warzone. Some of them still had the aquila stamped on the remains of their gear. Rust pocked every buckle and plate of their uniforms. Mould speckled the inside of their eyepieces. The guns in their hands should not have been able to function, but they would fire despite the muck coating them. Baeron fired. A bolt-round hit the figure at the centre of the ragged group. It was a metal-storm round, made to create a sphere of shrapnel. It hit the trooper in the torso and blew them apart. Shards of metal and bone ripped into the two nearest troopers. They fell. The others flinched. Then Baeron was amongst them. He did not shoot the rest. Ammunition and supplies had already become scarce, and besides there was no need. He took the first at a run, the knife blow rising to slice from groin to shoulder. The trooper came apart, all physical integrity vanishing in a burst of bowel fluid and blood. Then he was into the next one and the next, red spattering the dust of his armour. Behind him, the eyes of the human troopers watching him from the gun loops and firing steps. He cut the last trooper down and held his blade high as the gore pattered on his armour… In his mind, Gaellon could hear the cheer from the lines.

And then his memory and sight pulled back, so he saw Baeron at the centre of the painted image, a crimson angel with sword raised against a washed field of yellow and green. The shots of the soldiers firing from the lines were white dashes in the blur of ink, their shouts almost audible in the ripple of dried pigment and water.

Stillness.

A single moment of time inked and framed.

'I died and do not have to live with the future that is to come…'

* * *

White…

Blinding…

Falling…

Heat jolts through Gaellon's arm. The horned skull parts to the sword edge. The power field discharges with a blink of lightning. Blood jelly and red ectoplasm spatter his armour. He is screaming, shouting, roaring. The sound is pouring from inside him. He is in the middle of the daemons. They surround him. Their bodies are taut muscle and blood-slick skin. They hold swords of black iron which trail sparks as they cut. Their faces are skull grins of rage and slaughter-joy. They are of the Neverborn, bred by life's violence: by predation, by murder, by war. Fury, hate, and the joy of killing bleeds from living minds into the warp and gives them power. Normally they cannot come from the warp into reality, but the war, this last battle of battles, has broken the barriers between worlds. The Wasteland is a daemon realm.

Gaellon is far from the ruins of Hold Point 78 now. It lies in the distance behind him. He has waded out from that island of rubble, into the ochre dust and the tide of daemons. He is alone. If Su'lok and Nerron call to him from the shore he does not hear them. He kills.

The daemon he has just cut collapses into smoke and skin. Another takes its place. It is laughing, and the laughter is the sound of claws shredding feathers from an angel as it dies. Gaellon cuts it down. Then another and another. Swords find him. Claws open his armour. His blood is running to mix with the dust of the ground. But he does not stop. He cuts and hacks and roars and wades deeper into the tide, further from the shore.

His father is dead. The fact fills his mind. The pain of it reverberates through him, bouncing off the sides of the void it has opened in his soul. He is feeling the claws. He is rushing down through the last instant of existence into the maw of oblivion.

His father is dead.

Gaellon is dead.

The Blood Angels are dead.

There is nothing else. No other sound or sensation. The world is cold black and red rage.

Except, in this red-and-black-daubed world, the memory of Baeron speaks to him. A warrior who chose to see the world in the wash of colour under a brush and the bloom of ink on a blank parchment.

'It is better that I fell when I did…' says Baeron's voice.

A sword strikes Gaellon in the side. The black iron breaks the ceramite, cuts through to the meat and bone beneath. The pain of the wound vanishes into the abyss inside him.

'I will always be as I was. I will not live with what you must…'

Gaellon feels the blood pouring from the wound as the iron sword rips free of his side. It is a mortal wound, a death cut, but he is already dying, and his blood has already poured out to stain white feathers red.

He cuts the daemon's grin in half. Black jelly and ash fall from his sword, and the blow keeps going, cutting down through spine and torso. The pieces of the daemon fall, and Gaellon is already turning his sword to cut into another.

Red and black… Soot and blood, a bed of white feathers painted with the red of life.

The power field on Gaellon's sword fails. The lightning vanishes from the edge. A hound leaps at him. Its body is flayed muscle. Its mouth is a cave of splintered knives. Forge heat bleeds from the collar on its neck. Gaellon rams the tip of his sword up through the roof of its mouth. The tip punches out of the top of its skull. The hound's momentum pushes the blade down through the back of the skull and into its neck. The cutting edge meets the brass collar with a sound like a shattering bell.

Claws score into his shoulder through shattered ceramite. The pain of their touch is barely a note in the storm roar of pain and grief. The future is murder, here in the Wasteland where angels are corpses and rage drowns out all.

He has cut another three daemons down. He does not know how. He strikes another. A fanged skull shatters. Ichor has lacquered his armour from head to foot. He is aware of the island of rubble that is Hold Point 78 moving further away, growing smaller. Do Nerron and Su'lok still stand there? Had it been their voices he had heard calling above the roars of the daemons? Or was it another voice calling to him as he went deeper into the tide. His father? His brothers? Baeron? All of them gone, all of them calling to him from the grave, all on the shore beyond the black sea of death. He wants to join them. He wants this moment to end, for the world to return to a place where warriors mark parchment with ink, and dream in poetry, and where there is more truth in art than slaughter. A world where there are angels still.

Will he always be here? Will all the Blood Angels always be here? Red angels in the Wasteland, hearing the echoes of their father's slaughter? Will they ever reach the shore, or will they be dying for all eternity even if they live?

Cut and bleeding, Gaellon wades on. His sword has broken, but he does not stop. Daemons fall around him. His body is a ruin. The place where Baeron fell is out of sight behind him. The Wasteland has him now. Still he goes on, cutting, hacking, stamping, spilling blood into ochre dust. On and on, out of sight to where the red fades into a smudged horizon.

FULGURITE

NICK KYME

The vehicle column came into view through his scope. A chugging, fitting procession of battered transports, freight carriers and bulky Cargo-8s, fourteen in all, their fading paint abraded by the weather. Thick smoke plumed from their chimney stacks. Gunmetal shone in anaemic daylight. Or what passed for day. Even on the ridge overlooking the distant gulley, it was hard to tell precisely what hour it was. Light, dark, night, day; it had little meaning in the cyanotic pall over Terra. Even in these outer wastelands. The Palace was many kilometres distant, a muddy silhouette thronged by smoke threaded with flashes of fire. Like a world ending. And a strange aura that the scope and his Astartesian eyesight could not penetrate. He saw faces there, just the impression, and knew they knew he was watching them.

He turned away, recognising this madness, and the ones who served it. His zealot brothers. Those who bore the Word. It was known to him, the one on the ridge. It was known to him the moment he touched the fulgurite, that innocuous piece of stone that had the power to kill gods or men that pretended to be gods.

He had felt divinity then, *true* divinity, and in that moment of revelation known that his kin were false and unclean things. Aberrant.

He had but one answer to that.

The column was getting closer, the rattling cough of abused engines and starving fuel tanks patently loud. They would be passing through the canyon soon. He needed one of those vehicles, decrepit as they were. He needed to get to the war.

And as Barthusa Narek began to climb down from his vantage point, he glanced at the distant wreckage of the drop-ship behind him. He remembered the brothers he had killed, as the siege was reaching its dreadful culmination, and thought of the one he had come here to kill, the one called Aurelian.

They were screaming again, howling for death. For their false gods. It came from below, from the deepest part of the hold, the part usually reserved for cargo. Deeper still, behind a locked cage, the beasts had started up. Left over from the opening assaults, their reek swept through the ship's recyclers, infecting every nook and cranny. Bovine, caprine, and some that defied definition. Bleating and braying, as they rutted and fought, and ate the weakest. True children of the Four, the beastmen carried their marks branded onto flesh.

A guttural siren blurted. A series of lamps in the upper hold would be turning from dirty amber to red. The ship's chief 'muleskinner' was using gas to spur the bestial masses into feral insanity. It had many names. 'Slaught, psyk, frenzon. A melange of psychotropics chemically crafted to instil resilience and violence. Before the next assault run, before the murdering could begin anew.

It took effect quickly, a reddish fog swirling like churned milk. They drank it in, eager, hungry, afraid. It was pandemonium now, redoubled and compounded by thick steel and ceramite. A hotbox of uncontrolled wrath. They would blink and cry out as the light of Terran day hit their eyes. Blind, in pain and afraid, these unwashed hordes would fall upon the remnants of the terrified defenders, goring, chomping and stabbing. They would absorb the bullets, the las-bolts, the bayonets. They would storm the last redoubts, bereft of pain, of conscience, of basic humanity.

Then came the jolt, the steel-shrieking lurch of a sudden manoeuvre, and Barthusa Narek opened his eyes.

Battery fire. The defenders had sighted the drop-ship.

A small room came into focus, little more than a cell. A piece of stone lay in his outstretched hand, resting on the palm of his armoured glove. It gently vibrated, a subtle etheric murmur like a compass. Both guide and tool of destruction. He was sitting, his helmet to one side, eye-lenses facing the door.

A light was flashing, calling him to the hold. They were making ready for the attack.

Narek took up the Brontos-pattern rifle lying on the floor in front of him as he rose to his feet. He returned the piece of stone to a pouch on his belt. The helm he mag-locked to his hip. He'd need it soon, but for now he wanted to see with his own eyes. He took his knife, too, and sheathed it. Achingly sharp, it had sat alongside the rifle, his weapons arrayed beside him as he meditated. Concentration was paramount when you were planning on killing a demigod. Flak-fire rocked the ship.

But first he had to kill everyone else.

They looked scared. Scared and exhausted. The ones riding in the column. Army deserters, criminals and civilians by their uniforms and attire. Narek thought he saw a Palace enforcer in their midst too. He wondered how they got here, how they had escaped the opening salvos of the war. Or *thought* they had. The deserters were so weary they hadn't seen the hunters, the lupine forms capering silently behind them through the thickening sand drifts. A storm was brewing. A bad one. Narek had seen this too, in the eddies and whorls out in the desert. Farther still, he saw a half-hidden bunker entrance to some forgotten and disused silo. Perhaps it once held a stockpile of weapons or other materiel. He doubted it did any more. Terra would have been stripped for every resource, every weapon, even here in these hellish wastes. He was certain he had crashed somewhere west of the Thar. He was no expert in Terran geography, but felt confident of his reckoning. Sand-whips lashed the bunker, its badly abraded entrance like polished silver. The growing storm was obscuring sensorium and augur alike. Blind, deaf, mind-fatigued, it was little wonder the deserters had failed to see their doom approaching.

Halfway down the ridge Narek found a cranny, and with the Brontos strapped across his back he turned his body and pressed the scope back to his eye.

First he took in the column, humping and jostling over the undulating dunes. Their chassis worn down by sand and a rime of dirt gumming the edges of the armour plating. They had sealed their hatches now, the last of the passengers retreating into the relative cool of the interior as the wind brewed up. Blinder still, ignorant of the threat that came at them on all fours but was armoured like an Astartes and clad in legionary colours. Narek knew the panoply. Had fought beside warriors wearing those colours before. Emperor's Children. But not as he remembered them. There was nothing pristine or perfect about the malformed creatures he saw through the scope.

They ran on claws and talons that had pierced right through their armour, bounding bestially on splayed toes and fingers. Once men, they had been reconfigured, mutated. Remade. *Unmade.* Narek counted six. If even one reached the vehicle column… They moved easily through the desert and the shimmering heat, heads turned to the wind, scenting. Their faces had changed, too – that noble, haughty countenance, that decadent beauty. Transformed, malformed. Canine, caprine, ursine; only hairless and possessed of post-animalistic intellect. Creatures, not legionaries. Not any more.

God-Emperor, what have we done to ourselves?

He had been thinking it ever since his arrival on Terra, all those months ago.

Tucked into the side of the ridge, it took most of Narek's resolve not to try to kill them on sight, but he needed a vehicle and that meant not spooking the prey. He had selected one that looked the most hale and hardy, a transport, leading the pack.

The monsters in the drifts were still a few kilometres out. Stalking. They hadn't seen him. He had time. Climbing down the last stretch of the ridge, Narek reached the desert floor and took up the position he had prepared on the ground and laid his ambush. His second of the day so far.

The iron-sights blurred then snapped into sharp focus. He had the legionary in his crosshairs. A slow trigger pull, a gentle exhale as he squeezed, and Eheruk's head exploded like a frag grenade, spraying his warriors in blood and bone.

Vahreth turned at the death of his commanding officer, slowed by injury, his reactions blunted.

Ever serious was Vahreth, and devout as they came. He had not stopped murmuring his dark scripture throughout transit. The drop-ship was burning now, half buried in the desert, the beastmen Narek had unleashed still rampaging throughout the hold. Firefights had echoed from within before the ruptured fuel tanks cooked off, and the resulting explosion had killed almost everyone and everything inside.

Only a handful left. Like Vahreth.

Narek had not hated Vahreth; the zealot had kept his ravings to himself, which was more than could be said for many. He loaded another round into the breech with a satisfying snap of the mechanism. He fired, a soft sigh promising death. Vahreth, who had yet to fully conceive of the danger, fell with his chest torn open. A high-explosive round. Good for killing Astartes. Good for killing most things.

Vahreth joined six others Narek had already executed. They had staggered from the ragged tear in the hold, dazed and bloody. One of the Word Bearers had been creative and used grenades to blast a hole and escape the furnace. Because of that ingenuity, Narek reckoned maybe ten more would emerge, having survived the crash and the berserk beasts.

He shot another four before the other survivors finally caught on to the fact they were being picked off. Narek had never reached the hold. Instead, he had made for a saviour hatch and used it to exit the ship before it touched down, fusing shut the release mechanism with an incendiary charge after he made his escape. Sand made for a hard landing when struck at pace, but his armour and body had compensated. From there, he merely had to watch the lander's remaining trajectory and get set up for the killing to follow.

The fifth of his brothers, Utal, took cover, skidding behind a piece of fuselage broken off from the main hull. Narek could see the legionary trying to find the shooter. He'd even managed to draw a weapon, poking the bolt pistol's muzzle through a small gap in the fire-blackened metal. Snapping the scope to the rifle's stock, Narek tweaked the focus through the sighting lens and fired through the gap, hitting Utal in the eye as he tried to line up a target. The last of the Word Bearers came out guns blazing, firing indiscriminately into the desert murk, crying out the names of Neverborn and calling down curses.

Their hurled maledictions ceased after the fourth hiss from Narek's rifle. Hearts and heads. All kill-shots.

He racked the Brontos' slide, ejecting the brass casing, slung the rifle over his shoulder and began to trudge through the desert. The Palace was far off. He needed transport. Putting the scope to his eye, he saw a column of dust on the horizon heading east.

The trap was improvised. A line of frag grenades, shallowly buried under the sand, strung together by thin wire and connected to a rudimentary trigger plate. It was all he'd had time to rig up. But it would serve. Soon, as the lead vehicle hit the plate, a short timer would start; just long enough for maybe two or three more transports to pass through. The explosion would halt the rest and dig a deep enough trench that they couldn't easily follow. The narrow canyon, the quickest way through the kilometres-long crag where Narek had laid his trap, would keep the column in single file. As the deserters foundered, still wondering what had happened, he'd kill the drivers. If any passengers resisted, he'd kill them too. Then take the transport.

Not far off now… The vehicle column was gunning hard for the canyon mouth, unaware of what awaited them. They had no idea of what hunted behind them either.

Narek tracked the scope west, narrowing focus until the creatures resolved in his circle of vision. Closer, he discerned details. Markings, tarnished battle honours. Heliotrope armour buckled around gene-swollen bodies in half-split scraps. Sweat and slather splashed from hot bodies. Grotesque, depraved, howling in crazed relish of the hunt.

No, not howling…

Planning. Coordinating.

The creatures paired off, flanking left and right, whilst another two stayed in the middle. Even stripped of their honour and humanity, the Emperor's Children retained some of their tactical acumen. They were encircling their prey, cutting off any chance of escape.

He swung the scope back to the vehicle column. Still ignorant of the threat, still ahead.

Closer, ever closer… Narek gauged he'd have just enough time to take the transport and be on his way before the creatures caught up to the column. He gambled they'd be occupied eating, killing, or whatever they were planning for the passengers for long enough that he could slip away unnoticed. But if they sought him out, Narek had an answer to that too. He braced his rifle, preparing to line up a shot.

One hundred and fifty metres to the trigger plate.

Then the lead vehicle began to slow. Narek frowned, wiping grit from the lens before looking again.

Definitely slowing. The entire column decelerated. A Cargo-8 towards the back of the formation was ailing, black smoke spewing from its engine stack. They were really slowing now, reacting to the stricken vehicle. Then they did stop. A few feet short of the trap in the long shadow of the canyon mouth.

Narek cursed, still hidden in his nook, rifle braced.

A hatch opened in the lead transport and a woman leaned out, her head wrapped in a thick scarf, wearing goggles to keep out the sand lashing against the column. She was the enforcer he had noted earlier and spoke into a vox-unit held in one hand whilst pressing a pair of magnoculars to her eyes with the other. She looked in Narek's direction, but he was well enough concealed by the ridge to be certain of giving away no sign of his presence. Then she moved her gaze west.

And saw what hunted in their wake.

A panicked shout brought others from their vehicles, the entire column now slewed to a complete halt, engines idling. A rider at the back brought out a rifle with a targeter and looked behind them. He paled as he lowered the weapon, turning back to the woman to shout his confirmation.

The front vehicles started up again, sputtering and shuddering into an agonised crawl that pulled them out of column. The ones at the back filled in until the motorcade had reassembled into a defensive laager with the canyon at their backs. More and more hatches opened, both turrets and gang ramps. Men and women armed with carbines, shotcannons and pistols clambered out. They were draped in ragged cloaks that might once have served as blankets or sacking. Arms and legs were wrapped in cloth like a leper's bandages to keep out the sand. Some had goggles like the enforcer's, their heads and faces bound up the same. They had left one war and found another, perhaps something worse. Terra was hell now. There were no safe havens left. But they didn't know that.

Narek counted more than a hundred amongst the throng. A desperate expedition with no true understanding of what they faced.

Slaughter. And darker deeds besides.

He could wait, let the monsters have their fill, but the storm was coming, a fell promise on the horizon. At least, he told himself this was why he acted as he did.

Letting out another curse, longer and louder, Narek remotely deactivated the sensor plate on the trap and headed for where the deserters made their last stand.

The snap and crack of lasguns firing in concert with solid-shot weapons echoed across the desert plain as the laager's defenders did their best to fend off their attackers. Bullets and superheated beams rained down, but the creatures shrugged it all off, their armour scraps alight with sparking, ineffectual missiles. Even their flesh proved inviolable, readily suffering burns and shallow gouges. It didn't even slow them down.

As they closed an eager hunger flashed in their eyes, speaking of appetites too depraved to utter. An inhuman, ululating cry raked the air and Narek saw a legionary spring from its haunches and launch at a man with convict tattoos standing in a turret. He roared, the man, firing off an autogun. Shout turned to scream as the convict was ripped from the hauler and borne to the ground to be dismembered.

There was no time to be appalled as a second creature had reached the column and was amongst them. Rending, flensing.

Sustained defensive fire continued for a few more seconds as the deserters not currently being ripped to pieces by the legionaries tried to kill their attackers. Then even that failed as a blood-flecked conscript cried out and started running. He wasn't alone. More of the defenders broke ranks and headed for the open desert. Gaps appeared in an already fragile line as the last of the Emperor's Children struck at either flank. One man was split from crotch to crown, torn open and spraying his comrades with his blood. Organs wrenched from still-warm bodies were left to rot in the sun. A woman gave out a wail, choked off as a hulking thing in piecemeal ceramite leapt on her with fangs bared. Her short-lived screaming gave way to the sound of crunching bone.

Too late, the deserters realised the trap they were in. The enforcer, still fighting, tried to restore some order, but her troops either milled around in panic or ran.

Narek ran too. It had been seconds, but the laager was already a bloodbath. He slewed to a stop, dropping to one knee, and raised the Brontos. As a legionary capered into his sight, carrying in its claws the gory spine of some poor bastard, he fired. The round took it in the chest, shattering what remained of its breastplate and gouging a hunk of flesh. He was about to relocate to his next target when the creature, which had been lying on its back presumed dead, pulled itself up.

'Shit...'

Ejecting the spent casing, Narek loaded another round.

His second shot struck its head, blowing out a chiropteran ear and half of the legionary's face. It fell, dead at last. Narek spat in the dust. Others in its brood reacted, sniffing at the air and turning towards the threat. Narek moved, trying to get lost amongst the laager. Wind shrieked between vehicles, hot sand peppering metal as the storm rose up. Overhead, the sky had begun to darken. Hurrying between two Cargo-8s, he heard a chassis buckle as if from a heavy weight and raised his rifle just as a legionary sprang at him from a roof. The round struck it in mid-air, through the neck, and it landed hard in the gap between vehicles. Narek quickly put another in its head just to be sure. Then he broke through the laager and into open ground.

Grit scythed his armour, a great squall of dirt that lashed in a frenzy. Through the maelstrom, he caught sight of the enforcer. Scarf drawn up over her face, she was firing into the storm, the dulled flashes of her shotcannon like starbursts. He swore she glanced at him as he was glancing at her, something like hesitation and cautious hope hinted at in her body language.

Another legionary emerged through the darkening storm, seemingly unfazed by the gyrating whips of sand slowly cutting into its exposed flesh. It loped on four limbs, baying for Narek's blood.

He stood, angling his body slightly as he took aim. Airborne matter was fouling his scope, so he quickly disengaged it and lined up over the rifle's iron-sights. The crosshairs alighted on the creature's centre-mass. Even if he didn't kill it, the high-ex round would stop its charge.

Skin prickling at the back of his neck, Narek turned his head too late as a second creature barrelled into him and his shot went wild.

It was slashing at his armour before they'd even hit the ground, both wrapped in a ferocious embrace. He felt a stab in his flank, a dull alert chime in his ear from his armour's biological monitoring system. His sight blurred, the retinal lenses in his helm suddenly cracked, and his vision crazed with ocular static. Narek fended off hectic attacks with his arm as he pulled a bolt pistol from the holster on his belt. Pushing the muzzle of the weapon up against the thrashing creature's body, he held the trigger. Rapid-fire rounds punched upwards, hammering through plate, then through toughened skin. They broke the legionary apart, scattering it in various dismembered pieces. Shrugging off the wreckage of flesh and bone, Narek rose unsteadily. The Brontos lay nearby, but the other creature was already on him. He'd emptied the pistol clip into the shredded thing festering in the dirt and had no time to refresh another. He was also bleeding.

Trusting his soul to the Emperor, Narek drew his knife.

An explosion hit the other legionary, struck it in the side and sent it sprawling. A quick glance and Narek saw the enforcer, a tube launcher still smoking in her grasp. Elsewhere, everywhere, the few remaining survivors fought for their lives. As would he.

Snatching up the rifle, feeding a round into the breech, Narek took aim again as the creature scrambled to its feet like a canid briefly knocked off balance. It brayed, starved and lascivious at the same time. He shot it through the heart.

Four down...

He trudged on, siphoning off the pain of his injury into a vault of his mind. He didn't see the enforcer. She was either dead or had left her tank for better prospects elsewhere. There were plenty of others, though; their corpses littered the ground in charnel heaps, a hecatomb slowly consumed by the growing storm.

Rasping grit hit Narek across the body, the shoulders. He had to wrench off his helm; the retinal lenses were damaged and made him half blind. The improvement was marginal as he narrowed his eyes against the stinging sand, the tumult building to a roar.

Following the screaming, he found the fifth legionary. It had a man by the throat, its long clawed fingers tenderly caressing his bleeding scalp as it devoured his lower half. It convulsed as Narek shot it between the shoulder blades, its back arching, shreds of flesh and gristle hanging from its jaws as it bleated in agony.

Narek ended its misery with a shot through the ear, blowing out cranium and matter in a reddish stream.

The last one fled; he saw it capering off before the storm swallowed it and only dirt and shadow remained. Then a final cry just audible above the tumult... of rage, defeat? A second call, even more distant than the first, answered it. Then a third. Fourth. Many calls.

Narek let out an exhausted breath, his hurts rekindled like barbs in his flesh. He tried not to sag where he stood. Warnings sounded from his armour. He silenced them. Retreating to the relative cover of the laager, he crouched in the lee of a transport, its sides already banked with gathering sand, and checked ammo. He frowned as the gauge revealed the depth of his predicament.

He turned suddenly, pistol loaded and drawn at the figure standing at the other end of the vehicular corridor where he was taking refuge. A shotcannon cradled across her body, the enforcer looked back at him, wide-eyed through her goggles. A handful of deserters cowered behind her. Terrified, desperate.

'Can you help us?' The voice came from a vox-unit on her belt, distorted by the conditions and barely audible.

Narek wasn't here for them. He wasn't even here for the by-blows of degenerative science that had just tried to kill him. He needed transport, and a place to hide out the storm where the hunters would lose his scent.

Scowling at the survivors, Narek headed off into howling darkness.

And they followed.

Limping, Narek glanced back over his shoulder and saw the deserters still in his wake. He trudged on, head down, enduring the storm's wrath. Visibility was almost down to nothing, but he could just make out the fringes of the bunker up ahead. Every sense yielded to the churning swathes of sand. Every footfall brought agony, despite the efforts of his enhanced physiology to stymie it. He had slowed, but each step brought him closer to salvation. The krak grenades on his belt would have to be enough to break open the bunker. If not... Well, then nothing much would matter. He clutched the shard, not realising he had taken it from his belt, and felt the fulgurite's faint resonance against his armoured palm.

Feet dragging through the sand, an anchor dredged with every metre, Narek reached the bunker. He had primed the krak grenade, realising his consciousness was slipping. Blood loss, despite his Larraman's organ, and grievous physical injury had pushed his body to its limit. He'd place the grenade, the movement automatic. Then regroup.

I just need to regroup…

It took Narek a moment to realise the bunker door, emblazoned with the old sigil of Unity, was already open. The grenade fell.

Then so did he.

Cool, musty air touched his face and Narek opened his eyes.

A corridor resolved, deep, wide, dark. Metal walls, iron-grey. A distant shaft of light, the muffled howling of wind.

He rasped a laugh, despite himself. Still alive.

Four silhouettes resolved in the light. They were trying to push the bunker door shut. The survivors from the vehicle column, four out of more than a hundred. Two convicts in penal battalion garb, an Army deserter in an olive drab, and the enforcer in dirty grey armour he had seen earlier.

They must have dragged him. His rifle and pistol lay nearby within reach, knife still in its sheath.

He lurched to his feet, feeling his body reacting to trauma. Reknitting, mending, the furnace heat of accelerated healing dappling his leathery skin with sweat.

'Stand aside…' he growled, laboured steps taking him to the bunker door. They parted. He pushed hard and felt the pain of his wounds anew as he strained. It closed with an ominous metal clang and the darkness became nearly absolute.

A lume-stick flared and the enforcer stepped forwards, casting a pearlescent light over herself and the other survivors. They looked wary, afraid. She was pale-skinned but stocky.

'I'm Ebba Renski. This is Detof and Klena.'

She gestured to the convicts, rangy and tattooed specimens, red weals around their necks from where they'd removed their explosive collars.

'And the scruffy-looking soldier is Vuko.'

A bearded man with dark skin nodded, wearing the uniform of some obscure regiment. It had been painted in urban camo.

Ill-suited to the desert. He had a lascarbine, a knife strapped to his thigh. They had ditched the scarves and cloaks, and stood in their travel-worn clothes. The two penal battalion conscripts wore convict yellow and Munitorum-issue flak armour. It was cheap, barely serviceable. Crude autoguns were clutched in thin hands. The enforcer had decent enough kit, well-tended. Carapace armour over black fatigues, a functional tactical helmet. Shotcannon. No grenade launcher. He assumed she'd spent it during the fight in the desert.

Narek grunted. He cared little for their names or their attire. They'd be dead soon, anyway. Everyone on this cursed battlefield would be. He sagged against the door as if the world's gravity had redoubled and was pulling him down.

'You're injured,' said Renski, the enforcer.

She trembled, despite her best efforts not to – that heady blend of awe and fear that all unaugmented humans felt in the presence of an Astartes. The shotcannon in her grasp was loaded, but it was obvious she wished desperately not to have to use it. Passing the lumen-stick to Vuko, the soldier, she reached for a med-kit instead. The caduceus on the front caught the light.

'Sealant, stimms…' breathed Narek, feeling bones grate.

She rummaged around in the kit and came up with both. She pulled out gauze and bandages too.

'I don't need that,' Narek snarled. 'No use.' He took the sealant, using it to glue the gaps in his armour, laying the adhesive directly over skin and blood where he had to. The stimms he jabbed in his neck. Then another in his arm where the plate had been ripped away and was left ragged, half-chewed. He absorbed the concoction quickly, and felt the pain ebb to a distant thrum.

Awareness sharpening, he took stock of his surroundings. The door led to the storm and what hunted within it. Nothing to be gained that way. The other direction promised darkness and the vague impression of a chamber and more corridors beyond. Narek considered what this place was – a silo, perhaps a depot of some kind. Larger than it looked from the outside, and deeper. The shaft ahead sloped downwards. Hot air pricked his nostrils, and something else. Like meat left to sweat in the sun too long.

He felt the fulgurite shard throb in his hand, the fingers clenched around it like a vice. It was the Emperor's grace, a fork of psychic lightning crystallised in sand, fire turned into earth. Elemental transformation.

'Who are you?' asked the enforcer.

'Narek,' murmured Narek, taking up his weapons, making sure they still functioned.

'And…' she said, faltering, 'whom do you serve?'

He looked down, seeing the armour, the iconography and the sigils he despised.

'I serve myself. And I owe a debt of the killing kind.'

He trudged off, stiff-legged and raw with pain.

'I thought you'd kill us,' she called after. 'For leaving the defences. I thought that's why you had come.'

'Either die at the wall, if there are any walls left now, or die out here. It matters little to me,' said Narek, his voice echoing as he headed into the darkness.

'Then why help us?'

'I haven't. I needed a vehicle and would have taken one of yours if you hadn't slowed down. Don't see that for something it isn't.'

'Please,' she uttered, 'we can't survive alone. Not now. But we can be useful. We have weapons.'

Narek stopped, stared at her.

'So now you want to fight?'

'We want to live. If that means travelling by your side, then we'll fight.'

'Don't expect to live long,' Narek growled as he carried on his way, but he didn't stop them.

* * *

They found a generator, dust-caked and rusted with disuse, but it had power still. Weak lumens activated and threw wan light across old machineries, empty crates and other detritus. Servitors, crudely made, their remains calcified, stood around like petrified ghouls, trapped in whatever meaningless task they had been performing when they died. Several oozed a gluey mixture of blood, proteins, and whatever else was pumped into their cyborganic bodies to make them persist. Until they hadn't any more.

Narek gave them little heed. He had the shard and would follow its vibrations.

He will bring me to you, father…

A corridor ahead opened out into a large, circular chamber. In the deep and the chill, condensation glittered slickly on the walls, trickling down into a half-empty basin of brackish water. It was still deep. A cooling chamber. He had seen them before, used to prevent generators from overheating. Whatever this place had been for, it wasn't merely storage. A bridge had once spanned the basin but now jutted in a few broken pieces from the bottom of the half-drowned circular shaft.

A decent leap. Narek jumped, his legs leaden, and scarcely made it to the other side. He scrambled, the fingers of one hand dug into the shaft's edge, and hauled himself up and over. Pain flared, a familiar sting, and he took a breath. On his hands and knees, he glanced back and saw the deserters edging around the lip of the shaft, backs flat to the wall, taking narrow, perilous steps.

'Tenacious,' he muttered, and stood up.

Facing his father in such a state, he'd need to be sure of the kill. And then? Narek had given little thought to 'then', if even such a possibility existed. He knew from the skies and the hell unleashed through innumerable city districts that this was the end war. The last war. The death of everything. Not far off now.

The deserters met him on the other side, Renski first across.

'As I said,' she remarked, 'we want to live. Never underestimate a human's will to survive.'

'Survive...' muttered Narek with a wry yet rueful smile. 'Yes, that's what it's come down to, hasn't it?' He looked to the sickly light ahead, the seeming labyrinth into which they had blindly wandered. That smell again. Sweating meat. Spoiled. Rancid.

'Stay close,' he rasped.

The door would not budge. Narek readjusted his grip, hoping he could force the mechanism enough to widen the crack. He heaved, feeling bone fractures deepen, half-knitted skin and flesh reopen.

They had passed through several corridors and empty chambers, old stores and decrepit engines. All the while, Narek had followed the fulgurite shard, listening to its gentle tremors, smelled the sulphuric tang it exuded. It was not a compass in the traditional sense; this was more like scapulimancy or haruspicy. It required interpretation. Either he had divined poorly or he needed to pass through the door currently barring his path.

His last krak grenade lay primed somewhere in the desert, far from here now. The Brontos was an impressive weapon, but it couldn't shear bulkhead steel. The door's access panel was broken, inoperable. He'd levered off the face of the panel already, using the tip of his knife, but the wiring was burnt, its circuits broken. And he was no tech-priest.

He tried again, reaching under the door, searching for a release lever or a clamp. Something.

A hand touched his shoulder and he turned, biting back a curse.

'I think I can get under there.'

It was one of the convicts. Klena. She was rake-thin with narco-abuse, her frame skeletal and prematurely aged. Her lank white hair was like bleached straw, her rheumy eyes afraid but determined.

Narek glanced at the enforcer, who gave a nod that the woman could be trusted. Odd comrades, but then months of hell-war will breed desperate alliances. He stepped back. The stench was stronger here, emanating from somewhere beyond the door.

'A panel like this one,' he told her, 'or a lever. You will need two hands to move it.'

She nodded, about to get down onto the floor when he gently gripped her arm. He had to be gentle lest he break it by mistake.

'Do not linger,' Narek warned her.

Another nod, shaking now. Terrified. Of him, of this place. It scarcely mattered.

Klena disappeared through the narrow crack beneath the door.

It took several minutes, the humans fretting while Narek stood still as a statue, willing his body to heal, his strength to return. Then they heard a dull *thunk* of metal shifting and resetting, and the mechanism began to grind and turn. The door lifted, a few centimetres at first but then faster, until it stopped a third of the way up, the rusted gears unable to go any further.

Narek had to crouch low, as the others passed underneath barely needing to stoop. Whatever this place had been made for, it was large. Very large.

The door led to another chamber, this one much bigger than the others. Several lines of vats filled the expanse, brimming with viscous, briny fluids. The glass had fogged in the chill, ice-rimed and smeared with dirt. Several had smashed, and they found Klena standing in front of one of the broken vats, rigid with fear.

Something lurked within – fleshy, distinctly biological, sheened with frost, its eyes glassy with death. A huge thing, anthropomorphic but grotesquely so. Musculature too large for its frame strained the skin. The cranium looked overlarge, hooded. It had… claws. Chitinous plates bulged under its stretched flesh. And as Narek regarded it, he felt his gorge rise. An instinct, ingrained, atavistic, pulled at him to destroy this abomination. To cleanse this place with fire and see it turned to ash.

He went to one of the other vats, wider than him, much

taller. Encrusted dirt and ice yielded to his touch as he cleared a palm-width window into the depths within.

Matter lay suspended in the fluid: the approximation of faces, only distorted, strange. Distended limbs, some swollen, others pathetically wizened into drifting ropes of skin. Legs that ended in stumps or trailed into fleshy tendrils. Gene-craft. Narek pictured the monstrosities from the desert and saw in this horror before him something of their origins. In part, at least. This place had been remote and sealed away for a reason.

'What is it?' hissed Renski, a tremor in her voice. Behind her, the convict stared ahead, unmanned by the experience of looking into the shattered vat. The others stayed back, not wanting to look.

'Nothing good,' uttered Narek, and wondered if he should have chosen the desert.

That meat smell again. It was potent here, leading his eyes ahead to an archway and an antechamber. The fulgurite burned hot, its vibrations urgent.

Returning the shard to the pouch on his belt, Narek unslung his rifle.

'We are not alone.'

He advanced on the archway, moving quietly through the rows of abominations. In his periphery, he caught glimpses of leathern wings, a long proboscis-like tongue, scaled flesh. Several of the vats had been thawed, their contents excised. A gelatinous pool of fluids spilled outwards. In it, Narek saw footprints leading towards the arch. *Homo sapiens*, very large.

He heard the deserters follow, their fear of this place overriding their fear of him. Their rasped murmurings hissed like secrets as they saw the contents of the vats, and he suspected he was leading them to their deaths.

A twinge. A clench of the jaw. *What was that? Regret?*

Another door here. It had slid aside, bypassed, its locks eaten by acid. Narek crossed the threshold, passing beneath the arch.

He raised the rifle to his eye when he saw the legionary. The figure had his back to him, the fluted pack and gaudy heliotrope armour giving the Astartes' provenance away. A gilded eagle's wing glittered on the left pauldron. III Legion. Emperor's Children.

A haunting flash of revelation came swiftly. He had assumed the altered legionaries in the storm had been hunting. But what if they weren't... What if they were *guarding* something, or someone?

Edging closer to the figure, who yet appeared oblivious to his presence, Narek started to step obliquely to one side, trying to see what the legionary was doing. His back was arched as he leaned over a surgical table. There were more specimens here in this room, smaller. Organs and parts that were held in jars filled with aspic sat on rows of shelving. A more intimate space, a laboratory. There was equipment, much of it unfathomable to Narek. And tools on racks, both the mundane and the esoteric. A vault lined one wall, more than a hundred separate chambers, each stamped with an ident. Cold air drooled from a handful of these lockers, their contents ransacked. Parchment littered the floor, as if frantically read and then discarded. Scrolls lay piled on the table, their edges fringed in blood as the butcher-surgeon worked messily next to them.

Closer now, Narek beheld the razor-saw, the injectors, the red-rimed scalpels. There were basins. Organs, recently excised, steamed within. He stitched, the legionary, his narthecium vambrace to one side. An Apothecary's tool. The caduceus again, etched in red over white.

Each pull of thread was almost symphonic, the expert conductor at his podium. Here, the orchestra was a body: something huge, herculean. It barely fit on the surgical table. Its face, the parts of it which were not horribly disfigured, reminded Narek of something. *Someone*. White hair, pale skin like marble...

'It is not my father,' uttered the Apothecary, pausing at the apex of a pull, the thread taut like piano wire in his bare hand. 'Though it does bear some of his likeness.'

'What?' Narek heard himself say, mind and body warring with morbid fascination at the thing on the table. He had lowered his rifle without realising.

The Apothecary went on sewing.

'He did ask me once,' he said, his voice low and wistful, 'to remake one of them. Not him, of course, never him. The Phoenician is a perfect specimen, after all, what would be the point?' He spoke then against the side of his bloodied hand, as if he was sharing a joke or some scurrilous truth too heinous to utter openly: 'At least, that's what he claimed.'

He gave a dry chuckle, an awful dying-man's rasp.

'No, he wanted the other one. His brother. The dull, iron one. It was a flawed replication, I'm afraid. I required better materials. Something *original*.' He waved a hand, flicking drops of blood, the other still focused on its macabre art.

Narek found himself transfixed. Only when he felt Renski's hand upon his arm did he regain his senses. Her eyes implored him, *leave, leave this place now...*

But he couldn't leave. He had a mission, only he hadn't known this was part of it. The will of *Him* moving through Narek.

'All of this,' remarked the Apothecary. 'It is His. My father's father. They have a name for Him. They call him the Anathema. Puerile, if you ask me. He is a scientist. I can appreciate that as a vocation. To think, to create, to will that creation into being.'

He coughed, a seizure wracking his body that split the thread with the violence of his convulsions. Wiping a hand across his mouth, setting down his tools, the Apothecary turned to face them. Blood and other organic matter lathered his armour.

'Interesting...' He frowned. His arms were elbow-deep in crimson. Flecks of arterial red slashed a sharp face: intelligent, gaunt, all at once curious and cruel. 'Brutish countenance, thick brow and flat nose. Scarred, but not ritualistically. You don't look like one of them. A scholar. A priest. No, wait, what's the name they're using...' He paused, thinking. '*Apostle*. Are you an apostle, son of Lorgar, Bearer of the Word?' He read the ident on Narek's armour. 'Narek. I cannot say I have heard of you.'

Narek snarled, 'What are you doing here, legionary?'

'It's Apothecary, to be precise. I value precision. Apothecary Fabius.'

'I don't care.' Narek raised the rifle. 'Answer me.'

The Apothecary's gaze travelled to the humans. His eyes widened a fraction, hungry, lascivious like the creatures in the desert, though this one wore his deformities on the inside.

'I like its skin,' he said, referring to the enforcer. She retreated a step. 'Much suppler than yours, Narek. I think I'll take it, wear it as a coat.'

'You're insane.'

He should kill him, but Narek stayed his hand. Despite himself, he wanted to know what the Apothecary had been doing.

'Perhaps... but have you seen what's happening out there? Literal bleeding skies, Narek. Murder and nightmare made manifest. I prefer the biological over the etherical.' His eye drifted, ever evaluating. It alighted on Narek's wound. 'That looks painful,' said Fabius. 'Is it? Did you happen to meet my brothers out there in the desert?'

An ugly scowl curled Narek's lip. 'Those things are not Astartes.'

'They were. Flawed, like all of us, like all of *His* creations. My father thought so and tried to perfect himself. I wonder if he's happier now?'

'You made abominations.'

'I made them *better*. Stronger, faster, more ferocious. I am a healer, after all. Mankind must adapt if it is to survive.' Fabius coughed again, spitting up blood into his hand. He regarded it, displeased, before shaking it loose. 'But adaptation requires iteration.'

He stepped aside, Narek tracking his every movement. The thing upon the surgical table was revealed entire.

Naked, grotesque, its flesh a tapestry of scars and stitching. Tumours and obscene growths riddled its body. Swollen muscle shone sickly in the light. A monster.

'You're a madman…' Narek breathed, readying to fire.

'I'm a scientist.'

The fingers of the creature twitched and Narek turned his aim.

'You've inconvenienced me, coming here,' said Fabius.

A nerve tremor like a viper spasmed under the creature's skin, its arm slowly rising. Its mouth opened, releasing a tortured breath. Its first. Then it lurched to its feet, veiled in feverish sweat, clumps of amniotic jelly sloughing off its body.

'Emperor protect us…' Narek heard Detof mutter. He could not disagree.

He fired, but his shot skewed wide, catching the Apothecary in the shoulder as he vaulted the surgical table, taking cover. Fabius grunted in pain.

But now the creature from the slab was coming, steps faltering and unhurried at first, as it blinked in the light. Hurting. Trying to work out how to walk. One eye a perfect violet, the other a horrid, nacreous orb too large for the socket. Its pace increased, turning into long, loping strides, agony with every step.

It came for Narek, who fired again. The high-ex round tore away chunks of flesh that flopped and sizzled when separated from the host. He got off three shots before it was upon him, Narek already drawing his pistol even as he let the rifle fall from his grasp.

It hit him like a battering ram, lifting Narek up off his feet. His battle plate screamed a dozen integrity warnings, the metal shrieking as the creature squeezed. Huge beyond reason, it towered over Narek and was half as wide again, even in his armour. The pistol was gone, wrenched away as the creature bore him halfway across the next chamber. Back amongst the vats. Amongst further horrors.

Klena had been standing in its path, too afraid to move. She gave a stifled yelp before the creature crushed her like it was standing on an egg. The others scattered.

Narek's hand slid around his knife, his last weapon, and he stabbed downward, into the neck, searching for the carotid artery. Cascades of blood painted his armour. He could no longer breathe and felt his fused ribcage cracking under the extreme pressure.

Gunfire cracked nearby, solid shot rippling against the creature's skin. An irritant, nothing more. But as a burst of shot raked its face, the creature snarled and its grip loosened. Narek turned, drove his knife into the eye – that bulging, wretched orb.

It screamed, a low, ululating cry, and Narek fell, discarded, as the creature saw to its own pain. He scrambled backwards, his eyes on the thing as it clutched at its face, vitreous humour leaking down its cheek like wax. It was hurt. Angry.

Pain lancing through his own body, Narek dragged himself up, staggered. Unarmed, he had no chance.

Gunfire came again, left and right. The deserters had some fight in them after all. The creature turned, an arm raised to fend off the insect-sting of ineffectual bullets. It charged at Vuko, flinging out an arm and sending the soldier flailing into the vats. Glass shattered, fluids sluicing free, carrying with them the matter inside, a flood of offal and necrotised filth.

A desperate cry echoed from the other side of the chamber, bright muzzle flare from an autocarbine at highest rapidity lifting the shadows. Detof stood his ground, shouting vengeance for Klena. His volley hammered the creature's chest as it reached out for him. Then the convict was screaming, seized by both arms and ripped in two. The creature cast the bifurcated pieces aside like an unwanted meal before it advanced on Renski.

She ran. The creature loped after her, following some predatory instinct. Eager to chase.

Instead of running away, Renski drew the creature around the vats. Its rudimentary intelligence was too slow to realise it was being goaded. At least at first… until it roared, crashing *through* the vats in a shower of vital fluids and shattering glass. It paused to stare at the moist and shiny matter and alighted on a face, not so unlike its own, although more horribly deformed. It reached out with quivering fingers to touch its kin, something like melancholy hideously twisting its features…

It gave Narek time to retrieve his rifle and other weapons. Of the Apothecary, he saw no sign. His ambitions thwarted, perhaps Fabius had fled. More likely, he was observing from some hidden vantage, taking notes on his creation's performance.

About to load the rifle, Narek's fingers brushed the edge of the fulgurite shard.

The last of its kind. He had killed so-called immortals with the others. And now he could use this one to kill this creature.

He chose a high-ex round instead. The fulgurite shard had a name on it; Narek had etched it in his mind and it could be used to fell no other. Else everything he had done, everything he had *become*, would be for nothing. He needed another way.

He fired.

The explosive round hit the creature in the side of the head, splitting its ear, detonating in a shower of gore. A graze. Bellowing its hurts, ripped from the confusing pathos of seeing its malformed decedents, it turned on Narek with renewed vigour.

Out of the creature's eyeline, Renski had crept over to Vuko and was hauling him up, his arm over her shoulder, the enforcer taking most of the soldier's weight. She nodded when Narek caught her eye and he nodded back. Kinship of a sort. It had been a long time since he felt that, even this pale facsimile.

He tossed a frag grenade, leaving his bandolier empty barring one crude incendiary. It was used for fusing metal and it would not start a fire alone, although he did not doubt the fluid in the vats would provide a powerful accelerant…

The grenade blew a chunk out of the creature, staggering it

and allowing Narek to run clear. He followed Renski and Vuko, who were struggling and limping. Back out of the vat chamber they went, under the partially open bulkhead door and towards the tunnels.

Narek scrambled under after them, his backpack scraping against metal. He shared a look with the enforcer. Showed her the incendiary.

'I'll hold it off,' he said, probably about to die for these humans. Gallant. Stupid.

Renski nodded, the soldier scarcely conscious in her arms. They carried on. And Narek backed away from the half-open door, turning to face the creature.

How noble you are, brother... The voice of Valdrekk Elias returned like a revenant.

Distended claws wrapped themselves underneath the door, the creature's crude mind too dull to navigate by guile, and pulled. Wrenched metal began screaming and the door edged upwards, inch by shrieking inch.

Having waited as long as he could, Narek unclipped the incendiary and threw it under the door. It had a short fuse, but his aim was good and it rolled amongst the smashed vats, the spilled fluids lapping at its sides.

Then Narek ran. Back down the tunnels and through the darkness.

An eruption shook the laboratory complex behind him. It threw him against the wall, but he recovered quickly and kept on running as an ocean-roar grew behind him. The heat grew too, along with the stench of burning. Of chemicals. Of flesh.

A distant keening, half-swallowed by the tumult of fire, could faintly be heard.

The creature, dying.

He threw a glance over his shoulder as the sound of agony became louder, and he saw it then. Ablaze head to foot, skin sizzling... *dripping*, its gaping mouth a vortex of flame. But still coming, even as its flesh cooked and its bones baked to black.

Ahead of him, the circular room, the cooling chamber.

Behind, the creature chased by a rolling surge of fire.

Narek reached the chamber and leapt, straight down this time, into the brackish water. He found Renski and Vuko there, shoulders poking above the murk, alive but unable to clamber out. Renski gave him a fearful glance.

'Shut your eyes,' Narek told her, raising his rifle to his shoulder and aiming up at the lip of the basin.

He didn't have long to wait.

The creature appeared, a burning effigy now.

He shot it in the leg, and it faltered. Then another in the chest pushed it back.

And the roar grew, apocalyptic, deafening.

The rolling flame surge hit the creature, engulfing it, destroying it utterly and Narek dove down beneath the water, dragging Renski and Vuko with him.

Swallowed below as the fire raged above.

They found the vehicles again, half-buried in the sand. The storm had eased to a whisper and the Apothecary, wherever he had gone, had taken his hounds with him. No legionaries or things that had once been legionaries stalked this particular stretch of desert.

Fire had gutted the laboratory by the time they emerged from the cooling basin. Narek had scrambled to the lip and climbed out. Then he had reached down and pulled the others out too. The slow traverse through the still-burning, flame-scarred tunnels had been treacherous, but nothing had come after them. They were, it seemed, alone.

A silent trek through the sands followed, weariness stealing voices. And shock. At least for the deserters.

Narek preferred the silence. Inane chatter riled him, although he had become tolerant of a great many things, he realised. He had the fulgurite shard in his hand, its vibrations low but discernible. It had brought him to the Apothecary, he felt certain of that. Some animus of His will had led him there. To Fabius. But it wasn't over.

Father had yet to pay his due.

They managed to get two of the vehicles started, most of the others too sand-logged to function. Narek took the transport, as he had always planned to do, and Renski loaded Vuko onto the back of a Cargo-8. As she climbed into the front cab, engine sputtering as it idled in the heat, she made to catch Narek's eye. Her mouth shaped as if she were about to say something. Her thanks. Her prayers.

Narek turned away before she could utter them.

He wasn't here for her, for them. He started up the transport, turning it in a wide arc, and headed for the Palace. Towards the war.

The transport expired twenty-five kilometres north of the Palace outskirts. It slewed to an ungainly halt, hissing and groaning until it stopped entirely and did not start up again. On foot, Narek slogged for the front lines, but far from any kind of cohesion or strategy, he found only chaos. Madness. Strange lightning flickered in the firmament. Voices hissed and cackled on the wind.

Neverborn lurked in shadows, haunting the ruined places. They whispered to him, called his name, but none dared to creep close. Not with the fulgurite. He passed the outer precincts, staying away from the worst of the battle zones, his armour and his icons leaving him largely unmolested. Any who did come across his path, he either avoided or, if there were few, eliminated. Kill-gangs roamed in packs, hammering bodies to eight-pointed stars or hanging them in droves by the neck to jerk and dangle. They called out names into the darkness, names from languages unspeakable by human tongues. Chanting murmured on the air and the air murmured back.

Narek steered well clear.

He circumnavigated a vast slick of burning promethium, the flames clawing and black as they reached, trying to escape the horror. A Custodian stood staked to the ground like a crude scarecrow, impaled with sixteen spears. Its eyes had been put out and dirty iron nails rammed in their stead. He passed a graveyard of tanks, their crews curiously absent with no sign of their bodies. The tanks were seemingly untouched, purple ash piled in their interiors.

A felled Titan, its metal pitted and rotted through as if by contagion, made a bridge across a burning ravine that had once been a civilian square. Narek climbed upon its back, glimpsing between the gaps in its gargantuan limbs as he crossed. At the burning skulls in the ravine, their rictus mouths still screaming.

He followed the trails of the dead, the dismembered and crucified bodies, the rune-etched sacrifices laid out in ritual circles daubed in blood on the earth. The breeze had an unnatural flavour around such sites. It shimmered like oil on water, and Narek knew to stay well away.

Distant battles, skirmishes and larger more desperate conflicts, cracked and rattled on the air. He stayed away from these too.

And the fulgurite led Narek on, *His* will shepherding him.

To the Bearer of the Word, to his father. To Lorgar.

For a time, he hid, watching Terra burn from the shattered fortifications raised and then razed in its defence. He waited out a large battalion of loyalist fighters tramping by in battered tanks and on foot. Mainly Imperial Army, more conscripts like Vuko, and a handful of legionaries in dirty red and blood-flecked yellow. A grim assemblage, heading off to fight and die.

As they passed, Narek waited to ensure there were no stragglers and moved on.

The fulgurite thrummed in his palm.

And then stopped.

It had never done that before, not since he had arrived on the Throneworld. Hackles raised on his neck, the faint beading of sweat. Instinct reacting before thought…

…just a fraction too slowly.

He heard the blade before he felt it, that slick, impossible scrape through armour and mesh and then him.

Narek tried to draw his pistol, but he was sinking and his nerves dulling, hand slipping. On his knees, the fulgurite held in a clenched fist, head bowed.

Not a normal knife, he realised, nothing innocent about it.

Its wielder came to stand before him, there on the killing fields, amongst the dead places, in the shadow of once-impregnable bastions laid to ruin.

'I wonder,' said Erebus, his face arrogant, conceited, his bald scalp etched in Colchisian cuneiform, 'what you think you're doing here, Barthusa?'

Narek didn't answer. Couldn't answer. The blade had left something behind in the wound. In his blood. It spread like ice.

He managed to scowl.

'I cannot let it come to pass, whatever it is,' said Erebus. 'It ends here in your death.'

'Lorgar…' Narek rasped, teeth clenching, the taste of copper in his mouth.

'He is not here, brother. He never was. You have been following a false trail.'

The revelation of that stung, colder than the knife.

'Impossible, I was… it was…' The fulgurite felt cold, *inert*, in his grasp. How could he have come this far, done all that he had done for it to end here? In failure?

'None can contest the will of the gods, Barthusa. Not you, not even *Him*. A king will rise from darkness and all will be as it should be. As it was ordained. It has been spoken by their emissaries. I am merely their conduit.'

'You are a…' Narek spat blood, his wrath impotent but burning. 'A demagogue, a heretic…'

'The first, or so it has been claimed.'

Narek raged, he fought to stand, to reach for a weapon, but he was beyond that now and no amount of disbelief could change that.

'This isn't… it isn't… can't be…'

'Over? It has been over since the earliest millennia, since the primordial gods first enticed mankind. Such wilful, impressionable creatures we are, slaves to uncounted vices. How can a warrior, even one as determined as you, Barthusa, contest against that? Elias – you remember Elias, don't you? – he learned that lesson to his death. And so the lesson comes full circle to the servant.'

'I am no servant… I am…' Narek spoke through gritted teeth, but his throat had begun to lock up, his tongue like stone in his mouth. He trembled, trying to fight his imminent death.

Erebus looked upon the other Word Bearer, his eyes pitying. 'Such vengeful spirits,' he said, 'raging against the night…'

Narek watched the Dark Apostle turn and slowly walk away. The air changed, *thinned*, the scent of foulness fomented on the breeze, and fell voices thickened. Only for a brief moment and then gone.

And so was Erebus.

He left Narek to the cold spreading through his limbs, his back, his chest, his mind. The chill of unmaking. A deep plunge into primordial ice, the untethering of soul and the gentle bicker of daemons slowly returning, eager for their piece.

Another voice insinuated itself amongst the throng, weak at first, then louder.

Narek's fist tightened around the fulgurite shard, and he felt the faintest ember of warmth.

FRAGMENTS (ALL WE HAVE LEFT)

DAN ABNETT

All we have left now are stories.

There is no escape from this fate. There is no escape from this building. The enemy throngs at every exit and every entrance. There is no way out of here, so we will fight where we stand, and die where we fight.

Even if, by some chance, we fight clear of this hall, we would die in the courtyard outside, or in the street beyond, or perhaps the main processional beyond that. We will never escape the Palace. There is nowhere on Terra to escape to. We will never reach a port, or a ship, or make our way off the Throneworld. We will never escape this world to another planet, or some dim corner of far away, or an empty moorland where the air is fresh and clean. We will never make it to safety, or another life.

We have been going backwards for months, step by step, street by street. As the traitor Warmaster's grip on the planet tightens, our world grows smaller. We draw inwards as the walls fall, one by one, throttled by his grasp, our boundaries shrinking. Now all that remains is the Sanctum itself, and that is being choked too, squeezed shut. There is no escape.

Because my life is about to end, I can appreciate the whole of it. I can measure its highs and lows, because I can see it as a complete thing. There is no future in which other things might happen. I can see my whole story. All we have left now are stories.

Some may say there is no time for stories, but what is time? The traitor Warmaster has crushed time flat too. It is lifeless and does not move. I no longer need time to tell a story.

I will tell you one. My name is Aphone. The 'Ire' part came later. I do not know if my birth-mother chose a name for me, for I never knew her. Because of what I am, she rejected me soon after my birth. I do not know if my biological father had thought of a name for me, for he was long gone by the time I was born, unable to bear the void of me growing inside his wife's belly. At least, I assume she was his wife. I know nothing about it. My father couldn't bear me, and my mother bore me only because she had to, and had rid of me as soon as I was in the world. I was taken in by the Sisterhood, not out of kindness but, again, because of what I am. Thus I was raised in the order of the Silent Sisterhood, and they gave me the name Aphone. It was not chosen for any sentimental reason, or because it suited me. It was simply the next name on the list. They have a list of names, and those names are recycled when someone dies. I am not the Sisterhood's first Aphone, nor would I have been the last, but for the traitor Warmaster's uprising.

So 'Aphone' is, I suppose, more a label than a name. A means of identification, picked from a list. My mentor, Jenetia, once said that she had known an Aphone once. That's all. She seldom spoke – by which I mean used thoughtmark, as we all do, according to our Oath of Tranquillity – and shared her own stories even less often. But from the comment, I got the feeling that Aphone had been her sister, perhaps, or her daughter. Why would someone who said so little mention it at all if it didn't matter?

I don't know. Jenetia is dead, so I can't ask her. Perhaps this implied connection to another Aphone to whom she felt affection is just a part of my story that my imagination has embellished to make it more interesting. Perhaps she never liked me at all.

With us, it is always hard to tell.

But I liked that my mentor had mentioned it to me. It was something to cherish, something, if only imagined, that seemed personal. My mentor had lived a life of her own, a whole life, before she was inducted into the Sisterhood. Jenetia Krole… that was her actual name, not something chosen off a list. I envied her that. I envied the life she had led, however hard, before her induction.

I was simply Aphone for a long time, as I trained and rose through the ranks. After my first proper undertaking as a Talon of the Emperor, I was dubbed 'Ire'. Aphone Ire. This second name was given to me by my mentor, presumably to reflect the ferocity I had displayed during the mission. I can only guess. She never said so. But 'Ire' did not come from a list. Thus I prize that part of my name, because it is properly mine and was given to me.

That, then, is the story of my name. It is not a great story, I admit, but it is mine. I treasure it because it reminds me of my early years in the Sisterhood. They were not happy years. Our lives are bleak and friendless. But compared to what we are enduring now, those early years seem warm and reassuring, so I cling to my story. It is a tiny escape from this moment.

I have never told it to anyone. I only tell it now, Emil, because stories are all we have left.

The Archenemy bays outside and howls at the doors. I hear war-horns and chanting, louder than the roar of flames gutting the buildings around us. We are caught here, cornered. There is no escape.

The enemy soldiers are of the Tygris 14th Hussars, who turned to the traitor cause after the fall of Prospero. I know this from debased insignia I have seen on their corpses. They are drawn up in division strength. They were fine soldiers once, elite Excertus, trained and equipped to the highest standards of the Imperial Grand Army, but they are maniac berserkers now, so eroded by the action of Chaos that few of them wear human faces any more. Amongst them, there are other things. Rogue Traitor Astartes of the XII Legion World Eaters, who rage in like ambush predators, and dark horrors of the XIV Legion Death Guard, who plod through the smoke like rotting statues. There are other things too, worse things, things that were never born. My presence holds those things at bay, for now at least. The inert blankness of my kind is hard for anyone to bear, and to the Neverborn, it is anathema.

Thus, I am needed. For the very first time in my life, I find myself wanted. Tolerated. Almost welcomed. This is very strange to me. The loyal soldiers defending this building – almost all from the 24th PanPac or the Jorvio Milguard – were pleased to see me when I arrived.

I was not shunned, or regarded with disgust, or avoided, which has been the pattern of most encounters in my life. They saw me, and came to me, and smiled. They knew what I was from my vratine armour. Before that, even, they could smell and feel what I was from the emptiness in the air. But they weren't afraid of me any more. It is a mark of how atrocious this ending has become that the likes of me is greeted with a smile. I am hard to bear, but infinitely preferable to what is outside. Our fear is exhausted.

'What is your name, mistress?' the commander of the PanPac asked me when I first arrived. I could see the mild discomfort in him, the involuntary discomfort all sentients experience when they encounter my kind. But I could also see his smile, and the effort he was making to overcome his apprehension.

I am Aphone Ire, I replied. I made my reply in thoughtmark, which he could read easily, but I saw how he had focused his attention on me. Some of us, and my mentor Jenetia was one, are so profoundly null that it is hard for a sentient to even register them visually without trying. They pass by, all but invisible, but for the shiver of unease they leave in their wake. Most of us, like me, are less absent, but still I am often overlooked, or glimpsed only as a shadow. This man saw me, and saw me clearly.

'The Vigil Commander?' he replied. 'We are honoured.'

The news of my appointment had spread. It had been weeks since my mentor's demise. She had passed her rank and responsibility to me, personally.

'Do you come alone?' he asked. I could see him peering into the dusty air behind me, perhaps hoping there were others like me that had so far evaded his human eyes.

I do, my hands replied.

'So be it,' he replied, nodding. 'We are glad of you. Were you sent to us by the Praetorian–'

No, I responded. I didn't want to tell him that no one knew where the Praetorian was, or that he and the Great Angel and the captain-general had left this world at the Emperor's side to face the traitor Warmaster on his flagship. Nor did I want to say that they were all, most likely, dead, and that no one was in command, not even Lord Vulkan in the Throne Room. I didn't want to tell him that all was lost, and that no hope remained, and that all that remained of our stories was a fight to the death. We had to make good deaths, and so morale had to be preserved. *I was close by,* I said instead, *and saw this position under assault. I came to assist.*

'Close by?' he echoed.

A securement operation, at the Sigillite's Retreat, I explained in gesture. I did not elaborate. I could not say how I had assisted Hassan, Chosen of Malcador, in the recovery of the Terminus Weapon built by the abomination Basilio Fo. I did not say that the weapon was now being brought to Lord Vulkan for potential deployment. There was no telling if the device would be used, or if it would even work, and false hope can destroy morale as surely as grim tidings. *It is accomplished now,* I signed, *so I have returned to the field to do what good I can.*

He began to tell me how hard pressed they were, and the numbers in his cohort, and how they were deployed through the annex. He spoke so easily to me. I had never been addressed that way by humans of the rank and file, just as a person, not as an abhorrence. It was, I supposed, the sort of normal conversation that normal people have throughout their lives. It was alien to me.

What is your name? I asked him.

'Clade-Captain Emil Bleth,' he replied.

I am pleased to meet you, my hands said. *Continue.*

The Archenemy comes at us in waves, stirring up and then crashing at the walls. They assault the entrances and the windows. Bleth has built barricades across the atrium and the west postern. The facade of the annex has been so cratered by shelling it looks like the surface of a dead moon.

Within minutes of my arrival, the next wave of assault comes.

The sound of gunfire and screaming echoes from the atrium. We rush there at once. Bleth glances over his shoulder to see if I am following him, but I am not there. I am leading the way.

The Jorvio defending the entrance have been overwhelmed, and the enemy is already on the main staircase. Curtains of chain have been strung across the atrium space and the stairhead to block shrapnel and beam-fire. Some are holed and ragged, sections of chain-link glowing gold-hot along their edges. I meet the enemy troopers on the stairs as they plough up, hacking their way over the Jorvio dead. I am light of foot and fast, hard as steel and quick as a hawk. They do not really see me coming, but I see them flinch and baulk as they feel the numbing rush of my proximity, as though the air has been pushed from their lungs.

I hold a longsword, and have a short sabre on my back, and an autopistol on my hip. None of them are the weapons I began this war with. Those are lost and gone. Blades break, guns jam, munitions run out, and powercells deplete. War degrades and erodes resources, materiel and human. The longsword was made for a section leader of the Hort Palatine. It is straight and viciously sharp, and has a hand-and-a-half grip. I took it from the body of its previous owner after my last sword snapped off in the torso of a Word Bearer. It is a ceremonial blade, ornate and beautifully wrought, designed to be displayed on parade, and handed down as an emblem from one holder of the office to the next. I wonder that such quality is put into swords that are designed to be shown, not used. That seems a waste. It matters how things use, not how they look.

This uses well. Its reach is longer than the bayonets and trench mauls that the Tygris carry. I leap down the steps, whirling it. Soldiers topple away on either side of me, gut-cut, de-limbed, beheaded. Each contact puffs blood into the air, and the shock of each impact travels back along my moving arm. A man tries to spear me. I spin out of his thrust, and let momentum carry the longsword's edge around into the back of his skull. As he drops, I catch his falling spear in my free hand. I snap the captured spear backwards, and the knurled butt of the haft jabs the face of another Tygris, folding his nasal bone up under his forehead. I turn the spear as he falls, fore-haft along my forearm and the rest clamped under my armpit, and jab again, filling the howling mouth of a third Hussar with all sixteen inches of the spearhead. He jerks forward as I snatch the spear back out.

My sword blocks the down-strike of a Hussar officer. His sabre chimes against it. I shrug him off, and make a hard rotation on the blood-slick steps so that the trailing head of the spear sweeps the officer's legs out from under him. He lands hard on the edge of a stone stair, hard enough to crack his pelvis. I spike the sword down through his chest to make certain he will not rise again.

Some start to fall back from me, dismayed by the losses and unnerved by my vacancy. Others are too deranged by warp-madness to care, and bound up the steps, swinging. My longsword sends one off sideways, twisting, but another knocks me back onto the steps. I am prone as he lunges for me. I tilt the spear up, and he runs onto it in his glee. No one ever comes close to me except to try and kill me. My hold on the haft is not firm, but the butt of the spear is jammed against the step beneath me and cannot be pushed back. Yelling and snorting blood, he gets a third of the way down the spear before it kills him and he falls. I let the spear go with him. I do not have the grip to yank it free.

There is no time to fully rise. I roll up, one knee on a step, my other foot planted on a stair three steps lower. A Hussar runs at me with a trench pick. I swing the sword with both hands, low and lateral, and the blade severs both of his thighs. He is still screaming as I stand to kill the next man up.

Gunfire rakes from the stairhead above, cutting down soldiers in the well of the atrium and driving the invader mob back. I have held the stairs long enough for Bleth to rally his defenders.

I see some of his soldiers murmuring to each other as we regroup. They are talking about me. They have seen what I have done on the steps of the atrium. I have become a story to tell. But from the roar outside, it will not be a story that will last long.

All we have left are stories. The annex we are defending was once the record hall of the Symposium Geographica. Its inner chambers are lined with shelves full of atlases and portlans, treatises on Terra's geological history, and books that describe earlier periods of the Throneworld, its nations, continents and habitats. These works are scattered everywhere, torn and trodden, as worthless as our lives.

Between the waves of assault, Bleth's defenders huddle and try to steal what rest they can. Stress and fatigue have hollowed them out. Few are able to sleep at all, for the Archenemy besieges their dreams too. I see many of them at rest, hunched in corners, reading the books and files that have fallen from the shelves. I realise they are not reading to learn about the world, they are reading to escape it.

They read anything, everything, without discrimination. Scholarly essays on thousand-year-old tidal patterns, studious descriptions of mountain range formation, dry-as-dust texts about agricultural economies or fenland conservation. These are not books that any of them would have read willingly or voluntarily in the course of their lives. The works are academically demanding and dull, filled with charts of annual rainfall and tables of mineralogical comparatives.

Yet they read them, and they read them attentively. They read them because they are about places that are not here and now. They read them to shut out the world as it is and lose themselves, just for a minute or two, in some imagined other place. The prose may be rigid and formalistic, and often impenetrable, but in a colourless account of forestation, they glimpse the colours of an old forest, and in the indigestible record of river deltas, they visit lost rivers and extinct coastlines.

They read them to escape.

I understand this mechanism. The Sisterhood taught me to read, and I have escaped into books my entire life. A null like me has little exterior life at all, apart from our service. The world is cold to us, and unfriendly. It turns away and deprives us of social interaction or community. We learn, early on, that we will not have normal lives. We will not have friends or families. We will not know casual conversation or interaction, the warmth of company, the pains and pleasures of affection.

The silence enforced on us is eased by escape. In books, we find the solace of an interior life instead. We read of the things we will never be allowed to know, and experience them second-hand, and imagine them so fiercely that they seem real. The touch of another's hand. The tenderness of a parent. The delight in the face of a friend when they see us approach. The laughter of good companions. The kiss of a true love. True love itself.

Books have always been my escape. In stories, I can briefly feel what it is like to be the woman I can never be. I have yet to meet another in the Sisterhood who does not, like me, read voraciously, whenever they can. To us, books and stories are dispatches from a world denied to us, foreign correspondence from places we cannot travel to. They are minutes from meetings we did not attend, or mementos of events we did not experience.

Then again, I have yet to truly meet another in the Sisterhood. We are together, but apart.

As we wait for the next wave to break, I pick a book from a shelf, and open it.

* * *

The enemy comes at the west postern. I go to it and join the PanPac dug in behind the gate. Under fire, they seem glad to see me. My story – the story of me at the atrium steps – has reached them. Where they would normally be fearful and wary, they call out my name. Our plight is such that I am no longer the worst thing they will meet today. Extremity makes me *not* a monster.

I lay in beside them. An enemy bolt kills a PanPac gunner close by. I sheathe my sword, and pick up her stubber and her satchel of drum magazines. The stubber is a heavy thing. I loop the carry-strap over my shoulder, and brace it against my hip. I advance, firing, feeling its juddering weight, and the sting of hot casings as they fly out of it. When the drum is spent, I cast it aside and lock in another.

I walk into the mouth of the postern. I am an open target, but the enemy's shots go wide. It will take a few moments for them to understand me as a target, to draw a decent aim. They are flinching from my approach, distracted, unsettled, sighting badly.

I spray them with gunfire. I cut down Hussars as they advance through the gate. I rake them back against the postern's heavy walls, jerking and destroyed. I riddle the walls too, for the stubber has no finesse. The air fills with stone dust and grit flies in all directions. The marble and ouslite stipple with holes, and crack, and craze, and chip. Men are thrown back hard, shot through, and leave smears of blood down the walls as they slide to the ground. There is blood in the air, a vapour, and splashes on every hard surface, and droplets clinging to eyelashes and exposed rebar. In the powder dust at my feet, it soaks like spots of ink. I leave a trail of smoking brass behind me.

This cannot be sustained. But it doesn't have to be. Before the enemy can rally and draw a bead on me, before my last drum is spent, the PanPac surge forward, for the gateway is clear and the incoming fire reduced. They crowd in around me, firing, shouting, stabbing with their bayonets.

We focus our repulse, the impetus now on our side. The stubber grinds dry. I throw it at a Tygris coming at me, and the weight of it knocks him back long enough for me to draw my pistol and put a round into his face. The gateway space is close, and there are bodies churning and milling all around me. I draw my sabre, for the longsword is impractical in these conditions. I advance, one step at a time, shooting with one hand, and slashing with the other. The PanPac move with me, blasting, thrusting. Some are pushed back, grappling with the foe. Some drop from the line, caught by stray shots.

We drive the enemy out into the yard, and hold them at bay for a few long minutes, then draw back and re-barricade the postern with flakboard sheets and sections of the fallen gate.

'We would be dead but for you,' a PanPac corporal says to me.

You would have fought as you fought before I came, I reply to her in thoughtmark.

'So we would be dead,' she says.

I fear death awaits us anyway, my hands answer.

'These are better deaths,' she says.

They are not afraid, not any more. Everything they should have ever been afraid of is here, and they are no longer scared. We have passed that point. We have passed terror and anguish, dread and grief. Fear is exhausted. All we have left now are stories.

I cannot find the book I was reading before. It is lost in the dusty piles strewn across the annex floor, a cartography of geographies. I pick another. It is old, and in it a place called Albia is mentioned. Albia was part of my mentor's story, though she kept most of her story to herself, right up to the end.

I still wonder what her end was. She came to me, shortly

before the infamous Saturnine Defence took place, and told me she was leaving. It was a private meeting, just the two of us. Jenetia told me she was going to aid the defence of Eternity Port. This, I understood, was her own decision. It was not an order she had been given.

She already knew her story was coming to an end. She appointed me Vigil Commander, and handed her duties to me. She did not expect to return.

I do not know why she had made this choice. I felt it was important to her, so I did not question it. I prefer to believe that, like all of us, she went to the place she thought she could do the most good.

My last words to her were, *Come back*.

Her last words to me, spoken by her hands in thoughtmark as is our way, were, *I will*.

She never did. I like to think that she has simply not come back *yet*, but I am no fool. Eternity Port has long since fallen, and all there exterminated. Nothing and no one is surviving this.

Jenetia Krole always kept her promises, so to have broken one to me means she is no longer alive to fulfil it. I wonder, often, how her story ended. I doubt anybody knows. Our deaths are often unwitnessed, or overlooked, and they are never mourned, except by us. The end of her story, like the rest of her story, will never be told. It is a blank. An emptiness. No one saw it, so no one wrote it down. It is not in a book somewhere, to be read and wondered at. Our kind do not become myths, like the Astartes or the gene-sons of the Emperor. Our stories are never written, so that in books we might live on forever. I wish there was a book with the story of her end in it, so that I could escape into it and be with her. But there is none. Stories are all we have left, but there are no stories about us.

* * *

I read about Albia. The book talks only about its granite and its feldspar, its igneous formations and its alluvial deposits. But in those sparse words, I imagine empty moorland and breathe the fresh, clean air. I see wildflowers nodding in the cold wind, and a broad roof of sky filled with grey, rain-shot clouds. I see her standing there, on the granite and the feldspar. She is not smiling. She never smiled. That is all I have left of her.

Books are our only escape.

Bleth calls out and I am drawn back from the hills of Albia. There is a breach on the level above. The Archenemy has gained access because a neighbouring structure, a vestry, has slumped against the annex and formed a bridge of rubble they can scale.

Tygris breacher-troops have led the way in. They are more heavily armoured than the Hussars. They advance in the smoke-choked gloom of the upper floors like trolls in folklore. As the Milguard and PanPac start to fire from the stairwells, I advance into the smoke and my longsword leaves billowing lines in the thick air as I begin to slay the invader-trolls.

I read folklore too, when I was younger. Tales of giants and ogres and dragons. Stories of danger and peril. It seems strange to me now that there was ever escape in such tales. Who would wish to escape into books where death and monsters lurked at every turn? I did. I would have given anything to not be me in the cold and silent cloisters of the Sisterhood, but instead become some valiant peasant farmer or lone warrior facing trolls in a misty forest. My imagination let me.

There will be no remembrancers or witnesses left alive when this siege is finished to write our actions down so that they may be read by future generations, and there will be no future generations either. But if there were, but *if*... who would want to read them? Who would want to be here rather than wherever they are? Who would find escape in this bleak moment that I inhabit? I would rather be anywhere else but here.

The dark air is so full of dust and soot it seems solid. There is a glow of flames between the rows of stone columns. Everything is muffled and echoing. Everything is cold, except the blood that spatters on me. Shots scream past in the gloom, carving the smoke, tracer rounds and bright las-bolts. Each one is death and pain. The Tygris breachers are snarling animals that lunge from the shadows. My sword, hard and heavy, truncates limbs and lops heads. There is no escape here. There is nothing wonderful that the imagination can seize or long for. Even the beasts I am killing have no wish to be present, I am sure of that. This is a dull and gruelling hell. Everything is bitter and leaden, cold and hot, hard and cruel, indistinct and stark, loud and random. There is no story to follow, just a succession of impacts, a sustained terror, a catalogue of pain and exertion, a series of ghastly wounds, each one shocking in the chance originality of its trauma.

The breacher-troops have not come in alone. I smell an ogre with them. A World Eater. The rancid stink of it makes me gag. It turns from the scattered body parts of the Milguard squad it has just obliterated, flecks of meat spitting from its whirring chainsword. It can sense me. I am a space in the smoke it doesn't like. Its revulsion for me makes it frenzied.

The squealing chainsword clips a column in its haste to reach me. I duck and retreat, fragments of stone pinging off my wargear. The next swing catches my trailing cloak, and the cycling blade snags and snatches me backwards. I almost choke, throttled by my own cloak, but it shreds free, fibres billowing from the chainsword.

I spring and roll clear, but the ogre is fast. It lunges, roaring, crushing fallen stones and bursting the torsos of the dead under its stamping feet. It thinks I will run. I do not. I make my pass, and drive the longsword through its shoulder. The blade wedges fast in the ceramite, black blood pouring down the blade onto the hilt and my hands. It is scalding hot. I cannot free the sword. The ogre lashes with a fist. I let go of the sword and try to evade, but the armoured knuckles graze me and throw me across a heap of rubble in a clumsy cartwheel.

I am dizzy with concussion, and the pain of numerous contusions. I don't know if I can get up. The Traitor Astartes looms. It is laughing, sword raised.

Even if it will never be told, my story will not end this way. On my back, upside down, I fire my autopistol up at its groin and belly. It staggers, barely scratched, but the delay gives me time to scramble clear.

My destruction is the only purpose in its feral brain now. I cast my pistol aside. It is less than useless against such a foe, and it is spent anyway. I sweep out my sabre, but there is no great reach to it. How would my mentor win a fight like this? How would a peasant farmer, in a misty wood, in a story?

Stories have courage in them. Luck. Unlikely twists. Unexpected reversals. Million-to-one chances. That's why they are stories. There are none of those things here. I have nothing. All we have left now is nothing.

I break my silence and my oath. I scream. I have never raised my voice, not once in a life spent barely speaking at all. I scream in desperation at it as it kills me, a scream made of my anger and fear and disappointment and helpless frustration.

The ogre wavers. It knows what I am, and a scream was the last thing it expected from a silent null. My scream seems to amplify my blankness, to make it colder and more abrasive, to chill the heart of this black-hearted beast and make it recoil.

Just for a second. Less than a second.

I hook my sabre into its neck seal and tear out its throat.

It drops the chainsword, reaching for its neck, out of which a great quantity of blood is pumping. You have my sword, ogre, stuck through your shoulder. Now I have yours.

It is very heavy. Almost too heavy, the handgrip slick with grease. But once it is pressed against ceramite, the howling blade does not stop cutting.

When I am done, and the beast is dead, I heave the chainsword free, deactivate it, and toss it aside. I am strong, but I cannot throw such a heavy thing far, even when fired by adrenaline. It crunches onto the rubble beside us, and the black blood, flowing like oil, slowly glides through the dust to reach it.

No one has seen this happen. The smoke is too thick, and the confusion too wild. No one has seen this to make a story of it.

So I saw off the World Eater's head with my sabre and lift it up by the matted hair. It is heavy, unnaturally heavy, like the chainsword was. I walk through the smoke with it held aloft like a lantern. Head clutched in one hand, sabre in the other, drenched in the ogre's blood.

'Look at me!' I shout. It hurts my unused vocal cords to shout so. 'Look at me!'

I do not want their respect. I do not want glory. I want their fear. Fear is all we have left. We have spent too long living in fear of the Warmaster's menace. We have forgotten that fear can be a weapon that we can use too. Our fear is long since exhausted, but the enemy's is not. They have not felt it of late, and they have forgotten what it tastes like. Fear has not spoken to them for a while.

The defenders start back from the sight of me. The Tygris, the Hussars and breacher-troops, the Archenemy... They shrink from the blood-drenched revenant and her swinging trophy. They recoil from the thing that should not speak. They do not really understand what they are seeing, but it is enough to flood their guts with ice, and loosen their bowels, and make them understand that the Palace will not die without a fight.

There is no escape for us, but there is for them. They flee. They flee like rats, back the way they have come.

Clade-Captain Bleth has been shot in the fight. His troops have carried him downstairs and made him as comfortable as possible on a bed of books and charts. I can see that he is dying.

'You turned them,' he says. 'A third time, you turned them back.'

I will keep doing so, I reply. *Until I can't.*

'I know,' he says. 'But you are all we have left.'

He sighs and briefly closes his eyes. Blood in his mouth has stained his teeth pink.

'There is no escape,' he murmurs.

I think, sadly, you have found a way, Emil, I reply.

This makes him laugh. He laughs so hard I have to hold him steady as he coughs up blood. I have never made anybody laugh before. This is not how I imagined it.

'Talk to me,' he says. 'Tell me something.'

Like what?

'Anything. A story. Take my mind off… off this.'

I don't know any, my hands confess.

'You know your own,' he says. 'Tell me that. I know nothing about your… your kind. I have never even heard one of you speak.'

I shrug.

I will tell you one, I say. *My name is Aphone. The 'Ire' part came later. I do not know if my birth-mother chose a name for me, for I never knew her.*

He listens. He watches my hands intently as they talk. He does not speak or interrupt until I am finished.

That, then, is the story of my name, I sign.

He nods.

It is not a great story, I admit, I add, *but it is mine. I treasure it because it reminds me of my early years in the Sisterhood. They were not happy years. Our lives are bleak and friendless. But compared to what we are enduring now, those early years seem warm and reassuring, so I cling to my story. It is a tiny escape from this moment.*

'I am grateful for it, Aphone,' he says.

I have never told it to anyone. I only tell it now, Emil, because stories are all we have left.

A call goes up. Another wave of assault is coming at the atrium. I get to my feet.

'Come back,' Bleth says, looking up at me.

I will, I tell him. He will not be alive when I return, but I will keep my promise. No one has ever wanted my company before.

When I come back, he is gone and his story over. I sit beside him, and read a page or two from the book about Albia. For a moment, I stand on the empty moorland and breathe the fresh, clean air. I tell him what it feels like, even though he can't hear me.

There is no escape. He was right. The next wave, or the one after that, will be the one that crushes us. Not even the memory of us will survive. The future is sworn to silence, an elective mute like me.

No one is going to save us now. All we have left are stories, and mine will end here, in silence, as it began.

EX LIBRIS
JOHN FRENCH

'Flashbulb memory – *phrase from archaeo-psychology, denoting a memory of notable vividity and persistence triggered by a sudden shocking event.*'

– From the *Lexicon Psychologica*, only complete copy lost in the damage to Archive Collection 888 during the Siege of Terra

Ahzek Ahriman is leaving Archive Collection 888 in the Imperial Palace when the cataclysm takes place. He knows what has happened at the moment it begins. It is a psychic event, and because of that Ahriman understands it absolutely and instantly.

Horus has ended.

Ahriman is a psyker, perhaps one of the most powerful mortal psykers that has ever existed, or shall ever exist. He is the Chief Librarian of the Thousand Sons, and that is a role that makes him both a warrior and scholar supreme. He has great knowledge of both the occult and all the events that have led to this moment. He is also located in the Imperial Palace, close to the centre of the cataclysm. He is not at the zero point, but he is within the inner sphere of effect. If it were a bomb detonation then he would be so close that he would feel the blast wave strip flesh from his bones before he saw the flash. He is also partially in the warp.

Collection 888 is a library, perhaps the greatest library of occult works ever assembled. Physically it is located under the Hall of Leng in the Imperial Palace's Inner Sanctum. That has always only been mostly true. Now, at the end, it is most certainly a lie. The warp is in ascendancy. Reality has become subordinate to the powers of dreams and the whims of nightmare. Time's cog has jumped its teeth. Past and present have become the eternal now. The corridors of shelves in Collection 888 no longer join as they should or to where they should. Ahriman is trying to leave the library. He realised what was about to happen just before it occurred. Before the cataclysm came.

He is in a passage between shelves of books. Ahead of him is a door. The door is a frame of cut stone around a black rectangle. No light passes into or comes from the opening. It is a way out of the library, and the Imperial Palace. It leads to somewhere far away, to safety. All he needs to do is reach it.

All these things are facts. They make up the situation, the place and considerations. Ahriman knows them. Just as he knows, or maybe only fears, what is about to happen.

He is two strides from the black door.

There are candles burning on stands attached to the shelves on either side.

The flame light reflects off the gilded titles of volumes tucked onto the shelves.

The display in his helm visor is a simple set of golden icons showing his armour's power, the external air quality, and threat status.

Ahriman's foot rises to take the first of the two steps that will take him to the door. His armour whirs as it accentuates his movement.

Then…

… Now.

Everything is now.

Now is all there is.

Nothing is moving. Not the flames of the candles. Not Ahriman's step unfolding towards the door. Not the beat of blood in his veins.

This is what has happened.

Horus has died.

Ahriman knows it. He knows it because he just felt time and destiny jump the rails. He knows that the only thing now keeping him alive is that he hasn't arrived at the future. He is suspended in mid stride. His armour's power is suddenly about to fail. The physical reality of the shelves he is running past, and the floor under his feet, and the door ahead of him, are about to collapse into nothing.

The warp has rolled back from reality. All at once. Like a cloth snapped back from a table.

He is suddenly aware of every detail of his situation and his thoughts spiral out of control. He sees the frayed twist of the wick in the nearest candle flame, the gilt that is flaking from the spine of the copy of *Angelica Mystica et Incantartus* that sits on a shelf level with his right eye. It is not straight but tilted against the volume beside it. The angle made by the covers of the two books is twenty-two point two two degrees. Strange...

What is the significance of the number? Or is it the shape the angle makes? Or the books themselves?

He read *Angelica Mystica* once, but that was long ago, and he found that its insights were few, and its fabrications and errors many...

The candlewick? The shape of it resembles a serpent's head. A serpent's head in fire?

Simple, the serpent denotes the occult arts and the fire the power of the will. Yes, the symbolism is simple. Elementary. But does the fire spring from the snake, or consume it?

Or both?

Both, of course, but what is the correct interpretation to take? Which to take...

Which way through the door?

He can feel his thoughts sliding down a spiral. His mind is babbling.

Serpents in the flame, gilded truths of angels, bound in pages… Gilded words… Angels… Burning…

Cannot hear the right way to touch the book and choose the snake… before… burning…

The book has as many errors as truths, so which to choose? Which way to choose… out of the library…

'You need to stop that.' Amon steps from behind Ahriman. He looks as he did before he died, a warrior of the Thousand Sons in crimson armour, edged by ivory. His face is bare. His eyes are bright blue. He looks at Ahriman and shakes his head. 'You need to stop thinking. If you can.'

Ahriman just looks at Amon. His true-born brother has been dead for decades, yet here he is, as real as the candles and books, more real in fact. His presence is vivid, hard-edged, a solid fact in a contingent world. He looks directly at Ahriman and shakes his head.

'Your mental processes are not functioning,' he says. 'Your mind cannot dip into the warp. Your intellect has become so dependent on its presence that you struggle to function without it, and you are now drowning in simple reality.' Amon looks around at the surrounding shelves and books. He nods, shrugs. 'Like a fish left on the sand after the sea vanishes.'

Amon looks at Ahriman, smiling.

'I am not here, brother. I do not exist.' He moves to the candle flame and runs his finger through it. The flame does not move. He rubs his finger and thumb and looks at them. They are clean of soot and unburned. 'You know what a hypoxia hallucination is, of course – an acute lack of oxygen sparking images and delirium in the mind. Naturally, we are not talking about oxygen, but the analogy stands… up to a point. Your mind is reacting to the sudden lack of connection to the ether. It is disassociating, and trying to make sense of what is happening.' He turns and comes close to Ahriman. 'Hence my presence. I am your thoughts and experience of this moment pushed out in the shape of a memory, like a blister formed on the skin by impact. That's where we are, you see. In the instant when Horus ends, and just before the consequences really start to manifest. Would you like to see?'

Ahriman cannot move to reply. He cannot do anything.

Amon reaches out and pulls a book off the shelf. He does not look at the cover or spine, but simply opens it and holds it up. It's an image. It is a reproduction of the original, photo-mimetically printed onto the plasfilm pages. The book is 5th millennium, but the image on the page is far older. It blurs the deeper the eye travels along the lines of perspective. There are columns supporting balconies that run down the side of what might be a processional. Figures crowd the balconies. At a glance they might be human. It might be the quality of the reproduction, or a feature of the original brushwork, but there are hints of shapes that might be wings, or horns, or hunched cowls. Bronze-bodied serpents curl around the pillars, and breathe fire into the air. Are they supposed to be real or part of the architecture? Ahriman cannot tell. At the far end of the processional a red canopy spreads through the air. Here the image is little more than a series of smudged shapes and folds of colour. Every figure in the picture is looking to the point under that red canopy. A white figure stands there, arms raised. Even on the printed page they seem to glow, as though the light of the image were coming from within them. There are hints of wings on their back, of a crown on their head. The figures in the middle ground are raising their hands towards the luminous figure. Are they in ecstasy or torment? Praising or pleading?

Amon closes the book.

'Horus is…' he begins, then stops. His lips twitch in amusement. 'Horus was exalted by the powers of the warp. The false gods of the immaterium hungered so much for victory over the Emperor that they poured more and more of their power into him. He became their illuminated champion, a bright and shining tyrant through which the Great Ocean poured and poured. He became a conduit for all their might.'

Amon picks another volume off the shelf. Again he does not look at it. It's a holo-volume bound in brass, and its covers open with a click of cogs. The crystal leaves inside riffle like a set of cards in a rogue's hands before he deals. Light sparkles around them until they settle, and an image appears in the air above them. It's a picture of the galaxy, picked out in jewel-bright light, turning slowly.

'Everything has a centre. Just as planets turn around stars, and stars around the great dark heart of the galaxy, so too did everything revolve around Horus. Every ounce of immaterial power pressing in on the Emperor's mind, every daemon that danced on the burning walls, every nightmare in the minds of mortals, every crack forced in reality, every bolt of lightning pulled from the sky – all of it flowed from Horus. He is and was the core of this moment, the dark lodestar at the centre of all that has occurred… But the false gods overreached. They put too much of their power in Horus. And now, Horus is gone.'

Amon shuts the book with a snap. The image of the galaxy vanishes. Amon keeps pressing on the book's covers. The brass casing begins to bend. There's a sound of creaking metal and splintering crystal as the pages inside shatter. Amon keeps pressing. His face is twisted. His armoured fingers squeeze. The book's casing bursts. Shards of crystal and dust spill out, and Amon is still squeezing, pressing the brass into a ragged ball.

'Pressure,' he snarls. 'Pressure and more pressure, all constricting around one place, one moment, one entity… Pressure enough to break time, to remake existence.'

And now the candle seems to flicker and dim. The shadows in the shelves are deepening, flowing. Ahriman's view contracts so that now all he can see are his brother's hands and face. Light is shining from between Amon's fingers where they clamp around the remains of the book. The light is flickering as though the book's holo-projector is still functioning inside the crushed case. Images strobe in the beams: figures with hunched bodies and animal heads. There is a hound. Blood drools from its open jaws. Its tongue lolls over its teeth. Another has a crow head under a deep hood. Another is a skeletal vulture with strips of rotting flesh hanging from the bone. The last has the head of a snake with pearlescent scales. They reach towards the light coming from Amon's hands, pawing, eager, their eyes intent. Ahriman knows what the images represent. The symbolism is simple, but even so he feels the instinct to shiver. Amon voices his thoughts.

'These images are of the false gods of the Great Ocean, intent on the death of the Emperor, hungry for the souls of mankind. Can gods be blind? These are. All they have been able to see is victory, and so like all of the rest of us they haven't seen the true threat of failure...'

Ahriman does not need the explanation. He knows what is happening. He needs to reach the door. He needs to get out of the library. Two more steps, that's all he needs. But he cannot move, and Amon's voice presses on, insistent, louder.

'What happens when an object is placed under pressure and then that object vanishes?'

The light between his fingers vanishes.

'Implosion,' says Amon.

Then everything is rushing into the point where the crushed book was. Amon crumples, vanishing between his own hands. Ahriman's view cascades into the same point.

Blackness. Crushing blackness. As though the weight of an ocean were piled above him.

'Horus is dead,' says Amon's voice. 'The psychic pressure exerted through him by the false gods has collapsed into the void he occupied, resulting in an etheric implosion on a scale that has never been known. The psychic might that has flooded the Imperial Palace, Terra, the Solar System, all of it is in the process of pouring into the absence where the Warmaster was… Like a bomb detonation that sucks in oxygen and douses the flames around it…'

Ahriman could see the library again. Books were burning. Pages combusted. Scrolls became torches. Data-slates dissolved into ash.

'Or the earthquake that drains the water from the coast and leaves the fish dying on the bottom of the sea…'

Spines of books burst apart. Pages flutter into the air. Ahriman sees pictograms inked onto pages of skin flare to blue flame. He sees images of dead cities and falling skies shred to dust. Lines of poetry unravel into smoke. This was a library of works inspired by the warp. Every line of rhyme or lexicon of dead language was in some way linked to the Great Ocean of souls and dreams.

'Everything that is bound to the warp is now without it,' says Amon's voice.

Then Ahriman's view is moving out and up. Through the ceiling and layers of rock and metal of the Palace. The structure is coming apart. Time and space have become fluid as the warp power reaches its peak. The joins between place and time have found new configurations. Doors open into the past. The stairs of towers rise until they meet the ground. Broken bastions jut from the faces of great walls. The sky is red and ochre, and shivers like a sheet of bloody meat. As Ahriman watches, reality returns in a thunderclap. Time and space realign. Explosions light off as matter occupying the same space annihilates itself.

Ahriman sees it all in a single blink as his mind's eye rushes from his body. He cannot stop or control the vision. He is flying up and up into the vast shadow of the *Vengeful Spirit*. With him comes the warp, a great rolling ebb tide of psychic power, streaked with the colours of nightmare. Scraps of daemon essence fly past. Things made of eyes and claws and feathers wither as they tumble.

Down amongst the ruins of the Palace, Ahriman sees a daemon claw over a lip of red rock. The human troopers sheltering behind it are on their knees, weeping, gasping foolish prayers. The daemon is a bloated shadow above them. Antlers spiral from its skull. Fronds of mould and rot hang from its shoulders. Its bulk shivers like jelly. Its taloned arm rises to strike down. Then the implosion wave strikes it. Its essence blasts into smoke. Its body unravels in an eye-blink. It thrashes as it dissolves into black mist. Its screams are the cries of dying birds. The soldiers sheltering in the shadow of the rock do not look up but keep on praying. They will live for a little longer, but their souls are already broken, and they will never leave this moment behind.

On the remains of battlements, warriors in the colours of the Sons of Horus slump, suddenly weak. The Neverborn that they share their skin with have gone and now they are just shells of meat, bleeding pain from torn souls.

On and on it goes. Ahriman can see every individual detail and the full sphere of what is occurring. He is part of it, a watching eye spun by the currents of the draining ocean. It is beautiful, he realises, the most beautiful and terrible thing he will ever witness. Wave patterns shiver through matter and ether. As survivors move through the debris in weeks to come, they will find the implosion's mark left on everything, like a murderer's bloody fingerprints. They will find jagged ripples in blocks of stone that will cause anyone who runs their fingers over them to scream. The wind will blow through holes left in blast doors, and the sound will seem like laughter coming from far away. There will be water cisterns where the water will always be scalding even though there is no source of heat. Spirals of words in dead languages will appear on the pages of notebooks and sheets of parchment.

From his vantage point in the rip tide, Ahriman sees it all, sees the singularity at its centre. The hole in existence that was once Horus. A vortex. A spiral of unmaking. It will not last. It is an instant, a vast and echoing instant of eternity. When it does end there will just be dust and the echo of silence in the souls of the survivors. Ahriman will not be one of them, he knows. His being will vanish into the heart of the vortex. His body will rip apart. What of him will survive? Dust, perhaps. A thread of dust falling through darkness but never finding a place to land.

'This is the end, my brother,' says Amon's voice, so close that it feels like a whisper in his ear. Except it is not his brother. It is his own voice.

He is back in the library, back in the narrow space between the shelves with the candle flames. The door is there in front of him, still open. The darkness beyond is a promise of survival if he can step through. The door, though, is a conjuring, an opening to a corridor in the warp, and it is about to vanish. Time lurches forwards. The candle flames splutter. The stone frame of the door cracks. The opening narrows.

Ahriman feels his limbs inside his armour. They are heavy, drained. The servos that aid his muscles whine as they try to compensate, then they fail too. He draws a breath. The sound echoes inside his helmet. It is the only sound. Every movement is a slow creak of muscles and will pushing against the reality that wants to hold him in place.

Breathe in.

His foot shifts forwards.

The shelves bend inwards towards him.

His mind is spinning, rolling with images and thoughts that feel like they do not belong to him. Is anything he sees or senses now real, or is it all in his mind? Is there a difference? Does the difference matter?

He sees the collection. He sees the racks of scrolls and the lines of books, the recording devices and data readers, the wax cylinders and ceramic discs, the tablets and woven pictograms.

All ideas, all boats set on the sea of changing human knowledge and sent into the future. The pages of the books open and split, and the scrolls unwind without end. Needles catch dead voices from the grooves in cylinders. Images flash from turning pages, like the shell fire of dreams.

'This is a record made at the turning of the moon. I do not know if I will survive this endeavour…'

Green flowers opening on spring boughs that bend under the weight of birds with the heads of children…

A man with a burden on his back climbing towards a tower…

'Shall I speak of the place where the dead lie amongst, and the lemon blossoms bloom?'

Ahriman is a scrap of flotsam on the sea of knowledge, a piece of cargo jettisoned from the present by the cataclysm.

Yes… he thinks. All human achievement, mastery and failure is an ocean, a single pool of knowledge from which all thought flows and to which all returns. Collection 888, his own mind, the Emperor's failed vision, all of it is just a part of that great sea, a handful of dreams scooped from the waves, scattering droplets, already running through the fingers as it rises.

All thought is transient. All knowledge fleeting. To fail to see that was the great mistake. The Emperor and Horus thought themselves the end of knowledge. After them there would be no change, no alteration that was not part of their vision, and their will. They would become the ocean, the limits of their minds the horizon. Ahriman realises then that for all he has done to serve the visions of both Warmaster and Emperor, he shared neither viewpoint. There were no limits to knowledge, and to try to make it so was to make failure a certainty. And now, inevitably, here they are… Those dreams of tyranny, like all the rest, have failed. In a single flash of annihilation everything is returning to the sea. How much will be lost? How much will drown and never surface from the vortex?

Not I. The thought is a thunderbolt in his skull. He will not end. His brothers need him, his Legion needs him. He will not end with Horus.

The passage in the library fills his sight. The door is still visible at the other end. He wills his body to move...

The books on the shelves explode into multicoloured flame. They form images drawn from the dreams of the writers and artists who made them.

A ghost of a man in the robes of an ancient empire turns and reaches out a hand. His face is a ripple of blue flame. His eyes are holes. He beckons and behind him the shades of the underworld wait and shriek in torment...

'If from this savage place thou wouldst escape...'

A half-man, half-dragon uncoils in a brief inferno...

'What beast hath form'd this abominable void, this soul-shudd'ring vacuum...'

The stone feet of a dead and proud king who stands again in a blink of sparks, the darkness around him a desolation...

'Look on my works... and despair...'

Ahriman's foot touches the floor.

Breathe out...

Two more strides to the door.

The library is still shrieking as it burns.

Breathe in...

The candles burn down in an instant. Wax spatters on the paving slabs.

Ahriman pulls his foot from the floor. The shelves are not there any more. He cannot see the floor now. The door is in front of him. It is becoming narrower and narrower. The fire of the burning books gives no light as their voices reach for him...

'Worse than stagnation is the possibility of ascension...' speaks a voice from the flames. He knows that voice, those words. It is Hyposilia, a scholar of the 11th millennium whose writings were the only

thing to survive from three thousand years of absolute darkness. *'At its simplest, consider that if you fall from a stool you may suffer bruises, but scale the side of a tower and the same fall will be final. The higher we climb, the greater the consequences of our failures…'*

Horus, the Emperor… Two figures who climbed to the top of the tower while only looking up at the heights, never at the drop, never at what failure would cost…

Be silent! He pulls his own thoughts back into focus.

Breathe out…

His foot has reached the floor. The muscles in his lower leg tense to take his weight. Slow… Everything is being pulled out… Time stretches over an instant that is an age… The voices follow his slow tread and breath.

'And for that age there was a king, and with justice did he rule, and light from his throne shone across the land…' The Aquarian King… 20th millennium… based on the works of a previous age…

Breathe in…

'But there came another age, where suffering and loss were the kingdom's shroud…'

The arch of the door begins to crumble. Pieces of stone break free and fly past Ahriman as though he were climbing the wall of a crumbling tower and the drop were behind him.

'Oh, you who turn the wheel…'

Pieces of stone strike his armour. The sound of impacts chime in his ears. He thinks of rain falling…

'And the heavens poured forth…'

He raises his hands, reaching forwards. The doorway is a ragged hole now. The archway is crumpling inwards, crushed.

Breathe out…

His foot rises.

What will come next? What *can* come next? This moment is the knife-edge that cuts the chain of cause and consequence. All reading of the future from here is speculation. Blind luck, chance…

Two figures falling from a lightning-struck tower...

'We are in the moment after the thunder flash,' comes the voice at the back of his head. *'The moment when the tower falls.'*

The voices of the books fall silent. The library is not there. He is alone. Black oblivion surrounds him. In a moment that darkness too will vanish.

He can't feel the floor under his foot as it descends.

Is he... falling?

There is nothing more beyond the next second.

He hears his inhalation inside his helm, slow air dragging between teeth and into lungs.

In front of him. The arch of the door comes apart just in front of his reaching hand. Pieces of rock begin to spin outwards. The doorway is a blurred hole at the centre of the cloud of grey shards. The edge of the implosion wave from Horus' death has hit. The full force of it is there, looming in the darkness, a tsunami of unmaking.

Breathe in...

One more step... His stride reaches for the darkness between the shattered arch.

Horus got what he wanted in the end... he thinks. In death he has broken everything that the Emperor made. He has remade everything. The age that will come – if it comes – will not belong to the Emperor's dream. It will be an age shaped by this one moment, by what is left after death. It will be Horus' age.

Ahriman hears his breath leave his lungs.

Is it better to survive to see what will happen, or better to end now?

Oblivion a kindness. Life a punishment for the living.

Perhaps... But in uncertainty there is always hope.

The closing mouth of the door swallows him.

In Collection 888 the books are burning.

Far away, Ahriman half steps, half falls from a hole in reality. He drops to his knees and draws the first breath of an unwritten future.

SYSTEM PURGE

GAV THORPE

The scratching of dust and grit skittering against the hull of the ornithopter almost drowned out the strained whine of its engines as it fought through the storm. The gilding of its dragonfly wings had been flayed off just a few minutes into the flight from Station Nu-Zeta to Lion's Gate, and the thrash of their passage among the aerial debris made Pherezides-Qorph wince to hear it. Still, it was better than plunging three kilometres to the broken ground with clogged jets, or creeping across the wracked, ruin-broken, ashen wasteland that separated the great gate of the wall from the Lion's Gate space port. Plasma pools, radiation pockets, and rivers of slowly cooling molten ferrocrete made the surface as hazardous as flight. Not to mention the lingering threat of Horus' traitors, even now, just days after the Omnissiah's great victory over the Dark Architect.

'Your concern is unwarranted,' his companion told him, her voice slow and assured. It sounded human enough, but its measured tone betrayed a more mechanical intellect guiding the thought processes behind it. Sat in their secure harnesses, Magos Theokleia was a head taller than Qorph, her humanoid form extended by a metre, though gaining no bulk, so that she had the look of a lathe spindle. The cowl of her red robes – stained and patched from recent woes – was down, revealing a silvery head fashioned in the likeness of a woman's face. Not her own, he had learned. This was no death mask, but a homage to the great thinker Adaelion Akretes-Sigma-7. Hundreds of small mechadendrites cascaded from the scalp in an imitation of hair, each filled with a twitching life of its own. The neck was long, reticulated like an armoured power cable, and capable of rotating a full three hundred and sixty degrees in a manner that was quite disturbing even to one used to the physical eccentricities of his superiors. The neck disappeared into the folds of the robe, and the hands that protruded from the sleeves were likewise made out of carefully constructed banded digits, with data-plugs and other connectors for fingertips.

Qorph, lowly Second Beta in the Temple of the Matrix Watchers, was barely augmented at all. His brain had been fitted with neuro-filters to aid memetic assimilation and data processing, his lungs and heart cybernetically enhanced to survive on Mars – the beautiful plains and cities left behind when the Dark Mechanicum had usurped the Fabricator General. The only cybernetic of real note was his noospheric system, which overlapped his entire nervous system to add a digital extrasensory perception.

'The odds of arriving at Lion's Gate space port without dramatic incident are less than forty per cent,' Qorph reminded the magos. 'Worse if the operating malaise that befouls the systems of the space port and the inner defences has made its way into the systems of our craft.'

A burst of remonstration flickered across their noospheric connection as the magos replied, causing Qorph a tremor of discomfort in his cogitation cells.

'I personally inspected all code and machine script, and installed my latest purity remarks. These are backed up by double-blind thresholds between our navigational systems and the space port's guidance algorithms. Not a single character of infectious code can infiltrate our craft.'

'Others made similar claims for the systems on the wall and in the space port, yet the malaise found a way to circumvent their protections. If my theories about metapsykinetics are tr–'

'Your theories, if I must besmirch that word by associating it with your poorly conceived notions, have no basis in the realm of the Machine God.'

'Surely the Omnissiah Himself proves that there is more than just the physical and the spirit of the machine, but something betwixt th–'

'Enough prattling, Qorph. I have indulged these thoughts in private only to exorcise them from your processes by proving their error, but you will not mention this to our allies in the Emperor's service. We will locate the transgressive code and excise it from the Lion's Gate protocols as our Order are doing with the other systems still functional in the Imperial capital. Roboute Guilliman's reinforcements will be in orbit within days, and if they are to make swift planetfall the docks of Lion's Gate must be purged.'

'As you told me, magos. Delay risks the traitors recovering from the loss of Horus and striking again while we are still in disarray.'

'Yes. Such is our urgency that we risk this flight. But you are wrong. My calculations put our odds of directly reaching Lion's Gate at greater than fifty per cent. Be content.'

Yet it was not the calculations or even his theories that gave Qorph misgivings, but a very human dread of plunging into the unknown.

Qorph did not need an olfactory analyser to pick out the distinctive musty smell of mould and fuel that permeated the landing chamber. There was another smell too, stronger than the tang of disinfectants that had been used in an attempt to hide it. Faeces and vomit. Theokleia seemed unaffected as the pair walked down the ramp of the ornithopter, but Qorph's stomach clenched in threat of sympathetic ejection. The creak of the craft's settling blades added to a background noise of constant industry, but the hangar itself was silent. A hundred gunships could have been parked within the massive bay, but only the Adeptus Mechanicus lighter and a couple of other small craft were present.

A single figure in a dirty white robe waited for the magos and her novice. Qorph could see cyber-augmentation and recognised the symbol of the forge world of Metalica embossed into a brassy chestplate between the folds. Followers of the Machine God had been swept up from across the fledgling Imperium and brought to Terra by the treachery of Horus and his cohort. In earlier years the gradual reunification of the old Martian empire had been a cause of celebration, like long-lost relations brought back into the house of their great matriarch. Now it was fraught with the peril posed by the Dark Mechanicum and their perfidious ideas that were anathema to the Omnissiah and the Machine God. Qorph presumed their host had been properly certified to liaise with the incoming contingent.

'Magos Theokleia, apologies for the last turbulent minutes of your journey. The great upthrust of the space port creates immense vortices that were previously suppressed by artificial means, but they are not currently functioning.'

'There is very little that is in order, as I understand it, Magos Rakhbani. A malignant codeware is running rampant through the space port systems, corrupting everything from conveyor operation to environmental support. Most importantly, it has disabled the suborbital landing systems, rendering the upper decks virtually unreachable by large void craft. We are here to amend that.'

The other priest gave a small bow as Theokleia stepped off the ramp, ignoring Qorph altogether. Rakhbani was a short man, shorter even than Qorph, and below the chestplate his body splayed into six multijointed limbs, two tipped with manipulative appendages, the others with wheels that gleamed with a magnetic axle system. As he turned to fall in beside Theokleia, who did not check her advance in the slightest, he moved with a combination of rolling and striding.

Theokleia started asking detailed questions about the port's broken systems and the two magi switched to a shielded noospheric conference to speed up the discussion.

Qorph followed on, seemingly forgotten.

Theokleia and Rakhbani continued their private exchange as the latter led them deeper into the spire of the space port along corridors scoured by fire. Qorph recognised the telltale swirls of promethium on the metal floors, here and there criss-crossed by the jagged trails of phosphex. His olfactory filters detected high levels of anti-contaminant incense in the air and he noticed that Rakhbani had a censer hanging from one of his appendages, dribbling oily purple smoke. All hint of the Death Guard and their incorporeal allies was being cleansed, but Qorph could feel something was amiss.

The lingering silence of data-death hung around him as obvious as the stench of cleansing and the bullet and bolt scars on the walls. The few augmentations he possessed were geared towards a particular purpose, one that might prove essential here. Qorph was highly attuned to the spirits of machines both latent and active. To his data-sense, the conversation of his superiors was a faint buzzing at the edge of detection. Various devices about his person and his companions gave off a glimmer of artificial life. Until he had moved too far away, the systems of the ornithopter had been a melange of colours and noises.

But here… everything was dead. His awareness stretched for up to five hundred metres, but within that sensory sphere he detected nothing. Only the lifeless magnetism of dead cables;

the sparkless silicon of dormant circuits; a gnawing hollowness of cogitators thrumming with electricity but no life. To walk these corridors was to tread among the graves of a thousand deceased machines. Their absence weighed on Qorph's shoulders, crushing him down as they proceeded further into the port.

After another few minutes Qorph felt something flickering ahead, thrumming in tune with the frequency of the lighting strips. He hurried past the two magi, following the scent like a lord's bloodhound, picking up noospheric echoes from distant networks within the walls. Heat, light, life. Data. Not just one functioning spirit but a host of them, exchanging information, pulses of intelligence travelling at the speed of light along optical conductors. It was as though he had emerged from a dark, forbidding cave into a beautiful sunrise.

He spied a functioning terminal – the first since leaving the hangar – and allowed his noospheric presence to interrogate it. He expected to find some small trace of the malignant code that Theokleia had been dispatched to eradicate but found nothing. Not a single command or line of programming out of place. There was no evidence of reprogramming either. He basked in the pale gleam and warm stuttering of its harmonious computations.

'Magos!'

Theokleia and the other tech-priest had continued past as Qorph had lost himself briefly in the data flow. She turned at his call, her mask fixed in its expression of serene contemplation. Her tone was far from tranquil.

'You have interrupted a very important joint calculus. This had better be important.'

'This terminal… It is uninfected. There may be something to learn of the malaise by studying why that is so.'

'Curious.' Theokleia stepped back towards her acolyte, her noospheric field detaching from Rakhbani to extend towards the small antenna module of the terminal.

'There is no mystery,' declared Rakhbani, rolling backwards to keep abreast of Theokleia. 'Certain key areas were isolated by my companions during the siege. This docking level was one such area. All connections to the upper port were severed to create a local network.'

'That is unfortunate,' said Qorph. 'If the port is to be returned to any semblance of full functionality in time for the arrival of Lord Guilliman's fleet, we will need to re-establish integration from the highest docks to the command levels.'

'So?' Rakhbani's spindly limbs turned him a half-circle to face the acolyte. 'It is a matter of a few hours to reverse the protocols.'

'But we cannot access the main port systems remotely,' explained Theokleia. 'We will have to interface with an infected system directly. To open any network into the corrupted region will risk the quarantine you have created.'

'You intend to ascend into the Starspear?' Rakhbani's tone suggested this was a mistake of the highest order.

'If you mean the mesophex, then yes, that seems our only recourse to address the problem.' Theokleia loomed over the other magos, the gleam of the terminal screen throwing a jade cast across her impassive mask. 'We must encounter the code in its native state in order to devise a system of purging and inoculation.'

'The Fifth Legion are still conducting full combat operations to secure the Starspear.'

'Then we shall need to request their permission to proceed upwards, magos,' Qorph interjected. 'It would be unwise to enter a battle zone without first notifying the White Scars of our presence and intent. I trust you still have battle-automata available to provide escort.'

'Battle-automata?' Rakhbani looked from Qorph to his mistress and back again. 'We have a few, but I am not qualified for combat!'

Theokleia shook her head and turned away.

'Begin the protocols with the Fifth Legion immediately, Magos

Rakhbani. Qorph and I will attend to the other preparations.' Theokleia's statement seemed to settle Rakhbani.

'That would be more reasonable, magos. I am happy to coordinate your access.'

'*Our* access, magos,' Theokleia told him sternly. 'I am shocked you have managed to pass this last year without seeing direct conflict, but that will no longer be the case. Perhaps you viewed things differently on Metalica, but in the Solar System our duties are very clear. The moment the traitors drove us from the red sands of Mars, all tech-priests were qualified for combat. We will need your expertise.'

Rakhbani's limbs folded inwards, lowering him almost to the ground. Qorph was not sure whether it was a pose of submission or resignation, but it didn't matter.

'Look at it this way,' Qorph told him cheerily. 'Whatever happens to you in the mesophex, it won't be as bad as your fate if you're the reason Magos Theokleia fails in her mission. By the time she was finished, you would be begging her to make you into a servitor. At least this way you have a fighting chance. That's more than many of our Order were given.'

The scent of grease and fuel were to Tetzhou as grass and summer storms to his brethren. He dipped a broad, flat fingertip into the pot of unguent on the floor of the makeshift armoury and smeared it over the metal rein belt held in his other hand. He fed the newly oiled linkages back into the steering gullet of the jetbike, as carefully as his forefathers had nurtured a young foal or painstakingly riveted the links on a suit of armour.

'Whispers to Iron!'

Tetzhou chuckled as he heard Khulan Khan call his unofficial title. He snapped the last linkage in place and turned his head to see his commander stalking across the garage floor accompanied by a trio of tech-priests. One he knew. Rakhbani. The other two were newcomers, a magos and an acolyte by clothing and bearing, wearing the red of Mars and symbols of Fabricator General Kane. Other sigils about their person he did not know even though he had made it his business to study the machine-worshippers for several years.

'Time to ride the storm again, Tetzhou,' Khulan told him in Chogorian, coming to a stop a few paces away. He glanced back towards the great gates, already impatient to leave his charges in someone else's care. 'The servants of Mars wish to enter the Starspear.'

With a wince, Tetzhou pushed himself to his feet, the rough implants in his left thigh and lower back grinding against bone, tugging where they were crudely wired into nerve and muscle. 'You said I was more useful now with this.' He lifted the adjustable link binder in one hand. His other hand moved to the long curved dagger at his waist. 'Better than with this.'

'We each fly the wind that comes to us, you know that,' Khulan replied, his expression sombre. 'Had one of these metal-minded acolytes been on hand to tend your injuries, perhaps you would not be crippled.'

The khan meant nothing by the term, for the wounds that had severed Tetzhou's spine had been gloriously received, and moments later he had avenged himself on the Iron Warrior that had dealt them, but still it felt like a harsh judgement. There was no arguing though; Khulan was already turning to leave.

'Techmarine Tetzhou will be your guide,' he told the priests, switching to Imperial Gothic with a small bow of obedience. His last words were Chogorian again, tossed at Tetzhou as the khan departed. 'Don't get yourself killed for them, Whispers to Iron.'

Rakhbani roll-stepped forward but was overtaken by the other magos, whose mood was inscrutable, her face covered by an exquisitely rendered mask.

'You have your orders, Brother Tetzhou,' she said in quiet,

clipped tones. 'We require to enter and ascend the Starspear immediately.'

'I see.' Tetzhou gestured to one of his servitors. The half-man half-machine waddled over, face slack with unintelligence, eyes replaced with focusing lenses. It held out a cloth and cleanser, which Tetzhou took to remove the grease from his hands while he regarded the tech-priests in silence.

'I was led to believe the Fifth Legion were as swift as a bullet, yet you dawdle and gawp like your lackwit servitor,' rasped the magos. She turned her face towards the half-man, and Tetzhou could imagine an expression of distaste beneath the bronze. 'Was this thing cobbled together by the same idiot that threw augmetics into your body?'

Tetzhou smiled, her irritation fuelling his own placidity. He had something of the measure of her already. Her reaction spoke to a human mind, not some cogitator wearing flesh. She was clearly of rank, and accustomed to being attended without question. Such folk had taught him the way of machines.

'You are astute, magos. What is your purpose in the Starspear, so that I might better judge where to guide you?'

'We have arrived to remove the pervasive scrap code that has been plaguing the mesophex systems, in preparation for Primarch Roboute Guilliman. As you must be aware, his arrival is imminent and you have yet to return the Lion's Gate space port to low-orbit operation. We must ascend the mesophex without delay.'

'If by that you mean we are still fighting, you are correct.' Tetzhou gestured again to his mute servitor, which ambled away. He dropped the rag next to the open carcass of the jetbike. 'And it is interesting that you say "plaguing" given that the Death Guard have left their mark on this place very deeply. But I do not think your problem is scrap code. You see, the khan brought you to me because I've seen the shadow that makes its home in the cable forests of the Starspear. If you want to kill it, I am happy to help. But if that is the case, we will not ascend. No. To reach the lair of that beast it is far quicker to travel to the pinnacle and move downwards.'

The servitor returned with Tetzhou's gauntlets and assisted him in replacing them, locking the armoured gloves to his plate with a hex-driver fingertip. The Techmarine's ceramite-clad fingers moved and the machine-man slumped into its standby stupor.

'We have already travelled some distance from the magos' transport,' Rakhbani said apologetically. 'To return with the battle-servitors will take some time.'

'Worry not, magos.' Tetzhou looked around, his gaze encompassing the open space full of rundown war machines and half-built vehicles. 'I'm certain I can find us something suitable.'

That the battered cargo lighter that Tetzhou commandeered made it into the upper atmosphere on only one of its three engines was testament to the durability of the Machine God's will and the spirit of the craft; that the White Scars legionary was able to land it on one of the outer aprons of the suborbital port was testament to his skill at the controls. It was only in retrospect as he hastily followed the two magi down the loading ramp, uncomfortable and ungainly in a bulky, all-encompassing pressure suit, that Qorph appreciated both.

Having both feet planted on a firm surface was not much better. From this altitude, where Terra's atmosphere thinned and the void felt within reach of an outstretched hand, the sky was a deep blue in all directions save above. Looking up, Qorph could not see stars. In orbit over Terra was a litter of plasma clouds and debris, billions of pieces of broken ships and detonated reactors from the fierce void battles that had raged. Somewhere just beyond the cover of glittering shrapnel and multicoloured fog approached the immense fleet of the Ultramarines, guided by Roboute Guilliman.

Too late, thought Qorph, looking at the shattered hulls and broken starships that littered the thousand square kilometres of the space port's major landing area. Terra had held, but the cost had been too much. He had seen the powers of the traitors first-hand, witnessed unreal entities conjured from hate and despair. Somehow, by the grace and protection of the Machine God, he had been spared – for now.

'You say you saw a creature?' he asked Tetzhou when the White Scars legionary joined them. Rakhbani had moved to the back of the transport to usher out a quintet of bulky servitors armed with jagged motorised saw blades and heavy lasweapons.

'Yes. I saw it once, when I was fighting about four kilometres down from where we now stand,' said the Techmarine. 'A *jin-jiva*, metal made flesh and soul. One of your machine spirits given form.'

'Do not entertain such nonsense.' Theokleia slashed a hand as though cutting down Tetzhou's statements. 'We have both seen the depths to which the Dark Mechanicum have plummeted and the heresies they have committed. Doubtless this warrior saw some strange but wholly explicable construct, the workings of which are beyond a brain adapted for violence more than study.'

Tetzhou's laugh was distorted by his helm's vocaliser.

'You may be right, magos. On Chogoris, my world of birth, I was known to be gifted in the art of *wa-yangse-oh*.'

'A Chogorian battle technique?' asked Qorph.

With crashing feet and hissing pistons, the battle-automata arrived with Rakhbani herding them by short blasts of clicking, screeching binharic. Tetzhou hissed in distaste at the sharp noise, then turned to address Qorph.

'It is not a combat form, adept, but one of artistic writing. As a youth I used to compose poems, the letter forms inspired by the shadow-shapes the clouds painted onto the broad plains. Just child's rhymes, really. Before the brotherhood took me to the stars.'

'We are not here to chase shadows,' snapped Theokleia. 'An intrusive, self-replicating scrap code was introduced to the facilities of the Lion's Gate space port. First reports of its presence coincide with the arrival of the Iron Warriors' low-orbit assault, which to me suggests that its origin point would be somewhere close to your perceived encounter. It is my theory that if we can locate the source input of the scrap code and identify it, we can then use purification algorithms that I have prepared to revert the scrap code to its normal behaviour. By inverting the scrap code, it will replicate along similar pathways, cleansing the system by itself. Isolated pockets may remain, but we can quarantine and deal with them once the suborbital port is operational again.'

'We have seen the anticode work in the Lion's Gate itself, and a permutation of it is being used to safeguard the inner sanctum of the High Lords even now,' Qorph told Tetzhou, feeling he should support his magos.

They advanced across the pitted ferrocrete apron of the landing zone, heading towards one of the smaller conveyor shafts that were used to carry goods and people to and from the upper docks. The machine life here was fitful. Most of it was of standard nature, without noospheric resonance or links. Such mechanisms were barely more alive than a spanner, but still gave off the barest hint of signal here and there, like a crackle of distant static in Qorph's noospheric sense.

Tetzhou set a swift pace despite the inconvenience of his crude augmetics, putting himself ahead by a few dozen metres as the automata lumbered after, the two magi hanging back with their semi-human bodyguards. Qorph hurried ahead to speak with the White Scars legionary.

'You know something of the ways of the Machine God,' the adept said when he had caught up, out of hearing of his mistress. 'I am not fluent, but I inloaded a rudimentary understanding of Chogorian before embarking on this mission. Your khan called you the Iron Whisperer. That speaks to some degree of connection to our machines.'

Tetzhou grunted, perhaps uncomfortable with the questioning.

'I apologise if I am impertinent. Do not feel under any debt to answer my enquiries.'

'No, I'm fine with your questions, adept. I am surprised by your interest.'

'My mistress disapproves of my research, but I am fascinated by new lines of enquiry that have been revealed by the actions of the traitors, and in particular the hereteks you may know as the Dark Mechanicum. I seek to understand this new paradigm and that means I must collate information from the best sources. Given the reluctance of my Order to investigate, that means seeking knowledge from outsiders.'

'The Dark Mechanicum created those terrible engines that broke the outer wall.'

'Among many other disgusting and destructive artifices, yes. To do so they harnessed a power we do not widely understand.'

Tetzhou looked at Qorph with such suddenness that it made the tech-priest flinch. For a few seconds he felt himself scrutinised by the emotionless lenses of the legionary's helm. He was no stranger to being the subject of an inhuman gaze, not with Theokleia as his magos, and many others of the Martian priesthood had visual sensors far different to the standard human eyeball, but there was something predatory in the legionary's glare.

'Be careful what you seek, adept. It may have been a similar curiosity that started your fallen tech-kin on their path to ruin. On Chogoris, if one finds a dead animal beside a pool, one does not drink the water.'

'Because it may be tainted and thus the cause of the animal's demise?'

'Just so.'

Qorph glanced back. They were about a hundred metres ahead of the rest of the party and the tech-priest's robes inside the void suit were wet with his perspiration. He wished he could wipe his face – salty sweat stung the freshest of his implant connections just beneath the right side of his jaw.

'We should wait for the others,' he suggested.

'We'll wait at the conveyor,' replied Tetzhou, nodding towards the battle-marked upthrust of a building about thirty metres ahead. Qorph could feel a background hum of mechanical activity but nothing that suggested the conveyor was functional.

'How do you know we can get down this way?' he asked.

'This is the route I followed when I came upon the jin-jiva. I used this conveyor only three days ago.'

Tetzhou's confidence seemed misplaced when the conveyor call mechanism did not respond to his jabbed finger. No light or sound indicated the pad had registered the contact at all, and there was no sign beyond the heavy doors or in the engine housing above them that suggested the conveyor was on its way.

Tetzhou pressed the pad twice more, with increasing velocity, and Qorph intervened as he prepared for a third.

'I do not think the mechanism will withstand further investigation in this manner.'

Tetzhou looked away as he stepped back, fingers flexing in annoyance.

'It worked. Three days ago, it worked. Just came at the press of the button.'

'If that is the case, which I have no reason to doubt, then something must have occurred in the interim.'

Before he could do anything else, the vox-unit in the hood of his suit crackled into life with the voice of Magos Rakhbani.

'Is there some problem, Qorph?'

'A momentary delay, I am sure. A temporary lapse of function in the conveyor that I shall investigate.'

'No!' The sharpness of Rakhbani's injunction rang around inside the hood. The magos continued in calmer tones. *'This*

area is rife with the scrap code. I have some experience, unfortunately. Do not interface with the system. Await my arrival.'

Qorph looked back to see Rakhbani separating from the other group.

'It seems your superiors do not trust your abilities, adept,' Tetzhou said to him over his helm's external address.

'They are right to be cautious.' Qorph gazed at the control panel, wishing he could prise it open and delve into its workings. He had yet to see an example of the fully operational scrap code and, protected by a buffer of Theokleia's anticode, he was certain it would be safe.

Rakhbani arrived before obedience yielded to temptation, stepping past Qorph. A ribbed appendage snaked out and speared an interface key into a matching socket on the control panel.

A couple of seconds later the engine block growled into life. Qorph looked up in surprise, unable to see the workings behind the wall but aware via his noospheric sense that the conveyor was indeed operational. A chime followed by the crunch of the doors opening themselves drew his attention back down to the conveyor.

The next thing he was aware of was Tetzhou's massive frame slamming him sideways as something oil-slicked and jagged with blades whipped out of the conveyor cage.

Bolts from Tetzhou's pistol exploded across the metal-laced creature hunched within the conveyor cage, their detonations creating fountains mixed of oil and blood. He dimly registered a cry of pain from the tech-priest but was fully fixed on the foe, parrying a claw-tipped tentacle with his blade as he fired another bolt into the nightmare's midriff.

The thing inside the conveyor might have once been a legionary. It was about as tall as a warrior in Cataphractii Tactical Dreadnought armour, shoulders broad and chest covered in the remnants of what looked like a ceramite cuirass. Its exposed skin was thick with dark veins beneath stretched translucence, quivering with multiple pulses. Barbs of metal stuck through from within the muscle and exposed tendons glistening with fluid over reticulated metal bands.

The weapon-limbs were extruded from the beast's hips, four of them coming at Tetzhou like flails. Between their writhing and snapping he saw the face of his opponent and his gut turned in disgust.

A pair of all-too-human eyes looked out from a shifting mass of brass-like scales, beneath which spun delicate gears and axles, as though the rest of the face were made of intricate clockwork. Small cogs whirred as fat lips drew back in a grimace, initiating another flurry of attacks.

Feeling slow and awkward with his augmetics, Tetzhou backed off two steps, firing again – though the bolts had so far had no more effect than a man's fists against a steel door. One of the tentacles withdrew, coiling about itself. Impossibly the metal moulded with itself, forming a new shape: a muzzle, behind which now glared a generator that Tetzhou instantly recognised as a plasma chamber. He fancied he could feel the heat of it as his war plate systems detected the temperature rise and the whine of the charge building.

Lacking room to evade the coming shot Tetzhou launched forward again, driving his sword spear-like before him from inside the reach of the limb-gun. The blade pierced the widening eye of his foe and slid neatly into the cavity behind, but he felt the rasp of metal against metal rather than the smooth slip of blade through bone and flesh.

Twisting both wrist and waist he tore the tulwar free, scattering broken pieces of machinery, bone shrapnel and gobbets of torn flesh.

The thing slumped, folding slowly like a lifter that had lost hydraulic power, toppling backwards with a crash onto the metal floor of the conveyor.

Tetzhou watched for a few more seconds. Not even a twitch moved its armoured form.

'By the north winds, did you see that?' he muttered, taking a step back but with bolt pistol and sword at the ready in case the demise of his foe was not yet truly administered.

'I saw…' the acolyte replied weakly. 'It is as I thought. Meta-psykinetics.'

Theokleia arrived at speed with the battle-servitors a few strides behind. Air wheezed in and out of bulbous vascular tanks that had been fitted to their chests so that they could survive the near vacuum. Moisture crystalised in the freezing air and glistened as ice on their rubbery flesh.

'A construct of the Dark Mechanicum,' the magos snarled. 'Waiting in ambush.'

'More than a construct,' said Tetzhou. He looked again at the remains, but now that they were robbed of animus they seemed more mundane – a legionary with numerous implants melded with the remains of his war plate. 'Something else.'

'I do not see anything particularly strange,' said Theokleia. 'A perversion of the Machine God's will, doubtless, but rooted in the Major Mysteries of the cybernetica.'

'A corruption,' agreed Rakhbani, looking from the dead thing to the battle-servitors.

'He was a legionary,' argued Tetzhou. 'Not some vat-grown lump of muscle. What did you call it, adept? Metapsykinetics?'

'Superstition and…' Theokleia's remonstration trailed off as they turned their attention to the fallen tech-priest.

His faceplate was misted with condensation, but Tetzhou could see his face twisted in pain. A spasm of movement drew his eye to the left leg. It was pierced through and through with a blood-covered drill on the end of a long prehensile limb.

More crimson dribbled lazily from the wound and froze in the near void.

More urgently, a vapour cloud of escaping air was coalescing around the punctured suit.

'Get something to clamp that thigh,' Tetzhou barked, holstering his pistol. He sheathed his sword and grabbed the inert form of the dead cyborg in the conveyor. With his own cybernetics grating inside he heaved the mass into the open, leaving enough room for three or four of them to enter.

Too slow, he chastised himself as he hauled the tech-priest over one shoulder. Half a second quicker and he would have been between the traitor and the adept rather than having to shove him aside. *My khan was right to leave you off the front line, you clumsy oaf.*

'One of you with me, one comes down next with the servitors,' he told the two magi. 'Some of the levels have been resealed and pressurised, fortune has it that our goal is in such a place.'

'I'll remain with the automata,' Rakhbani said immediately, withdrawing a couple of metres on his magnetic casters. The other magos offered no argument and stepped into the conveyor.

Tetzhou's last glimpse of Rakhbani was of the magos looking at the broken machine-carcass of the dead legionary. The doors closed and they were plunged into darkness, the lamps no longer functioning. Suit lights sprang into life a moment later, cutting the gloomy interior with cones of yellow.

A thought occurred to Tetzhou as he lowered the tech-priest to the decking and placed a massive hand around the breach in the suit. Rakhbani had been standing at the controls, right next to the conveyor entrance. Yet the traitor had ignored him and attacked Qorph. It might mean nothing, but Tetzhou wasn't happy to dismiss it just yet.

Numbness down his left side alerted Qorph to the fact that a suite of pain receptors had been switched off in his brain, presumably due to some trauma. As neurons fired into life, the recollection of the entity in the conveyor flooded back. He could hear the clank and wheeze of its movements, the crackle of energy weapons and discharge of bolt propellant followed by the crack of detonation.

As brain activity increased he came to the conclusion that the noises were not a memory. There was a firefight raging around him.

He forced an eye open, to be confronted with the slack-mouthed visage of a combat-servitor leering at him upside down. Alarmed, he opened his other eye and saw a dribble of saliva from the biomechanic's mouth, foamed with pink blood. Its vacant gaze was not unintelligent – it was dead.

Moving his head slightly, wincing as bullets whipped past too close for his liking, Qorph moved his gaze to the torso of the servitor. The fist-sized holes revealed the remains of pulverised organs through the mesh armour that had covered its torso. Bionic enhancements still whirred and clattered around its cardiovascular system, but a severed artery simply vomited out the artificially circulated blood, creating a spreading pool that was about to reach Qorph.

Flushed with distaste, the tech-priest rolled to the other side and unsteadily regained his feet. His void suit had been removed, but the red of his robe by his left leg was far darker, heavy with blood. He had no recollection of suffering the injury, but the pain that threaded through the blockers was very real as he tried to put his weight on that side. Through a slit in the crimson he saw a binding of white – Rakhbani's robe he realised – tight around his thigh.

Beyond the dead servitor was another, but it looked very different to the warriors Rakhbani had assembled, being of flatter, more brutish features, which he realised reminded him more of a legionary than a normal human. Cybernetics pierced its flesh, its arms and one leg had been replaced with augmetics, and a heavy cannon connected to a backpack by a belt feed lay close by. The silvered armour and yellow-and-black stripes were reminiscent of the Iron Warriors – perhaps a failed aspirant to their ranks donated to the Dark Mechanicum as part of some unholy contract?

The small expedition was in a chamber about thirty metres long and five wide, erratically lit by malfunctioning lumen strips and muzzle flare. At the door at the far end were two more enemy constructs – armoured, human-sized, more metal than flesh – and three of their number lay broken across the floor of the chamber, likely charting the advance of Tetzhou as he had counter-attacked. Another allied servitor was missing a leg, leaning against pale, blue-painted ferrocrete to the left, its multi-laser tracking back and forth while in the shelter of its bulk Rakhbani and Theokleia hunkered close to the wall.

'Assistance would be good,' shouted Tetzhou between Chogorian curses and battle cries. He smashed his bolt pistol into the face of one of his foes – evidently unable to reload in the melee – and hacked into its reeling form with his sword.

'We brought the servitors for a reason,' Theokleia replied coolly.

'I am not cleared for combat duties,' Rakhbani reminded them.

Qorph staggered over to the pair just as Tetzhou spun away from his opponent. The nearest combat-servitor responded to the freshly revealed target, its multi-laser strafing red blasts across the traitor construct's midriff and arm, flashing past into the corridor beyond. Tetzhou had reloaded in the two seconds of respite this brought him, firing a trio of shots directly into the head of the stumbling enemy, blasting its skull apart from within. A crackling mace wielded by another foe crashed into the chest of the legionary, throwing him backwards.

'Late intervention will not preserve us,' Qorph pointed out as another clanking monstrosity appeared at the doorway, a pair of triple-barrelled guns where arms would have been.

Through his noospheric awareness Qorph could tell there

was something different about this new arrival. Its signature churned constantly, changing ratio and aspect every few milliseconds, stuttering like an indignant archmagos. He had seen similar activity in previous encounters during the siege and he pronounced his discovery with a shudder.

'Neverborn-infused construct,' he warned the others. 'Ignore the head! Breach its soul chamber.'

Disturbing runes glowed with a melange of colours inside a ribwork of iron and bone. Tetzhou was separated from the horrifying creation by the mundane battle-servitors, resorting to crude hacking as he tried to sever a tree-thick limb pinning him against a wall.

An electronic sigh issued from Theokleia and she stepped out from the shadow of the bodyguard. Instantly, the possessed engine-warrior turned a many-lensed, insect-like face in her direction. She reached into her robes as the six barrels of its guns started to spin, pulling a thick-barrelled pistol from within.

A momentary glimmer preceded a blast of orange that struck the Neverborn engine square in the chest, melting the protective cage in an instant to punch through into the soul canister. Pierced, the canister cracked open from the warp pressure within, its runes separating like a mess of wires untangling itself, purplish light blazing from the breach.

Theokleia fired her volkite serpenta again, hitting almost exactly the same spot. Molten metal spumed from the back of the tottering creature and a wail erupted directly inside the head of Qorph, bypassing conventional sound waves. For a moment its noospheric aura took on the faint form of a Neverborn – a contorted, squat creature with no head, its raging face set into its torso, fangs of fire bared in a maw of void black.

Then it was gone, disappearing like autogun discharge, its animated mechanical body clattering to the ground in component parts.

Tetzhou burst free from his predicament as his attacker's arm spun away trailing a mix of oil and blood, his bolt pistol firing into the exposed backs of its knees to sever the frayed metal ligaments. Unable to hold itself up, the combat-servitor tried to twist as it fell, ripping apart its own leg in the act.

A noospheric burst accompanied by a binharic command erupted from Rakhbani into one of the battle constructs. It responded by powering forwards, spinning saw blade slashing into the neck of the stricken Dark Mechanicum creation. Tetzhou leapt at the last foe as it exchanged shots with the other servitors, ramming his blade point first between two armoured plates on its lower back, severing the spine within. The legionary wrapped a ceramite-clad arm under the construct's chin and twisted in what was obviously intended to be a throw. The servitor parted where the spine had been severed so that the White Scar ripped it in half instead, pulling thorax, head and arms away from the rest. Spinning, Tetzhou smashed the flailing upper half of the construct into the unyielding floor, contacting his arm so hard that its exposed jaw and skull shattered.

'Where are we?' Qorph asked, turning to Rakhbani. 'What did I miss?'

It started as a presence, not a voice or sound. It pricked Tetzhou's awareness like a change in the wind. A herald of something more significant to come. As when he had ridden the plains of Chogoris his focus was on his surroundings, but he allowed instinct to monitor that other presence; to listen to the voice of the wind.

It sat uneasily in his subconscious as the group pushed through the zone secured over the previous days by the White Scars. The evidence of recent fighting was abundant: corpses, spent rounds, scars from bolt and laser. The festering dead of Mortarion's servants had been burned, but the corpses of the Iron Warriors that had preceded them were everywhere, abandoned by their own and ignored by the Death Guard. This place had been changed rapidly by successive occupations of several masters, and their touch was layered over the Lion's Gate space port like the paint on Tetzhou's war plate. For decades it had been home to humans – regular people charged with the mundane but essential job of ushering goods and people to and from the Throneworld of the Imperium. Few of them remained, but pockets of survivors had been discovered in isolated boltholes, miraculously protected from the bombardments and assaults of the traitors, overlooked by Neverborn interlopers. Haggard and close to madness, if not already driven over the edge by their harrowing experiences, they perhaps suffered a worse fate than those that had perished.

The sons of Dorn had come next, fortifying, regimented and solid, breaking and erecting walls, phalanxes of gun and blade ready for when Perturabo and his Iron Warriors arrived. The White Scars had honoured the dead of the Emperor's chosen as best they could, but the unnatural taint had been upon many of them and they had been turned to ash and blackened ceramite along with their corruptors. Malignant Neverborn and lethal poxes remained though Mortarion had fallen to the fury of the Great Khan, who even now still lay at the brink of slipping into the endless sleep, kept alive by the ministrations and machines of Terra's finest chirurgeons.

But it was the Iron Warriors that now occupied his thoughts, and the legacy of their brief time as lords of the Lion's Gate that drew Tetzhou and the others towards the core of the Starspear. And as they neared their destination, Tetzhou's vigilance increased. Now he was no longer the rider on the plain sifting the whispers of the wind for signs: he was the mouse scurrying from shadow to shadow knowing that the hawk glided overhead – and he was the hawk with eyes that saw all, searching for its prey.

While the half-knowledge of being observed nagged at Tetzhou, part of his brain registered the ongoing debate between the tech-priests. At times he understood none of it, spoken in sharp exchanges of their machine tongue that set his teeth on edge. Now and then they spoke plainly, but even then he was able to follow the argument only occasionally, as now. They passed into a vast turbine hall, the five mammoth generators that provided power to this sector dormant, the light provided by his suit and lamps mounted upon the combat-servitor that advanced a pace behind him.

'It was not the same,' contested Qorph. 'Though my recollection is fragmentary, and my sample of short duration, I am certain that the entity in the conveyor cage was closer to an exploited code system than a living being. It had a noospheric register different to both corrupted servitor and Neverborn-hosting engine.'

'What you claim is simply not possible,' replied Theokleia. 'While there is a motive spark in flesh, machine and warp, the three are still separate. Even the sorcerous engines we have faced that are machine in build but powered by the immaterial denizen are animated matter. This is no different to a void-shield generator, in principle.'

'An infection of the type you posit would be impossible to restrain,' Rakhbani added as Tetzhou and the servitor came to the tall arch at the end of the turbine hall. It led into a room of monitoring stations, their screens dead and broken. Looking at splintered glass and shattered circuits made Tetzhou's implants rasp at his flesh. The sensation was not pain in the normal sense, but it grated on his thoughts as he limped into the control chamber.

'That is entirely my contention,' said Qorph. His voice echoed from behind, still in the larger space. Tetzhou became aware of the far more cramped confines of the control room, narrow so that he had to take the lead, blocking the combat-servitor. 'This is not merely scrap code we are dealing with, it is a power that has the ability to rewrite the physical makeup of any system it encounters, including genetic data and programs, treating them the same. The data is very raw, but in time we shall understand this as a new state of matter and energy.'

There was a harsh crackle, laughter from Theokleia, accompanied by the ring of their footsteps inside the control chamber. Their strange snaps, buzzes and creaks reminded Tetzhou of what they were: agents of an inhuman cult that believed machine was superior to human.

Could he trust them? The adepts of Mars certainly had kept their own agenda since being reunited with Terra. They considered legionaries to be a strange, indulgent experiment of the Emperor – the Omnissiah, they called Him – that were inferior to their own cyberised military.

And that magos... So dismissive. So arrogant in her mechanical certainty.

Moving through the twisted remains of a blast door into a broad corridor, Tetzhou paused and allowed the combat-servitor to come up alongside him. He glanced up at the mute. Built for violence. And servility. Is that how the magos saw him? A construct of flesh rather than metal.

They were getting closer to the lair of the creature.

'Another five hundred metres ahead,' Tetzhou told his companions. 'A tertiary control chamber.'

'The noospheric signature here is very different,' remarked Qorph. Tetzhou glanced back to see the adept looking back and forth along the dead consoles as though his eyes were an auspex.

Which they probably were, the Techmarine realised.

The foreignness of the metal and plastek inside Tetzhou's body made him wonder how the Martians tolerated it. For them perhaps it was an improvement, but his body had been forged by the artifice of the Emperor – may the winds carry His name forever – already superior in every way to the unaugmented human form.

He recalled the thing in the conveyor cage, how it had blended machine and flesh as one. Not meshed, but seamless despite the protestations of the rude magos. Tetzhou wondered how his ravaged skeleton and muscles would feel if he had that kind of symbiosis with his own artificial parts.

'Tetzhou!'

The Techmarine realised it was the third time Qorph had called his name. The adept's gaze was fixed on the hand of the legionary where he had paused for a moment, bracing himself on an outthrust console of a terminal as his implants had spasmed.

Tiny tendrils of wire had wormed their way from beneath the rune pads and screen and were questing at the ceramite of his gauntlets, a few strands burrowing into the flexible interstitial layer. Like pin pricks he could feel them trying to pierce the thick skin of his fingers.

He pulled his hand away with a cry, stepping back as thicker cables ripped out of the console and lashed at him with sparking ends and flashing plugs. Sheathed copper threw itself around his arm in quick coils as he tried to slash his blade through the serpentine mass. The glowing termini of optical cables plinked against the lenses of his helm, trying to crack through to plunge into his eyes beyond. Around them the lumens flared and dimmed, creating an inconstant movement of light and shadow, the darkness itself seemingly alive.

Tetzhou's bolt-round detonated inside the console. Glass and circuitry showered across the chamber, revealing innards that looked as much like the pulsing organs of a living creature as they did a construction of artifice and electricity.

The servitor lumbered around, its multi-laser swinging back and forth uselessly as it failed to identify a target, A pulse from the magos' volkite pistol tore a blistering gash through the living machinery that caused its appendages to flex back in shock.

'Go!' bellowed Tetzhou, breaking into a run down the corridor. 'We must tackle the machine shadow in its lair.'

'The sanctum is secure-vaulted,' barked Rakhbani. 'I will overload the security protocols from the antechamber.'

Before anyone could object, the tech-priest rolled back into the room they had just left.

Clear of the thrashing cable-tentacles, Tetzhou slowed to a more tactical pace, his lopsided stride creating an offset double clang on the metal mesh underfoot. He glanced down, anxious of conduits and other machinery that might be beneath him, but there was nothing but ferrocrete below the ironwork.

The heavy clump and lighter treads of the adept and the magos followed him a few seconds behind, but his attention was focused on the space ahead. The corridor opened into an octagonal chamber with a similar shaped vault within, the remnants of more broken machinery, hanging cables and pipes like gala flags criss-crossing the space between. The lumens flickered arrhythmically, crafting images that looked like faces from splinters of glass and ruptured cable housing. Sparks pulsed along exposed wires, their crackle and snap sounding like the machine language of the Martians.

The closest door to the inner sanctum wheezed open, the moist air within turning to vaporous cloud as it came into contact with the near-freezing atmosphere outside. Swirls of mist coiled from the vents of Tetzhou's armour as he took up a balanced stance, bolt pistol leading, sword held out to one side.

Tetzhou thought he could see lit rune pads and data scrawling across screens within the sanctum, but after a moment a shadow eclipsed them.

The thing that came out of the doorway was impossible. Its whole form was neither fixed nor fluid – at one moment easing its way through the portal, at the next a thing of solid matter, bearing whirring saw blades and guns that gleamed with las and plasma power. Its innards glowed like a reactor, glimpsed between plates of metal and ceramite that shifted and locked as it moved, assuming a form as large as a Contemptor Dreadnought, more than twice as tall as Tetzhou and far broader and heavier. Exposed bone sheathed in molten ceramic hardened into curved and spiked surfaces. The main sarcophagus on what must surely have once been a Dreadnought assumed the leering features of a horned Neverborn face, sculpted from cable and pneumatic pistons.

Pale-yellow lumens regarded the arriving group with what Tetzhou thought was interest rather than hostility.

'We require a servitor of more mass,' whispered Qorph, coming up to stop a few steps behind Tetzhou. A little further back, the rude magos' intermittent bursts of machine tongue gave the impression of maddened babbling.

Prompted by the adept's words, Tetzhou couldn't hear the signature thud of the servitor. He dared not take his eyes from the monstrosity assembling itself in the outer chamber a few metres away, but the absence of the construct made him want to tear his gaze away to check on its whereabouts. Instinct screamed at him that something was wrong.

'Adept,' he growled. 'Where is the servitor?'

Confused by the legionary's question Qorph turned, confident he would find the servitor just a few metres behind them.

The half-man construct was further back than he expected, about twenty metres away. Qorph found himself staring down the lenses of the multi-laser barrels, backlit by the flickering strobe of the corrupted lumen circuits in the ceiling. An aura of tainted noospheric data surrounded the combat-servitor, like a sickly melange of scrap code and nonsensical bursts that shrieked and blistered through Qorph's noospheric awareness.

He could sense that the influence stretched back along the corridor, emanating from the command chamber where Rakhbani was operating the controls. Concern for the magos spiked for a split second until realisation dawned on the acolyte.

'Rakhbani is corrupted! He's turned the servitor against us!'

With a speed possible only to the augmented and noospherically aware, Theokleia snapped a data-cordon out across a new noospheric connection, momentarily cutting off the baleful influence from the traitor magos.

'A simple enough proof of concept,' Theokleia calmly announced, packets of modified data-code streaming across the link even as the viral taint of Rakhbani's control started to eat away at the quarantine. 'Once the vessel is cleansed, I shall use the evolved data to purge the master system.'

<Foolish priests.>

The words rumbled out from the nightmare apparition in the sanctum in a combination of sonic and data-waves so as to nearly overwhelm the senses. The bark of Tetzhou's bolt pistol seemed tinny and distant. White armour blurred across Qorph's vision as he looked back at the master-beast, to be swatted away by a still-forming limb made part of flesh but studded with metal barbs.

<I am beyond your petty alphanumeric bonds.>

Tetzhou recovered with a roll, slow and awkward compared to the legionary Qorph had seen fighting within the inner walls of the Imperial Palace. With almost languid ease, twin whips of ribbed plasteel flexed out across the White Scars legionary's chestplate, almost ripping it from its mountings as he again tumbled across the sanctum floor.

'Empty boasts!' Theokleia's code was replicating at an exponential rate, burrowing into the combat-servitor's systems like armour-piercing bullets against unprotected flesh. 'Nothing stands outside the great Cosmic Artifice. All can be rendered to our knowledge through the wisdom of the Machine God.'

<You know that she is not right, young one.>

Qorph couldn't keep his attention on both the giant machine-creature and the ongoing data battle, flicking his senses from one to the other and back again. Each time he looked at the behemoth that had once been a Legion war engine, he caught glimpses of Tetzhou swinging his blade and firing his pistol, neither with any noticeable effect. Shields and phasing fields sprang into life around the creature, deflecting shots, absorbing the energy of the legionary's blows.

<I am the obliterator. You cannot destroy me.>

Broken screens flickered into life across the sanctum, displaying the same twisted Neverborn face but with varying expressions of joy, hate, anger and misery. The voice boomed from a dozen external address systems and crackled across a score of data-conduits.

<You cannot keep me at bay forever. I sense the approach of your ships. They do not know what awaits them. When they reach out, blindly pushing through the data-fog and the last of the warp storm, I shall be waiting for their signal. I will ride the data-waves and take command of them as I command this station. And as the messenger of the One Destroyer, I shall have your vessels to take obliteration across the void.>

'Magos, your anticode will not work, you have to listen to me.' Qorph grabbed Theokleia's arm as he entreated her, earning himself a glance from her mask that managed to convey bottomless scorn despite its lack of expression.

'Unhand me! You are no better than this misguided traitor.'

'It's not working!'

Qorph could see the obliterator infection gathering against the code-wall, not just pushing against it but becoming attuned to it, turning anticode into versions of itself. Even as Theokleia's countermeasures weakened, it was growing stronger.

With a boom of laughter from the sanctum the obliterator presence gnawed through the last of Theokleia's data-shield, racing back into the systems of the combat-servitor.

The barrels of the multi-laser glowed for a split second and then the magos disappeared amidst a hail of light beams, cut to pieces by the fusillade.

Qorph reacted without thinking, diving through the archway into the sanctum, closer to the obliterator fiend. It was the only place out of sight of the servitor. He heard its crashing tread as it advanced, impelled forward by the will of the obliterator via Rakhbani.

<The clumsy hybrid legionary would not listen to me, though I offered him the cure to his ailments.>

The obliterator had finished building its new form inside the sanctum's outer chamber and turned its bulk towards Qorph. Broken faces on the screens focused their attention on him, eyes glittering with scrolling lines of code.

<You understand the secret of obliteration, I can read it in your data-aura. Align with me and you will possess all the knowledge you seek, and great power to see your will is done.>

For a few moments the voice lulled Qorph into a data-dream, returning to Mars as herald of the obliterator, ripping open its archives of the forbidden, raising up mighty edifices to the glory of the Machine God as the One Creator. A million servile priests laboured at the data-mines for his enrichment and his name was spoken as one of the prophets of obliteration.

'False promises,' spat Tetzhou, hacking off a limb that had grown into a plasma muzzle. Superheated matter exploded across the floor, melting plasteel tiles. 'The *quest* for knowledge has true meaning, not the finding of it. I am my pain and my weakness. In time it shall make me stronger. Without effort there is no earned reward, just gratification. Its words are the shadows of clouds on the plains, do not give them form.'

A fist like a battering ram smashed the legionary from his feet, hurling him into a wall of terminals. Amidst the spray of sparks, Neverborn faces glowered at him from the cracked screens while wires slithered out of split plastek casing. On the obliterator a new plasma gun formed from the ruin of the old, coalescing into being from raw material made from regenerating flesh. In seconds it would blast the Techmarine into oblivion.

It would obliterate him.

'I've seen your soul, Neverborn filth,' snapped Qorph, running forward to spear a data-spine into an exposed part of the obliterator's flank, just above an armoured hip. As the tip pierced matter, Qorph unleashed his own data-flood. Unlike Theokleia he had studied the metaphysical elements of the Neverborn closely and, with the last pieces provided by the tendrils of obliterator code that had been trying to invade his noospheric senses, he had the antivirus. Not just a cleansing of scrap code but a flex of warp-derived, ever-shifting algorithms. They quickly took on their own life, combining and feeding on the obliterator code itself.

The obliterator bellowed in frustration as Qorph hauled himself backwards. Confused, the combat-servitor opened fire, blasting lethal red beams into the sanctum, slashing wounds across the metal and flesh of the beast. It responded against itself without thought, plasma and shells ripping apart the servitor.

Shrieking from back down the corridor announced that the antivirus had expanded through to the other chamber and was cleansing Rakhbani, shredding everything it found, data and biological consciousness combined.

The vectors of the obliterator contagion itself supplied the mapping for the new code to follow, Qorph's antivirus now honed to delete this specific strain. It flowed into systems throughout the inner space port, leaping from terminal to terminal, turning the obliteration against itself. In Qorph's senses it blossomed like a magnificent, destructive black flower.

Shuddering, the obliterator stumbled back, unable to keep one form, haphazardly growing limbs and faces, guns and blades, while vents gushed blood and oil spewed into the air from breaking blisters. Plasma fumes wreathed from a plethora of iron-fanged mouths.

A massively powerful hand grabbed Qorph's cowl and yanked

him from his feet. For a moment he feared Tetzhou had been turned.

'We have to get clear of the blast,' the legionary snapped, lifting Qorph to his shoulder and breaking into a lopsided run.

He looked back as Tetzhou raced along the corridor. Plasma glare grew brighter and brighter. The purge and the explosion would gut the heart of the space port – not exactly restoring the systems as they had been tasked to do. Even so, Qorph felt a moment of satisfaction as the brightness became white hot and his noospheric sense burned with the screams of fracturing meta-code.

They rounded a corner and kept going, the lumens falling dark around them, environment filters and fans becoming stationary. The whole level was dying around them.

'Why did you not accept its offer?' The question nagged Qorph, and if he were to die in the next few seconds he wanted to know that of all things. 'And who cursed you with such crude bionics?'

'I did,' grunted Tetzhou. 'Well, through my servitor. I used it to rig them out of war plate parts when I was the only survivor of an ambush. I would have died not far from here otherwise.'

'If you get me out of this alive, I will get them replaced for you.'

'We'll live, and I'll keep them. It's good to remember that flesh and machine are meant to be separate.'

'Though it will displease my Order, I feel I must agr–'

A boom and sudden noospheric static swept over them, followed by silence. Tetzhou slowed to a stop, keeling to one side in his discomfort like a holed sailing ship.

Qorph felt nothing. Not even simple electrical impulses, except for Tetzhou's war plate and his own augmetics.

Total system purge.

AFTER THE DAWN, THE DARKNESS

GUY HALEY

To the south there was lightning of gold, purple, blue and black, unnatural colours. The sky was still tainted, and the refugees kept their heads downcast, eyes firmly on the dirt, not wishing to see. It could have been night, but the days were equally dark, except when the lightning flashed. Then the shadow was stripped away, and ruin was revealed, broken hab-spires leaning in mourning on each other, mountains of rubble from which rose the sickly odours of decay, slumped mounds in place of Imperial glories. At least in the dark, the people could pretend not to see. The lightning mocked them, highlighting the wreck of Unity, of hope, of everything. It made them look at what they had lost.

As bad as the lighting was, for the ten thousand survivors in the camp the accompanying thunder was worse, for it recalled the war. When the thunder rolled, the survivors retreated into private hells, memories of when the walls of reality broke and nightmares spilled out from their proper places. Each crackle in the cloud brought a scream from somewhere, sometimes near, sometimes far, but consistently, like an echo.

Katsuhiro did not scream. He was on the move, doggedly picking his way across the uneven ground, placing his feet carefully to avoid sprawling legs. Others were shuffling through the dark, those with enough energy to get up and move. There was precious little shelter in the camp. It was, in truth, a containment area, not a place to live. Three high fences of razor wire butted up against a scorched wall of rockcrete, the only surviving side of some building or other that had been atomised in the conflict. If you looked through the cracks in the wall out of the camp, there was a rippled field of glass behind, perfectly round, preserving the vitreous after-effect of an energy cannon fired from orbit.

'Hush now, hush,' Katsuhiro said to the bundle clutched to his chest, though the child was quiet, eyes shut, fingers twitching in his dreams. He seemed peaceful. The child slept soundly through the worst of the storms. He had been born into this world after world's end. Violence seemed not to affect him.

'Hush now, hush,' Katsuhiro said again, anyway.

The wall was ahead. Katsuhiro crept through the people on the floor with a slow tide of other ghosts, seeking shelter by the stone. He would not try the handful of tents bellying in the rising wind. Those already within might let him in. People knew him. Some cared that he carried the child. But status aside, kindness aside, the truth was that space, mass and time – all the things that made the universe work as it should – had once more become absolutes, and there would be no room.

There was not enough of anything. Not water, nor food, nor shelter. The war was over, the struggle went on.

Katsuhiro was half the man he had been, in the most literal sense. Never big, he was now a wisp, skin wrapped awkwardly over bone. The coat he wore had once fitted him, more or less. Now it was as voluminous as one of the shelters, and stiff with dirt, so that sometimes he had the bizarre idea it had grown into a suit of angel's armour, and that he had not shrunken so.

He did not like to look at the sticks his limbs had become.

Within the coat, the child was warm. In the manner of fathers since the dawn of time, Katsuhiro rested his face on the top of the child's soft head, breathing in his gentle scent. That was still there, under the grime and the filth of the camp. He wasn't the child's father. He often wondered who was, but he felt he had earned the right to take comfort in his smell.

'Hush now,' he muttered, though the child slept on.

The other bowed figures split off, they all had their favoured spots, like Katsuhiro. He always had somewhere, someone, something, often by chance. Maybe that was why he had survived when so many others had not. Chance. Not the Emperor. Definitely not that.

'He protects,' Katsuhiro said. 'Hah! They're the biggest fools of them all. If that were true, where is He now? He's dead. He protects!' Katsuhiro scoffed.

You're still alive, said a more reasonable voice in his mind.

He ignored it.

The storm gave a terrific bang, and the child jerked in his sleep.

'Hush now, just the storm,' he said. 'It's moving in closer, off the plains to the south.' The plains he had first fought on, when it all began. The plains where he had seen ancient hells disgorge all their evils.

This he did not say.

He reached a fan of rubble slipped down from the wall and started to climb, exaggerating his lean forward so that if he did fall he would catch himself, and not hurt the child. Up he went, lumps of rockcrete slithering away under his feet. Everything was bone dry. The dust sucked away what little moisture his skin had held onto. His hands were cracked and sore. He was severely dehydrated. He had given most of his water to the child, along with most of his food.

He got to the top. The wind was blowing strongly, uphill from the plains of Ind, a reverse of the usual direction. Nothing was as it had been.

There was a ledge at the top of the rubble, a part of a floor jutting out from the side. It was big enough for him to sit with his legs stretched out in front, while he rested his back on the wall. His boots scraped away the dust accumulated on the floor, revealing tiles of black and white. He was always surprised to see them. They were covered over each time he came.

He was tired. The climb, though short, had depleted his meagre stores of energy. At times like this, the child was the heaviest burden in the world, and when he put his head against the rockcrete of the wall, he thought he might never be able to lift it up again. But he could not close his eyes. They remained fixed on the skies to the south.

The lightning gave a terrific display. The colours were unnatural but beautiful, and he watched safe in the knowledge that there was nothing at play in the heavens.

'Look, look, no monsters in the sky,' he said to himself. 'They are gone.'

What awful being could overcome such creatures? Katsuhiro knew. He thought of the light in the Hollow Mountain, of Keeler's ecstasy. That horrible, pressing presence. The lightning was a reminder of that. He wanted to turn away, as he had in the Astronomican, as he had turned away from worship, when he shut his eyes against that all-consuming fire.

He made himself watch the lightning.

They called the camp 1207-Alpha 23, Montagne Wall, though there was no wall left to speak of, only a mountain range of rubble. He wasn't entirely sure where the camp was in relation to where things used to be. The Palace's topography had been erased blast by blast. When the haze cleared enough, he could see what he thought was the Eternity Wall space port. Or perhaps it was Lion's Gate? They were near one of them, he was sure of that. Sometimes he thought he had himself oriented, only for something huge and undeniable to loom up out of the murk to prove him wrong. If this were Montagne, he thought, and he faced it, then the Eternity Wall space port should be to his right, and Lion's Gate to his left. But he could not be sure. One of the others had a compass, a simple device with a magnetically charged needle, a design as old as time. The needle had spun slowly round and round, like an old man with a failing mind who, disoriented, cannot find his way out of a familiar room.

In better weather, void-ships came down, emerging through the cloud base with unexpected roars and the glare of nav-lights. Many ships. Rumour had it they were bringing aid to the beleaguered capital world. Normally, he could hear them when he could not see them. Today was not one of those days. Too dangerous. The sky belonged to the lightning alone.

The wind picked up some more. Showers of grit pattered on the rockcrete – the rain of this new, ruined world. There would be no liquid precipitation again, he feared. He huddled deeper into the coat, sinking out of the neck and pulling the collar tight, making a tent for him and the child.

Debris rattled off the dirt-stiff cloth. He and the baby were safe inside.

The child gave a little noise that reminded Katsuhiro of a faulty engine trying to start, failing, catching. He gave a thin wail, then he began to cry.

'Hush now, hush,' said Katsuhiro.

Katsuhiro had had a sister once. She had been alive and well when he had left the east, but he doubted that was still the case. When he was a boy, she had sung to him, back home in the Dragon Nations. Her song rose upon his lips.

'Rose and rain, and petal on the bough,' Katsuhiro rasped. 'Oh, where will my heart find true home?'

The wind tugged at his coat. The storm boomed. Someone down on the ground was screaming loudly, 'Stop! Stop! Make it stop!'

'Rose and rain, leaves on the trees, oh, when shall my heart be yours?'

The child quietened.

'Hush now, hush now, it will all be all right,' he said. He tried to sing some more. 'Rose and rain, rose and rain…' His voice gave out. It was raw with dust. He attempted to clear it, failed. His mouth was too dry to muster a dribble of spit. 'It will all be all right,' he repeated.

Even as he said it, Katsuhiro knew he was lying. Nothing was all right, and never would be again.

He cried a little, dry tears in scratched eyes.

Curled over his charge, Katsuhiro felt his head nod. The tempest rumbled, and for him too, like for so many in the camp, the thunder became once more the roaring of guns.

Katsuhiro was back on the wall. The dead were coming in an endless mass. Clouds of insects swarmed over them, each as long as his thumb. When he faced them, he had not faltered. He had not run. He had not stopped firing.

In his dream, the lasgun hung limply from his hand.

The dead staggered to the foot of the wall, hands outstretched, as if beseeching him. They were far away, but according to the logic of nightmares he could see their faces clearly: Captain Jainan, Steena, Runnecan… so many others he had fought beside and lost. All known to him. All calling to him.

A moan rose off the crowd.

'Help us, help us.'

He stood, slack mouthed. He could do nothing. There were no other defenders, only him, the dead, and an infinity of insects. Close by, heavy guns boomed without effect. No explosions, no destruction, only the noise.

'He protects, He protects!' Katsuhiro said desperately.

But there was no Keeler, no angels, no light of the Emperor, only darkness and death. Nothing and no one was coming to save him. The dead mounted the wall as if it were a set of steps, and flowed upwards, a treacly tide of despair.

'Help us, help us,' they moaned.

'I can't help you. I can't!' Katsuhiro shouted.

Finally, he found the strength to turn and run.

He banged into a solid wall. An angel blocked his way: Baeron, a son of the IX Legion who had commanded on Marmax. He appeared as he had the moment he died, as a broken thing, war plate shattered, livery stripped back to a battered ceramite grey. Only in the crevices did it preserve some of its bold red lacquer. A horrific wound opened his chest wide. Dying organs twitched within.

'You did not flee,' Baeron said. He grabbed Katsuhiro's shoulder with a mutilated hand. Only forefinger and thumb remained, smearing Katsuhiro with his blood. More blood poured from his mouth, painting his armour red once more. 'You will hold this section!'

A gun roared nearby. A child cried in terror.

Katsuhiro awoke. The echo of the thunderclap was still bouncing off the ruins. The boy was wailing. Thin, grey light that signified day shone through the gaps in his coat.

In the camp, reveille clarions sounded. Groggily, Katsuhiro gripped the squalling infant, and staggered down to be counted.

The morning roll call revealed gaps in the ranks. A score of people had died in the night, more than a few by their own hand. The child wailed right through the shouting of names. Katsuhiro almost missed his being called out.

'Here!' he shouted. 'Here!'

The commander, a man like the rest of them who dwelled in the camp but who had the distinction of having been an officer once, gave him a stern eye and moved on to the next name on the list. Responses marched off down the lines.

'Can't you keep the boy quiet?' The woman who spoke was called Elantra Katamana. He knew this because they always stood in the same place for the calling of the roll, in alphabetical order. Elantra had one arm, the right. Her left was a stump wrapped in dirty bandages. Her hair was prematurely grey under its coating of dust. Her eyes were sometimes wild, always sad. The camp did not provide an atmosphere conducive to small talk. Katsuhiro knew nothing else about her.

'He's hungry. He needs feeding.'

'You need to calm him down,' Elantra said out of the corner of her mouth.

'He doesn't care about schedules,' said Katsuhiro. 'He's just a baby. They understand that.'

The child wailed on.

'They don't,' she said. 'Look at them. There's no humanity left here.'

Presently, the roll call finished, and the commander began to speak. Katsuhiro caught none of it. The child's cries drowned out every word.

Katsuhiro patted the boy and jiggled him up and down, earning him a glance from one of the camp enforcers patrolling the lines of refugees. The child would not be silent.

'Give him to me before you earn yourself a beating,' Elantra said.

'No,' he said. 'He is my responsibility.'

'Raising a child is too big a responsibility to carry alone at the best of times. Give him to me.'

Katsuhiro put a protective hand around the boy.

She pulled a face. 'I'm not going to eat him,' she said. 'I know some tricks.'

Some in the camp would have eaten him. Katsuhiro shook his head.

'I...' Elantra began. Her eyes reddened, and bulged. Her head went at an odd angle, as if she was trying to keep something terrible from showing. 'I... I was a mother. Before all this. I can help. I promise I won't hurt him. You're doing it wrong.'

Carefully, unable to keep the suspicion off his face, Katsuhiro handed the boy over.

'There, there,' she said, taking the child awkwardly into the crook of her one arm. 'There, there.' A change came over her face, an inner light making it the brightest thing Katsuhiro had seen since the dark first fell on Terra. The boy quietened.

An enforcer approached. Like the others, he had been chosen from among those who had been soldiers before the invasion, and he wore the remains of his uniform still. It was a meaningless distinction. Every single person in that camp had fought. Everyone was a soldier.

The enforcer held a smooth baton in his hand. They all had them. They were among the only new things in the camp.

'I'm sorry, sir,' said Katsuhiro, holding up his hands. He did not fear a beating, his worries were only for the child.

'Shut up,' said the enforcer. 'You will have missed all that.' He waved his stick at the commander.

'I did. I'm... I'm sorry, sir.' He dropped his head humbly.

'Then listen now.'

A synthesised trumpet blast blared from the voxmitters set at regular intervals around the camp. The assembly began to break up. Katsuhiro and Elantra remained where they were, blocked by the guard.

'Everyone's being processed. You'll get ration cards. You'll be assigned work duties.'

'Good,' said Elantra, 'I'm tired of sitting around.'

The enforcer looked at her with sad, tired eyes. He returned his attention to Katsuhiro.

'Take the child with you tomorrow. Make sure you get a card

for him too. You look weak. Are you feeding him off your own allocation?'

'What else am I supposed to do?'

'You can't protect him if you are weak, and you can't work. Make sure you get him his own card.'

Katsuhiro stared.

'Don't you understand?' He pointed with his baton at the boy. 'That is the only child in this camp. It is a source of wonder that he has survived. He brings a little hope here.'

The word you are looking for is miracle, Katsuhiro thought.

'You cannot let him die, is that clear?'

'Yes, sir,' he said.

'Good,' said the enforcer.

Katsuhiro took the baby back.

'Maybe I'm wrong,' said Elantra philosophically as the enforcer walked away. 'Maybe there is some humanity left, after all.'

Processing took place a kilometre away at what had been a crossroads, but now resembled the meandering meeting of four mountain paths. Katsuhiro set out early, Elantra, unasked, at his side. There was nothing else to do. The walk was over quickly, even at their starved pace, and they came to a halt at the appointed place. More people were arriving from other camps, and the crowd grew into a great throng.

Functionaries gathered behind a cordon of chain looped over whatever would support it. As protection, it was a fiction. The refugees numbered in the thousands. They were hungry, and traumatised, yet some deference to authority remained. They made no move on the field office being set up in front of them, but waited in eerie, hopeful silence.

Battered Cargo-8s carried containers converted into mobile offices. Exhausted scribes laboriously arranged three long desks on a patch of ground bulldozed more or less flat. They brought out cogitator terminals with dangling wires, and placed piles of plastek flimsies beside them. A few cyber constructs buzzed back and forth in the air. Some of the scribes even had functioning data-slates. They looked tired, but unharmed, and they were better fed than the crowd.

'Where'd they unearth this lot from?' Elantra said in amazement. 'They look untouched.'

Katsuhiro shrugged. He was just as surprised, but for all matters excepting the child he felt only an unshakeable lethargy.

The near-total silence of the refugees was unnerving. The scribes glanced suspiciously at the ragged crowd as they set up, then kept looking off past them, up the street. Their leader had more iron in him, and chivvied his underlings along to little effect. It was plain they were waiting for something.

That something came soon enough. A steady thump of armoured feet grinding rubble to dust that Katsuhiro had not heard in weeks.

They all knew that sound. The crowd became agitated.

Space Marines.

There were four of them, jogging up the debris-choked street towards the processing office. They wore the deep blue of Lord Guilliman's Legion, and their armour was dusty, but unmarked.

The crowd parted to let them through. When the warriors passed, the people shrank back in fear.

Their leader approached the chief scribe. The scribe wanted to put on a show of annoyance, it seemed, but it was tissue-thin. The warrior replied, his vox-grille harshening his voice.

'We were delayed, you have my apologies.'

Katsuhiro had a flash of other voices like that, issuing from the armour of monsters. The roar of boltguns. A dying angel.

'You will hold this section.'

He shook the image away.

'What is the scribe saying?' he asked.

'What?'

'What is the scribe saying? I can't hear him. You can hear better than me,' said Katsuhiro. He tapped the side of his head. 'A blast ruptured my eardrums at Marmax South. They've not been the same since.'

'Oh,' Elantra said. Unconsciously, she touched the stump of her left arm. 'He's complaining about the angels arriving late and that there should have been more.'

The Space Marine said something Katsuhiro did not catch. Now the scribe erupted in anger.

'Wah, wah, wah-wah-wah,' was all his anger sounded like to Katsuhiro. He looked to Elantra.

'He's complaining that they're only getting one guard,' she explained.

A single word from the sergeant silenced the official, and the chief scribe shrank in on himself.

Katsuhiro looked behind him. The crowd resembled a stand of drowned trees – grey sticks rooted in inimical ground. They couldn't fight off a dead canid.

'One is enough,' he said.

The sole Space Marine guard was directed to stand behind the scribes. The rest departed with their sergeant, jogging off at machine-boosted speed into the ruins of the city. It was bizarre to see technology that worked. He'd never expected to see such things again. Katsuhiro felt dazed by it, like walking into the past.

With their guardian watching over them, the scribes seemed to find more purpose. They arranged the crowd into lines. Six sat down in pairs at the desks, one behind a pile of flimsies, one behind a cogitator. Another scribe unclipped the chain and ushered the first of the survivors forward. Three lines, three desks, thousands of the dispossessed. Soon the queues stretched back out of sight.

Katsuhiro was hundredth or so in line. Elantra somehow got further ahead. Their conversation cut off.

The day was sultry. Katsuhiro figured that so much energy had been discharged into the atmosphere in the war that it had heated the world. He felt faint from it and the lack of food. The child jiggled in his harness on Katsuhiro's chest. Only the pain as the straps dragged at his shoulders kept him from passing out.

Names were called. The line shuffled forward one painful metre at a time. Katsuhiro's entire world had narrowed to the calling of names, the making of lists. At least no one was shooting at him. He snorted with laughter at the thought. The man in the next line scowled.

Time stretched, drooped, boneless as melted plastek. The day grew hotter. Katsuhiro raised his canteen to his lips, but it was empty. He had given all his water to the child.

'Next! You there. Come forward.'

Somehow, he was at the head of the queue. The desk and the scribes were not three paces ahead.

'That must be you, void head,' said a voice behind. A hard hand pushed him forward. 'Get on with it.'

Katsuhiro staggered with the blow towards the desk. 'I don't hear so well,' he croaked.

'I'm sorry?' The clerk looked at him expectantly, electrostatic pen ready over a flimsy.

Katsuhiro knew what to do in these circumstances. He stood to attention.

'Katsuhiro, conscript of the Kushtun Naganda, of the Old Hundred.'

The man behind the cogitator clattered some keys. The ritual begun, the first scribe played his part, asking questions and ticking boxes on the flimsy, the second staring at his device. On the screen of the cogitator Katsuhiro saw a grainy pict of himself, taken before the siege began. It didn't look anything like him now, but that didn't bother him. He was astounded. They had records, still? How?

'No surname, family name, patronymic, demonym or other distinguishing marker?'

'It's just Katsuhiro. My clan only use the one name.'

The designation was on the screen. He wrote it down anyway.

'Camp?'

This too was on the screen.

'One-two-zero-seven-Alpha Twenty-three, Montagne Wall.'

'Origin?'

'Hokkaidan mega-hive, Dragon Nations.'

Another tick.

'What was your profession before the war?'

'Agricultural enumerator.'

'Specialisation?'

'My clan grew algae,' Katsuhiro said. He had a sudden vision of the subterranean halls, and the vast glass tanks a hundred metres tall stretching off to a distant vanishing point, each filled with an ocean, each ocean full of life. He was there again, in the cool, underwater.

He supposed it was gone.

This was duly scribbled down. The second scribe seated behind the data-terminal took the sheet and began hammering his machine. Neither of them made any enquiry about the child, though the boy was clearly visible.

The scribe took out a thick sheet of card, slightly bigger than Katsuhiro's palm, placed it on the table, stamped it twice with a red stamp. The card was such poor quality that the ink soaked into it.

'Your ration card,' the scribe said. 'Do not lose it. Food and water can be claimed from the labourer's kitchens at your work site.' He handed it over.

'Work site?'

'We've no need for agricultural specialists right now. I am going to assign you to clearance duty.'

Another card, this one yellow, printed letters blurred by ink bleed. Katsuhiro picked it up. He could make no sense of the data on there. All he saw was meaningless sequences of numbers and letters.

'I can't work.'

'You must. Everyone must work.'

'I want to, but I have other responsibilities.' Katsuhiro opened his coat a little, to make sure the scribe had seen what he carried. 'More important responsibilities.'

The child, bright-eyed, gurgled.

The scribe looked a little shifty. 'That's, ah, not my problem.' He said so guiltily. Katsuhiro seized on that.

'Aren't you going to fill in a form for him?'

'No need, citizen.'

'I can't work *and* look after him.'

'Then leave him with someone who is too injured to work. There's plenty of them,' said the scribe.

'It's not safe.'

'Nowhere is.'

'Fine.' Katsuhiro leant forward, far onto the desk. The child swiped at the flimsies with a pudgy fist, and missed. 'Say I do find someone to look after him. I'm not going to leave until you give me a ration card for him. You can do that for me, at least.'

'Get back,' said the scribe.

'Ration card,' said Katsuhiro, planting his knuckles on the desk and leaning in closer.

The scribe looked over at the Space Marine standing guard. The data operator licked his lips. He looked scared. Katsuhiro realised then just how fragile the situation was. The scribe did too. He raised a hand.

'Call for the angel if you want,' said Katsuhiro quietly. 'A lot of these people probably don't care, but I'll bet more of them care than don't. Imagine how it will look, you putting a babe in arms in danger after all we've been through. He's the only child I have seen in this blasted wreck of a city. If you can't help him, what's the bloody point?'

The scribe did not call out. His hand dropped.

'This is irregular.' His protest was, however, feeble.

'He needs feeding. He is a human being – therefore, he is entitled to aid. How is it irregular?'

The scribe looked at the boy.

'It's irregular because there is no provision in the regulations for children.'

'Why?' said Katsuhiro.

The scribe lowered his voice, ashamed. 'Because we did not expect any to have survived.'

'This one's alive,' said Katsuhiro. 'Help me keep him that way.'

The skin around the scribe's eyes creased in thought. 'All right. Just because there is no provision, I don't see how he would not, as you say, qualify. An oversight. That's all.' The man spoke with brittle authority, more to convince himself.

'But, Klavius–' his colleague began.

The scribe, Klavius, waved the other quiet, got up slowly on painful limbs, and went away. He was gone for several minutes. The line behind Katsuhiro got longer. Some of the people began to complain.

'What's all this about two cards?' said the man behind, who'd crept close. 'You getting two cards? Why?'

'It's for the child,' Katsuhiro said, not turning. The hand that had pushed him grabbed his shoulder and spun him round. The owner was as rough as his voice suggested, tall, with cunning eyes that held no glint of pity.

'What do you mean?'

'For this child,' said Katsuhiro. He rested his hand on the boy's head. The man's expression only became more wicked. Katsuhiro half turned, sheltering the boy. The man still had his muscles; he was better fed than anyone else in the queue, and that could only mean he'd taken more than his share. He looked like he'd have no moral qualms stealing from babes.

'Get off me,' Katsuhiro said, and shrugged the hand from his arm.

The burly man smirked. 'Why don't we split it, you and I? Two cards? You're going to need protection. I can give you that.'

'It's for the child,' Katsuhiro reacted, harshly this time.

'Him? He's probably better off dead.'

A hot flush of anger took Katsuhiro.

'Don't say that. Don't ever say that.' His fists clenched.

The man drew himself up, but something in Katsuhiro's expression made him back down.

'Fine,' said the man. 'You better watch yourself. No one round here likes freeloaders.'

'I'm no freeloader,' said Katsuhiro, and pointedly turned his back. 'There are two of us. Two cards. One each.'

Back down the line people were stirring. 'He's got a baby!' someone said. The rest of what was spoken was indistinct. Katsuhiro ignored it.

The scribe came back. He sat down more quickly than he had got up, as if he hurried to give himself an air of legitimacy, or to get past an act that might get him into trouble.

He laid a second flimsy down.

'What's your son's name?'

'He doesn't have one, and he's not my son.'

'When was he born?'

'I don't know.'

Klavius quickly scribbled something on the new flimsy in the box for the name. Katsuhiro did not see it.

'He is your son now.' The scribe put a sheet of rough card on the table, and stamped it twice. Once more, red ink bled into the rough pulp. He held it out.

'Thank you,' Katsuhiro said. He grasped the card, but the scribe did not release it.

Klavius' face paled. His gaze flicked sideways to the Space Marine again.

'He protects,' the scribe whispered. 'Your child is proof of that.'

Katsuhiro held Klavius' eye for several seconds. 'Does He?' said Katsuhiro. 'I thought so too, once. I'm not so sure now.'

Klavius let go of the card. 'Next!' he bawled.

Katsuhiro turned away. The burly man jounced his shoulder, making the child jump.

'Watch your back, freeloader,' the man hissed.

Katsuhiro hunched down and tucked the second card into his coat, hiding it away from jealous eyes.

'They say I can't do heavy work,' Elantra said, cradling her stump. 'So I convinced them my work should be looking after him.'

They'd approached each other with the same idea, that Elantra look after the boy while he worked. Even so, Katsuhiro did not want to give him up.

'He's being watched. I'm being watched.' She nodded her head back at one of the enforcers. 'They all know how important he is. He'll be fine. He has friends here.'

He frowned.

'You've changed your song,' he said, but undid the knots in the ragged straps holding the boy to his chest anyway.

It felt like it would have been easier to hand over his own bloody heart than the boy, but then Elantra took him, and cooed over him, and Katsuhiro felt a little better.

'What's his name?' she asked.

'He doesn't have one,' said Katsuhiro defensively, annoyed about the scribe and his uninvited filling in of boxes. It felt strange not to have the child's constant weight pulling at him, dragging him forward.

'He has a tooth,' said Elantra. 'Yes he does!' she said to the boy. 'Yes he does!'

The child giggled.

'He does have a tooth,' Katsuhiro agreed.

'If he has a tooth, then he needs a name.'

'When I'm ready,' said Katsuhiro. Work transports were pulling up at the gates to the camp, blaring their horns. Even he could hear that.

'I think *he's* ready,' she said. 'Think of him. Never mind how you feel.'

There was shouting, the clanging of metal loading gates.

'I'm not ready,' he said again. 'It has to be the right name.' He took out the child's ration card from his coat and held it out. 'Take this.'

Elantra held the child in the crook of her arm and took it with her single hand. She looked at Katsuhiro as if he had given her the most amazing treasure.

'Don't let anyone know you've got it, all right?' he said. Clarions and horns sounded again, more urgent. Katsuhiro looked over his shoulder, to where people were piling into the trucks. 'I have to go. Look after him until I return.'

He hurried away, unable to look back.

The workers were crammed into flatbeds more suited to carrying cargo. Bars for covers arched over the bed, but they were bare of canvas, leaving the passengers exposed to the dust, the heat, the desolation. Katsuhiro felt every lump the truck crossed through the metal seats bolted to the deck, bashing himself hard against some man he didn't know. The man didn't react, staring ahead and muttering frightened nonsense the whole time.

The people were a mix from several camps. It had called at

a couple of others before Katsuhiro's, and called at four more afterwards. At the last stop, Katsuhiro noted the burly man from the processing centre. He saw Katsuhiro when he clambered aboard, and glared at him as he took his seat. There were around a hundred people on the truck, and there were twenty trucks in the convoy, which then became hundreds as they filtered into other convoys. Dust hung heavy over them. Katsuhiro wrapped a tattered kerchief about his mouth to keep it out – his respirator was long gone. Others had theirs though, and donned them. Those that opted for no protection were soon coughing.

The truck rumbled on man-high wheels through the wreck of humanity's dreams for hours. Tall buildings had been cast down, their corpses filling the highways. New roads had been pounded into the rubble that the trucks were obliged to ascend like passes. Sometimes, when the truck reached a high vantage, Katsuhiro could see clusters of standing structures in the distance, some with glass still winking in the dim day. But where his truck drove, all was ruination. The heavy miasma of decaying flesh choked the streets. Only the walls had any form left, though much of them were eroded, and in places there were breaches in the fortifications, wide lacunae that left tower stumps as lonely mesas.

Definitely heading towards the Lion's Gate space port, Katsuhiro thought. Heading north.

Nobody spoke, except one man. There is always a talkative man in every group. Often, everyone wishes that man would be quiet.

The talkative man was oblivious to the signals conveying this sentiment. He carried on talking, talking, even though he was obliged to shout over the grinding of the truck's engines.

'They say anything about that?' The talkative man looked around the open truck bed. 'Anyone meet anyone else who got a different job? Everyone I've spoken to was assigned to clearance duty! Why do they ask, that's all!' He laughed and shook his head – not entirely sanely, Katsuhiro thought. 'So why do they ask, eh?'

'Shut up,' said the burly man.

'I'm just saying.'

'Don't. No one wants to hear your blather.'

On that, Katsuhiro and the burly man could agree.

'My name's Irun,' the talkative man said brightly, as if the burly man had said something altogether more pleasant.

The burly man hauled himself up from his seat. Using the bare cross supports he half walked, half swung his way across the bouncing flatbed.

He put his face aggressively close to the talkative man's.

'My name's kick your face in if you don't shut up!'

'Funny name,' said the talkative man, but he was cowed, and his quip came out weakly.

The burly man snorted, and ape-walked back to his seat.

After that, Irun ceased to speak.

Three hours passed. Katsuhiro grew worried. If they were driving so far, he might be expected to stay in a different camp, and so how would he get back to the child? He began to fidget and turn around in his seat. They were driving now along the foot of the Ultimate Wall, towards the Lion's Gate itself.

There was a statue lying on the ground, a huge thing, forty metres tall, and that only a fragment. It was of a man, broken off at the waist, wearing archaic robes and carrying something Katsuhiro had always taken to be a book of laws. His other arm stuck out, jammed into the ground, but it had had an open-palmed hand on the end, a gesture to stop.

It had not stopped the enemy.

Katsuhiro knew all this because the statue was familiar. He had walked past it dozens of times upon the wall. That could only mean…

'Marmax,' he said.

Shadow swallowed the truck as it passed under the lawgiver. His blank stone eyes stared back with benevolent authority, for the statue did not know it had been toppled. His outstretched hand had singularly failed to stop anything; still he smiled on, as if nothing had changed at all.

With a snort of tired engines the truck heaved itself out from under the statue, and Katsuhiro's eyes were drawn upwards.

The Marmax bastion soared skywards, hundreds of metres tall, yet humbled. Most of its features were sheared away, exposing the hyperdense core and adamantine rebar. The firing galleries, turrets, and gun platforms were gone. Scree slopes of architectural flinders skirted the base. As a vision of ruined strength, it reminded Katsuhiro horribly of Baeron.

It took a long time to drive past the tower. He kept staring at it until his neck hurt. When the slopes of rubble pulled in tight to the corner as the fortifications returned to the main wall, he twisted in his seat.

All that blood. All that death.

He thought of the child, now hours behind. The great massif of the Lion's Gate reared ahead, battered, but unbowed.

He dropped his hands between his knees, and stared at the floor.

'Where are we going?' he said to himself.

The man to his left, who had not stopped muttering all the journey, turned his haunted face upon Katsuhiro.

'The Inner Palace,' he said. 'They're taking us beyond the Ultimate Wall.'

'I have to go back,' Katsuhiro said.

Another desk, this one of bare, dusty wooden boards. Another functionary, just as tired as the last, this one military rather than civilian. All the world had become one stage set of rubble and grit. All the players upon it were the same character.

'You can't go back. This is your work detail. Priority clearance is to be conducted here, within the Inner Palace, as a matter of priority.' He repeated the sentiment mechanically.

'You don't understand. I have a child. He's been left behind.'

'Every man, woman and child of the Imperium is expected to make sacrifices to consolidate our great victory over the traitors.'

This same slogan blasted periodically out of voxmitters mounted on tall poles. Their cables hung loosely, just above ground level, snaring feet.

'How many children have you seen?'

'There are some,' the man said. 'They are our future.'

'Then let me get back.'

'He is your son?'

'Yes. No. Sort of. You don't understand. An angel gave him to me,' said Katsuhiro. 'He's my responsibility.'

'An angel?' An expression passed over the officer's face; it said that he realised Katsuhiro was mad. 'Others will take on your responsibility, you have fresh ones.' There was sympathy in his voice. 'Go line up, we must serve the Emperor as we can.'

Katsuhiro opened his mouth, but he had nothing more to say.

He went across the yard.

He was in a new camp of different appearance but identical spirit. It was contained in a grand courtyard, the buildings around which had the appearance of grand corpses, pockmarked with bolt craters, and every window an eye put out. He reckoned they were in the far precincts of the senate. When he exited the courtyard he was upon a huge square, and from it he could see the broken dome of the Senatorum Imperialis like a great cracked egg, dirty sky clearly visible through it.

It was dawn, though the atmosphere was still unbearably fuggy; there was no let up from the stifling heat of triumph. It had taken them days to arrive. Katsuhiro had barely slept with worry. Men with shock goads herded the survivors together into squares thousands strong. The animal reek coming off them made Katsuhiro dizzy. Many were sick, or injured, or both.

More roll calls, more men ticking sheets, more directions.

Vox-hailers barked orders and incomprehensible motivational speeches. Katsuhiro was moved from one place to another, until he found himself in a line of workers. There were even more dirty desks with more harried functionaries. There were piles of boots and gloves on the table, all bearing the look of recent mass production; they were conspicuously clean.

'Gloves, boots,' a woman said – she almost sang it, like a lament. Another uniformed woman shoved the items at him. There was no attempt to check his size.

'Have you ever used a lascutter?' the next functionary asked him.

'Not really,' said Katsuhiro. He could not focus. All he could think of was the child.

'You look relatively strong. Take a prybar.'

He was pushed along.

The gloves were too big. The boots were about right, which surprised him no end. They were badly made, mono-plastek extrusions. They probably had about a fortnight's wear in them. Nevertheless, they were better than the boots he was wearing, and he swapped them gladly.

A pile of picks, shovels and pries waited in a tangled mess. He took a pry, as instructed. Nearby there was a rack of lascutters. When he thought of lascutters, he thought of the small scalpels that the medicae used, or the short-bladed industrial sort. These were enormous things. Katsuhiro was glad to be given a pry.

A man in adept's robes blew a whistle.

'Detail Four-zero-zero-three, form up. On me!'

A reluctant column formed.

Another peep on the whistle. 'March!'

Apparently, they were going to walk wherever they were going. So Katsuhiro walked.

They were sent to clear the Via Principa heading towards the innermost Palace. It was vast, half a kilometre wide. The centre was almost clear, but rubble banked up to a depth of a hundred metres at the sides. Thousands upon thousands of people worked at clearing it, by hand. There did not seem to be any machines. Katsuhiro saw one giant dozer under machine spirit guidance trundle by, but it did not stop, and headed away to some more important rendezvous.

They worked without rest. The sound of picks on masonry blended into a continuous clattering. The lascutters were brought in to slice through plasteel. Circular saws chopped through blocks too large to move. Every so often a klaxon would wail and a whole section of workers would retreat from the rubble face. Explosions followed, bringing down sudden slips.

Soon Katsuhiro's eyes were red with grit. His throat was raw. A tankbearer came by every hour, doling out ladles of water, but it was never enough, and it tasted of metal and death.

A dead giant rested on a bed made of a smashed-in monument: a Titan, its mechanical bones bigger than the world. To the north, the Bhab watched them, somehow whole, a rotten tooth in a ruined gum. Beyond that was the Eternity Gate, beyond that the Emperor. His presence dominated that part of the city, and it did not feel protective at all. Katsuhiro felt judged by Him. He avoided looking in that direction.

The work was monotonous. Katsuhiro fell into a rhythm, prying huge blocks of stone out of the compacted rubble that were lifted up by others and dumped into the wheelbarrows of others still. Picks clattered. Looser material was shovelled. Miraculously, it seemed to work. The line of debris was nibbled back, centimetre by centimetre, uncovering the ground floors of buildings, toppled statues, broken lamps and vehicles – all the wreck of empire.

Corpses, oozing and black, were taken away by luckless teams. Katsuhiro pitied them. No consideration had been made to the corpse-bearers for the difficulty of their work, and they were filthy from it.

Katsuhiro slammed his pry into the wall, then hauled back upon it. Loose debris slithered down to be collected by waiting shovels, blocks by sweating men. He went to the next block, rammed in the pry, levered it back. Rubble fell, blocks slipped out. Step back. Step forward, ram, haul, step backward. Step, ram…

The iron point clanged on something. He saw a flash of colour. He reached down, cleared some little rocks away.

Lacquered ceramite.

He stepped back. Rubble fell after him. A Space Marine was entombed in the strata of war. Only his upper shoulders and helm were visible, as if he were tucked up in a stone bed. His armour was the green of deep alien seas. The armour was whole, but the eye-lenses smashed. The unmistakable stench of death rose from them.

Work came to a halt around Katsuhiro. Upon the Space Marine's pauldron was the hated Eye of Horus. Katsuhiro stared at it. A shoveler came forward and spat on the emblem. Someone else ran off shouting.

Katsuhiro looked at the Space Marine. He did not seem so terrifying dead. He looked human, even. Katsuhiro wondered who he was, and why he had turned on the Emperor.

The runner came back with an overseer.

'Right. Astartes,' said the overseer, as if he had been expecting this event. 'Clear this section. You, you and you, ten metres right. You,' – he pointed at Katsuhiro – 'you and you, ten metres left. Keep on working.'

A specialist team arrived to dig out the body. They had a machine equipped with industrial lifting claws. Katsuhiro watched them drag the giant out of the mess and up, so that he was dangling like a gargantuan marionette, until the overseer shouted at him to get back to work.

* * *

When night fell, they were taken back to the camp. The workers were separated by gender and directed into small cities of tents. A field kitchen served up watery stew. His ration card was stamped. They ate, then they were sent to their rest, twenty men to a tent.

The burly man was assigned to his group. Luckily, they were all too exhausted to talk or do anything else, like knife each other for ration cards, Katsuhiro thought.

He protects. Yeah, right.

They fell into their cots, and soon snores sawed and whimpers were called up by nightmares. In the distance, Katsuhiro heard the roar of void-ships descending. His cohort was resting, but work continued on elsewhere, giving the night a voice of constant hand-tool clatter and the grunting of machines. Light from glaring lumens seeped through the thin plastek tent. Katsuhiro was exhausted, but he could not sleep.

I have to get out of here, he thought. *I have to get back to him. He's my responsibility. If I stay here in this camp even one more night, the work will crush me. I will become a human automaton, and I will forget my responsibility. I have to leave now.*

He was out of his bed before he had finished the thought. He stood silently, a shadow. Nobody moved. He decided to say he was visiting the ablutorial if anyone asked, but nobody did.

First, he went to the kitchen. There were guards on it, of course, but he had become wily and slipped past them, filling up his canteen quickly from the bowser behind the tents. The food was locked away in large steel cabinets, but he found a mesh box of root vegetables someone had left out. They were shrivelled almost to the point of inedibility, but they would have to do. He stuffed as many into his pockets as he could, then he stole away.

He slipped through the tent city, heading for the perimeter. There were floodlights over the gates, but the chain-link fences were mostly unlit. He ran along it quietly, checking the joins in the fence panels for loose connections. Sure enough, he found a hole.

He was about to step through when the burly man emerged from behind a pallet of boxes to Katsuhiro's front.

'Quite the night you've had,' he said.

The talkative man came out from a tent behind him. Two more men stepped into view to his side. All of them were carrying pick handles.

'I wonder what reward I'll get for turning in a thief like you?' said the burly man. 'Two ration cards, and now stealing food.' He tutted. 'You should have taken me up on my offer before. We'll turn you over, once you've given me that other card.'

'I don't have it. It's with the boy.'

'Liar,' said the burly man. 'All that play-acting. I bet you murdered that kid. Sickening.'

Katsuhiro lunged for the gap, but it was narrow and the wire ends snagged his clothes, trapping him.

He cried out when the first blow hit. The pain was immense. A strike to his elbow filled his head with vicious stars. He was dragged roughly back from the hole. Another blow to the back of his knee made him drop to the floor, and he curled into a ball as more rained down. Some detached part of him thought how ironic this was, to survive a war of gods only to be beaten to death by starving mortals.

Death did not come. Whistles blew. Stab-light beams punched the dark away. There was shouting. The crack of a las-blast fired overhead.

'Drop your weapons!'

'We caught him, we caught a thief!' The burly man was so excited he sounded almost childlike, like a boy exulting in a petty act of cruelty in the scholam yard.

Lights shone down on Katsuhiro's face. Hands grabbed his

arms and dragged them off his head. He could see nothing beyond the glare.

'You've beat him half to death,' said a voice behind the light. 'You'll suffer for this.'

'But we caught a thief–'

'The giving of discipline is to be left to the appropriate authorities,' the voice said. 'We'll let the commander deal with this.'

Katsuhiro was dragged up off his feet and taken away with the rest of them.

He was hooded, his hands bound behind his back, and then pushed into a truck. He was dizzy with pain, and though he did not pass out, the world retreated from him a little. When they stopped, he was dragged out of the truck and frogmarched into an undamaged building, the first he'd been in for weeks. He could smell the damp of poorly proofed plascrete, taste the effusions of bio-lumens. His poor hearing did little to fill in the rest of the picture, but after he'd been thrust into a chair he heard the whining growl of power armour, and he nearly soiled himself with fear.

The bonds were snapped. They were pointless. What chance had a mortal against an angel? He'd been taught that lesson over and over again.

The growl of active armour came close. He could smell the strange, semi-human odour of the Astartes under the scents of oil, lapping powder and hot machinery. A gentle tug pulled his hood free.

'Katsuhiro,' said a warrior he at once recognised. He had spent half a day with this man what seemed like a lifetime ago, but angels are by their nature memorable, and this one was unforgettable.

He wore the colours of the White Scars, and his hair was dressed in a topknot. He was heavily scarred and much of his body had been replaced with mechanical parts, including his left eye. He had a tanned face of a slightly golden hue, epicanthic folds around his remaining eye that recalled Katsuhiro's own, as if their nations shared kinship – and maybe they did, thousands of years in the past. For the angel was of Chogoris, not Terra. He lowered himself into a squat so as not to tower over the seated Katsuhiro. Even then, he was taller.

'Shiban,' Katsuhiro said incredulously. 'Shiban Khan.'

'That is who I am, yes. You are Katsuhiro,' he said, as if gently reminding an amnesiac of his identity.

'You remember me.'

'I am of the Legions. I remember everything,' Shiban said.

'What are you doing here?' asked Katsuhiro. 'My lord,' he remembered to add. The Space Marine did not seem to mind.

'The siege is over. We are needed everywhere. I and some of my kin have been placed in command of this area, for a little while at least.'

The White Scar was quiet, almost pensive.

'I see.'

'I ask the same of you. What are you doing here?'

'Digging,' said Katsuhiro with a shrug.

'Ah,' said the khan. He dropped his eyes to the metal table between them. Five sorry-looking turnips were lined up. Katsuhiro shrugged again.

'I gave you a duty. What became of it?'

'Believe me, my lord, I have tried my utmost to fulfil my promise to you.'

'Then where is he?'

'The child was with me until a few days ago, at camp One-two-zero-seven-Alpha Twenty-three, Montagne Wall. We were separated.' Katsuhiro pointed at the pathetic vegetables. 'I was trying to get back to him. That's what those were for.'

'You would have died. It is hundreds of kilometres. All is waste between here and there.'

'Maybe, but I made an oath to you.'

The khan looked at him appraisingly. 'That is foolish, but it is also good and noble.'

'I keep to what matters. The child *matters*,' said Katsuhiro. 'Can you help me?'

'I will help as much as I can,' said Shiban Khan. 'It would honour me. But–'

Katsuhiro gave a laugh that, on reflection, sounded just a little bit crazy. 'I don't want any more honour!' he interrupted. 'I am choking on honour, and there is no water anywhere to wash it out of my throat. I just want some help. Do you understand? I want to fetch the boy, and raise him. I want him to have some kind of future, even if I don't, and...' The catch in his voice surprised him. He didn't want to start sobbing in front of this demigod, and he knew he would not be able to stop if he started. 'I want to go home.'

'Home?'

'The Dragon Nations.' His voice hitched. The request was as much of a surprise to him as it was to Shiban. He had not thought about home in so long, not properly. 'I want to go home and see what is left of my clan, if anything, and if I can find anyone left at all of my people, I want to raise the child among them. Home.'

'Katsuhiro,' said Shiban Khan gravely. 'All Terra is wounded.' A troubled look settled onto his features. 'I saw things outside the lines, before I met you. This world is not the same as it was. Your people are likely dead. Everything has to be remade.'

'Then what does it matter if I am here or there? At least the memories there include some good. Here there is only pain, and horror. I've had enough of it.'

'You have been given a role. There are procedures to be followed, and orders to be obeyed. The fight is over, but the struggle is only beginning.'

'You gave me a role,' said Katsuhiro, getting to his feet. 'A more important role than shifting rocks. What about that? Surely your command to me counts for something.'

'It was not an order, it was a request.'

'I've nearly died trying to fulfil it!' Katsuhiro said. 'Please, help me. Help the boy, once more, just once more. How long do you think the child will survive this hellhole?'

Shiban Khan smoothed down his long moustache and opened his mouth in thought, then he stood – a swift, unexpected movement that took Katsuhiro unawares. For a moment, he'd forgotten how dangerous the transhumans were.

'It could perhaps be arranged. Come with me.'

Elantra crouched over the boy. Feeding him was hard. There was no milk. Katsuhiro had mixed up food powders, when he had had them, with the brackish water rations. When that hadn't been possible, all he could do was chew the child's food into a slurry for him. Katsuhiro had not thought that ideal, but it was often the only way. Elantra was doing that just then, softening pellets of hard tack and pushing it into his mouth in such a tender manner, Katsuhiro felt something other than sadness. She was totally focused on the child and did not see him approach, so he watched for a few minutes, how the child's arms and legs jerked with pleasure as she tickled him and fed him. He could have watched for hours, he thought, but one does not keep a Space Marine waiting.

'Hello,' he said.

Her expression betrayed a complex set of emotions. Part of her, he thought, hadn't wanted him to come back. He understood that. She had purpose again, with the boy.

'I didn't think you were going to return,' she said.

'I almost didn't,' he said. He crouched down next to them. The child rolled his head around to see his visitor, and shrieked with delight when he saw who it was.

'That's the biggest smile anyone has smiled in the Palace since forever,' she cooed at the boy, but she was sad, Katsuhiro could tell.

'We're leaving. The child and I,' he said. 'I've managed to get passage home to the east.'

'How?' she said. She rested her hand on the child's stomach, a protective gesture, the same as Katsuhiro had used himself so many times.

'I don't know. Coincidences. Luck.' He glanced over his shoulder towards the Inner Palace, and its sombre airs. Maybe... He could not countenance that. 'You have to give him back. I'm taking him home.'

She hesitated, then nodded. She let her hand linger, then removed it. Katsuhiro bent low and scooped up his charge. He drew in his soft, infant's scent, and kissed his head.

'I'm sorry,' he said to the boy. 'I'm sorry I had to go.'

He had a thought.

'You can come with me, Elantra. It'll be safe, getting there at least. I have an angel as an escort.'

Her eyes widened.

'A Space Marine?'

'It's a long story,' he said. 'He's the one who gave me the child. Come on, come with me. Help me raise him. I don't mean as a wife or anything like that, it's an honest offer. No conditions attached. I see how good you are with him.'

Her gaze drifted down to the child with tenderness, then back up to Katsuhiro's face.

'Why me?'

'Why not?' said Katsuhiro. 'Do you have anywhere better to be?'

'No.'

'Then come.'

She looked like she might cry. 'So He does protect after all,' she said. 'I heard that, on the line.'

Katsuhiro had once been sure He did. Images of Keeler, the light, the faithful. Simple words of faith throwing back the monsters of the enemy, the great burning wash of grace and terror that had erupted in the Hollow Mountain. There was something there, or someone. Then, all this… The child surviving was a miracle, the chain of events that had led him here almost beyond the scope of coincidence to provide. Surely, some of that had to mean something.

'Perhaps He does,' he said, and almost meant it, but when he looked again towards the north, he felt a shiver run down his spine.

Shiban Khan sat in the pilot's seat of a sleek combat skimmer hovering a few metres in the air. A Javelin, Katsuhiro thought it was called. Its engines growled, making it seem angry and alive. The space beneath danced with dust caught in complex anti-gravitic currents.

Shiban's helmed head looked down at them.

'You said only two. You and the child.'

'Well, now there are three,' Katsuhiro shouted over the noise of the machine. 'We'll fit. I'm sure if that machine of yours can carry two fully armoured members of the Legiones Astartes, it can accommodate two half-starved mortals and a baby.'

The khan grunted in amusement. 'There is a lot of spirit in that small frame, Katsuhiro. You've no fear.'

'I've had enough of fear,' said Katsuhiro. 'Now, are you going to bring that thing down so we can get in, or are you going to sit up there all day?'

The khan shook his head.

'You are a most peculiar man, Katsuhiro.' He depressed a button and the vehicle sank down to the ground.

'I'm surprised you came yourself,' said Katsuhiro, as the Javelin came level with him.

'I said it was a matter of honour,' said Shiban, 'and you are not the only one who wishes to get out of the Palace.'

By now a crowd was gathering. The people kept their distance, and Katsuhiro ignored them. He clambered into the immense seat well of the gunner's station. There was easily enough room for him and Elantra. He took the child off her, and helped her up with his free hand. They sat side by side, legs touching with a companionable warmth. The child reached out a pudgy fist to the angel, and smiled.

'I have your papers. I do not have the woman's,' Shiban said.

'I don't think it matters,' said Katsuhiro.

'I see you named the child,' Shiban said, as he handed over a satchel. Inside were the plastek flimsies confirming Katsuhiro and the child's identity, a little food, and a canteen full of water.

'I didn't name him. The Administratum did,' Katsuhiro said, somewhat sourly.

'It is good that they did. Cole said he needed a name. He was right, and it is a good name they chose for him,' said the White Scar.

Katsuhiro read the flimsy. *Oriens Katsuhiro*, it said.

'Consider keeping it.'

'Why?'

'Because in High Gothic, Oriens means "the dawn". I cannot think of a better name for one such as he.' Shiban bent over the machine's controls. 'Be still. We have a long flight ahead of us.'

The Javelin's engines lifted them into the air. The crowd of upturned faces dwindled into a sea of dots on grey. The air thinned. Katsuhiro worried he would suffocate, but the Space Marine stopped before he rose too high.

A bar of orange light fell over them. Katsuhiro looked west, where a break in the choking dust let the evening sun creep under the pall, so that it hit the broken city, casting shadows across the land. These lengths of blackness crept up and over the debris, like arms, fingers jealously reaching for the warmth of living bodies.

The shadows would not catch Katsuhiro. Shiban was bringing the Javelin around, facing towards the indifferent grey skies of the east. Somewhere, thousands of kilometres away, were the Dragon Nations.

'Oriens,' he said. 'Oriens.' It seemed like the right name.

The child, Oriens, smiled.

Jets choking on the dusty air, the Javelin accelerated and was away over the walls of the Palace, out into the mountains the Emperor had chosen for His eternal seat, then beyond, heading home, heading towards the dawn.

HOMEBOUND

CHRIS WRAIGHT

Maybe she should have felt guilty. She'd felt guilty before, often, but now she couldn't summon anything. The sense of impropriety, that she was alive – again! – when others had been butchered in the trenches, just couldn't be sustained forever. All she retained now was a vague numbness, a cold nothing that rose up from her fingertips and made her heart and lungs ache.

But it wasn't guilt. All those things were for the past now. A chapter in the story had ended violently, closure had finally come. How long had it been, then, in all? The best part of eight years devoted to this grinding horror show. Getting over the finishing line, bruised and bleeding, felt nothing like a victory, because it wasn't, but it was a change. It consigned a great deal to the past, all to be locked away now, shoved out of view. Even more would be buried soon. Layers of earth would be heaped over the bodies, the still-hot gun barrels, the cursed metals and the cursed flesh. The soil would be pushed down by trembling hands, each of them numb like hers, and then those who had witnessed these things would die, the earth would subside and harden, and even the memories would be buried.

When the news came in, the confirmation that the Arch-Traitor was dead, she was standing at her workstation, her thin grey hair loose around her face, hands limp by her sides. Ilya Ravallion, decorated general of the Imperial Army, honoured sage of the V Legion, took in one weak breath, then another. People were moving around her, shakily, feeling their way across the wreckage in the chamber. She paid them no mind. They were lost in their own worlds of shock, unwilling to believe it was over no matter how many urgent comms came in telling them the news. Every pict-lens swam with empty static, useless now. The lumens were down, save for a couple of low-power emergency strips, so it was dark, just as all moments of creation were.

She had wanted him dead. She had wanted his ship to be destroyed before it got to Terra, or blown apart in the opening barrages from the surface. Then she had wanted him to come down to the planet himself so he could be torn apart in front of his own hateful armies. She'd wanted to watch that happen. He'd never come. He'd never set foot on the world he'd sworn to take. His end had come, as it had had to, in the heavens, the realm of gods, not mortals. That made it all seem unreal, like a myth, despite the reality of the blood and the bodies.

So, what now? What was left? What had they saved?

Rumours were still swirling. That the Emperor had died. That He was merely wounded. That Guilliman was here. That the Lion was here, together with the Wolf, poised to reconstruct and to restore.

All those things might have been true; they might not have been. Months would pass before any true certainty arrived. Until then, Terra would be fogbound, a realm of doubt and whispers, a planet frozen by its own psychic agony.

She looked down. She lifted her hands, saw how her fingers

trembled. Each of her nails was bloody, worn down to the quick by nervous biting. The flesh was puckered and dry over the bone. All of a sudden, from nowhere, she had a memory of doing the same thing as a little girl, decades ago now. She had lifted her hands and studied them, caught by random awe at the sight of ten pudgy fingers, all of them hers, stained with the dark earth of her home where she had been grubbing in the topsoil.

Home. A modest house. A yard. Flowers in pots, a cold blue sky above her. She had always meant to return. Always.

Withdraw, she reflected, ruefully. *Then, only then, return.*

A shadow fell over her. A familiar aroma filled her nostrils: the engine-stink of power armour, undercut with dried blood and burnt soil.

She looked up. It was Halji. No, Halji was dead. It was Sojuk. Attentive, diligent Sojuk. So he was alive. Good. Good.

'*Szu,*' he said, using the Legion honorific. His voice was cracked, hoarse, as if he'd been shouting for so long his throat lining had ruptured. 'You are preserved.'

She issued a wry smile. 'Not really. I thought you'd gone out there to die.'

'I expected to.' Sojuk was unhelmed, his forehead a mass of bruises and scabs. 'But there have been surprises.'

'Really?' She looked around her bleakly. 'I don't see any.'

'He is alive, szu.'

Her gaze snapped up. 'What do you mean?'

'I came to get you. To take you to him.'

'Did he ask for me?'

'Can you come? Now?'

Her body ached. Her temples throbbed. She was malnourished, badly dehydrated, sleep-deprived. The final barrages still rang in her ears, hours after they'd stopped. Her pulse felt weak in her veins, because her old heart – and she only had one – was finally on the verge of giving up. If she lay down here, in the tangled detritus of the Rotunda's interior, she could finally close her eyes. She could set her head on the rubble and start to forget about it all. They couldn't ask for more. They'd already asked for more than was humanly possible, and, somehow, she'd given it.

'Take me,' she said, reaching out for his hand. 'Take me there.'

Sojuk knew the way. He had the perfect recall of the Astartes, that innate ability to commit tactical landscapes to memory, and even the ever-disintegrating Palace ruins – now a three-dimensional labyrinth of collapsed foundations, open shafts and crumbling walkways – gave him no trouble. He limped, though. Limped badly. Ilya wondered if he'd taken a wound that even his physiology wouldn't cope with.

After they'd clambered down from the Rotunda's outworks, picking their way through cliffs of rubble and rusting rebar, they started the long slog down into the catacombs. Ilya got a brief view of the Delphic Battlement, just before the arched roofs closed overhead again. Those proud ramparts were high slopes of gravel now, scooped and swept into curves by the wind. It all smelled strongly of carrion. A diamond-shaped patch of sky shone with ongoing chemical fires. After so long being a deafening cacophony, the narrow vista was almost silent now, except for the crackle of the flames and the distant, booming hum of electric storms.

Then they were back into the dark, both of them limping now, ducking under lintels and squeezing along narrow corridors cut into heavily cracked and pitted rockcrete. Sojuk activated his armour's lumens to guide them both, and the hard white pools of light slipped and slithered across bare masonry.

She remembered marching down similar walkways before she'd left Terra for Ullanor, data-slate in hand, heels snapping smartly on polished floors. She remembered staggering through the very same corridors not so long ago, fighting physical and mental agonies after the assault on the Lion's Gate port. They had all been filled with the clamour of military preparation then, bodies moving swiftly past one another, orders shouted. Now the bodies lay still amid the ankle-deep ash. One corpse had a stiff hand outstretched, fingers curled, as if reaching for a hand up, but its hidden face was buried in dust, expression unreadable.

Pride forced her to keep walking, to give away nothing to Sojuk, who could go on forever. She'd have to stop at some point, humiliatingly, sink down into the filth at her feet and take some deep, sour breaths. She gritted her teeth, balled her fists, forced herself to recite the mantras Qin Xa had taught her on the *Swordstorm*.

'We are here, szu,' Sojuk said, startling her out of her reverie.

She squinted in the gloom. This was not the place the two of them had visited before, just after their nerve-flaying journey by Thunderhawk at the height of the final assault. It might have been even further down, sunk far into the thick-layered crusts of civilisational sediment that ran under the Palace's ancient foundations. The stone arches above them, barely clearing Sojuk's head, were worn smooth by winds that had not blown for millennia.

'This is *his* place,' Ilya breathed, referring to the Sigillite. 'Is he here?'

'No. His people do not answer questions about him.'

She guessed the reason why. One of Malcador's Chosen shuffled up to them out of the darkness, still wearing her battle armour.

'Who is this?' she asked, looking doubtfully at Ilya.

'You will let her pass,' Sojuk said, flatly.

'She is of the Legion?'

'Very much so,' Sojuk said.

The woman hesitated, then backed down. 'If you say so, lord,' she said, in a tone of voice that seemed to add *as if it matters any more*.

More Chosen emerged, some robed and cowled, some in

battle dress, all carrying an air of faint dissolution. Ilya and Sojuk were ushered along more interminable rock-cut tunnels, ones that throbbed with geothermal warmth in the deep shadow. Eventually they reached a sealed doorway, and the attendants melted away as silently as they had come.

Ilya looked up at Sojuk. 'You've been inside here?'

'No. You will be the first.'

That was said so casually, as they often did, and yet the gift, the privilege of that… She was a mortal, a mere human, whereas the primarch was a part of them, a continuum of genetics and fealty and brotherhood that defied easy description.

The honours they heaped on her could become oppressive at times, hard to deal with, not that they would ever have known it.

She reached out for the door. The heavy panel swung inwards, revealing a large chamber beyond, bare stone, faint strip lumens, batteries of gently ticking medicae equipment. Cables coiled across a vapour-covered floor like torpid serpents. The place smelled of counterseptic and sorcery.

A single slab dominated the room's centre, an oblong of black stone five metres across and three deep, smooth and dully reflective like smoked glass. A translucent canopy hung over the slab, glowing acid-yellow from some diffuse inner light source. Tubes cobwebbed the canopy like veins, making the fragile covering shiver.

Ilya edged closer. An opening had been cut at one end. The interior of the canopy was filled with a dense fog of the vapour, continually refreshed by outtakes so that it spilled down the sides of the slab in slow-moving cataracts and spread out across the chamber floor.

She instantly recognised the profile of his face silhouetted against the ambient glow. The high forehead, hooked nose, and lean, bony features. He was lying on his back, his eyes open and unfocused. She could hear him breathing, a movement accompanied by the wheeze and tick of mechanical helpers. He had not responded to her approach, but remained totally still, as if locked down in time, a graven image lost amid all the other statues down here, just one more of the Sigillite's discarded relics.

She crouched lower, bringing her head level with his. Sojuk hovered close by, saying nothing. For a long time she stared at the inputs, the cables, anywhere but the shrouded face she had known so well.

'Sage,' he said eventually. His voice was a hoarse hiss, barely audible over the clank of the devices keeping him alive.

'Khagan,' she replied, softly.

She couldn't make out much detail amid the backlit smoke. She caught glimpses of charred-dark flesh, of exposed sinew and flecks of visible bone. He still looked more corpse than man, though he could clearly speak. She saw an eye blink, the halting rise and fall of a cavernous chest.

His bloodshot eye swivelled in her direction. 'He's dead,' the Khan said. 'My brother.'

'He is,' said Ilya. 'Damn him to the hells.'

'I felt it. The loss. Immense. *Immense.*'

His voice cracked as he spoke. Grief. He was grieving. Ilya didn't know what to say to that. How could he possibly feel that way? She wanted to reach out, try to brush away the clouds of condensation that pooled and trickled down his ravaged cheeks, check that it was really him.

'His essence is gone,' he said. 'Destroyed. My father enacted vengeance, in the end. He found the strength for it. I never knew if He really would.'

The Khan was rambling, falling over his words as he struggled to get them out. Perhaps he was still under the influence of sedatives.

'Victory is ours, though,' Ilya said, weakly.

'No, no,' croaked the Khan. 'No victory now. He is destroyed. His soul annihilated. I never knew if He would actually do it.'

Ilya glanced over at Sojuk, who returned a look of quiet alarm.

'So then, are you… recovering?' she asked.

The Khan didn't reply immediately. 'I walked strange paths,' he said, his voice now little more than a whisper. 'I saw the hidden realm. For a time, I was a part of it. I was in it. I searched for him. My brother. And when I couldn't find him, I knew the end had come. So I had to come back.'

It was all about Horus.

'Yes. Your people need you now,' Ilya ventured. 'When you are restored, back to health, they will need you with them again.'

He looked briefly confused, as if he couldn't remember anything about what he had done.

'I am not… what I was,' he mumbled.

What did that mean? That he was weaker? That his role had changed, as everyone's had? Or something more profound, more worrisome?

'You will be,' said Ilya firmly. 'You must be.'

The lone bloodshot eye fixed her again. 'Nothing can be the same now, sage. Nothing. All the more so for those who have crossed the boundary.'

The boundary. Life and death, the fixed border that had been ruptured by the forces unleashed on this world. Once a breach had been established, it would be hard to close again. She found herself wanting to ask much more: what he'd seen, where he'd travelled to, what that meant for the future of them all.

But then his expression changed, a sudden rearrangement of those bloodied, tormented features. He smiled crookedly, and for a moment it was almost back as it had been, as if the two of them were on the *Swordstorm* again.

'I remember when you met us for the first time,' the Khan said. 'You remember it too? On the ship, over Ullanor. I thought you'd pass out when he walked in.'

Despite everything, she smiled at the memory. It felt an age away, part of another reality now, but the shock of meeting a primarch – *two* primarchs – for the first time left its imprint.

'Both of you had that effect,' she admitted. 'Yesugei did try to warn me.'

'Who?'

But that cut her, sudden, like shrapnel to her heart. The Khan, noticing her expression, immediately lost his smile. Then he looked anguished. 'Targutai,' he whispered. 'Of course. It is all so… hard to remember.' His voice trailed away, miserably.

Ilya shuffled closer. She badly wanted to reach out, just touch him, reassure him, even if such intimacy was surely forbidden. 'You *will* remember. It will return. You will recover.'

He looked at her, and said nothing, but the expression was one she had never witnessed on him before. Fear. Terrible, deep-seated fear. That something fundamental had gone, never to return. That he still bore the same name, still possessed his title and his privileges, but that the Deathlord had taken something away that could never be returned.

The price had been high, for what he had done. It could never have been otherwise, not in this galaxy, where every gift given had to be paid for in full, but the full toll was still excruciating.

'You saved your people,' she told him, hoping the words counted for something. 'You brought them deliverance, on Terra, just as you did on Chogoris. You will remember it all, and be yourself again, and lead them again. Believe that.'

He did not reply. His breathing became shallower, his bruised eyelids closed.

Exhaustion had returned. He slipped back into unconsciousness, and across his sarcophagus warning lumens blinked on.

'We must go, szu,' Sojuk urged.

But it was hard to pull away. She knew already this would be the last time she would ever see him. They would never converse again over an evening game of go, never discuss strategy and tactics by the light of candles, never exchange wry asides over the insanities of the Imperial bureaucracy. This was it. The final parting, and yet he was so damaged that she barely knew who she was saying farewell to.

Perhaps, if he had been himself, the parting might have been impossible. The pressure to stay, to rebuild, might have been too much to bear. So maybe this was the way it had to be. A formal renunciation of her commission, a withdrawal, and then keeping the memories intact. What she had before her now was not the Khan. It had been, and maybe in the future it would be again, but for now it was a dream remnant, a half-shadow, spun out of the warp's sudden retreat and still struggling to breathe the real world's air.

'You showed me another world, lord,' she said, her voice cracking a little. 'When you can, return to this one.'

After leaving the medicae chamber, they met another warrior of the Legion coming the other way. Ilya recognised him immediately. Despite all the work done to improve and conceal his augmetics, Shiban Khan's profile had been forever altered by the war. He looked in the very worst shape she'd ever seen, with his white armour now blackened and encrusted in layers of stinking grime. He was helmless, and his heavily scarred face with its tufts of scratchy beard made him look like a wild man stumbling into a village from out of the wastes.

All she had known during her time at the Rotunda was that Shiban had been fighting on, isolated and far from any possible help. No details had made it through after her return to the core. To see him alive, walking, breathing… A grin of pure relief broke out across her face.

'Tachseer,' she burst out, limping towards him.

He took her hands up in his gauntlets, clasped them tight.

'Szu,' he said. 'No one could tell me anything. But this… *Hai.* It gladdens my heart!'

Ilya laughed suddenly, a release of pent-up sorrow and tension. She wanted to hug him, to draw him into her embrace, but even if she could somehow have managed to get her arms across his huge frame he'd never have allowed it.

'How many others?' she asked, meaning the defenders of the port.

Shiban drew in a breath. 'We were tested. Not many.' But then a sly smile. 'We held out long enough. Did what we came for.'

'You did,' she said, with feeling. 'You did, Shiban. They're already telling stories of it. There'll be songs before long. Ever imagine that? Terrans! Terrans, singing about a bunch of savages from the grass!'

Shiban's face darkened. 'But… him? You've been inside?'

'I have. He'll want to see you. You, most of all. But I would wait a while… You should be warned – he's not recovered. He's not himself.'

'In what way?'

'I… don't know. Not yet. Something's changed. How could it not have done?' She shook her head, forced out another smile. 'It will pass. He was *dead*. Of that I'm certain. So it will be difficult. Give it time, though, I urge you. Make no hasty judgements.'

Shiban winced. 'You sound like a Stormseer.'

'I doubt that.' She squeezed his hand. 'It is a new dawn for the Legion. We are the witnesses of it. For those who remain, it may be brighter than we expect.'

'So we will need you. More than ever. Naranbaatar is gone, half the command staff are gone. We are just bones and gristle now.'

Only then did she disentangle her fingers from his. 'No. No, do not make me doubt. I can't.' She looked up at him. 'I wish

I could. I wish I had another twenty years, the strength to get back on a ship again, to finish what we started.' She sighed. 'But look at me. Look at this body. I'm done. There's nothing left. Nothing at all.'

He resisted. Was he surprised? Did he really think he could persuade her? Or was that a kind of politeness? Maybe neither. Maybe just an unwillingness to accept the hard truths.

'The challenge ahead of us will be greater than we have ever known,' he said. 'Everything lies in ruins. We must rearm, rebuild, and swiftly. No one could guide us better than you. We need you.' A look – almost – of yearning. '*I* need you.'

That might even have been true, and so, listening to the flattery, that nagging, treacherous doubt returned. Maybe she could do it. Hold it together, train up a replacement. Just a few months. Put things in order for them before nature finally exacted its delayed price for her continual postponement of the inevitable. She owed them that, and it would prevent all her old work from going to waste, forgotten in the whirl of fresh fighting that would come again soon.

Ilya closed her eyes briefly, allowed herself to smile again.

They are perilous, these people. Their courtesies, their hidden weapons.

'No. I steeled myself against this. The decision has been made, and cannot be changed.' She opened her eyes to look at him squarely. 'Yesugei thought so highly of you, Shiban. They all did, the masters of your Legion. Now you are their inheritor. This is your task.'

They never queried it, when she made her judgements. This time was no different, for all that it clearly pained him. Shiban drew in a long breath. He crossed his arms, stood back, regarded her.

'Then what will you do?' he asked. 'Where will you go?'

'To the place I came from. My home. Terra is my world, and I will see it cleansed of the Traitor's touch.'

'Not alone.'

'I will not take strength away from where it's needed.'

Shiban looked over at Sojuk, who was standing close by. 'You will accompany her,' he ordered. 'Her life in your hands, her blood warded by your blade.'

Sojuk bowed. Ilya almost protested, but a quick glance at Shiban's face told her it would be futile. The indulgence they extended towards her had always been just that: a grant of generosity. At bottom, they were still lords of battle, capable of almost anything, as far above her in capability as the gods were to humanity.

And yet, just then, Shiban bowed to her deeply, took her hand again, and dropped to one knee in the manner of a warrior giving fealty to his warlord.

'It will be remembered. All of it. Know that you have been venerated. You have been *loved*.'

She'd almost avoided the spike of tears – she'd been determined to – but that was too much. This, the second great parting, was harder.

'And I, too,' she said. 'More than I'd ever expected.'

'Then you must go in joy,' Shiban said. 'We have mourned enough. We have grieved enough. We will learn to laugh again now, just as we used to.'

'May that be so,' she said, gripping his hand hard. 'May that truly be so.'

Only then did she leave the Palace.

In normal times, they would have taken a flyer, but there were no flyers left. It proved hard enough to find a ground transport, for most had been destroyed and those few capable of combat operations were still badly needed. In the end, Sojuk managed to unearth a wrecked civilian transport upended in a blast crater. After nearly an hour of work, he was able to coax the machine spirit back to wakefulness, haul it out of the mire, and get the soot-belching engines shaking into noisy life.

Ilya clambered up into the cab. She was wearing an environment suit, full rebreather. The back of the transport was filled with all the supplies they'd been able to find at short notice. They hadn't hunted too hard for those. Starvation would soon raise its head over the ruins, even if the incoming loyalist supply fleets got here soon, so they'd taken the minimum they judged necessary.

She already felt nauseous as she settled in, her stomach empty and her head light. Her emotions fizzed, making her fragile and morose. She shuffled back against the hard seat, took a pill from her rapidly diminishing stash, let Sojuk take responsibility for driving. Through the smeary forward viewers she watched what was going on around them: the few survivors emerging from their bunkers and standing around in twos and threes, gazing in stupefaction at the extent of the devastation. Ilya had been told that serious work was already going on in the heart of the Sanctum Imperialis, and that the advance units of the incoming reinforcements had gone there first to shore it up. The entire structure was in danger of collapse, she understood, and tens of thousands of people were still working inside its essential control chambers. On the surface, though, the whole place looked abandoned, an ancient set of crumbling monuments amid a static ocean of blasted stone. Above them, the storm clouds still boiled, no longer ruptured with orbital las-fire but messy and lurid from the backwash of fires. Her chrono told her it was mid-morning, though it looked like dusk in winter, and probably would do so forever now.

'Ready?' Sojuk asked, preparing to test out the transport's doubtful powers.

She was. This was the correct path now, for all the pain of it. She thought back to the Khan, for so long her master, buried under kilometres of earth, clawing his way back to a new life.

She thought of Shiban, with the weight of reconstruction ahead of him. She thought of the survivors at the port, of Jangsai Khan in particular, whom she dearly hoped had lived to see another age. They all had wars still to fight, and would have to summon the strength for them soon. Hers, though, at last, was over.

'Ready,' she replied, biting back the tremor in her voice.

Sojuk started the engines. The ignition spluttered, kicked, then thrummed into life. Then they were moving, slowly, skidding over the treacherous terrain, heading north.

It took them a long time to reach the Palace's nominal boundaries. Ilya gazed out of the viewers for a while, but soon became dispirited. The old gaudy complexity of the vast city-world had been reduced down to grinding tedium: kilometre after kilometre of undifferentiated wreckage, gently smouldering like slowly cooling lava. Under every levelled block festered hundreds of thousands of bodies, a hot stew of decomposition that would soon bring plague in its wake. The greater majority would be humans just like her, defenders and attackers alike, subject to two different species of delusion, now destined to rot away into the undercrofts of their origin world together.

Some sights were striking. She saw a Stormbird gunship suspended between the teetering flanks of two skeletal hab-towers, its earthward plummet arrested as it wedged between them, nose down. It was still on fire somehow, a crackling torch held a hundred metres from the ground, placed there like a warning. She saw headless Titans in the distance, a whole phalanx of them, static and shrouded in roiling clots of mist. She saw the immense carcass of a void-going ship that had crashed over an industrial area, and marvelled at the inferno that landing must have kindled. The entire district was a colossal cat's cradle of black spars and gaping thruster housings, as silent and wind worn as everything else.

The going was slow. All transitways were blocked, or pitted with craters, or lost under the deep tides of rubble. Sojuk drove hard where he could, at times scaling steep slopes of scree before sliding and skidding down the far side. It was an oddly natural landscape, like a stone desert that had existed undisturbed for millennia. No sign of any living thing – no warriors, no civilians, no animals. For a theatre of war that had been teeming just weeks ago, filled from horizon to horizon with the largest armies ever assembled in human history, the emptiness of it now was astounding.

'Where did they all go?' she murmured to herself as the transport laboured. 'Were they really here at all?'

'Oh, they were here,' grunted Sojuk darkly.

All the same, the landscape became increasingly dreamlike. Smoke rolled across the ruination endlessly, thick and tox-heavy, snagging on the edges of eyeless buildings before wafting back into the heights. Burned-out military vehicles littered the terrain like the discarded shells of enormous crustaceans. At times Ilya thought she caught strange noises on the wind, like screams, or maybe laughter.

Night fell before they reached the city's edge. Sojuk drove on through while Ilya drowsed fitfully, her head jerking up whenever the transport's wheels snagged on an obstacle. The light slid out of the turbulent sky, turning an ash-grey horizon a deep unbroken black. In the extreme west, lightning forks flickered, white-silver flashes that briefly exposed the jagged ruin-profile, but otherwise it felt like tunnelling back into the world's core.

Ilya awoke just before dawn. Sojuk stopped the transport and she stiffly dismounted. He was on edge the whole time, unwilling for her to leave his eyeline, but she had human requirements – and a need for privacy – that he didn't. He was happier when she was back at the transport again, chewing weakly at a carb bar and sipping from one of the canisters.

Travelling was tough; she felt worse than she had for weeks. The adrenaline that had kept her on her feet, just about, during the siege itself was dissipating fast.

'Close to the edge yet?' she asked.

'The scanners are malfunctioning,' Sojuk said, doubtfully. 'But yes. One more day, then out onto the plains. You will have to guide me after that.'

That might be hard. It had been years since she'd been anywhere close to the old lands, the oblasts of her youth. Every trip she'd ever taken down to the Himalazian heartlands after that had been by flyer, and summoning up cartographs was impossible now. Still, it was possible some of the big multi-lane transit corridors were intact, as well as the cities that had spread steadily across the high plains. It should be possible to orientate via those, even if they were ruins too. Her memory was still good, at least her long-term memory. That was almost the last thing she felt she could rely on now.

They set off again. Ilya let Sojuk drive – he could do so for hours at a stretch without tiring. She attempted to stay awake herself, but struggled as the hours passed. At times it felt as though she was drifting through a semiconscious fever, punctuated by brief interludes where a jolt would force her to open her eyes, stare out at the world beyond, before lapsing back into an uneasy reverie.

Eventually, the transport crawled its way to the remains of the Palace's great northern wall systems. Sections of the structure were still intact, rearing up into the haze like geological features, their outer flanks shorn cleanly to expose honeycomb innards. Quagmires of broken masonry and metal still glowed hot from the munitions employed to break the outer perimeter, and the air crackled with electrostatic. Bodies were plentiful here at least, or pieces of them, lying out in the open pressed up against one another, piled high, loyalist and traitor alike, dotted with the larger wrecks of attack walkers and troop carriers. Every surface was coated in a thin film of sooty black.

'Bastion Ledge,' Ilya said, grimly, squinting up at the profile of the high parapets. 'I didn't even know they'd broken through here.'

Sojuk regarded it dispassionately. He stopped the engines, got out, stalked over to some troop carriers. He came back with armfuls of power packs, some ammunition magazines, a couple of water canisters. 'I detected movement,' he said, starting the ignition and slamming the cab door. 'Not everything is dead.'

They pushed on, grinding over the heaps of corpses, shoving their way through old barricades. Even once free of the wall-line, the crowded landscape of limbs and torsos still stretched off into the distance, punctuated by derelict Titans and artillery pieces. The transport travelled for fifty kilometres, Ilya reckoned, without the wheels touching dirt, just churning up the desiccated remains of the infantry hordes. The survivors, when they got here, would have to burn these corpse fields. Was there enough promethium left in the reserves for that? The entire plateau would be like this now. The soil of the future, all of it rad-scarred and phage-rich.

Night fell again before they cleared the traitor rearguard zones. As the last sunlight died, Ilya caught sight of some big troop landers, the vast ships that had made planetfall out of the range of the Palace wall guns to unload their cargo. The ridged spines of the storeyed crew compartments towered a hundred metres into the dusk half-light, immense and empty, like tombs built for impossible giants, before slipping behind them again and dissolving into the gathering dark.

Sojuk kept going. He was steady, implacable, pushing them onwards without pause or mistake. Ilya fell asleep again, this time deeply. Getting out of the Palace seemed to trigger something within her, some kind of release valve, and after losing consciousness she didn't even dream.

* * *

When she next awoke, it was still dark.

'How long was I out?' she murmured, blearily.

'All night, all day,' replied Sojuk, smiling. 'We have made progress.'

She rubbed her face, stretched out, gingerly pushed her aching body higher up in the seat. Looking out of the viewports, she saw that the city was long behind them. The landscape was empty and featureless in all directions, a true desert now, stony, pale under the night sky, free of vegetation. The cloud cover was less complete here, exposing a couple of diamond-like stars between the drifting shrouds. Portions of an old transitway – a fifty-metre-wide ribbon of asphalt – still lingered in broken patches, and Sojuk threaded a path along the extant passages. A cluster of immense fuel pipes ran parallel alongside them, breached at regular intervals, and Ilya could smell the acrid tang of spilled promethium.

'Signs of life?' she asked, peering out into the night.

'Not much.' Sojuk adjusted the controls, keeping the speed steady. 'The outer cities are dark. Maybe bombarded, maybe evacuated.'

Ilya nodded. She remembered some of the early transmissions, back before the orbital barrage had made comms beyond the Palace almost impossible to pick up. The tributary cities of the high plains had been planning to hold out for as long as they could, even to open second fronts once the traitors had made planetfall. Some regiments of the Army had been stationed for that very purpose, though if any counter-attacks had been launched they had certainly failed. Most likely those urban zones had been overrun in the first few days, reduced to playgrounds for the millions of murder-hungry troops waiting for their summons to the main prize. It wouldn't have been good, to have ended up stuck there. Not good at all.

'Can we stop, just for a moment?' she asked.

Sojuk's eyes narrowed. 'This is exposed. Not a good place.'

'Do you expect to find a good place soon?'

He thought about that, then pulled the transport to the ragged edge of the old transitway. 'Quickly, please.'

Ilya pushed open the door and stiffly clambered down. The air was cool here and smelled less foul than in the Palace. She limped towards the transport's rear end, trying to get some blood moving through her system. Her joints protested, her hands started to shake. She reached for the canteen at her belt, and unscrewed the cap with trembling fingers.

The wind was howling down from the line of dark mountains to the south, and her loose hair flapped around her face. Nothing much to stop the gales here, not for hundreds of kilometres, just like the country she'd been raised in. She drank, and the cold water quelled the worst of her shakes. She closed her eyes, listening to the howl again for a moment. It felt like it was all around her. Closer than it should have been. She opened her eyes again, and saw a dozen pairs staring back at her from the dark.

'Sojuk!' she shouted, scrabbling back towards the cab.

The eyes moved, leaping out of the murk, bounding towards her, turning into heavy silhouettes of animals.

Ilya ran, almost reaching the cab, the scatter of paws on scree in her ears, the hot panting of canid breath on her back, imagining the inevitable leap, jaws agape. She wouldn't make it. She twisted around, back to the transport's edge, fumbling for her blade.

They had once been dogs – strays, or even pets. Now they were changed, engorged, their skin split open, their eyes wide and rolling. Spines had erupted along their backs, claws from their pads. Their hides were skin-pale and glistening, their flayed muscles obscenely bulked out.

The first one leapt at her; she flailed clumsily with her knife.

The creature yowled, jerking away and crashing into the side of the transport, before dropping low and growling, coming again more carefully.

Except that Ilya hadn't touched it, she hadn't got close. Sojuk was there, silent out of the dark, pulling her back and shielding her with his body. His own blade dripped with blood. The pack closed in on them both, limping and lurching, a misshapen gaggle of hideous, famished mutants driven into the empty lands to starve.

Another one leapt and Sojuk lashed out, severing its bulbous head and sending the heavy body crashing to the ground. He pushed Ilya up the cab steps, then lunged back into the gathering pack, laying into them and killing two more. Ilya, breathing heavily, palms sweaty, reached over to the engine controls and got them going. The howling got worse. More were coming.

She grabbed the control column and the transport began to move. Sojuk scrambled up through the open door and slammed it shut behind him. As he did so, one of the canids pounced, hitting the armaglass and raking it with its claws. Ilya had a brief, freeze-frame vision of manically snapping jaws against the pane, bloody eyes, vivid pink flayed flesh.

Then it fell away. The transport picked up speed. For a while the howls kept pace, but after a few minutes of pursuit the creatures lost ground. Ilya had her foot on the accelerator the whole time, bouncing and jarring across the pitted terrain. Her fists clenched the controls hard, painfully hard, and she found it difficult to breathe.

Sojuk reached across to her, gently, placing his gauntlet on her shoulder. 'They are gone,' he said. 'Please, a little less speed. You will crack an axle.'

He was right. The transport was already battered, and she was smashing it around badly. She couldn't stop. She couldn't relax, her limbs were rigid, her jawline tight.

Slowly, slowly, she got herself under control. The transport's crashing progress slowed, and the engine whine fell back into the normal range. She forced her shoulders back, her muscles to unclench.

'They were horrible,' she muttered.

'Left behind,' Sojuk said. 'I do not think they will last long.'

Ilya snorted. 'Maybe they will. Maybe they're the only thing that will.' Her panic was turning to anger. 'These places had been *tamed*. It's all gone. It's all ruined. It's all–'

Again, the gentle pressure of a hand on her shoulder. 'They were remnants. They will not endure.'

Ilya tried to listen. For some reason, she didn't want to hear it. She found herself wanting to wallow in the grief for a moment, to give in to it, to believe that it had all been for nothing, that everything had been a waste and an exercise in folly. 'Where are the people?' she demanded. 'Where are the *people*?'

'The people will return.' Sojuk never raised his voice. He was just like they always were, damn them – reasonable, measured. 'The cities will be remade.'

She couldn't maintain her fury for long; fatigue returned too quickly. Once the cortisol drained from her system, the old ailments and the nausea reasserted themselves, dragging her back into the state of resigned weakness she loathed.

Someone, in time, would have to plan out the purging and resettlement of these places. Someone would have to coordinate the demolition teams and the construction crews, manage the logistics of supply and migration, liaise with the incoming repopulation fleets. Whoever it was, they wouldn't do it as well as she would have done. They wouldn't have the attention to detail that she did. Things would be lost. Mistakes would be made.

She found herself wishing she'd never lived to see the prospect. To glimpse the problem, and be too decrepit to address it. That was worse than ignorance.

She sighed, concentrated on what she was doing, on the broken road twisting off into the night, a patchwork of asphalt blocks picked out by the transport's weak lumens.

'Why am I even going back?' she murmured, half to herself. 'It's just a city. Just a house. I don't even know who lives in it any more, I lost touch years ago. Why do it?'

'Because it is the right thing to do,' said Sojuk. 'Because it is honourable, after all you have achieved. And because you wished it, and deserve to have that wish fulfilled.'

She blurted out a laugh, suddenly amused by that. 'Or maybe just stupid,' she said.

'Maybe,' said Sojuk. 'If so, though, you have earned the right to be.'

She glanced over at him. 'Do you feel the grief of it, Sojuk?' she asked. 'All that we've lost?'

He paused for a while. She knew just what he was thinking of – the last days, out beyond the Delphic Range, the fighting he never spoke about – and regretted the question.

'I do, szu. Very often.'

'You don't show it.'

'When I have a blade. Then it shows.'

She nodded. 'We should be glad the time for that is over, then.'

He said nothing in response to that. For all that, Ilya knew what he was thinking.

It is not over. It will never be over now.

She kept driving.

Days passed, one after the other in numbing succession, and the landscape barely changed. These regions had always been empty, even during the great population boom of Terra's recent history. They were wide, flat, featureless places, traversed at speed by travellers, traders or armies looking for somewhere more amenable to linger. Even after Unification, when so much of the planet's long-tormented terrain had been cleansed and placed back into productive life, these vast highlands had never become crowded. Their few cities were clustered around natural resources, and resembled enormous manufactories rather than natural settlements. You could still see their decaying hulks on the eastern horizon from time to time, slowly rusting away as the storm clouds raced above them.

The road took them very close to one such place. Sojuk hadn't found a way to bypass it, so they drove through the outskirts, keeping their speed up, watchful for threats. Ilya looked up and around as they travelled under the enormous labyrinths of pipework and scaffolding. The place had the look of an ore-processing module, something the Mechanicum would have laid out to standard templates – core workforce of a few hundred thousand, a support population maybe three times that. The once-booming forges were silent, the furnaces empty and the conveyer belts static. Catastrophic damage was evident all around – an absolute hurricane of artillery must have been unleashed to wreck it so completely. The desert gravels had started to filter in from the outside, running up against the corroded walls in shifting piles. Partly mummified corpses littered every unsheltered area, their exposed skin wax stiff. One zone must have been hit with some kind of arcane chem-weaponry, freezing an entire mob of terrified civilians in place even as they ran. The transport passed close by them, and Ilya couldn't resist looking at their expressions, still intact after months: fear, panic, horror, even anger. Men, women, children clutching toys, thousands of them, locked in position until the city fell apart around them and the sand reclaimed it all at last.

'Did the Legions come this far out?' she asked Sojuk. 'The traitors, I mean.'

He looked uncertain. 'I do not know. I saw reports of the Third leaving the walls. They must have gone somewhere.'

Ilya shuddered. Of all the Legions to be let loose on civilians, they might have been the very worst. 'Maybe Traitor Mechanicum.'

'Possible. They would have relished destroying these places.'

Likely no one would ever know. A small atrocity, in the scheme of things, one that would be erased by the elements long before reclamation squads made it here. Still, the faces were all individual. The families clutching one another's hands, the fathers reaching out for sons, the mothers cradling daughters. They had a monument to their suffering at least, as grotesque as it was.

The transport passed back out onto the open road, and Sojuk carried on tracing out the long north-west road, keeping the mountains to the south, heading further and further away from the Palace.

As the long hours passed, Ilya found her grip on reality start to slip. She flitted in and out of wakefulness again. On one occasion she was sure that it was Shiban sitting next to her, as if they were back on the bridge of the *Swordstorm*. On another, she thought she was back on Ullanor in the transport she'd taken to find Yesugei. She knew all those things had happened, but could no longer be sure in exactly what order.

'I find it harder and harder to tell the difference,' she muttered.

Sojuk glanced at her. 'Between what?'

'The real and the unreal,' she said. 'The ghosts and the living.'

'I am real,' he said. He thumped the dashboard. 'This is real. As are you.'

Ilya smiled sadly, feeling an exhausted sleep coming for her again. 'For a little while, Sojuk. A little while.'

When the towers crested the forward horizon, she recognised them at once. They were grim hab-blocks, rectangular slabs of cheap rockcrete, but they had been home, and they gave her a sudden pang of familiarity. She shuffled upright, peering through the viewport.

'There it is,' she said.

Sojuk kept driving, watchful as ever. He had been doing so for days with only the scantest breaks for rest. His endurance was phenomenal – uncomplaining, solid, remorseless.

The outskirts drew closer. Ilya recognised it all: the moisture traps on the outer limits, crumbling and paint-flaked; the big water towers; the hydroponic gardens with their fraying plastek films. Orchards had lined the roads in the old days, and the trees still lingered amid the rubble and rubbish, overgrown and untended, but alive. Like everywhere else they had passed, signs of combat were plentiful: bullet-pocked walls, belongings strewn across roads, empty vehicles overturned on the edges of cratered roads. Here, though, it didn't look quite as bad as other places. This was a long way from anywhere, so far from strategic targets that an enemy would have had to be particularly determined, or badly lost, to have gone for it.

The transport crossed the boundary, rumbled down deserted streets. Empty windows looked out at them from the tenements on either side. One of the public announcement boards had got stuck in a loop, flashing its warning message over and over in faded phosphor dots: *The Traitor Has Landed. All Civilians To Designated Evacuation Points. The Traitor Has Landed. All Civilians…*

'They didn't fight?' she mused, resting her chin on her hand.

Sojuk shrugged. The administration of the isolated stretches hadn't been a priority. 'They could not hold everywhere.' His voice gave away a certain disappointment, though.

Ilya pursed her lips unhappily. It wasn't as if she'd have known anyone here any more – it had been decades since she'd been home, and she had no family to come back to. Still, some evidence of resistance would have been nice.

In the event, they found that soon enough. The centre of the city was dominated by its administrative core, a monolithic dome of rockcrete with a black-green patina creeping up the exterior. Decomposed bodies lay in clumps all around its blasted walls, clustered around barricades and piles of sandbags. A few fixed artillery pieces still looked functional, but otherwise the destruction was ruinous. The dome itself had been ruptured by missile fire, and its cracked curve gaped like an enormous black-toothed mouth.

Sojuk ran a scan. 'This was months ago,' he said, sweeping the auspex around him. 'No active signals remain. The attackers have moved on.'

Ilya nodded. So at least some of them had tried to hold what they had. It had never been much, but the fact of it made her feel a little better. She wondered who had come for them – dregs from the traitor rearguard, most likely. Deserters, rampaging across a world largely stripped of its defences in favour of the Palace. Maybe the marauders had kept on going, burning a path towards softer and softer targets, or maybe they'd been stopped somewhere. She hoped so.

She looked up at the heavily damaged buildings around them, tried to get her bearings. 'We need to push on,' she said. 'Past the dome, into the hab-zones beyond. I can find it from there.'

Sojuk pushed the controls and the transport rumbled over the wreckage. They soon moved back into a suburban sprawl of low-rise buildings, though this time the hab-clusters looked a little better built, a little cleaner. These places had had gardens, some of which were already bursting at the seams from overgrowth, sending foliage spilling up and over the cracking hardstanding. Save for the plentiful, wind-dried corpses, the smell and the occasional ruin, it might have been anywhere in post-Unity Terra – modest, decent.

When they finally reached the street she'd been born in, and she caught sight of the old house, Ilya's hand flew to her mouth. She hadn't expected it to hit her so hard. For a vivid moment she had the same vision she'd had at the Rotunda. She was a young girl again, playing in the dusty road with the rest of them, her cheeks dirty but flushed, her eyes squinting against an old sun, long before careers and wars and travels into the void.

The place was still standing, at least, though many of the lots around it were fire-damaged. It was a single-storey unit, an old-style prefab dwelling set in a square yard and surrounded by a low wall. The neatness she remembered had largely gone – it was now overgrown, the render cracked and falling off in slabs. Metal gates hung from their hinges, exposing the uneven path up to the open doors. It had clearly been deserted for a long time. The family who had lived here after Ilya had left for the Palace would have cleared out with the rest of the evacuees, assuming they'd survived the fighting. She didn't know their names or anything about them; they were just transient episodes in a long story, hopefully carrying on somewhere else.

Sojuk halted the transport. Gingerly, with a buzzing in her ears both from fatigue and the constant drone of the transport's engines, Ilya got down from the cab, limped up to the gate. Sojuk came with her, saying nothing. The two of them passed inside, up some steps to a veranda, then through double doors and into a low-ceilinged living chamber. The place had been ransacked – the furniture pulled apart and clothes strewn over the wooden floor. An old vid-projector lay smashed in the corner, and more doors leading further inside hung from their hinges. A standard-issue image of the Emperor and His eighteen sons in a cheap plastek frame had hung on the facing wall – it had done so for as long as Ilya could remember – but it was on the floor now, the glass cracked. Someone had scrawled over the old mount unintelligibly. It might have read *Damn them all*, or maybe *Help us all*. It was hard to tell.

She reached for one of the chairs, pulled it upright and sat in it. Sojuk watched her.

'This is the place?' he asked, carefully.

She looked up at him. A whole stew of emotions boiled within her. She felt at once young again, and older than ever. It smelled the same. Despite all the wreckage, the general fug of decay that hung over the city, the long occupancy of people she didn't know, she could still smell the old aromas: fabrics, polish on the floor, engine oil from the generators in the rear yard.

She had begun to doubt on the journey. Whether it was worth all the effort. Whether it meant anything. Whether the gesture, such as it was, was entirely pointless, just a piece of indulgence that she'd regret. Now, though... Now, the old place seemed to shrink comfortably around her, just as her own body was shrinking. Unlike the vast sarcophagus of the Palace, gigantic even in its ruin, this was more her size. And it was still here, just as she was, clinging on, battered, the outer shell ravaged but the heart still beating.

'It is the place,' she said, leaning her head against the chair's frame. 'Throne, at last. It is the place.'

Sojuk moved the transport some distance away, hiding it from prying eyes and taking all the supplies from its hold. Between them, they cleared the worst of the rubbish from the hab's living chambers. Ilya got tired very quickly, frequently having to sit, panting weakly, as Sojuk did all the work. It was faintly ludicrous to watch him, with his heavy battle armour still on, picking up scraps of clothing or broken furniture and neatly stacking it all up for her to go through. She wondered what he really thought of it. Only days ago, he'd been fighting a battle of vengeance in the heart of a living hell, the war to end all wars where the fates of new-cast gods and devils were being determined. Now he was looking after an old woman on the edge of the world, stooping under her low lintels, bumping his outsized shins against the room's flimsy paraphernalia.

He only hesitated once, when taking out the dagger Qin Xa

had given her years ago. That was one of the very few relics of the war she'd had the time and inclination to bring with her from the desolation. Perhaps he thought it inappropriate for her to be carting something so precious around. She didn't really see why. It had never been drawn, and was virtually the only physical link she now had to her life in the Legion.

'Put it on the case, over there,' she told him, pointing across the room. 'It will remind me of better times.'

Later, as evening fell, the two of them sat together on the veranda. As the light reduced, the rows of tenements started to blend into the grey-blue of the desert beyond. Sojuk had arranged a couple of portable lumens, strung from the veranda's ceiling and swinging against the ever-present whine of the wind.

'We are running low on supplies,' he told her, standing at her side. 'I will need to go into the city at first light.'

He attempted to hide it, but he was very weary. Weeks of non-stop fighting against the worst enemies imaginable, followed by days of unbroken wakefulness carrying deep wounds, had taken its toll even on him.

'I'm grateful, Sojuk,' Ilya said, pulling a blanket around her shoulders. It would get cold soon, and they would both need to sleep. 'I'd never have made it.'

Sojuk bowed. 'You say that. I think you would have found a way.'

She smiled wryly. Always with the compliments. 'So, what now for you? Your duty is done here.'

'I will stay.'

'Shiban will want you back.'

'He ordered me to ward you.' He left the rest unspoken: *until the end.*

Ilya took a sip of water from the canister she'd carried with her. 'And after that? Things will change.'

Sojuk looked equivocal. 'The Khagan will rule.'

She shivered slightly – the shock of seeing his alteration hadn't faded. Maybe his gene-progeny would be blind to it, once the Khan recovered. Perhaps it wouldn't matter. Or perhaps it would alter everything. It felt very strange, knowing that it would all take place without her.

'We used to speculate,' she said. 'In the Departmento. About what would come for the Legions as the crusade ended. I doubted anything would happen because the primarchs were so powerful. Even then, it was hard to imagine imposing anything on the expeditionary fleets. But now... I really don't know.'

'We may go back to Chogoris,' Sojuk said. 'The oath was fulfilled.'

'You might, and it was. But would you be allowed that luxury?' She shook her head, doubtful. 'They were lenient with you before. They could afford to be. Now it's about survival. They will not want to lose control of one of the few Legions they still have here.'

'The Khagan will not be compelled.'

'No, maybe not. But there is more than one primarch on Terra, and they're only nominal equals. Watch for Guilliman, would be my advice. The Wolf has no desire to control anything, and the Lion was always too busy with his own world's intrigues. Guilliman, though, he's a man after my own heart. An organiser. A builder of systems. If the Emperor fails to speak again, watch that one.'

'I shall pass on the advice.'

'Do. Look, you were a shambles when I first came among you. Don't slip back now.' Her expression became more serious. 'It could all fall apart. It's a dangerous time, just after the guns fall silent. You have few natural allies on the Throneworld, despite all your heroics. I wouldn't like to see you swallowed up by them, your identity lost. That will be the instinct – to impose control, to erase the past. Fight it. Maybe the new masters of the Imperium will be wiser than those who commanded us, but I fear the best are gone now.'

Sojuk folded his arms. 'Or it may be better. Renewal may come. Things were not perfect before.'

Ilya sighed. 'They were not. Anything is possible. Still.' She trailed away. Every part of her ached. Her forehead felt hot, and she guessed she had another fever coming. 'I'll do my best to write down my thoughts on how the bureaucracy works. You can take them back with you. You'll have to work with the politicians, the power brokers. You'll need the tools. Your tulwars won't frighten them.'

Sojuk looked at her tolerantly. 'Szu, we have just arrived. You need to rest. These things can wait until some strength returns.' He looked up, over to the west, where the sun was sliding below the horizon and embossing the churning clouds with grey-pink. In the evening haze the worst of the damage to the urban structure was obscured, and the distant peaks were traced with slivers of intense gold. 'I like this place. It has a good sky.'

Ilya let her head fall back, giving in, her dry lips twitching with a smile.

'You're right. It does.'

The next few days passed in a strange kind of companionability. Ilya, when her strength allowed, did what she could to put the house in order. For all that it had been inhabited by strangers for so long, very little of substance had changed. She would surprise herself to enter a room and have a memory of long ago immediately pulled into her mind: a gesture, a word, a laugh, an injury. At times she almost expected to hear her mother shuffle out of the hallway to nag her about getting married and giving her grandchildren, or her father grumble about the draft for the Army stripping the young from the city or ask for help with the maintenance of the cold-frames. She remembered the day she'd buried both of them, just weeks apart, in the municipal cemetery on the city's edge. She remembered how that had hollowed her out, made her feel more alone than she'd ever felt, and how after that the house had seemed both too big and too small. Too big for a single soul, too small for the ideas that had already clustered in her active mind.

So she had left. Studied for the Army exams, travelled five hundred kilometres away to the regional proving centre. She was older than the average, but progressed quickly. All those memory tests her father had instilled into her, all those mathematical treatises he'd forced her to plough through, proved their worth then. Progression up through the ranks felt as easy as anything. It had been rapid, painless, and she'd loved the work. The old house was swiftly forgotten, lost in a welter of troop planning and ledger creation. The stars had to be conquered. The race into the void had to be won. In time, she'd left Terra entirely, never once regretting it, marvelling at the beauty and the splendour of her new life, the shimmer of the galactic swirl against the deep dark, the fires in the abyss, the glittering fleets and the alien worlds.

And now she was back, and it all felt like a sham. A huge wrong turning, one that she should have seen coming. Who would have thought that the void-ships she'd travelled on – so colossal and unbreakable – were all destroyed now, whereas this little house was intact? It had been here the whole time, cradling the smells and sights of her earliest days, keeping them ready for her return.

She might have relished it more had the pain been less. She tried to hide the worst of it from Sojuk, who would only fuss, but she slept more than she waked now, and even hobbling out into the yard to feel some weak sun on her face took up most of her energy. Her lungs were tight, a result of all the toxic air she'd breathed in during her time in the Palace bunkers. Maybe the filth from the Lion's Gate space port had pushed her a little further down the slide. The corruption there had been worse than anything she'd ever experienced during the worst of the fighting to get back to Terra.

So she sat more than she'd have liked and walked even less. She ate less too, and drank less. Some cleaning up was done, but most was left to Sojuk. She found some old bulbs in her father's ramshackle shed, and spent a long and exhausting afternoon clearing the dust-covered earth and planting them in a row. Sojuk had wanted to help her, but she'd shooed him away.

'I can do this *one* thing,' she'd snapped, angrier at herself and her decay than at him.

For his part, Sojuk did his own recovering. He found medicae supplies from somewhere, some tinned rations, a source of purified water. Astartes were astonishing things. Given just a little time and a few calorific inputs, his wounds seemed to fade away into nothing. She often wondered if he was keeping in touch with the Palace somehow, even though the range was great and all the comms networks were down. He would have to go back soon. It was still amazing to her that Shiban had even countenanced his absence for so long, but then the Scars had always been generous to a fault.

She did not venture much into the city itself. Sojuk told her a little about it – that the emptiness appeared to be complete, that all the fighting had taken place a long time ago and no one appeared to have come back. On the few occasions she limped out of the front door and walked along the street, the echoing silence unnerved her. The stench of death was harder to ignore somehow, and the rapid erosion of the environment made her despondent. It had been a tidy place, once. Nothing glamorous, far from the bright centres, but the streets had been clean and the dwellings well kept.

The nights were worse. Strange noises were carried by the wind, just as had happened all the way along the journey. She had dreams about the feral canids, and feared they would follow the scent. She had dreams about the siege, especially the terrible last few days in the Rotunda, and woke often covered in freezing sweat. When she dreamed of the Khan, though, the images were all from the earlier days, before the war had really started, when he had been vital and imposing and alive. Those had been the best days, the ones that had been so busy that she'd barely slept, filled with an almost febrile level of discovery and enchantment. For a scant few moments, sunk within those dreams, the old reality was back, the one she had felt, at the time, would last forever.

As the days went on, Sojuk began to become increasingly concerned for her welfare. She felt the rapid weakening herself, but it no longer bothered her. What could she do? She sat in the yard as much as she could, blankets heaped over her even in the faint grey sunlight, and watched for germination from the bulbs. Sojuk told her he'd seen contrails from aircraft a few times, far to the south, but at least it was evidence of activity. He'd picked up signals from land vehicles too, but too far for him to investigate. A convoy, he had thought, but they hadn't been interested in the city, and he couldn't tell where they were headed.

Little else punctuated her fading existence, just the ancient rhythms of light and dark, wakefulness and forgetting. She began to feel primordial. Nothing to do, nowhere to go, just a state of being, herself alone, everything else stripped away.

'Turning to stone,' she murmured. 'Just like everything else.'

Days later, some warmth returned. The cloud cover was sporadic, and patches of wan light speckled the ruins. The vegetation continued to grow, pushing up the asphalt into liquid-like ripples, prising apart cinderblock foundations. It was all already beginning to look parched, but maybe rain would come soon. Who knew what the weather systems were doing now, or how they would develop. Life would find a path, in one way or another.

Ilya woke from one of her shallow naps. She blinked, waiting for the room around her to come into focus. It took her a while to remember what was going on. Sojuk had gone out again some time ago, to collect more water, she thought. She had the place to herself. Again.

She tried to lift herself, felt shooting pain in her arms and chest. Stiffly, she pulled upright, shuffled to the lip of the chair's seat. The room around her was dark, the blinds lowered, though thin strips of sunlight peeped in around the edges.

An odd smell wafted in from somewhere. Sojuk had cleared the corpses from the nearest hab-blocks, but the city still reeked when the wind dropped. Ilya sniffed. This one was foul, far worse than usual. Maybe something had got into the old cistern.

She got up awkwardly, rooted around for her stick, hobbled towards the rear doorway. As she did so, she heard a low machine grind: a whisper-soft purr of ancient servos, damaged and erratic. She turned her head, and saw the light strips under the blind interrupted. Something heavy was moving in front of the windows, coming for the front door.

'Sojuk?' she asked, tensing. She knew the sound of power armour, the way it moved, but the smell was getting worse.

Then the door opened, and a monster came in.

Even in her diminished state, despite all the corrosion and mutation of the battle plate, she instantly recognised the sigils. III Legion. Fulgrim's sense-addled degenerates. The monster was huge, as they all were, barely squeezing under the door frame. Its armour was incomplete, some plates missing, some fused with fat-pale flesh that rippled unnervingly around the edges. Scraps of other unfortunates' skin hung from rivets and spikes, flecked with dark bloodstains. The monster was helmless, and its ruined face peered, birdlike, into the gloom. It had no eyes. Its ears had been sewn shut. Its mouth was only loosely human, crammed full of curved needle-thin teeth and with a lacertine black tongue.

A few scraps of thin hair clung to an otherwise naked scalp. It carried no weapon, but its gauntlets had been refashioned into cutting tools. It stank of perfume, chems and rotting flesh.

It turned its eyeless head towards her, sniffed, smiled.

'I came this way before,' it said. Its voice was like tangled steel pulled across glass. 'No one was left. I ate this city. I ate it all. Then how are you here?'

Ilya could hardly breathe. The creature filled up the entire space, dominating the tiny chamber, looking almost as if it might keep swelling until it squeezed her up against the walls.

It took a step towards her. Just a single step, on a leg of exposed muscle, pinned skin pulled back from the sinews, old ceramite of lurid finery now cracked and faded.

'I slept for a long time,' it said. 'Gorged on the gristle of your kind. Now I awake again, and nothing is left. The Warmaster is gone. My people are gone. Has the world ended? Has it all ended?'

Ilya remembered the dome at the city's heart, the one like a broken jaw. Had this thing been slumbering in there? Wouldn't Sojuk have detected it? It felt like a fist had rammed itself down her throat, choking out the words from her mouth. *Not like this!* she wanted to scream. *Not like this!*

The monster's knife-fingers snickered against one another. 'I shall starve, if I do not eat. I shall starve. Shall I eat you? How long will your flesh keep me alive?'

The monster was insane. It seemed barely sensate, as if its sensory inputs had all been burned out. It panted, it drooled.

Then, suddenly, she was angry. She remembered what the III Legion had done to the Scars at Kalium. She remembered what these bastards had done to a thousand worlds, how much they had ruined, how much pain they had caused, and for *nothing*, because they themselves had been destroyed too, they had dragged the whole species down with them, and for all their power and their strength they were to blame, the Astartes were to blame, and it had been her kind, the baseline humans, who had kept things together for their masters while they swaggered in their blood orgy across the stars.

'Get out of here,' she croaked, balling her veined fists. 'Get out of this place.'

It sniffed again, grinned, its tongue curling around skinless lips. 'I can already smell death on you,' it said. 'It hangs over your shoulder, close, close. Lucky you. I can give you a remarkable death. An extraordinary one. I made a scream last for a whole day, once. Shall I best that record with you?'

No fear remained. She was furious. She was beyond fury. Her cheeks flushed, her nostrils flared. 'They will drive you out,' she spat. 'They will drive you from this world and hunt you into the void. You have failed here. Nothing awaits you now but oblivion. They will never let you back.'

That halted it. For a second, it hesitated, as if stung by the words. It cocked its avian head, considering.

Then it grinned again. It raised its bladed hand, extended the fingers. Bars of shadow fell across her face.

'You might be right,' it said, advancing. 'But, just for now, your shrieks will light up the empyrean.'

Neither of them saw Sojuk coming. Just as before, with the canids, he was suddenly there, piling through the door, tackling the monster and barrelling it past her, the two of them carried together by his momentum and slamming into the far wall, denting the masonry and making the ceiling above it sag.

Ilya fell to her haunches, fighting against hyperventilation, instantly reduced to a spectator as the armoured leviathans went at it. Sojuk had his blade drawn, slashing wildly and tearing loose flesh from the beast. The traitor lunged back at him, punching its knives at the White Scar's throat and torso. The monster wailed horribly as it fought, an eldritch squeal, while Sojuk fought with silent determination.

The monster would win. She could already see it. It was faster, stronger, still benefitting from the gifts it had been given despite its debasement. Sojuk hammered at it, gauntlets flying, but the thing seemed to absorb every punishment. The margins were tight, just as all combat between Astartes was tight, but this could only have one outcome.

She would not allow it. This was *her house*. Trembling, she got up, staggered over to the pile of old cases, grabbed Qin Xa's dagger and unsheathed it for the very first time. A white metal blade glinted in the pale sun, and it felt light in her hands. She clutched it two-handed over her head, took a deep breath, and threw herself at the monster.

Sojuk reacted immediately, seeing the opportunity, slamming his adversary around in an all-in move that rocked it into her path while sacrificing his defence. Ilya thrust the dagger point down, putting every last morsel of her strength into the blow. It penetrated the nape of the monster's neck, jarring on bone before sliding deep into the spinal cord.

The monster screamed, thrashing wildly and throwing Ilya free. Her hands slipped from the dagger's grip and she thudded to the floor, skidding along before smacking into her chair. The blade had bitten deep, and Sojuk now had the opening he needed. He punched three deep quick thrusts in succession, tearing up the creature's chest and sending its armour panels clanging to the ground. It tried to respond, its throat filled with blood now, its limbs half hanging, but missed its aim. Sojuk spun viciously, whipping his tulwar laterally across the traitor's neck. The blade lodged deep, dislodging Ilya's dagger. The traitor's huge, raddled corpse teetered, swayed, then crashed down, cracking the floor and making the walls around them shiver.

Ilya could feel herself losing consciousness. She tried to get up, and failed. Through blurred vision she saw Sojuk hurrying for her. He knelt down, his hand lifting her head up gently.

'Did it strike you?' he demanded urgently.

Ilya glanced over at her blade, bloody on the floor beside her, used for the first and last time, her gift from the greatest blade-master the Legion had ever produced.

'No,' she whispered hoarsely, passing out but still angry. 'I struck *it*.'

She never asked Sojuk what he did with the corpse. She was out for so long that by the time she came around, it was almost as if it had never happened. The wall was still damaged though; the smell lingered. It *had* happened.

Once she was fully awake, Sojuk took her out into the yard. She sat in the wicker chair, covered in blankets, shivering under the warm sun.

'So you are one of us at last,' he said, a weak smile on his worried face. 'Blooded into the Legion.'

She tried to laugh. It was too painful. After that, they sat together for a long time without saying anything. She looked out over the little yard, the patches of earth she'd cleared, the tools tidied away and hanging neatly.

'This will enter the annals,' Sojuk added, sticking to his theme. 'Shiban Khan will want it recorded.'

Despite everything, she couldn't help feeling a glow of pride at that. He was right, after all. She'd ended a Space Marine. It had come late in the day, long past the real fighting, but military reputations had been built on far less. Sojuk had taken some nasty wounds, but they would heal up. She, on the other hand, could feel the internal damage. The last test. A good one to go out on.

'I want you to remember what I told you,' she said, her voice a faint hiss now. 'About the Legions, about Guilliman. Do not return to Chogoris too soon. The Khagan needs to see to that.'

Sojuk nodded, taking it seriously. 'But do not–'

'My collected data-slates might still be in the Rotunda. Someone should retrieve them. They have documents from the earliest surveys of the Legion, ones that will be useful for reconstruction.'

'They will be–'

'You need alliances with Mars, quickly. Get the ships rebuilt. That's your great asset. Even the Thirteenth can't master the void like you can.'

Sojuk smiled to himself, defeated. 'Anything else?'

She thought about it. For some reason, she suddenly remembered Yesugei's calm face then, on Ullanor, the very first time she'd met a Chogorian. 'Be careful,' he'd said. She'd not heeded that advice. She'd never been careful, and it had – mostly – been wonderful.

'When the Khagan is returned to himself,' she said, 'thank him.'

'Thank him?'

She looked up. 'For bringing me home. From there, where I didn't belong, to here, where I do. Do that for me, Sojuk. Thank him.'

After that, the weather warmed further, a steady heat now, gathering strength day after day. The worst of the storms faded, and even the wind dropped a little. No one came to the city, no more monsters were uncovered.

One morning, Sojuk entered Ilya's room. It was late, and over the past few days he had been helping her walk to the row of bulbs she'd planted to see if they would germinate. He found her lying on her bed, one arm limp against the floor. He went to her, kneeled down close, checked for breathing, checked for a pulse.

Then he sat back, and rested his chin on his chest for a long time. Then he reached up and made sure her eyes were closed. He rested her hand on her chest, and arranged the covers around her. And then he wept.

If Ilya had been Chogorian, her body would have been left for the sky. But she was Terran, so Sojuk buried her in the yard of the house where she had been raised. He left no marker, just in case an enemy should come again and recognise the name, but placed the dagger beside her in the earth. He wondered if she'd known just what a priceless gift it was, and how few blades of such quality had ever been made. He guessed she had done. She had probably known all about it, and been embarrassed by it and flattered at the same time.

After that he spent a long time in the house. He repaired the damage caused by the fight. He put the last of the old mess in order, just as she would have wanted it. He found things to do. Eventually, he couldn't think of any more tasks. He would go to the transport, take it back to the Palace, report to Shiban Khan and set in motion the things that needed doing. It was where he belonged, and the work was both necessary and honourable.

Before he left, he went into the yard one last time. The light was weak, greyer than it had ever been. A rumble of thunder sounded from the south, where the clouds were thickening against the distant peaks. Despite his efforts, the place looked shabby, bereft of colour, as if the materials themselves were mournful. The growing heat didn't feel natural. It didn't feel like it would ebb again.

He crouched down by her garden, checking the soil. Nothing. Too soon, surely. Maybe if it got warmer, something would push through. Maybe, by the time explorators got here, a new garden would be blooming. Or maybe the poisons ran too deep, and nothing good would be ever raised on this world again.

She had planted, though. Right at the end. She had performed the labour. That seemed like the important thing. The rite. The activity. She had always been busy, always diligent.

'*Untakh, szu-khundet*,' he said, softly. 'To your rest, honoured sage.'

Then he left the house, closing the door behind him. He shut it before heading back to the Palace, closing it tight on a life, on a war, on an age.

THE CARRION LORD OF THE IMPERIUM

AARON DEMBSKI-BOWDEN

I

I was there, the day Prometheus stole fire from the gods.

Haedo would chide me for that phrasing. Ra would smile in that sad way of his. Samonas would sigh and call it melodrama. Were any of them here, that is. Were any of them still alive.

But I was there – as were they – on the day our king did what He should never have done. With great engines of scientific violence, He plunged His metaphysical hand into the realm behind reality's veil. When He withdrew His questing touch, still burning with the violation of breaking the dimensional barrier, there it was. A divine and malignant light.

We asked it then, as you ask it now, as it will be asked in the darkening millennia to come:

Why?

We weren't enough, you see.

Every one of us represented years of the fleshcrafter's toil. Each one of us was something bespoke, something wrought just so. We were His guardians in times of war and His conscience in times of crisis. But He could not build an empire with us alone. We were a mere ten thousand souls. If the galaxy's song is the screaming fusion of a hundred billion stars, our presence was less than a whisper.

There are already scribblings that tell of an accord being reached, a deal being made, or – and one must pay heed to the phrasing of this one – a pact being sworn. I saw no smirking godlings or capering sprites offering to sell tainted souls at midnight. I saw machines. I saw machinery torn out of a bygone age, when humanity had mastered marvels to put our greatest achievements now to shame. Our king hadn't invented these, any more than He invented the Golden Throne. His genius was never in creation but recreation. His mastery was in dredging the truths and promises of the past, pulling them up into the dim light of today. His vision for humanity's golden future was built on the technoarchaeological bones of the past.

The engines I saw began as charcoal on parchment, evolving into hololithic schema written in flickering light through the stagnant air of the Palace's catacombs. Where these ancient engines called for elements of Abominable Intelligence, from the era when robots could think and reason, our king patchworked biotechnical solutions blending engineering and necromancy.

The function of these machines was unknown to me. Unknown to all of us. Their purpose, yes, that we knew. Their operation owed as much to magic as it did to manufacturing. And that, too, we knew.

So, there we gathered. Not all of us. Not even most of us. Just some of us, those that happened to be present by luck, destiny, or design. The others – those of the Ten Thousand whom our king trusted above all others – had voiced their hearts and thoughts before. But this was it. We gathered there, in the stark-lit dark, where it always felt no torch's light ever did more than stab at the gloom.

And, one by one, we told Him:
No.

– Epistle I:I, *The Master of Mankind*
by Diocletian Coros

'Humans,' says Constantin, who is never the first to speak, and often the last. His face isn't bleached of emotion tonight. That masquerade has no place here: it's a performance for other audiences. Nor is his voice the stern and stoic baritone of a being expecting his lessers to hear and obey. There's passion in his tone. He means what he's saying.

'The people,' he says, and his words have the ring of a promise. 'The people of the Imperium.'

This is an argument they've all heard before. Many of them agree with it. Amon nods in the wake of Valdor's words. He is one of the Three Hundred, as are the others gathered here in the rattling and clanking heart of the Imperial Dungeon. When any of the Ten Thousand speak, the Emperor always deigns to hear their words, but the Three Hundred are granted indulgences even beyond that. Rank and battle honours mean nothing; none of them has ever really known what qualities they possess that brought them into the Emperor's innermost circle. They know only that they are the chosen of the chosen.

'And we will lead them,' Amon tells his king. 'The Ten Thousand shall lead the armies of the Imperium into battle.' Amon is loved by all present here for a lifetime of forthright speech and fraternal honesty. His voice is as rich as Constantin's, flooded with that same belief in what he's saying.

Ra is one of the Dynastes – called the *Lords of Terra* with a smile that could be kind or unkind, depending on who wears it. He was a child of the Emperor's gravest enemies, stolen from his parents as punishment for their sins, now grown to primacy among the Emperor's elite. Like Constantin, like Amon,

Ra was one of the very first to wear a Custodian's pale and cold Imperial gold.

He pulls his gaze away from the machines that spark and crash in their housings. Softly – for though he shouts orders across a battlefield, he's never been as strident in questioning his king as some of the others – he lends his voice to Constantin's and Amon's.

The others speak, too. All of them. Their protests and promises echo throughout the grand chamber, over a syncopated backbeat of machines drilling their way through the dimensional barrier. Diocletian listens to all of them, though his eyes never leave his king.

He feels strange being here with only his kindred in gold, though he doesn't know why. The truth is, he's not alone in this sensation. It's a hollowness that plagues many of the Custodians, for they're created as only half of a whole. In years to come, when the Great Crusade is born and the Imperium begins claiming the one million worlds that comprise its core, the Legio Custodes will be joined by others just as alien to baseline humanity as they are themselves. There will be unity, synergies yet unimagined, between the Emperor's finest genetic creations and his warriors born without souls. Together, they will be the Talons. Decades from this moment, Diocletian will be by Kaeria Casryn's side; long since used to interpreting her thoughts through flickers in her facial expression, knowing her meaning by the weave of her hands in the air as she forms the wordplay of thoughtmark.

But here, now, those nights are far in the future. Of the Silent Sisterhood, only Jenetia Krole exists, and she has yet to cut out her tongue. She stands some way from the Emperor, sensed by all but seen by none. They know she is here somewhere. They register her presence as a distracting absence, like words on a page that never come into focus. She is a sentence you read three times and still miss its meaning.

When every objection has been made and every alternate path suggested, the Custodians fall as silent as Krole.

The Emperor turns to the only one of the Three Hundred that has not yet spoken.

'Diocletian,' He says, in a voice that His false sons will one day say is kind, unkind, angry, and calm, no matter its pitch and tone. To Diocletian, He just sounds tired.

Dio isn't sure what to say. He lacks Constantin's soulful composure, or Amon's gift for abrupt rhetoric, or Ra's poetic sincerity. He worries, in his quiet moments, if he is worthy of inclusion within the Three Hundred. He wonders if his king made a mistake by appointing him.

Everyone is watching him. Waiting for him to speak. Waiting for him to join the chorus of oaths that their blades will be enough, that the Custodians will lead the armies of the Imperium into battle, and that those armies will be human. Not Legions of transhumans. Not led by godling generals. That all this work, all these machines, are unnecessary.

You don't need to do this, he could say. *You don't need to steal the warp's essence. You don't need to create these things, these… primarchs.*

Diocletian tells the truth, as he always does to the Emperor, as they all always do. It's just that, tonight, his truth is different to theirs.

'I don't think it matters what I say.' Dio leans on his spear and inclines his head to the Emperor. 'I don't think it matters what any of us say. With respect, my king, I think you're going to do it anyway.'

II

Immortality.

There is no greater gift, and I have no time for those that decry eternity as a burden. Humans have always soothed their fears with fantasies of what awaits them at the end of life, and it's hard to respect them for warming themselves with lies.

I try not to judge. Truly. But I am so sick of their prayers.

I am so tired of hearing the people scream and shriek and mumble and murmur of an afterlife at the Emperor's side. Their prayers reach our ears even here, creeping, spreading, an infection of faith overcoming the species. I don't want to enlighten them. It isn't malice that motivates me. But in the name of the man they believe is a god, I wish they would cease their wailing.

We know what happens when a soul leaves a body. The fortunate enter swift oblivion. The unfortunate are the playthings of daemons, forever. It is the fundamental truth of reality, and the one thing our king never wanted the species to know.

We don't die as other beings die. We don't age as mortals age. For us, death is a misfortune not an inevitability. We can be killed, of course. Many of us have been. Nevertheless, we represent the pinnacle of genetic archaeoscience. One of the Dungeon's laboratory menials spent her life studying my blood – she grew old and died before there was any change in the blood cells under her monoscope.

For the longest time, we didn't even know if we aged. The Astartes can grow ancient, and their genetic code was always something mass-produced and imperfect. But we would reach a state of healthy middle-age and then… stasis. Was there some temporal sorcery used in our creation? Something undetectable, that our king never shared with us?

We suspect not. We aren't made the way the primarchs were made, with tampered metaphysics and borrowed essence. We aren't flawed from the very start.

There are those of our number that believe, not without precedent, that we don't age if we remain in our king's presence. That it is He – something about His body and soul – that binds us to immortality. No one has ever been gone from the Emperor's side long enough to test this notion; at least, none that have ever returned.

This raises questions better answered by men like Constantin, or Haedo, or Ra. Is there something inside us, some aspect of our loyalty, founded on selfishness? That immortality is ours – but only if our king lives? These are the secret questions my kind has asked one another since our creation, and the kinds of philosophic quandaries we once brought to our king.

I never asked Him such things. Back then, I wore my simplistic demeanour as a badge of honour. I used to tell Ra that I didn't care about the answers. Sometimes, walking the halls of the catacombs as they are today, I ask myself what I never considered in those long-lost days: if He kept the truth of reality from the humans, and the truth of obsolescence from the Astartes, was there some truth – magnificent in its darkness – that He kept from us?

Did I keep silent because I trusted my king, or did I never ask anything of Him because I feared what He might say?

– Epistle V:IV, *The Master of Mankind*
by Diocletian Coros

It is their first funeral. They don't know what to do.

The Ten Thousand are no strangers to death, and such is their education that they can summon to memory the graveside rituals of innumerable cultures. But they don't have their own funeral rites because none of them has ever died. All that knowledge of death was academic until now. Sagittarus was the first to suffer terminal wounds, his dying form infused with alchemical and technological life-sustainers and interred in the cradle-coffin of a Dreadnought. He slumbers often to ease the weight of his dislocated mind. But he still lives. After a fashion.

And there are others beyond Sagittarus. The Moritoi. The living, wounded unto death but saved from the grave, still able to wage war.

Xerxes is dead, though. Truly dead. How should they mark the loss of one of their own?

They ring his body now, shielding it from view. Curiously, it's the men and women from the Imperial Army that grant the

Custodians the most privacy. With the battle won, they tend to their own wounded and deal with their own dead. These duties may be sorrowful for them, but they're hardly unfamiliar. They leave the Custodians in peace, sensing that something momentous has happened here today.

The Legio Cataegis knows no such etiquette. The warriors of the Thunder Legion come sniffing around, some curious, some conciliatory, neither of which the Custodians have any interest in hearing. The proto-Astartes are sent away with polite dismissals and the occasional wordless grunt.

Diocletian stands with Juhaza and Mycorian, two of Ra's *Lords of Terra*, the Emperor's precious Dynastes. Haedo looks down at the body, what's left of it: Xerxes is a thing of meat and broken gold, and it makes Dio's skin crawl to even glance downward. Gore holds no unease for him, let alone disgust. It's just that the corpse's existence feels at odds with reality.

Ra and Amon converse in low tones a short distance away, their armour burnished amber in the light of the setting sun. Diocletian can hear what they're saying and has no desire to join in. Should they return the body to the Palace? Should they make a cairn? Should they burn the remains? And if so, do they do it alone, or place the corpse with the fallen humans to be incinerated on the mass pyre?

There are political considerations, too. Several of the others have already noted them. The humans would feel honoured if a Custodian was burned in a pyre with the Imperial Army's slain. Is that an honour that should be conferred upon them? Is their morale a factor for the Ten Thousand to take into account? Would Xerxes have willed it this way? And whether he would or not, do the wishes of the dead even matter?

Diocletian has no answers for them. He can still scarcely believe that he's looking at a corpse.

Later – when most of these new emotions have lost ground

against the mundane realities of troop transports, drop-ships, resupply runs, and the hundred other tasks of lifting an army from here to there – Diocletian comes upon Constantin. They're still on the field of battle, their boots still muddy with the blood-reddened muck of the land they were told they had to take.

At first, he doesn't approach. Constantin stands not far from the edge of a cliff overlooking the ruined cityscape below – a vista of tumbledown grey and pillars of smoke that reach the cloudy sky. Constantin doesn't move. He watches the aftermath of compliance. The wreckage. The fires. The death of a culture that dared resist the precious homogeneity of Unification. Regardless of all else, it paints a picture: the captain-general, first of their kind, radiates solitude.

In the quiet, away from everyone and everything, Diocletian hears the low, emotive song on the air. Realising his intrusion, he begins to turn away.

'Dio.'

Diocletian turns back at the sound of his name. Constantin is watching him now, the captain's eyes betraying a soulful nature the enemies of the Imperium will never know.

'I didn't mean to intrude, Con.'

'All is well.' There's a hesitation, three heartbeats in duration. When he speaks again, Constantin's voice is edged with something subtle and wry. It makes him seem human. Almost. 'I take it you heard me.'

Now it's Diocletian's turn to hesitate. 'I didn't know you could sing. It sounded… sad.'

That isn't the right word, and he knows it, but no word seems righter in its place. Ra would say something like, *It sounded melancholy, like you mourned a future that will never come to pass,* but the day is unlikely to dawn when Dio phrases things in those terms. Ra tends to sound measured and thoughtful with his eternal sincerity. Diocletian suspects he'd sound far less insightful if he tried to mimic it.

'It's a lament,' Constantin admits, scratching his unshaven jawline. Diocletian is one of the Ten Thousand that prefers to be clean-shaven, while Constantin always seems a day or three distant from a razor. 'There was a Nordafrik tribe, a century ago. The Abar. Do you know of them?'

Diocletian does, though he wasn't present for the war that annihilated them.

'I've seen their entries in the Palace archives. Nomads of the Zu'har Expanse. Matriarchal. Spiritual. Dedicated to ancestor worship.'

Constantin nods. 'They'd sing dirges by the pyres of their fallen.' For a moment, he lifts his dark eyes to the occluded sky. 'Believing that their words join the wind with their loved ones' ashes. And so, the dead are sent into the afterlife with the blessings of the living.'

Diocletian has never been a passionate student of history.

'Such fascinating heathens,' he says.

Constantin smiles. 'Sarcasm is a keen blade, Dio. Try to wield it carefully.'

Diocletian grunts, the closest he's come to laughter in days. He adds nothing to it, and Constantin senses the unspoken question, the reason Dio approached him.

'Ask,' Constantin presses.

Diocletian gestures west, towards the great golden drop-ship nestling on the churned earth, its wings spread wide. Before he can ask the question, Constantin smiles again.

'Ah,' says the First of the Ten Thousand.

Dio asks it, nevertheless. 'Why doesn't He tell us what to do?' There's something not a thousand leagues from frustration in his tone, giving flavour to his curiosity. 'Why doesn't He tell us how to deal with Xerxes' body?'

He can see in Constantin's eyes that Con doesn't have the answer, either. What Constantin has, as he so often does, is more questions.

'When has He ever told us how to manage our inner selves?'

'Ugh. You sound like Malcador. Stop trying to *impart wisdom* upon me. Just talk to me.'

Constantin takes a breath, searching for the right words – or the least-wrong ones.

'I don't know,' he admits, 'and you know I don't know. Perhaps He keeps His distance because He comprehends that something seismic has occurred in our ranks. Or perhaps He's already musing over the logistics of His next conquest and the emotions of His creations are a matter of absolute indifference.'

Diocletian gives him a look. 'You're not saying anything I've not already considered.'

'I think I am.' Constantin is patience incarnate. 'It doesn't matter why He leaves us alone tonight, Dio. All that matters is that He does.'

Ra has a word for conversations like this about their king. That word is *ineffable,* and it makes Diocletian grind his teeth.

'We're the ones who will make the choice,' Constantin says. 'So let us make it.'

Diocletian joins Constantin on the ridge overlooking the dead city, and the two secular demigods speak of heathenry across history. They search for the right rites to honour the first of their kindred to die, knowing that whatever they decide will shape precedent for the second, and the third, and every life they lose in their king's long war for the soul of the species.

III

It's said that almost none of the Ten Thousand are able to dream. The biological and psychological truth of the matter is beyond me, though the oneiroscists of my king's court have theories on the necessity of dreams and the corresponding stability of a mind. It's commonly believed by the survivors of the Ten Thousand that we all dream, as do all sentient beings, but something in our physiology prevents the evidence of firing synapses showing in machine analysis, and keeps us from accessing those memories.

But I remember mine. Constantin once ventured that it was an intentional adjustment in the Emperor's genetic masterwork: that our king manipulated each use of the Custodian gene-process in unique and subtle ways, defining us as individuals. There's no way to know if that's true. Con knew our king as well as any living being could, but I can't conceive of why the Emperor would leave me – or imbue me – with the capacity to dream.

My king once asked me to ensure the details of my somnolent visions were entered into the Tower of Hegemon's archives. I don't know if He ever read them when He still walked among us, but since His installation upon the Throne, I've considered abandoning the practice. It's a tedium I could well do without. I did it only because He asked it of me, in an age that is already slipping away from mortal memory into immortal myth.

Yet I allow it to continue. It was one of the few times my king asked something of me personally, without it being a command to the Ten Thousand or a specific order given in the line of duty. He came to me one day and He asked for it. I find that I can't, in good conscience, refuse Him even now. Even now, when it no longer matters.

For most of my life, scribes have painstakingly preserved every one of my dreams, recording my dictations first as simple research, now increasingly as holy writ. As the years pass, what was once a scientific curiosity is taking on a more religious weight, and I see the scribes – ever more faithful, ever more ignorant – clutching the rolls of parchment with a disconcerting fervour.

The nature of my dreams is detailed in thousands of dictated scrolls already. This includes the way they changed from seemingly random firing of synapses invoking scraps of memory and imagination, into something focused and sour. I won't relate any of them here. I will only note that when the scribes ask me if I reflect on the way my dreams changed to nightmares, I admit that I don't.

But I often reflect on the day that changed them.

– Epistle X:III, *The Master of Mankind*
by Diocletian Coros

Diocletian is in the Dungeon when the Emperor's dream dies. He knows the moment it happens, not because of some over-tuned transhuman sense, but because the entire Eurasian landmass quakes with sudden torment.

He sprints through the chambers of the Imperial Dungeon, through packs of confused and panicking technicians and scientists, towards the screams, the gunfire, the thunder; the sound of empire strangling on its own ignorance. He runs as he's never run before, with every iota of his physicality devoted to motion. He is a machine; a weapon being drawn for the fight about to take place.

Though less than a minute has passed, by the time he tears into the central chamber the burning avatar of Magnus the Red is gone, driven back by the onslaught of the Ten Thousand and the revelation of its own catastrophic success. In the wake of Magnus' banishment, disorder reigns. The webway gate is a wound wrenched wide, vomiting inhumanity into the Throne Room. Things, creatures that use humanity only as a mocking baseline from which to diverge, spill into reality, exalted by Magnus arrogantly tearing open the path before them.

'To the Emperor!' Constantin is shouting above the uproar as he spins and cleaves and carves and kills. 'To the Emperor's side!'

The Emperor is already ringed by fifteen of His golden elite – Con is one of them – and Diocletian is halfway to his king's side when the Emperor throws His hand forward, fingers curled into a claw as if He could tear at the webway portal from where He stands. Dio sees the scream in his king's frantic stare before it leaves the Emperor's lips.

'Into the breach!' the Master of Mankind cries out, and His voice is broken, heart-struck. He wears the face of a man watching his hopes die.

The Custodians obey their king, killing their way forward, advancing through the dissipating muck of daemons. The sheer density of corpses forces them to crush underfoot the bodies of butchered Terran scientists and viziers of the Martian Mechanicum. Diocletian is in the front ranks, at Ra's side by virtue of instinct or fortune. They share a look as they draw closer to the screaming portal. In temporal terms, the glance lasts barely half a second. More than long enough to convey the weight of what both men fear.

For Magnus the Red to have reached the Throne Room, and for Hell to have followed in his wake, there's a chance that every single Imperial soul on the other side of the portal is already dead. Magnus, through intent or ignorance, has killed thousands of men and women, Martian and Terran, in the span of seconds.

Ra rams his spear through the throat of something shrieking and horned and ultimately nameless, and he plunges forward into the portal, only a step behind Constantin. Diocletian feels as he always feels when he approaches the webway gate: that it wants him to enter and that he has no right doing so. It's a breach in existence as sure as the warp – the high arcane art of a long-dead species that considered the laws of the physical universe something beneath them, a malleable joke rather than inviolate reality.

Diocletian turns back, seeing the warriors of the Anathema Psykana forming squad-ranks, the Sisters of Silence gathering into their packs and bracing to follow the Custodians. He sees more of his own kind entering the chamber, surging forward; more of his own kind around him, the power fields of their spears crisping away the daemonic blood trying to cling to their blades. He sees scientist-priests of the Mechanicum unlocking never-used protocols to bring weapons of devastating misery to full power; he sees these holy souls bear them on their shoulders or pull them from beneath robes with unfamiliar grips.

He sees Kaeria. She is *his* in a way that veteran soldiers will know without needing words to qualify. He is *hers* in the same way – a bond defined by its supreme intimacy in absence of sensuality. The same way Constantin has Jenetia Krole, and Jenetia has Con. The same way Celia Harroda has Ra, and Ra has Celia.

It isn't love. Between many, it isn't even affection. It just *is*. The bonds that form on the front lines between the chosen few entrusted with the secrets of the galaxy. Bonds mandated at first by a king that needed His precious elite to know, see, and do things far beyond the scope of any others in His kingdom. These bonds will grow in the coming decade, in the war that has literally just begun in the webway. In the case of Ra and Celia, that bond will also end there.

Dio sees Kaeria gathering, arming, with her cadre. She sees him in the same second, and her hand cuts a single slash of thought-mark across the distance. *Endure*, that curved slice of her hand says, the way someone else might say *Stay alive* or *Good luck*.

Diocletian sees and processes all of this in the time it takes a human to blink. And there, at the heart of this madness, is the Emperor.

Other recollections of this moment will cite that the Emperor raged at what fate had dealt, or was perfectly calm, or said nothing at all. Diocletian will disregard these alternate tales. He sees now what he will always remember seeing: he sees the Emperor distraught, ordering His finest and most loyal souls into the breach, and that in itself is a new kind of agony. He's never seen his king weep before. Until now, he hadn't been sure it was possible, whether there was enough humanity in the man for such a human reaction.

Diocletian turns back to the gate. Its alien light screams against his armour.

He steps forward.

* * *

IV

If there is one subject which has had more breath committed to questions than any other, and more ink committed to parchment in its analysis, then it is this:

Why did they betray us?

Haedo once asked a more pertinent question, one that haunted me in its aftermath: Why did it take them so long?

There's a question behind this question. It was often said, in doggerel screeds and propaganda offered up by remembrancers, that the primarchs each embodied an element of the Emperor. Some say they even carried His soul, portioned away into pieces.

This is a lie. At best, it's a half-truth. There was no division of soul-stuff, no imbuing of the Emperor's attributes into the gestating monsters that thought they were His sons. Stories have always simplified the nature of gods and heroes by telling tales of children inheriting this virtue or that flaw from their divine sires and mares.

The most evident and crucial divergence between my king and His creations is thus: the Emperor existed for unification. To unite the lost worlds of humanity. To unite an Imperium in echo of the human race's lost interstellar empire. To unite the species and protect it from unseen adversaries.

The primarchs, from their first steps out into the galaxy, existed in a state of disunity. They distrusted one another. They resented each other's glories. They fought amongst themselves even before the great rebellion. Each one of them knew best. Each one of them believed their way was right; no compromise, none.

Yet Haedo's question remains.

Was this tendency towards infighting because the Emperor had sliced away sections of His spirit and gifted them to His creations? Were they spiritually, fundamentally, incomplete?

I believe not. I believe the opposite. They were perfectly complete. The Emperor succeeded too well in His undertaking.

Each of them embodied their creator in something close to His entirety. Each of them possessed the same messianic urge for absolute unity that the Ten Thousand saw in our king. They didn't fight amongst themselves because the Emperor left them incomplete. They hated one another because each of them was an Emperor.

– Epistle XLI:I, *The Master of Mankind*
by Diocletian Coros

It is the final days of the primarchs and their Legions. Soon, they will be exiled from Terra as the new leaders of the Imperium close the tome of history on the age of gods and demigods. A new age of stagnation and fear is dawning, built over the bones of truths best left forgotten.

Diocletian is going to kill Roboute Guilliman.

He knows it with the surety that he's ever known anything, that unless the self-proclaimed *Lord Commander of the Imperium* doesn't fall silent at once, Dio and the Custodians at his side – and the remaining, furtive, persecuted Sisters in this grand chamber – will draw their blades, and they will kill the creature that believes itself heir to the empire.

Time and again they have endured Guilliman's speeches, his declarations of intent, his orders that counter even the wishes of his own brothers to the point there are already whispers of another war. A war, this time, over Guilliman's vision for the Imperium.

'Are you listening, Diocletian? I call for unity, at a time when we need it most.'

Diocletian is listening. He doesn't hear calls for unity. He hears demands of obedience. The time they most needed unity was decades ago, when half of Guilliman's breed set the galaxy aflame.

'Are you finished?' Diocletian asks softly. 'Are you done?'

This is how Diocletian looks to the world outside his brothers and Sisters. He is almost entirely without warmth and without humour. His genetic lessers irritate him, and he regards no being as his genetic superior. He is decisive, authoritative, and absent of all patience. This perception doesn't grieve him. He truly couldn't care less how he's perceived by others. The perceptions that mattered belong to men and women that are, mostly, now in their graves.

Metaphorically, that is. Many are decomposing unburied in the webway, their bones gnawed by daemons. Many others were incinerated on the Palace walls, their ashes scattered to the Terran winds. But the sentiment stands.

'I grow weary of your mistrust,' says Roboute Guilliman, saviour of Terra, Lord of the Armies of Humanity, Avenging Son of the Emperor. And then he says Diocletian's title, which was once Ra's title, in a tone of voice that, to human ears, is perfectly smooth, perfectly calm. *'Tribune.'*

Diocletian stops moving. He stops breathing. He's an animal in that moment, a thing of urges and desires, frozen in place as he feels his heartbeat quicken. If he isn't careful, if he doesn't master his instinct and his rage, then the Imperium will lose another primarch this day.

He isn't convinced that wouldn't be for the best. Perhaps it would be. But he doesn't believe it's his decision to make.

The others sense it, too. It passes between every Talon in the chamber, as wordless and true as a Sister's hand signals. He sees Haedo shift position, ever so slightly adjusting his balance. He sees Kaeria tilt her head a fraction of an inch and, by her thigh, she taps her first finger against the tip of her thumb in silent signal. He sees others, Custodians and Sisters in absolute harmony and absolute unity; if he acts now, they will act with him before the *courageous and honourable* fools in blue can even aim their bolters.

'My mistrust,' Diocletian repeats. His tone is that of a man seeking clarity. He wants to be sure he heard what he thinks he heard. '*My* mistrust.'

There is so, so much he could say to Roboute Guilliman.

He could state, calmly, clearly, that tens of millions have died on worlds that the Legions deigned not to defend, regardless of orders from Terra. He could remind the Lord Commander of the lives lost in the months it took the Khan to decide what side he was on, and ask just how many war fronts lacked Legion support because the Warhawk couldn't decide whether to betray the man he insists is his father.

He could ask how many Imperial Army regiments went unsupported, on how many worlds, because the primarchs enacted their own crusades instead of aligning with the Imperium's defence. He could ask how many lives were lost on the Throneworld, and across the galaxy itself, because the mighty Lord of Ultramar squatted in his petty kingdom and only set sail at the eleventh hour. And they'd have their reasons, of course. They have their familiar excuses.

But he could ask how many lives will be lost in the years to come because these creatures disagree on whether the Legions should be broken apart, with Dorn on one side and Guilliman on the other. How many Imperial souls will die in that war, just so one brother can see his vision come to pass over his rival's?

As if that would be any different to Horus' war. As if the primarchs haven't done enough damage to the human race in their ceaseless martyrs' quest to be the protagonists of the species.

And this, all of this, is to say nothing of the others, the *traitors*, the broken monsters that followed Horus into treachery fuelled by ambition, vanity, madness. Sol would burn out before Diocletian could completely speak the roll of their sins.

He could say all of this and more. And he wants to. He burns to. The Ten Thousand know all of it is true, as do the surviving Sisters, even as the Imperium turns its ire upon them as witches, even as the shroud of ignorance begins to fall.

He wants to say it, and he knows what he would say.

I watched the death of my king's dreams, and then the death of my king. I watched half of your kind rebel against the empire it took us almost three centuries to build, and I watched you turn it to ash.

I've watched even the most loyal of you scheme against your brothers, whine about who was favoured over whom, and go to war over your arrogances, heedless of consequence, like some moronic pantheon of ancient gods. You, and the malformed coven of tainted genetics you call a family, have no right to set foot upon this world.

You say you lost a father. But you didn't. You lost the scientist that created you. You lost the visionary that had such high hopes for you. But He was never your father. Your fathers *love you dearly,* primarch. *Even now they dance through the warp, laughing at what good boys you've all been.*

You say the Emperor would trust you now with the resurrection of the Imperium. If He trusted you, why did He need ten thousand bodyguards? And why weren't you one of them? Why weren't you called upon to defend the webway? Why did He entrust that most vital task to His true chosen? Why, whenever He related the truth of the galaxy, was it never His 'sons' that He told?

Diocletian could say all of this.

And it would be so satisfying. So vindicating.

Or...

He forces a slow breath from his body. It takes all his self-control to do so. Next, he forces his knuckles to unclench from the haft of his spear.

'Talons,' he says. 'With me.'

Diocletian leaves the chamber, the weight of Guilliman's eyes on his back, and the incessant sound of praying rising to his ears from outside the walls.

Kaeria, at his side, gestures in an elegant flourish of thought-mark. Her sentiment is cold, but it warms Diocletian with its sincerity. She can smell the stink of defeat on Guilliman, like an aura around him. She believes he will die soon.

'They all will,' Diocletian replies. 'They weren't built to last forever.'

* * *

V

To my core, I am tired of these prayers. The ones whispered in monasteries that were once laboratories. The ones wailed at the Palace walls. They infest my thoughts in a way the cries of daemons never could.

I dream of them. I dream of the suffering cried into the skies of every world in the Imperium. I dream of an empire's worth of pain and loss and zealotry and fear, all focused towards one man. Some nights, the few nights I require rest, I wake anyway, sheened with sweat and hearing the voices of men and women and children whose prayers cannot ever be answered.

I don't think this is real. I'm not cursed with a psyker's genetic spiral-code. Nor am I a fool, to believe these are anything more than portions of my slumbering mind coming to life in ways I wish they wouldn't. They're dreams. Just dreams.

Tonight, I will wear gold for the first time in what seems like an eternity. I will forgo the black helmet of my shame and the symbolism of my bare skin. I will instead go to my king armed and armoured, the way things used to be before we failed Him.

I am going to ask Him a question. Something I have always wanted to know the answer to. Something I regret never asking Him before.

– Epistle XCIX:CXXV, *The Master of Mankind*
by Diocletian Coros

It feels at once strange and perfectly natural to be wearing his armour once again. The strength it pours through him is utterly familiar, a homecoming, though he feels subtle deviations in his movements that aren't quite what he expected. A purr in the servos of his hip there, a tightening of the knuckle joints there. His armour has been maintained (religiously maintained, to his weary disgust) for all these long years, but little vicissitudes have been introduced into its function purely by the fact he hasn't worn it in so long. It was made to be worn, to function in bond with him.

Were he inclined to the Martian way of thinking, he might say the armour's machine spirit resented him for abandoning it. He believes in machine spirits – it's a common enough thing for a warrior to believe a weapon has a soul – but not in the absolutist terms proclaimed by Mars.

Clad in Imperial gold, Diocletian Coros makes his way through the Palace. He passes pilgrims that pray to him, that plead for scraps of his cloak, that beg for blessings. He ignores them. He always ignores them.

He moves through museums to lost ages and cloisters dedicated to a new and powerful faith. He walks on, through libraries that are now convents; across avenues now bedecked in religious iconography. Down he goes, through halls of statues dedicated to the fallen, through chambers of reliquaries housing meaningless bones and stasis fields cradling weapons that will never work again.

He hesitates only twice in his night-long journey. The first is when a beggar-child bars his path, gazing up at him with amazed eyes. Diocletian remembers a time, long ago by his measurement of things and practically prehistorical to the pilgrims and beggars surrounding him, when he'd been with Zephon, the Bringer of Sorrow, and another child stood before them in a similar way.

So much time has passed since then. So much has changed.

'Are you the God-Emperor?' this child asks. Past and present collide. Diocletian's throat closes.

He goes down to one knee, still towering above the youth. He can see the gold of his war plate reflecting in the child's eyes.

'No,' Diocletian tells the boy. 'My name is Dio. But I know the Emperor.'

He unbuckles his scarlet cloak, marked with the Palatine Aquila, the Emperor's own symbol. He bundles it up and hands it to the filthy child, who takes it in trembling hands. Perhaps it will serve this boy as a blanket for the rest of a long life. Perhaps the child will be killed by jealous relic-hunters. Diocletian knows which is more likely in this new dark age, but he hopes he's wrong to think it.

The second time he pauses in his journey is at Kaeria's grave. There's no grand monument to mark her passing, no ornate tomb worthy of one who served the Emperor and humankind so ardently, for so long. It's a plaque in an ossuary. A space in a wall. Her bones aren't even interred there.

Many of the Sisters' original tombs were looted by mobs of Imperial faithful as the zealotry of their beliefs grew fiercer with time's passing. The bodies of the 'soulless witches', long gone to nothing but bone, were immersed in holy water and subsequently incinerated on pyres, surrounded by the God-Emperor's joyous and weeping worshippers. Some of the corpses were put on trial, their bones bound together with sanctified rope, while priests and priestesses of the most holy, most hateful, most loving God-Emperor judged the dead witches guilty of the blackest heresy.

Kaeria's original tomb was one of those defiled. He'd never recovered her body. Only her blade was buried here, in her new grave. He'd tracked her stolen sword to a black market in Ashripur, on the other side of Terra, before returning it to the Palace and placing it here himself.

Tonight, he runs his fingertips along the plaque marking her life and death, lingering only long enough to say farewell. He hates coming here. There's no closure to be found, only the rawness of a wound that won't seal.

He goes deeper into the Palace. Deeper. Deeper. Through doors that no human has seen in generations. Past members of his own kind, those that share his age and experience, and those they've created in the time since – those that never heard the Emperor speak in life; those that only know Him as the God-Emperor in death. Some address him by the rank of tribune. Some call him Dio.

Down. Deeper.

Through the doors, the secret doors, the ones behind those

renowned gateways decorated in trappings of glory. Past the graven image of the Immortal Emperor: a skull-faced warlock on a mighty throne, eternally alive on the edge of death, imposing in His majesty.

Through that final door, which opens only to droplets of a tribune's blood, and whose impenetrable locks take an hour to unseal.

Inside the innermost sanctum, where the architecture of the walls is uncomfortably organic, strangely spinal. Diocletian approaches the Golden Throne, such as it is, and his kindred – naked but for their cloaks, loincloths, and black helms – move aside in his honour.

He ascends the steps. Slowly. Not without reverence, but without the abject worship expected by the people of the Imperium. They would be horrified by its absence; but then, everything about this place would horrify them. It's why they will never be allowed to know of it.

At long last, Diocletian stands before his king.

He looks past the hanging wires that resemble intestines, and the clicking, ticking life-support engines, and the preservative mist sprayed into the air in nine-second intervals. He looks past the blood bags and vitae-packets linked intravenously to the thing on the throne, which is just a chair compared to the great and grand artworks: a throne without the capital T that makes it both a curse and the salvation of the species.

He looks at the revenant husk of something that was somehow once, somehow still is, a man. Something that shouldn't be alive, and arguably isn't, by any mortal measure. Something tortured by its own impossible continuation – physically starved and psychically bloated on the feast of souls it's forced to devour every day of its endless and agonising existence.

Or is it forced? Maybe it craves this. Maybe it hungers.

Diocletian removes his helmet and kneels before his king. At first he says nothing, his head hanging, his eyes closed. Here, of all places, there's no hatred of the primarchs, no anger at the Legions' betrayal, no bitterness at humanity's self-destructive nature. The weight of the centuries lies heavy on Diocletian's shoulders, here in these quiet seconds between a warrior and his liege. He feels the weight of his failure to protect this man; the knowledge that had the Ten Thousand done what was needed of them, then the Emperor would still be with them. Their king would still be a man, not a skeleton silently screaming into the midnight reaches of the universe just to give humanity a few more millennia.

Diocletian lifts his gaze. He stares into what's left of his king's features, and in that moment, they appear as two sides of a coin: created and creator – an ageless countenance opposite a living carcass. Each breath he takes draws the scent of the Throne into his body: a stinging reek of overworked metal unable to entirely mask the fainter smells of alchemical solutions and biological waste. Beneath it all, and worst of all, is a wisp of decay.

Diocletian rests his spear before the God-Emperor's feet, and he asks his question.

'My king. Do you dream?'

ABOUT THE AUTHORS

Dan Abnett has written over fifty novels, including the acclaimed Gaunt's Ghosts series and the Ravenor, Eisenhorn and Bequin books. His work for the Horus Heresy includes the first book in the series, *Horus Rising,* and the three-volume-long conclusion, *The End and the Death.* He also wrote several novels in between: *Legion, The Unremembered Empire, Know No Fear, Prospero Burns* and *Saturnine.* He scripted *Macragge's Honour,* the first Horus Heresy graphic novel, as well as numerous Black Library audio dramas. He recently penned the Warhammer 40,000 novel *HIVE,* as well as *Interceptor City,* the eagerly awaited sequel to fan-favourite *Double Eagle.* Dan lives and works in Maidstone, Kent.

Aaron Dembski-Bowden is the *New York Times* bestselling author of the Horus Heresy novels *Echoes of Eternity, The Master of Mankind, Betrayer* and *The First Heretic,* as well as the novellas *Aurelian* and *Prince of Crows* and the audio drama *Butcher's Nails,* for the same series. He has also written the Warhammer 40,000 novels *Spear of the Emperor* and *Ragnar Blackmane,* the popular Night Lords series, the Space Marine Battles book *Armageddon,* the novels *The Talon of Horus* and *Black Legion,* the Grey Knights novel *The Emperor's Gift* and numerous short stories. He lives and works in Northern Ireland.

John French is the author of several Horus Heresy stories including the novels *The Solar War, Mortis, Praetorian of Dorn, Tallarn, Slaves to Darkness* and *Sigismund: The Eternal Crusader,* the novella *The Crimson Fist,* and the audio dramas *Dark Compliance, Templar* and *Warmaster.* For Warhammer 40,000 he has written *Resurrection, Incarnation* and *Divination* for The Horusian Wars and three tie-in audio dramas – the Scribe Award-winning *Agent of the Throne: Blood and Lies,* as well as *Agent of the Throne: Truth and Dreams* and *Agent of the Throne: Ashes and Oaths.* John has also written the Ahriman series, the Age of Sigmar novels *The Hollow King* and *The Dead Kingdom* and many short stories.

Guy Haley's work for Black Library spans the depth and breadth of the Warhammer universes. He is the author of several Horus Heresy novels, including *The Lost and the Damned, Titandeath, Wolfsbane* and three titles in the Primarchs series. He has also written many Warhammer 40,000 books, including *Dawn of Fire: Avenging Son,* the Dark Imperium trilogy, and the Belisarius Cawl novels *The Great Work, Genefather* and *Archmagos.* For Age of Sigmar he has penned the Drekki Flynt novels *The Arkanaut's Oath* and *The Ghosts of Barak-Minoz* as well as many other stories. He lives in Yorkshire with his wife and son.

Nick Kyme is the author of many Horus Heresy novels, novellas and audio dramas, including *Old Earth, Promethean Sun* and *Nightfane.* His novella *Feat of Iron* was a *New York Times* bestseller in the Horus Heresy collection *The Primarchs.* For Warhammer 40,000, Nick has written *Volpone Glory* and the Dawn of Fire novel *The Iron Kingdom.* He is also well known for his popular Salamanders series and the Cato Sicarius novels *Damnos* and *Knights of Macragge.* His work for Age of Sigmar includes the short story 'Borne by the Storm', included in the novel *War Storm,* and the audio drama *The Imprecations of Daemons.* He has also written the Warhammer Horror novel *Sepulturum.* He lives and works in Nottingham.

James Swallow is the author of the Horus Heresy novels *Fear to Tread* and *Nemesis,* which both reached the *New York Times* bestseller lists. Also for the Horus Heresy, he has written the Siege of Terra novella *Garro: Knight of Grey,* the novels *The Flight of the Eisenstein* and *The Buried Dagger,* and a series of audio dramas featuring the character Nathaniel Garro, the prose versions of which have now been collected into the anthology *Garro.* For Warhammer 40,000, he is best known for his four Blood Angels novels, the audio drama *Heart of Rage,* and his two Sisters of Battle novels. His short fiction has appeared in *Legends of the Space Marines* and *Tales of Heresy.*

Gav Thorpe's long and prolific career with Black Library has seen him write across the depth and breadth of the Warhammer universes. Author of the Horus Heresy novels *The First Wall, Deliverance Lost, Angels of Caliban, Corax,* and novella *The Lion,* he has also recently written the titles *Luther: First of the Fallen* and *Rogal Dorn: The Emperor's Crusader.* His Warhammer 40,000 work includes *Indomitus,* the Dawn of Fire novel *The Wolftime,* and the fan-favourite Last Chancers series, amongst many others. For Age of Sigmar, Gav wrote the novel *The Red Feast,* and in 2017 he won the David Gemmell Legend Award for his novel *Warbeast.* He lives and works in Nottingham.

Chris Wraight is the author of the Horus Heresy novels *Warhawk, Scars* and *The Path of Heaven,* the Primarchs novels *Leman Russ: The Great Wolf* and *Jaghatai Khan: Warhawk of Chogoris,* the novellas *Brotherhood of the Storm, Wolf King* and *Valdor: Birth of the Imperium,* and the audio drama *The Sigillite.* For Warhammer 40,000 he has written the Space Wolves books *Blood of Asaheim, Stormcaller* and *The Helwinter Gate,* as well as the Vaults of Terra and Watchers of the Throne series, *The Lords of Silence* and the Dawn of Fire novel *Sea of Souls.* Additionally, he has many Warhammer Fantasy novels to his name, and the Warhammer Crime novel *Bloodlines.* Chris lives and works in Bradford-on-Avon, in south-west England.

MORE FROM BLACK LIBRARY

ASHES OF THE IMPERIUM
by Chris Wraight

It's the beginning of an epic series. Find out what happens after the cataclysmic events of the Horus Heresy, as an unsteady Imperium must find its footing and learn how to exist without the guidance of the Emperor.

For these stories and more, go to **blacklibrary.com**, **warhammer.com**, Games Workshop and Warhammer stores, all good book stores or visit one of the thousands of independent retailers worldwide, which can be found at **warhammer.com/store-finder**

An extract from
Ashes of the Imperium
by Chris Wraight

The error of history is to assume greater awareness of circumstances at the time than ever existed; to imagine those of the past knew precisely and with insight what was the case then, what was about to be the case, and what they must do to bring about their desired outcome. So it must be with those days, the days I have made my own study. Will the age come to have its own marker, as the Age of Heresy now has? Will the period become a byword for some particular human failing or accomplishment? Surely it will. And yet, even now, so long after the ashes have cooled, I do not know what it shall be. I propose this, with caution: the Age of Confusion. Or maybe, the Age of Ignorance. For it was this way; there was no certainty, and no ready means of discovering it. As a gravely wounded Terra emerged from its seven-year trial into the fog of a new era, be sure of this one truth: nobody, not a soul, from the greatest of generals to the humblest of soldiers, had the faintest idea what to do next.

– Diomedon of Luna, *A Study of the Reconstruction*

Now run. Run hard. Nothing else exists. Run, then run some more. You will be doing it forever now.

Those were the words, in the rare moments of clarity, the brief pauses in the headlong rush for doubtful sanctuary. It seemed that this was just the start, the movement into a new way of life that would become eternal. Was death preferable? Maybe another fighter would have thought so. They might have turned, weapons held wide, bracing in defiance before the crash of fury-surf that would dash them away.

But he was not made that way. None of his Legion had been made that way. Iron within, iron without. Live. Survive. Fall back, regroup, rebuild. No pity – not for self, not for any living thing. Run. Run hard. Find a place, a distant place, where you can turn at last, and do so from strength.

A place will be found. It will. That was the other truth: the wheel shall turn. Only live long enough to see it.

So run. Run now. But no, not forever.

He had once had a reputation. The earth itself moulded and turned under his hands, they had said. He would gaze at a landscape, a terrain, a scarp that rose and fell like a drape of cloth, and know how to bend it to his will. He would gauge the substrates, the underlying strata and the surface conditions, his grey eyes glittering while his body was held perfectly still under the glow of massed augur readings.

After a minute, or an hour, or days – however long it took – the orders would come. He would signal for the machines to roll into their positions. The drills would start up, the shafts would be delved, the courses dug out. Pumps would begin to churn, soundings would be made. As he continued to observe, arms folded across his chest now, patient, still silent, the levies of slave labour would march into position, tools at the ready. The earth would be changed. It would protest – the screams and bellows of upended stone, the crack of ancient sediments being wrenched into the open – but his will was the mightier.

Always, the mightier. The earth was his servant; he was its master.

Thus it had been before the great schism, the years in which he had fought under the banner of the Imperium. Thus it had remained after the break, as victory drew ever closer – the turning of fate's thumbscrew, when his Legion threw off its long humiliation and turned its talents upon old tormentors. The tools remained the same throughout. Not for him the doubtful advantages of the daemonic, the sprites and delusions of weaker minds and souls, just the old, familiar instruments, the physical things: the hammers, the machines, the hands, the mortal minds and sinews.

Bitter, they had been called. Resentful, reclusive. Well, there was a reason for that. A host of reasons. And the Emperor, for all his sins, had never forged a weapon without a purpose. You needed to be bitter to do this work. You needed to put your back into it, to channel all that surliness, to direct the force of it into the soil. Because the deep places were bitter too. They were foul and they were deep, the accumulated spoil of a thousand buried lifetimes, all of it stinking, pulling at your boots and dragging at your shoulders. Only the sour-souled endured that. Only a stomach of wormwood could out-spite the earth.

So they twisted and changed the worlds they found. They sunk their fingers into them and made the terrains into stages of death. Sometimes it was defensive – earthworks and palisades against which armies broke like sheets of glass. Sometimes it was offensive – encircling trenches that covered the advance of the Great Machines and suffocated the life out of enemy fortresses. The result, in the end, was the same. Corpses rotting into the mulch, walls slumping into the mud, war engines condemned to slow rust, and the banners of the IV Legion – the Iron Warriors – raised high once again.

It was methodical. It was patient. It had been perfect, so

perfectly planned, from start to finish, the product of a mind of hard genius, and one under whom he had been so proud to serve.

The Master of Sieges. That's what they'd called him back then. Ortag Theokon, the Earth-Tormentor. Honoured among a people who only honoured the most strenuous arts, those of the tool and the instrument, the gauge and the theodolite.

What did it mean any more? There would be no building now. No patient remaking of the earth. Only running, headlong, panicked.

The humiliation of it. The raw, unbearable humiliation. That was the worst wound, far worse than any physical flesh-breaking.

Run. Feel the abjectness, the white-hot shame. Run hard.

He'd got close, though. He still remembered it all, vivid as a shell-burst in his mind – the Palace itself. Months of toil it had taken to get that near, and at times the fatigue had been too crushing even for them, but they'd made it eventually, cresting the slag heaps with their engines and gazing at last upon the wounded prize.

By then, Terra had been sunk deep into the oily embrace of the warp and everything was shifting under their feet. You'd fight your way down a processional for a week only to find yourself back where you'd started, or pursue the enemy into a dead end only to find yourself ambushed by hundreds more spilling out from new roads that had never been on the cartoliths. It had sickened him, he remembered, making him frustrated and impatient. His master had long quit the field, perhaps out of the same disgust, leaving only the most committed of the IV behind. Theokon had hauled his engines out of cussedness towards the end, losing thousands of slaves with every painful advance, no longer caring about the waste, just committed, absolutely committed, to being there when it mattered.

And he had been. He'd seen the pinnacles of the final redoubt with his own eyes, swimming amid an ocean of empyreal saturation. He'd got near enough to train his guns on their faltering structures. He'd been poised to level them all, just as he'd levelled so many other fortresses in the past.

For a moment, for one intense moment, he'd revelled in it. They had won. They *had won*. The sacrifice, the compromises, the pain – it had been worth it at last. The Tyrant would be overthrown, the Reign of the Astartes Unfettered would begin, and this time the Imperium would be constructed and maintained without lies or compromises.

Theokon did not know if he had ever been *happy*, not like they said the baseline humans were capable of being, but that moment surely got close. He'd grinned under his rusted helm, felt all the fatigue melt away, clenched his fist high. The moment he unclenched, the engines would go to work – the earth would shake, the sky would split, his accumulated hatred would pour onto those walls and render them down to ashes.

He never got to give the order. It had all happened so suddenly, so completely, so utterly without warning. The entire vista had rocked, slammed over, flexed, shuddered. The crimson skies had flared, the stars had blazed. Fires had leapt up from the earth, spontaneous, almost gleeful. These were no munitions, no fresh weapons firing – this was the universe itself in both rapture and agony, a shaking of its primordial foundations, a snapping-back of reality like a dislocated limb being reset.

The daemons were torn out of reality, howling with horror and disbelief. The warp sky exploded and then gusted back into darkness. A great crack rang out from horizon to horizon, deafening for a split second, blinding for a mere instant, then just an echo – the resumption of physical law, the wrench of the immaterium being hauled away.

Elation was replaced, instantly, with terror. Real fear. A whirl of vertigo, of stomach-churning horror. Hardened Space Marines around him fell to their knees, dropped their weapons, looked to the heavens in dumb amazement. Theokon himself staggered, all thoughts of conquest suddenly gone, barely noticing as the greatest of his precious engines disintegrated from within. A gale whipped up, churning dust and ashes into the already filthy skies. Rumbles of collapse juddered across the poisoned soils. A greater roar rose, gathering strength, resounding and voluminous, coming now from far, far above. So he looked up at last, barely aware of himself or where he was, and saw them: the enemy, not crawling across the landscape in scraps and rags but swarming from the heavens, rank upon rank of them – drop pods, landers, heavy carriers laced with friction lightning. Where had they come from? Who *were* they? How was this *happening*?

'Fall back!' came a cry, a strangled outburst of wild astonishment.

Theokon might have resisted that, but then the bombardment began – curtains of fire, vengeful fire, lancing down from the hurtling atmospherics, crackling and splitting the air itself. The concentration of it was phenomenal, as if ranks of calderas had tipped out their white-hot contents in unison, dousing the surface in a tide of sizzling ingots even as more were lined up to come.

So he ran. He turned heavily, slipping in the already-boiling mud, limping back the way he'd come, along with all the rest of them, sliding and skidding and dropping to all fours, leaving weapons, leaving shields and trophies, dropping it all, forgetting it all, just scrambling out of that inferno before the waves of pain overtook them and dissolved them down to nothing.